The
Sound
of the
Wind

The Sound of the Wind

THE LIFE AND WORKS OF UNO CHIYO

Rebecca L. Copeland

University of Hawaii Press
Honolulu

for my parents

© 1992 University of Hawaii Press
All rights reserved
Printed in the United States of America

97 96 95 94 93 92 5 4 3 2 1

Library of Congress Cataloging-in-Publication Data

Copeland, Rebecca L., 1956–
    The sound of the wind : the life and works of Uno Chiyo /
Rebecca L. Copeland.
        p.   cm.
    Includes translations of The puppet maker, The sound of the
wind, and This powder box by Uno Chiyo.
    Includes bibliographical references (p.   ) and index.
    ISBN 0–8248–1409–6 (acid-free paper)
    1. Uno, Chiyo, 1897–   —Biography.
    2. Japanese authors—20th century—Biography.
    I. Uno, Chiyo, 1897–   . II. Title.
    PL840.N58Z58   1992
895.6'344—dc20
    [B]   91–48130
                                                          CIP

All photographs unless otherwise noted have been provided
courtesy of Uno Chiyo.

Designed by Paula Newcomb

Contents

Preface

Uno Chiyo has lived the depth and breadth of life—fashion ingénue, magazine editor, kimono designer, celebrated femme fatale. That she is also a significant writer sometimes escapes notice; indeed, my Japanese colleagues are often surprised that I have chosen to study this author. "Why not Natsume Sōseki?" they ask, suggesting one of Japan's literary heavyweights. Even the grand lady herself has been somewhat perplexed by the flurry of attention her works have received recently. She is no stranger to the limelight, but usually the focus was on her life, her loves, her scandals—not her writing.

Initially I was distressed by the lack of appreciation for Uno Chiyo's literary accomplishments. After all, her works have been accorded several of Japan's highest accolades—the Noma Prize among them. But later I came to understand that this skewed perception of Uno was not so much a result of the quality of her works, which few would dispute, but of the content of her life.

Uno never lived the life of a dedicated writer; she was always busy with other projects and enterprises. Serious writers are meant to suffer; they struggle courageously with poverty, with periods of emotional trauma, with self-doubt. True, Uno's masterpiece *Ohan*, barely one hundred pages, did take over ten years to complete, so careful had she become with her craft. Yet her stories read as though she spun them effortlessly from the threads of her own life. Uno would have it appear that she never suffered. She has said that she never cried, never knew a day of pain, never even had a headache! There are those who would believe such exaggeration, so full of vitality and joy is the life she has described.

"I have always done whatever I wanted to do, whenever I wanted to do it. I never looked back. I only looked ahead." This seems to be Uno's motto; and true to form she raced through pre–World War II Japan at a pace, dizzying even by today's standards. "Married" for the first time at fourteen, she went on to have three other husbands and several celebrated lovers. "It got to the point where I was adept at breaking up," she has said. "I'd cry quietly for a bit, then put on my best kimono and head out the door for another man." Old age, though tempering her appetite, did not remove her from the path of passion. At ninety she acknowledged a marriage proposal from a man half her age. (He is reported to have said she was "more womanly," even in her old age, than today's young women.) She turned the suitor down but at the same time rejuvenated her image as a woman whose thirst for life is insatiable.

Uno has never been loath to divulge the secrets of her affairs. She eagerly describes her many loves in the several memoirs and autobiographies she has penned, the most recent being her best-seller *Ikite yuku Watashi* (I Will Go On Living, 1983), which was serialized in the *Mainichi Shimbun* newspaper before being published in book form. These works, all written when Uno was advanced in age and years removed from the events she relates, tend to look over her past experiences with a fond detachment. She distills from memory those moments that appeal to her and in so doing rewrites her life, reinvents herself. The Uno we meet in these memoirs is delightfully carefree. She dances from one adventure to the next, never turning back, never losing momentum.

And yet the Uno of these memoirs is not always the same woman we find in her fiction. Here we have not the reckless femme fatale but a passionate, highly intelligent woman whose quest for authenticity renders her vulnerable. She writes of women who, endeavoring to follow the voice within themselves, inevitably encounter doubt and uncertainty as they surge ahead, closing doors resoundingly behind them. The poignancy and simple eloquence of her stories fill out the portraits she paints of herself in later years. As gratifying as her life has been, she did not sail through it unscathed, never knowing a day of pain, never crying. She suffered, but she did not allow suffering to define her life. She used her pain as a stepping stone to greater self-discovery, and it is this rocky passage to authenticity and happiness, so carefully chronicled in her fiction, that I find compelling.

Why Uno Chiyo? Because her stories are at once challenging and engaging. They are replete with an earnest optimism that will appeal to readers sated with the darkly brooding vignettes long the staple of Japanese literature. Her life is equally compelling; she dared to demand her right to happiness and self-determination at a time when most others—men as well as women—would not have dreamed it possible.

Acknowledgments

I owe a debt of gratitude to a great many people for their generous and invaluable assistance and guidance, and it is with pleasure and pride that I now take this opportunity to express my appreciation. I began this study while a graduate student at Columbia University, and I wish to express my sincerest appreciation to Edward Seidensticker, my dissertation adviser and friend, whose rigorous criticism and positive direction proved an invaluable asset in the dissertation, and whose unflagging support and sage advice have given me the confidence necessary to present this study. I would also like to thank Paul Anderer for having the foresight to suggest Uno Chiyo as subject matter; Donald Keene, who allowed me to read drafts pertaining to Uno Chiyo from his *Dawn to the West* (1984), and who was ever generous with advice and guidance; and Saeki Shōichi, who kindly met with me in Tokyo on several occasions to discuss Uno and the Japanese narrative. A special word of thanks must also be extended to the Fulbright-Hays Doctoral Dissertation Research Abroad Fellowship Program for funding my preliminary research in Tokyo.

The translations included herein could not have been completed without the generous assistance of a variety of friends and teachers. Moriyama Tae and Higashi Akiko spent many hours with me reading through "The Puppet Maker" and *The Sound of the Wind.* Appreciation is also due Anthony Chambers and Aileen Gatten for the many incisive suggestions they made about the former story. My colleagues at International Christian University, particularly Tanaka Mari, were great sources of advice and encouragement; and my sisters Judy and Beth generously read through early drafts.

PART ONE

The Life

I

A SPARTAN

BEGINNING

Objective information on Uno's childhood is scarce, though much can be gleaned from the highly detailed accounts she has offered in her memoirs and autobiographies. She was born November 28, 1897, in a section of Iwakuni known as Kawanishi, "west of the river." Her father, Uno Toshitsugu, then forty-one, had moved to this small town on the Inland Sea the previous year with his twenty-three-year-old bride, Doi Tomo. They set up residence in what had been the village master's old estate. The main house, with its sloping eaves and latticed windows, though not particularly large, was surrounded by an imposing wooden fence. Behind the house was a bathhouse, a storehouse, and a stable. To the east was a well-appointed garden and to the west an orchard.

Toshitsugu was the second son of Uno Mokichi, the patriarch of the affluent Unos of Takamori. The Unos had been sake brewers for generations in Takamori, a tiny mountain hamlet west of Iwakuni, and they wielded a fair amount of influence. In her autobiographical essay "Nokotte iru hanashi" (The Story That Remains, 1980), Chiyo traces the Uno clan to an ancient Korean king but notes that their more recent progenitor was Uno Masatsune, Lord Governor of Chikugo (Saga Prefecture, Kyūshū), and a chief retainer in Lord Sugi Takayasu's retinue. In 1554, when Lord Sugi's castle on Kuragake Mountain was besieged by the powerful warlord Mōri Motonari, Uno Masatsune and 1,370 other retainers committed seppuku along with their lord. Uno Masatsune's three sons fled. The older two entered the priesthood, but the third escaped to Shikoku, where he became a farmer. Several centuries later, his descendants returned to Honshū and settled in Takamori as sake brewers, and it is from these Unos that Chiyo's family is descended.

As frequently happened to second sons, Chiyo's father, Toshitsugu, was sent to live in his uncle's house. Several years later Mokichi, concerned by the fact that his first son, Masanosuke, suffered from a congenital physical disability, brought Toshitsugu home with the hope that he would succeed to the family headship. But the young man spurned his father's offer, took his share of the family wealth, and traveled to Kyoto and Osaka, where, in true prodigal fashion, he squandered his fortune on women and gambling. Even after Toshitsugu returned to his native province and had seemingly settled down with Doi Tomo, he did not mend his ways. He continued to lead a life of dissipation until his death.

Not much is known of Doi Tomo. She may not have been Toshitsugu's first wife; it is clear that Toshitsugu was not her first husband. She had previously been married to Fujimoto Kakutarō of Kojiro, a village not far from Iwakuni. Apparently their marriage was happy and produced at least one child, a son, Etsutarō. But Tomo's husband was not able to provide adequately for his family. He had inherited a dye business but lost it due to incompetency. Later he tried his hand at sake brewing, but when this business failed as well he was forced to eke out a living as a scrivener. Tomo's parents compelled her to divorce Kakutarō in June of 1896. She had to leave her son behind as well; according to the law at the time a mother had no claim to her children. Shortly thereafter she married Uno Toshitsugu, though their marriage was not legally registered until October 1897, a month before Chiyo was born.

Tomo contracted tuberculosis after Chiyo's birth and was removed to a seaside village to recuperate. However, her condition worsened, and she died on July 13, 1899, just short of her twenty-sixth birthday. Toshitsugu sent Chiyo to Takamori to live with Masanosuke and his wife as their adopted child. The following year Toshitsugu married Saeki Ryū, a young woman from the neighboring village of Kawashimo, and Chiyo was returned to her home in Kawanishi. In her autobiography *Ikite yuku Watashi* (I Will Go On Living, 1983), she describes her first meeting with her stepmother:

> "She will be your mother from now on," Father told me. I stared in amazement at this mother who had appeared out of nowhere. She was pretty and fair-skinned. I had absolutely no memories of my real mother, no way to compare my new mother to her.[1]

Toshitsugu had destroyed Tomo's photographs and had disposed of all her possessions. There was nothing in the house to indicate that another woman had even lived there. Toshitsugu never spoke to Chiyo of Tomo but led her to believe that Ryū was her natural mother. In her autobiographical novella *Aru hitori no onna no hanashi* (Story of a Certain Woman Alone, 1971), Uno writes of her two mothers:

> Did Kazue [fictionalized name for Chiyo] believe that this was her new mother? In Kazue's mind there was no difference between her first mother and her new mother. She did not know that her real mother had died. She could only believe that her new mother had always been in the house.[2]

Chiyo was very fond of her beautiful new mother, and Ryū took good care of her young charge. Even after she had given birth to children of her own, four boys and a girl, Ryū continued to treat Chiyo with great affection. If anything she doted on Chiyo to the exclusion of her own children, making certain that Chiyo was always the first to eat, the first to bathe, and the first to receive whatever treat a neighbor or relative might pass along. Had Chiyo been a stepson, this behavior would not have been unwarranted. But it was unusual, at a time when such dicta as "men first, women to follow" or "respect men; despise women" were widely propagated, for a mere daughter to be accorded this privileged treatment, especially when a legitimate son was present. Uno later claimed that her sense of self-worth and bold independence were all due to Ryū's preferential treatment of her as a child.

Ryū's gentle nature sharply contrasted with Toshitsugu's moodiness and ill temper. Uno described him as being "like someone out of the novels of Balzac or Dostoevsky."[3] He was a dark, brooding man, unpredictable and often abusive. He never sought any sort of employment but instead fancied himself a gentleman of leisure. He kept race horses and expensive carp, and he raised canaries, linnets, and doves. Behind the house he planted an orchard where he grew a variety of citrus fruits. He even had a small grape arbor. Toshitsugu was a great habitué of the Daimyō Koji, the Iwakuni pleasure quarter, and he was evidently a popular patron of several establishments there. Stories of his escapades in the teahouses and brothels were widely circulated and eventually reached Chiyo's ears. Later many of these accounts would form the basis for her own stories.

In addition to Toshitsugu's reputation in the Iwakuni demimonde, he was known to the local police as a gambler and was often jailed for his illegal activities. Yet despite Toshitsugu's debauchery—or perhaps because of it—Chiyo professed a strong admiration for her father. In her short story "Kokyō no ie" (My Old Home, 1974) she describes the mixture of sorrow and pride she felt as a child waiting for her father to finish his business in a high-class restaurant and sometime house of assignation:

I would stand out in front of the house; I never once went inside. The word-less sense of loneliness that I felt then still lingers in my heart. No, it wasn't loneliness that I felt—it is difficult to believe, but even though my father was involved in what could only be termed "debauchery," I felt that whatever he did was special and above reproach. As I waited outside I was enveloped in a deep awe for him. Why did I have this kind of image of my father when I was a child? Even now I am not certain. All I can remember clearly are the feelings I had for him. He could do no wrong. Even if what he did hurt my mother, my siblings, me—it didn't matter. If he did it . . . it was good. For me, as a child, the more immoral my father was, the more I admired him for his immorality.[4]

And the more Chiyo admired her father, the more it seems she longed to win his favor. But Toshitsugu was not an easy man to please. When he was not gallivanting through the pleasure quarters he sequestered himself in the Clock Room, the family parlor so named for the ornamental clock that graced one of its walls. He rarely spoke to his children, but when he did, it was usually to bark a command. As the oldest, Chiyo was responsible for car-rying out his orders. He would summon her in a gruff voice and require her to kneel on the cold wooden floor outside the Clock Room until he saw fit to admit her. At times he made her wait for over an hour in the drafty cor-ridor.

"Chiyo!" he would call out, and I would answer immediately, "Yes!" just like a retainer before his lord. I always answered, "Yes!" Even when asked to do something I didn't want to do, I jumped up, "Yes!" This was my way of overcoming the unpleasantness.[5]

Usually Toshitsugu's errands involved running out late at night to pur-chase sake or other treats. Frequently Chiyo was asked to wait on him, sit-ting silently by his side, carefully keeping his cup full, while he drank. Some-times she would also be asked to massage his legs. If she failed to please him, he would verbally or physically torment her. In an early work, "Michiyo no yomeiri" (Michiyo Goes to Wed, 1925), Uno describes what happens to Michiyo (Chiyo's surrogate) when she fails to satisfy her father.

It happened long ago when she was still a child. Her father was in the Clock Room . . . drinking sake from a bottle he warmed over the hearth. For some reason, no one else was in the room with him but Michiyo. She sat obediently at his side and poured his sake. He twisted his face into a hideous smile—the likes of which she'd never seen before—and peered directly into her eyes.

"Today I'm going to buy you whatever you want," he said. "Whatever Michiyo wants she can have. Well, what'll it be?"

Michiyo shrank back slowly. She said nothing. She could not trust her father's face. When he saw this, he repeated over and over, "I'll buy you anything."

Suddenly Michiyo realized that her father was playing a game with her. . . . She thought it would be fun to play along, maybe even tease her father a bit, too. She laughed happily. There was something she wanted. "A red ribbon. I want a red ribbon!"

Her father put on a different mask. He spread his arms out wide and seemed ready to pounce on her.

"You want a what? A ribbon? You shameless little fool, you wasted no time spitting that out!"

He looked around the room for the sash her mother used to carry the baby on her back and found it tied to the pillar behind him. He trussed Michiyo hand and foot and hung her from the ceiling like a rabbit. Her tiny head, caught between her shoulders, fell backwards. Tears ran in a line down her cheek. She thought she would die.

Her father sat beneath her drinking his sake. Had he meant to teach her a lesson? Was she supposed to respond, "No! There is nothing I want!" whenever asked about her needs? Or, was her father simply amusing himself with her because he was drunk? Michiyo thought about it for a long time. There was that sort of meanness in the man.[6]

Toshitsugu was relentless in his demands that his children conform to a strict code of discipline. They were to be ever self-denying and obedient. Chiyo later described her upbringing as "Spartan." Having no income of his own outside of gambling, Toshitsugu relied entirely on his elder brother for financial support. Twice monthly Masanosuke sent Toshitsugu an allowance in a gold-trimmed, black-lacquer money box, delivered by a servant on horseback. Toshitsugu spent most of this in the Daimyō Koji. Ryū and the children were forced to manage with a mere pittance. When Chiyo began school in the spring of 1904, there was not enough money to buy her school supplies. She wrote her lessons out on the margins of old newspapers and used her pencils until they were stubs too tiny to grip. Later she claimed this practice affected her penmanship and was responsible for her now rather famous crabbed characters.

Toshitsugu's selfishness also denied Chiyo the money for proper clothing. She never had adequate footwear. If it rained or snowed, Toshitsugu forbade her to wear her everyday sandals of roughly woven grass; she was to go barefoot. Toshitsugu reasoned that the moisture would rot her sandals, forcing him to buy more, but that a little dampness would not hurt her feet.

The Uno children were poor but not destitute; they had a house to live in and enough food to eat. Yet they were denied the comforts befitting their social status. The Iwakuni townfolk treated Chiyo with the respect due a niece of the prominent Uno family. But the sight of this well-born girl running barefoot through the snow must have seemed incongruous. And Chiyo, clearly, was sensitive to their stares.

> When Kazue walked home she never took the road through town. She took the road by the drainage ditch, going around the embankment behind the town. Here no one would notice her. She hated it when the others looked at her and said, "Such a shame! There goes Miss Kazue barefoot again." Even if she did go barefoot in the snow, Kazue was not to be pitied.[7]

Chiyo did not think she was particularly unfortunate. "Others said I was pitiful, but I didn't think I was. I was doing my father's bidding, and that filled me with pride."[8] Chiyo's determination to fulfill her father's bizarre and often cruel requests is surprising when one considers the nonconforming free spirit she later became. But when asked why she never tried to assert herself in her father's presence, Uno answered simply, "Resist him? I never once considered it."[9] During the Meiji era, when Uno was growing up, it was literally unthinkable for a child to go against the patriarchal authority. Young girls in particular were made to understand that blind obedience was a virtue.

But this does not mean that Chiyo approved of her father's bullying or that she never resented him. In small measures, she managed to assert her will. When he insisted that she deny her interests in literature, Chiyo found ways to read on the sly. In her essay "Mohō no tensai" (A Genius of Imitation, 1934) she describes how she discovered her father's cache of literary magazines:

> Magazines and newspapers were forbidden me by my father, who was very strict. I read them secretly in the outhouse anyway, not minding when my bottom was chilled by the cold air creeping up from underneath the toilet. The newspapers in those days serialized modern stories such as "One's Own Sin" or "A Bride's Abyss." I didn't quite understand what these stories were about, but the mystery of the adult world swelled in my imagination like a dangerous boil. I don't know how many times I was spanked after being caught by my father when he came to use the outhouse. I thought the world of fiction was endlessly fascinating, and the stricter my father was, the sneakier I became. I looked for all kinds of ways to read stories. Once, I discovered piles of very old newspapers and some magazines called *A Flower of the Capital* in the corner of the storehouse; I read them by the dim light from the windows until it was dark.[10]

Public education, as well, had little tolerance for fiction at the time. In the Iwakuni Higher School for Girls, which Chiyo entered in 1910, the subjects covered were limited to those that would make "good wives and wise mothers." Fiction, it was feared, would corrupt "shallow-minded" girls with unhealthy fantasies and immoral suggestions. Emphasis was placed instead on sewing, cooking, childcare, and the fundamentals of the eighteenth-century Confucian treatise on female subservience *Onna daigaku* (Greater Learning for Women).[11]

In the summer of 1911, at age fourteen, Chiyo had the opportunity to put her learning to use, for Toshitsugu decided it was time for her to marry. The average marriage age for women in the early Meiji era was fifteen or sixteen, so even by traditional standards Chiyo was being wed young. But Toshitsugu was now suffering from consumption, and it seems likely that he was eager to have his oldest daughter's future secured before his death. She was to marry her seventeen-year-old maternal cousin, Fujimura Ryōichi, a boy she had no recollection of ever meeting.

The marriage was simple. One summer night Ryū took Chiyo into the bath, scrubbed her down, and dressed her hair. Ryū was crying, but Chiyo, little understanding the role that awaited her, felt only excitement. She was led to her cousin's house by an old neighbor couple carrying red lanterns. Here she and her groom exchanged the traditional sake cups. But the marriage was not to be consummated immediately. Chiyo stayed in her aunt's room for the first week. During the second week Mrs. Fujimura instructed Chiyo to sleep in Ryōichi's room, but the young man, dissatisfied with his child-bride, refused to come home and instead spent his nights in a cheap inn nearby, apparently with a woman of questionable virtue. Mrs. Fujimura was not alarmed. She simply bade Chiyo to prepare Ryōichi's bedding and to keep his bedclothes ready, in case he put in an appearance.

Chiyo performed this vigil for ten nights or so, but then one day after school she found herself racing down the familiar path to her Kawanishi home. Humiliated and homesick, she refused to return to the Fujimuras', and her aunt did not demand that she do so. The "marriage," having never been officially registered, was not legally binding, and all promises were dissolved.[12]

Toshitsugu was by this time too sick to reprimand Chiyo for her "waywardness." As his illness progressed he began coughing blood. On February 8, 1913, he grabbed a knife from the kitchen and staggered out to the road in front of the house, where he angrily flailed out at anyone who attempted to subdue him. "Don't come near me!" he cried, "or I'll cut you down." Three days earlier there had been a heavy snowfall in the area, a rare event for Iwakuni. Snow still covered the ground. Toshitsugu, now on his knees, continued to rant. Ryū and the children spilled out into the street to help him, but he would not let them near. Soon he collapsed, spattering the snow with blood from his lungs. A few minutes later he died.

Toshitsugu's last frantic moments made an indelible impression on Chiyo, leaving her with a vision that would haunt her indefinitely. In all her endeavors she would never quite escape nor deny the power her father had held over her—a power made more intimidating by the horrific nature of his death. She describes the moment in an autobiography she wrote years later:

> Snow is a strange thing. It is now already seventy years since my father died, but, because of the snow, the strangeness of the snow, the horror of that scene has evaporated.
>
> I think I know just what it was my father was thinking at that instant. It remains in my mind like a picture. . . . Did he want to injure himself with that knife? Did he want to hurt whoever tried to help him? No. No, he wanted neither. But isn't this what my father wanted to say? . . . "I am dying. If I could I would start over from the very beginning and lead a life true and respectable in the eyes of the world."[13]

Toshitsugu may indeed have had such thoughts as he faced death. Yet if he had lived his life over in a way that was true and respectable in the eyes of the world, very possibly we would not have benefited from the passion and verve of his daughter, for much of her daring and unconventionality can be traced to him and to the relationship they shared.

Chiyo's reaction to her father's death was twofold. She was, of course, overcome by a sense of loss. She had lived in awe of her father; all she wanted in return was some recognition of her worth, some form of approval. But reverence of this sort is binding, inhibiting; only in his death did Chiyo find release from his tyranny. In "A Genius of Imitation" Uno writes:

> My father died when I was sixteen. After offering their condolences, the neighbors said to my mother and me, "But I'm sure your life will be a lot easier now," and they even congratulated themselves on his death. . . . I cried bitterly, but somehow I was happy at the same time, thinking that I could now do whatever I wanted.[14]

Chiyo began to indulge her own interests with a vengeance. She devoured newspaper and magazine novels and pored through the latest copies of *Seitō* (Bluestocking), a radically feminist journal.[15] When her teachers admonished her for these activities, she charged that their "ideas about discipline proved to be no more effective than my father's."[16] With five other students she formed a literary group of her own, the Kaichō-on (Sound of the Tide). They secretly compiled their poems, essays, and stories into a journal imitating *Seitō,* and even submitted some of their works under pseudonyms to the short-lived journal *Joshi Bundan* (Women's Literary World). They were soon discovered by the principal, however, and forced to abandon their literary aspirations.

Toshitsugu's death, while liberating the family emotionally, fettered them financially. Masanosuke discontinued the periodical allowance and virtually cut all ties to Ryū and the children. Ryū had to take employment at the local spinning factory, where she worked for nearly twenty years until failing eyesight forced her to quit. When Chiyo graduated from the Iwakuni Higher School for Girls in 1914, she desperately wanted to follow her classmates to women's normal schools in Tokyo and Kyoto. But Ryū could not afford to send her off on such an adventure; Chiyo had to seek employment in Iwakuni. As a child she had toyed with the idea of becoming a geisha, the kind of woman her father had loved. But she had neither the money nor the patronage to establish herself. Instead she became a teacher's assistant at the Kawashimo Elementary School.

Chiyo began work in May of 1914. She earned eight yen a month, which she turned over triumphantly to Ryū. That year during her summer vacation she made two important changes in her life. The first was a change in residence. Her step-grandmother helped her find a little cottage for rent in the Kitamura section of Kawashimo, so close to the elementary school that she could hear the bell toll in the morning. Moving out of her Kawanishi home and into a house of her own gave Chiyo a new sense of independence.

> I realize now that this first independence of mine . . . was just the beginning of a long life of wandering, a life that has pulled me along through the years.
> I can remember watching the minstrels, famed for their jaunty ballads, shouldering their cloth-encased *shamisens* and setting out for some other town after their performances at the two-bit inns along Okinomachi. How I longed to follow after them!
> I suppose I was answering this wanderlust when I left my mother's house and moved into the Kitamura cottage. This move was my first step in a life of wandering, the very life my late father had forbidden, terrified that his children would make the same mistakes he had.[17]

While on her own, Chiyo made a discovery that, trivial as it may seem, had a tremendous effect on her life. She discovered the mysterious benefits of makeup. One summer evening while taking a bath at her old home, she happened upon her mother's face powder. Crouching before the mirror in the dimly lit bathroom, she brushed the powder on her damp skin and was startled by the difference it made in her appearance. Chiyo had a naturally dark complexion, so dark in fact that her father had nicknamed her *Iroguro* (Blackie). He and others taunted her, telling her she would never find a man willing to marry her. Chiyo took the threats to heart; to a young girl in turn-of-the-century Japan, the threat of being abandoned by suitors was terrifying. As Uno said much later, "Now I do not feel that my dark complexion is any cause for regret. But at the time, the way country folks saw it, there was no one more pathetic than a dark-skinned girl."[18] Chiyo resigned herself to a lonely life, until, that is, she learned of makeup. A generous application of powder transformed her into a fair-skinned beauty.

She began wearing makeup daily, never leaving the house without it. She would rise at dawn and then elaborately wash, rinse, and powder her face and throat. Next she would apply rouge and eyeliner. Since Chiyo was working within a budget, she had to learn to improvise. A burnt match tip worked well as an eyebrow pencil. (She claims the practice rubbed her eyebrows entirely away, and now she must paint them on or go without.) Once her grooming was complete, a process she eventually managed in forty-five minutes, she proudly likened her painted face to "a tree peony in full bloom."

Chiyo did not limit her attention to makeup; she also concerned herself with clothing. She could not afford new garments, but she found a hand-me-down here and an old kimono there and with clever needlework (her girls' school education had not been wasted after all) altered them to suit her needs. Her daily teaching attire consisted of a purple *hakama* (pleated trousers) and a splash-patterned kimono, onto which she had sewn an undercollar (to make it appear as if she were wearing an underkimono) of embroidered peonies. Her efforts did not go unnoticed. School teachers were expected to maintain a more subdued appearance, and the sight of Chiyo sauntering by like a painted geisha raised more than a few eyebrows in that rural town. Soon the local pastime was to ogle her whenever she led her class to the schoolyard to exercise.

> There I was, the young teacher, leading the exercise class in my splash-patterned kimono with tight-cut sleeves, my purple *hakama* trailing about my heels.
> "Now, arms out straight and one, two; one, two."
> I pushed my young charges through their paces. And what do you suppose happened? In no time at all a large crowd would gather around the exercise grounds. The grounds were beside the road that ran from the Oki fields to the

town hall and the middle school. The barbershop and sweetshop boys, on their way back from errands, would lean their bicycles against the wooden fence of the exercise grounds. The young farmers on their way to the fields would tether their oxen to the fence. The middle-school students and the young town officials, even old men and women, would flock to the fence to gape at me as I led the exercises.[19]

Chiyo did not devote all her time to her appearance or even to her teaching. With six young men and women she started the literary group Kaichō (Seabird). The group met regularly in Iwakuni teahouses to discuss literature, to gossip about the sensational events of the day, and to parade about in what they imagined were the latest Tokyo fashions, the men with straw hats and walking sticks and the women clutching parasols. They compiled their literary efforts—stories, poems, and essays—in a typeset magazine also known as *Kaichō*. The magazine was abandoned after only three issues. And Chiyo, for her part, was now very much involved with a new interest; literature would have to wait.

> Yes, I was in love. It was joyful to be young, to be alive. Instead of thinking I might be the sun, I now felt I was a butterfly. I stopped writing verses and essays. I had no time to spare. Instead of writing about my emotions, I acted upon them. I was in love just like the characters in the stories in the typeset magazine we had published. I thought I had no need to write anymore.[20]

Chiyo was in love with a handsome young teacher who had recently joined the Kawashimo Elementary School staff. He was soft-spoken, wore wire-rimmed glasses, and was so fair-skinned that his cheeks glistened blue from the traces of the razor. Chiyo was smitten. During class, while her pupils busily read or copied out their lessons, she sat at her desk and wrote one torrid love letter after another. She folded and knotted them, just as lovers had done in the old romances, and had one of her pretty girl students carry them to his classroom. At night she would tear through the darkened fields to his boarding house, where she gave herself over to reckless ardor. Her lover cautioned discretion, but Chiyo was too impassioned to care about anything else. Soon gossip was rife. Chiyo lost her job, and her partner was given a reprimand. Although she did not find this unfair, she did think the cold censure she received from those around her unjust.

> I love the plays *Osome and Hisamatsu* and *Oshichi, the Greengrocer's Daughter.* But Osome and Oshichi exist not only in the world of the theater, but in the

real world as well. If they were here today, they would be "modern girls."
Whatever they wanted to do they would do at once. And, since they would not
bother about what others thought, they would stir up trouble. In the real
world this kind of girl worries her mother and older sister, and the neighbors
label her a "troublemaker."

Then why is it that when the life of a girl who is a "troublemaker" in the
real world is dramatized on stage, she appears so very beautiful? I do not understand why the theater world and the real world must be so different. . . .

Back then, I just wanted that teacher to look at me and think, "My, what a
pretty girl!" Forever. That is what I wanted him to think of me forever. That
was all I wanted. Indeed, in a similar situation the heroine Oshichi took it into
her head to burn down her house![21]

Chiyo did not burn down her house. But, because of the furor over the
affair, she was forced to leave Iwakuni. She traveled to Seoul, Korea, where
an acquaintance helped her find work with various Japanese families, cleaning
and baby-sitting. The working conditions were miserable and included washing diapers outside in the bitter cold of the Seoul spring. Chiyo's only conso-
lation was her warm thoughts of her lover; she wrote to him constantly. He
responded only once, and then to ask her not to write again. Chiyo was
incensed. She packed her bags and took the next steamer bound for Japan. At
Shimonoseki, while she was waiting for the train to Iwakuni, she happened
upon a brightly lit hardware store with a glittering display of knives. She
claims that as she gazed at the knives she recalled her father's last frantic
moments. On impulse she rushed into the store and purchased one of the
knives; her mother must need one, she told herself.

Once in Iwakuni she set out with all her baggage to her lover's new boarding house. (He had transferred to another school to free his name of scandal.)
It was a long walk, and by the time she reached his lodgings it was well after
nightfall, and he was asleep. When Chiyo called to him from the garden he
flung the door open and glared down at her. Joining her outside, he ordered
her to leave, and when she protested he gave her a shove, causing the knife to
fall from her sash. It clattered to the ground, where it lay menacingly under
the moonlight. Assuming she had brought it to use against him, he grew
livid. He pushed her toward the road so roughly that she lost her balance and
tumbled into a ravine. He hurled her bundles down after her.

My kimono wound up around my waist, and I skinned my backside. My basket of belongings from Korea came bouncing down after me, spewing my personal things in all directions. The doll I had bought for him in Korea—a
singsong girl—my powder puff and my rouge went flying. And all I could

think to say as I rolled deeper and deeper in the ravine was "Oh dear, I'm falling!"[22]

She prefaces this account with a word of advice: "Listen, all you young lovers out there, take a tip from me: Do not ever, ever sneak up on a nervous lover."

Hindsight brings humor, but it cannot disguise the pain and humiliation Chiyo must have felt. She brushed herself off, straightened out her kimono, and returned to Ryū, where, as always, she was met with love and understanding. "My mother never voiced one word of reprimand. She never asked me why I did what I did. She simply, silently enfolded me in her arms and let me rest. She was my mother. Not my stepmother but my one and only mother."[23]

During the *Obon* season of that year of 1915, Chiyo again met her maternal aunt, Mrs. Fujimura, who immediately began scheming to have Chiyo united with her younger son, Tadashi, then a student at the prestigious Kyoto Third Higher School. Her aunt needed someone to look after Tadashi while he was away from home, to do his laundry, fix his meals, and clean his room. She hinted none too subtly that this would be an ideal arrangement for Chiyo, as it would eventually lead to marriage. Chiyo's reputation was so tarnished in Iwakuni that she had little hope of marrying there. Her aunt felt that she was offering Chiyo a generous alternative. Ryū reluctantly consented and saw her wayward daughter off once again.

Chiyo and Tadashi lived together in the Chion-in temple boardinghouse for students. They had only a six-mat room and had to share toilet facilities with the other students. Tadashi instructed Chiyo to refer to him as "elder brother" and to keep their true relationship a secret; Chiyo complied. As cousins they looked enough alike to pass for siblings.

Chiyo lived with Tadashi through the bitter Kyoto winter. Funds from the Fujimura household were unexpectedly reduced when Mr. Fujimura retired early, and there was not enough money to support the young couple adequately. Chiyo pawned her extra garments and all of Tadashi's school books in order to buy charcoal and food. She also worked briefly teaching Japanese to a Chinese student; for this she received an allowance of rice. Chiyo admits that she rather enjoyed those lean days with Tadashi in Kyoto; they were impoverished, but they were also in love, and Chiyo found that struggling to keep her lover comfortable gave her great happiness. In the spring of 1916 Tadashi graduated from the Third Higher School and entered the Law Department of Tokyo Imperial University.

2

"Painted

Face"

Once in Tokyo Chiyo and Tadashi settled in a shabby flat above a beauty parlor on a back alley in Koishikawa. They were within walking distance of Tokyo Imperial University, where Tadashi was matriculated. As funds from home were meager, he was forced to seek employment and managed to secure a position with a government office.

Despite Tadashi's income, finances were still short of supporting the two in Tokyo, and Chiyo found it necessary to work as well. She had little trouble securing part-time jobs, as there were plenty of positions for young women in the capital at the time. Chiyo ran the gamut; she was a hotel maid, a waitress, a model, a tutor, and a bookkeeper, among other occupations. Most of these jobs lasted only a week or two; Chiyo was proud, and it was difficult for her to submit to the humiliation the work often entailed. She had dreams for her future. She would be a stage actress like the famous Matsui Sumako, whom she idolized.[1] She struggled to project an air of studied sophistication; one measure she took was to keep a ponderous philosophy book held open on her lap whenever she rode the streetcar. She had little interest in or comprehension of the text, but she would pretend to be enthralled, turning the pages and knitting her brow knowingly. As women normally were not expected to display such a wealth of knowledge, she imagined that those beside her were impressed, perhaps even shocked, by the sight of a pretty girl poring over such a massive book. When she got off the streetcar, she always carried the tome clutched tightly to her breast with the title conspicuously displayed.

Chiyo combed newspapers and magazines for audition announcements. Most of the calls she answered were disappointing, or worse, humiliating.

She remembers one that turned out to be nothing more than a one-day job for female extras in a still photo to be used on the cover of a children's magazine. The photograph depicted the actress Umemura Yōko as a fairy princess surrounded by butterfly attendants. The director handed Chiyo a flimsy costume and told her to change on the spot. Like most women at the time, Chiyo was wearing a red *koshimaki* (tightly wrapped underskirt) beneath her kimono but little else. Realizing her undergarment was inappropriate, she found herself in a terrible quandary.

> Giddy with excitement, I clutched the costume in both hands and ran off alone to hide behind the farthest tree. So this was it. This was my first costume, but I could hardly strip naked and put it on in front of all those people. The costume was as sheer as a cicada's wing. I was certain people could see right through it. I was an old-fashioned country girl and had never even seen a pair of bloomers much less worn any. I stood in embarrassment for a long time.
>
> "What are the other girls doing?" I wondered. "They're probably all sophisticated and, wanting to become actresses, are wearing bloomers!" I made up my mind. Leaving my hips swathed in my red kimono underskirt, I pulled the flimsy butterfly costume over my head and emerged, not a white butterfly but a rose-tinted one.[2]

Perhaps the steadiest and least offensive position Chiyo found that summer was with a magazine office in Hibiya. She worked in the bookkeeping department for thirteen yen a month, a sum she imagined would bring instant wealth. At the office she was exposed to the professional side of writing.

> "The man going up the stairs now is Mr. Tanizaki, you know," Hanako, the girl sitting next to me, would say. "And look, Mr. Hirotsu is with him!" I would look up in surprise only to glimpse Mr. Tanizaki's dark blue *hakama* or the tip of Mr. Hirotsu's shoe as they disappeared up the stairs. Famous writers visited our office any number of times a day. From my desk at the foot of the stairs I could see them as they went up to confer with the editors.
>
> "That's it! I shall become a celebrity, too!"[3]

Writers at the time were indeed celebrities. Traditionally a lowbrow occupation, fiction still carried with it the taint of scandal, and the writers themselves were somewhat notorious for their choice of careers. Several women writers had emerged by this time, encouraged by *Seitō* and other feminist movements. Most celebrated among them was Tamura Toshiko (1884–1945), a writer Chiyo clearly admired. Tamura began as a stage actress but eventually established a name for herself as a writer. Like so many women writers who followed, she could not easily reconcile her ambitions with society's expectations. In 1916 she left her husband of five years, took up with a young, married man, and fled with him to Canada. Her actions sent shock waves through the public but nevertheless brought Tamura a degree of admiration from similarly inclined young women.

Chiyo, too, planned to be a celebrity. When acting became a hopeless dream, she turned her sights on writing, much as Tamura had done. She visited Ogawa Mimei (1882–1961), a writer she had admired since her Kaichō days.[4] Every young writer needed a mentor to break into the publishing world, and Chiyo hoped that Ogawa would take her under his wing. But Ogawa, impoverished himself, was not in any position to offer favors and nothing came of their meeting.

What most influenced Chiyo's interest in literature was her brief sojourn at the Enrakuken, a fashionable, Western-style restaurant situated diagonally across from the Red Gate of Tokyo Imperial University. At the time, working in a café was considered by some to be a desirable, even glamorous, occupation. Kon Tōkō (1898–1977), an Enrakuken regular, equated it with today's fashion modeling.[5] Curiously, quite a few women writers—foremost among them Sata Ineko (b. 1904) and Hayashi Fumiko (1903–1951)—began their careers in such establishments. But the status of the women who worked in these places and the definition of their tasks were often ambiguous and dangerously close to prostitution. It was just this ambiguity that Tanizaki Jun'ichirō (1886–1965) despised.

> I have a strange aversion to cafés. The reason is that they appear to be places for eating and drinking, whereas in reality eating and drinking are secondary to having a good time with women, and yet the women aren't always at your side to wait on you. Such a shady, ambiguous setup is distasteful to me.[6]

Uno emphasizes in her autobiography *I Will Go On Living* that the Enrakuken was not such a place. "I was not a serving girl. The Enrakuken was a high-class, Western-style restaurant, and the waitresses simply carried the food to the customer's table. Nothing more. We were not even allowed to pour the beer in the customer's glass."[7] Because of its proximity to both Tokyo Imperial University and the Chūō Kōron publishing office, the Enrakuken's clientele consisted largely of the literary elite. Akutagawa Ryūnosuke (1892–1927) frequented the restaurant along with Kon Tōkō, Kume Masao (1891–1952), Satomi Ton (1888–1983), and Satō Haruo (1892–1964). Although Chiyo worked at the Enrakuken for only eighteen days, the impression she made on the customers there, and they on her, had a lasting influence.

> The people I met while I was a waitress those eighteen days were the so-called writers of vogue in the *bundan* (literary world). Meeting them was the origin of my later decision to become a writer. No one ever knows what will become of the acquaintances made during one's life. But I wonder if there is anything stronger than the impressions one leaves the young. Before I was even aware of it, something had been planted deep within me.[8]

Early reports of Chiyo inevitably describe her as a beauty. Photographs reveal that though she was not exceptionally pretty, there was a liveliness about her features, an arresting capriciousness; clearly it was these qualities that so intoxicated the Enrakuken clientele. Kume Masao, for example, was desperate to win her affections. He waited outside the restaurant for her to finish work, and, though waitresses were not allowed to meet customers after hours, he walked her home on several occasions. Once he even took her to the seashore near Kamakura for a stroll along the beach. But Chiyo adroitly avoided his advances and nothing came of their relationship.

Others vied for Chiyo's attentions. Takita Choin, the editor of the prominent journal *Chūō Kōron*, was a contender, though he conducted his suit with greater circumspection than his younger rivals. He came to the Enrakuken daily for lunch and made it a point to sit at Chiyo's table. After each meal he would leave a fifty-sen piece for her beside the plate, a substantial tip in those days. Although not much was made of their acquaintance at the time, Takita Choin eventually became instrumental in launching Chiyo's writing career.

Biographers and critics often suggest romantic ties between Chiyo and Akutagawa Ryūnosuke, ties Uno has laughingly dismissed. Akutagawa was at the height of his career; he was a god to her, "above the clouds," and she was just a waitress. Apparently on at least one occasion she attended the literary salon that he frequently held. But, awed by Akutagawa's august presence, she cowered in the corner the whole evening.[9] A more mature Uno Chiyo might not have been as reticent, but Chiyo of the Enrakuken was still just a country girl in the big city. She lacked the nerve and the confidence she would later enjoy.

Perhaps Chiyo's most successful suitor at the time was Kon Tōkō, a typical Taishō dandy. Highborn and sophisticated, he dabbled in poetry, art, music, and drama and was a prominent habitué of the cafés and concert halls of Hongō. He often sported a silver walking stick, a burgundy ascot, and a black fedora. Chiyo found him extremely attractive. "An unrivaled Adonis," she called him, "with the fairest skin imaginable, big beautiful eyes, and a luxurious mane of jet-black hair."[10] The two spent many an evening strolling along the streets of Hongō. On occasion Tōkō would take her to dinner or a concert. Once he even had her over to his house while his parents were out of town. His younger brother, Hidemi (1903–1984), describes Chiyo's arrival:

> She was standing in the entrance hall wearing, unlike the day before, a kimono of a subdued hue. Even so, she was beautiful! I showed her to my brother's room on the second floor. I found it incredible that such a beautiful woman would visit Tōkō the Bookworm. But then, there's no accounting for taste![11]

The Chiyo-Tōkō courtship continued for several months, well after Chiyo had left the Enrakuken. Their romance was a great source of gossip among the Enrakuken clientele, and Akutagawa wrote a short story about the two, using material gleaned, most likely, from Tōkō's confidences. The story "Negi" (Leeks, 1919) is not counted among Akutagawa's finer works, but it is a charming roman à clef, offering a bright and humorous glimpse of Chiyo's Enrakuken days.

> In a certain café in the Kanda-Jimbōchō area there is a waitress named Okimi. They say she is fifteen or sixteen, but she looks older. Her nose may be a bit upturned, but her skin is fair and her eyes bright. All told, she is a beauty, though not extraordinarily so. Standing before the piano in her white apron, her hair parted in the middle and adorned with a bauble shaped like a forget-me-not, she looks as if she just stepped out of a Takehisa Yumeji painting. I was told that one of the habitués of the café nicknamed her Melodrama because, I imagine, she so resembles a Yumeji girl. But then she has many nicknames. Because of the flower that decorates her hair baubles, some call her Forget-me-not. Because of her resemblance to an American actress, others call her Miss Mary Pickford, and because of her indispensability to this café, Sugar Cube, etc., etc.[12]

Chiyo made a tidy sum of money from her tips. But her career as the "sugar cube" of the Enrakuken was not to endure. It seems that appearing before the pampered sons of the elite as a mere serving girl was somehow repugnant, despite the financial rewards. As Uno put it, "I suppose the idea of exposing myself to the scrutiny of others as a girl who meticulously makes up her face, though she must wear a makeshift kimono, was too much even for me to bear."[13] Akutagawa seemed to sense this mood of despair in his waitress' life. His story ends as Okimi, strolling by the gaudily festooned stores with her rich lover Tanaka, suddenly sees a greengrocery with leeks prominently displayed at four sen a bundle.

> The visions of roses, of rings and nightingales, the Mitsukoshi Department Store streamers were suddenly swept from her eyes. Instead, the room rent, the rice bill . . . and all her other expenses, all her bitter past experiences, swarmed before her like tiger moths clustering around a light.[14]

Okimi dashes in among the fruits and vegetables and finds two bundles of leeks which she buys at a bargain and triumphantly shows her lover. But the acrid odor of the leeks she cradles so fondly only reminds him of the meanness of her condition. She is no longer the beautiful heroine in a melodrama, but a shabby little girl smelling strongly of banality.

On August 29, 1919, Chiyo and her cousin Fujimura Tadashi married. In all the references to Chiyo made by those who knew her at the Enrakuken, no mention is ever made of Fujimura Tadashi. The two kept their relationship a secret, as they had in Kyoto. It is unclear why they felt compelled to be so discreet. Since they were acting with their parents' consent and with the assumption that they would eventually legalize the arrangement, the fact that they were living together without the benefit of marriage would not have been cause for censure. Yet it should be remembered that the couple was terribly poor at the time. Uno recounts that they frequently went without proper nourishment, so desperate were they to make ends meet. Perhaps the young couple reasoned that for the sake of Chiyo's employment it would be best to keep their relationship secret; it was easier for a young woman to find a position if she were unmarried and unattached. There is even the suggestion that Chiyo, perhaps at Tadashi's bidding, used her charm and her assumed availability to attract wealthy men. Although it is unlikely that Chiyo ever resorted to prostitution, it is clear that she was aware of the possibility. Many of her early stories, based loosely on her experiences in Tokyo, feature impoverished women who support hapless lovers, aged fathers, or ambitious brothers by selling their bodies.

In March 1920 Tadashi graduated from Tokyo Imperial University and took a position with a bank in Sapporo, Hokkaido. The couple lived briefly with Chiyo's paternal uncle, who had been instrumental in helping Tadashi secure his position. Before long they moved into a large, ramshackle house that they had bought with money Chiyo won in a lottery. In order to supplement their income, they took in boarders. Never one to sit idly about the house, Chiyo busied herself with one enterprise after another. She sold charcoal with a neighbor woman, and she took in sewing. Known affectionately

throughout the neighborhood as Sister Seamstress, Chiyo made a modest reputation for herself. But Tadashi was far from pleased. He did not think it
proper for the wife of a Tokyo Imperial University graduate to work, and
especially not at such menial occupations. However, Chiyo persisted until the
heavy winter snows made it impossible for her to receive and deliver orders.

She now spent her afternoons quietly curled up by the open hearth darning
socks, reading books, and daydreaming to the tune of distant sleigh bells.
When evening approached she applied her makeup and dashed out into the
snowy darkness to meet Tadashi on his way home. "When I think back on it
now," she later wrote, "my life was never so full of promise as it was that
year and eight months with my husband in Hokkaido. That was the only
time I ever lived the well-ordered life of an ordinary woman."[15]

Then Chiyo became pregnant. It is unclear whether this was her first preg-
nancy. Itagaki Naoko, in *Meiji Taishō Shōwa no joryū bungaku* (Women's Literature in Meiji, Taishō, and Shōwa, 1967), states that Chiyo's only child was
born while she was in Sapporo and that the child, a month premature, lived
only three days. Chiyo refers occasionally to this child in her short stories and
essays and usually describes the baby as being conceived and born in Tokyo.
The following is an excerpt from her lovely memoir *Ame no oto* (The Sound
of Rain, 1974):

> The second year after our move to Tokyo we had a child, a girl. I had always
> thought that if I had a baby girl I would name her Chōko. I wanted to use the
> character chō from the word chōai, "beloved." The baby sleeping beside me
> was my Chōko. Someone took a picture of her as she slept. In the picture her
> eyes seemed to be protruding, I suppose because the eyeballs were so big behind
> those closed lids as she slept. They looked like the closed eyes of a chick. I do
> not know what happened to that picture. It went the way of the picture of my
> real mother, who died when I was a baby, and the picture of my father. It sim-
> ply disappeared.
>
> Chōko lived in this world for three hours. It was a cold night and the mid-
> wife slipped a hot-water bottle into the bed with us. They said that it came too
> close to the baby's heart and that is why she died. But I do not remember ever
> blaming the midwife. The baby was premature, born in the seventh month.
> From the beginning she was not expected to live.
>
> The baby's corpse was placed in a tiny coffin the size of an orange crate. They
> put the lid on the coffin and began driving in the nails. From my bed I could
> hear the sound of the hammer hitting the nails. The tears fell from my eyes
> without stopping.[16]

Uno was later asked to "mother" her lovers' children, but she never again
bore a child.

Writing began to occupy more and more of her time. She took an English-language course and began trying to read English books.

> I began to study, more than ever determined to become a celebrated woman. I placed a board over the *kotatsu* and on top of it arranged my paper and pens. Then I retrieved Bebel's essays on women from my husband's bookshelf and set about "translating" them with great earnestness. "Perhaps I will be like Hiratsuka Raichō or Yamakawa Kikue!"
>
> My husband came home late one night while I was hard at work. "What's this, 'And then Sukopenhua said . . .'?"
>
> "Well, it's somebody's name!" I snapped.
>
> But I had mistranscribed Schopenhauer as "Sukopenhua." Tadashi roared with laughter for the longest time. I put my pen down and sighed. What a long winter this was. I lowered the curtain and began darning socks again.[17]

Chiyo was soon to tire of her pose as an English scholar. She abandoned translating and resumed writing stories of her own. In the winter of 1920 she entered a seven-page story in a short-story contest sponsored by the newspaper *Jiji Shimpō*. In January of the following year she learned that the story "Shifun no kao" (Painted Face) had taken first prize. She was ecstatic; there on the first page of an established newspaper was her name, Fujimura Chiyoko, in large print along with her photograph.[18] Next to her picture were smaller pictures of the other winners: Ozaki Shisaku (Shirō) in second place, and Yagi Tōsaku in third. Kanemitsu Sama (Yokomitsu Riichi) was given an honorable mention. Satomi Ton and Kume Masao had judged the contest, and apparently the competition was severe. Satomi scored both Chiyo's and Ozaki's stories equally at seventy-two points, reserving his highest mark of seventy-five for Kanemitsu Sama. Kume put Chiyo over the top with a score of eighty-three, whereas he gave the other two authors scores of eighty-two and seventy respectively. Chiyo won by a single point, thanks to Kume Masao—one of her most ardent admirers at the Enrakuken. Both judges claimed not to have recognized Chiyo because she used her married name. Yet, since her photograph accompanied her submission, one wonders how impartial they really were.

"Painted Face" is a minor work in comparison with Uno's later masterpieces. As might be expected, the story is immature and unformed, lacking the cohesiveness and control of her more mature works. And yet it evinces a certain freshness and liveliness. The story concerns the plight of Osumi, a poor but moderately attractive café waitress who becomes involved with Hüber, the Swiss manager of a Yokohama-based silk-exporting business. Hüber offers to provide Osumi with sixty yen a month, and, though he never makes clear what is expected in return, Osumi accepts. On the day she has agreed to meet him at the horse races, she watches dismally as he falls in love with a younger, more presentable Japanese woman.

> That evening a letter from Hüber was delivered by express mail. Oh, she had expected such a letter, she just hadn't expected it so soon! To the very end, Osumi simply could not understand how disillusioned Hüber had been seeing her peony-blossom, painted face under the bright autumn rays of the noonday sun. A feeling of irritation lodged in her heart, not to be removed for some time. The ordeal had not been worth the sixty yen![19]

Chiyo received two hundred yen for "Painted Face." The prospect of earning money encouraged her to continue writing. She is not reticent about the fact that, at first, writing was a way to earn a living. " 'You mean you can make money like this with writing?' This was not an inappropriate thought for me. I had been poor all my life. I made up my mind then and there that I would write for money."[20] But a writer needed a mentor to succeed, and Chiyo turned to Takita Choin, the editor of the *Chūō Kōron*.

> Suddenly the face of one of the customers at that fancy restaurant where I had worked flashed across my mind. He had come every day for lunch. The other girls called him Kintarō. Mr. Takita Choin, our Kintarō, worked for the Chūō Kōron Publishers, whose offices were on the third floor of the bank across the street. As soon as the noon bell chimed, he'd appear at our door. In fifteen minutes flat he'd eat a five-course meal, and, after downing his beer in a single gulp, he'd be on his way, tossing a fifty-sen piece on the silver serving tray. With that fifty sen I could buy ever so many things! That's it. I shall see if I can't get that man to give me fifty sen again.
>
> I wrote every day. I didn't know if what I wrote was a novel or not. I just wrote what I was able to write leaving out whatever I couldn't. But I was able to write at length, and, when I had written over one hundred pages, I gave my work the ponderous title "Haka wo abaku" (Opening the Grave).[21]

Shortly after completing "Opening the Grave" in November 1921, Chiyo sent it to Takita Choin. She expected to hear from him shortly, but when month after month passed without word, she imagined her precious manuscript lying forgotten on a desk in Takita's office. In April 1922, when the snows were melting and the violets pushing their way up through the soggy ground, Chiyo bade her husband goodbye and boarded a train for Tokyo. Once there she walked to the Chūō Kōron office, where she obtained an audience with the famous editor. He took one look at her and tossed the May

1922 issue of his magazine her way. "Opening the Grave" had been published.

The work, based on Chiyo's experiences as a school teacher in Kawashimo, is quite unlike her earlier story. Instead of flashy verve and facetious coquetry, "Opening the Grave" is burdened with misery and brutality. A deaf student is cruelly turned away from school, an outcast girl is shunned, and another girl violently beaten, all while school officials scramble to show off before provincial politicians. The work, with its never-ending parade of sorrow, is hopelessly flawed and now forgotten. But, despite its weakness, the work is important for one reason: it represents the direction Uno's writing might have taken had she been so inclined. When she wrote "Opening the Grave," Chiyo was clearly inspired by and imitative of the Socialist works that were fast becoming the dominant trend on the literary front. During her stay in Hokkaido, she had pored over the works of August Bebel, a leader in the German Social Democratic party and an inspiration to many Japanese socialists. She was even more entranced by the courageous rhetoric of feminists like Hiratsuka Raichō and Yamakawa Kikue. After finishing "Opening the Grave," she fully expected to become another Chūjō Yuriko (1899–1951), a writer with Socialist sympathies who had made a sensational debut six years earlier at the age of seventeen. In fact, Chiyo's work is not unlike Yuriko's "Mazushiki hitobito no mure" (The Flock of Impoverished, 1916); both authors deal sympathetically with the squalid lives of the rural poor.

Socialist works, which emerged during the so-called Taishō Democracy period (1912–1926), meant to challenge society by embracing the downtrodden and exposing the tyranny of the bourgeoisie. Chiyo does just this in "Opening the Grave" by providing an outspoken condemnation of the provincial educational system, among other assorted ills. Moreover, in an obvious attempt to mimic stock Socialist issues, she focuses on Korean-Japanese disparity and the plight of Japanese outcasts. Her prose style, though generally following the rhythms of her native dialect, is overwrought at times and highly rhetorical as she incorporates the conventions and formulas of Socialist literature. She frequently uses terms like "civic outrage" and "rebellious spirit," and has her heroine's "heart harden with resistance, as if she were glaring into the sharp eyes of some dark monster."[22] Her description of a family of outcasts "crawling over the black earth like ants" is typically formulaic,[23] as is her description of the deaf-mute's father who grows angry over his son's unjust dismissal. "He turned a fiery red with anger down to the very roots of the hair on his naked chest. He bared his yellow teeth, and his jaw began to waggle as if he wanted to continue speaking. But the muscles in his cheeks froze."[24]

Perhaps "Opening the Grave" received the attention it did because it so neatly incorporated the aims and interests of the newly emerging Socialist literary movement. And, since Socialist works have rarely been noted for their outstanding literary merit, it would not have been surprising had Chiyo's work been published in a small coterie magazine that espoused Marxist issues. But "Opening the Grave" hardly deserved printing in the prestigious *Chūō Kōron*. The fact that it was leads some to suspect that Takita Choin was too impressed by the memory of the pretty Enrakuken waitress to view her work impartially. Chiyo seems to have had this in mind when she sent him the piece.

> Mr. Takita had probably read my manuscript out of curiosity . . . a waitress he used to know had written a story. A waitress who writes a story, I thought, had a definite advantage over, say, a young woman from a good, middle-class family. In the same sense, I now feel lucky, being born a woman.[25]

With "Opening the Grave" Chiyo proved that she had the material for social criticism, but she lacked the temperament for it. She would never attempt such a work again, and in her succeeding works she was to turn increasingly to a literature of private emotion.

3

THE MAGOME

LITERATI

VILLAGE

Uno did not return to Sapporo imme-
diately, as she had promised Tadashi. In fact, she did not return at all. When
Takita Choin handed her the May 1922 issue of *Chūō Kōron*, he also handed
her an envelope of money. Her 130-page work had netted 366 yen, which she
calculated at approximately three yen per page—a sizable income for one who
had earlier earned just eight yen a month as a teacher's assistant. It seemed she
was on her way to becoming that "celebrated woman." But if she were to
accomplish her dream, she would have to stay in Tokyo, the hub of literary
activity. Nothing would come of her if she buried herself once again in the
snows of Sapporo. Uno wired Tadashi that she would remain in Tokyo for
several weeks, write a story or two, and set the publishing wheels in motion
before returning. She made a quick trip to Iwakuni, where she lavishly spent
her earnings on Ryū and on her siblings, showing the country town just
what big-city success had done for its prodigal daughter. It seems she even
paraded gleefully before the school teacher who had earlier spurned her—
revenge was sweet.

When Uno returned to Tokyo she rented a small farm cottage in Sugamo
and began writing. In June she published an essay in the *Yomiuri Shimbun* and
in August her second story, "Chimata no zatsuon" (Harbor Sounds),
appeared in *Chūō Kōron*. Shortly thereafter she met the young writer Ozaki
Shirō, the man who had won second place in the *Jiji Shimpō* short-story contest. Accounts differ as to the circumstances of their meeting, but it seems
once they were together Ozaki began to discuss his forays in the Yoshiwara

pleasure quarter. Apparently he meant to intimidate the young woman who had bested him in the contest, but far from shocking Uno, he left her smitten.

> I imagine I was captivated by Ozaki Shirō from our very first meeting. It is now well known that he stutters. But back then his stuttering was especially severe. Every time he started to say something I was so taken with him that I wanted to help him. I wanted to speak for him. His hair was cropped short in a tousled mass. He was very fashionable, yet with an air of nonchalance. I was completely disarmed. Yes, there I was, a silly country girl knocked senseless with one glimpse of a handsome boy.[1]

Uno followed Ozaki to his room at the Hongō Kikufuji Hotel, a first-rate inn not far from the Enrakuken. He discreetly rented the adjoining room for her, but apparently it went unused. One biographer put it thus: "Judging from the mountain of *donburi* bowls stacked outside Ozaki's 'Plum Room,' rumors went the rounds that the two were involved in lovemaking day and night."[2]

Many years later Uno conceded that leaving Tadashi was one thing in her life that she regretted. He had been a good and gentle husband and abandoning him without a word of explanation was shameful. But Ozaki reawakened a passion in Uno that had lain dormant while she was with Tadashi. She could not bear to deny this passion and resume her life with a husband who, for all his kindness, was little more than a brother to her.

> "What you are doing is adulterous! A heinous crime! Stop now before it is too late and return to Hokkaido!" Had someone admonished me thus, as I was on my way in ecstasy to visit Ozaki, I would have been too lightheaded to have minded, too carried away with rapture. "Don't worry," I would have said. "This is not a crime or anything of the sort. It's just that I'm so happy. I'm sure if you told him this he'd want me to be with Ozaki as well."[3]

But adultery *was* a heinous crime at the time—at least for women. Years earlier it had been punishable by death, and, though the penalties were not as severe in 1922, it was still a civil and criminal offense. Women could be not only divorced but imprisoned for up to two years if their husbands chose to prosecute. Tadashi did not press charges, nor was he particularly interested in divorce. However, when it became increasingly clear that Uno had no intention of returning, his family intervened and had her name stricken from the Fujimura registry. Uno and Tadashi were officially divorced in April 1924. She married Ozaki shortly thereafter, though their marriage was not regis-

tered until February 1926. She dropped the name Fujimura and began using
Uno. She never again adopted her husband's name and became known in
both professional and social circles as Uno Chiyo.

A year earlier, in May 1923, Uno and Ozaki had bought a house for 140
yen in Magome Village, Ebara County, on what was then the outskirts of
Tokyo. Actually, what they had purchased was a farmer's two-room storage
shed in the middle of a radish field. They floored one of the rooms with
tatami mats and the other with concrete. There was no kitchen; Uno cooked
on a small stove under the eaves. Gradually they were able to remodel the
house. They added an octagonal bay window to the tatami room, as well as a
red carpet, blue chintz curtains, and a piano. Several years later they added a
new wing.

In this tiny "love nest" Uno and Ozaki began their "fairy-tale" life.
Ozaki, with his dark kimono and crisp Hakata sash, was more the romantic
hero in an old drama than a progressive intellectual from Waseda University.
Uno dressed the part of the amorous wife of yesteryear. She sewed black satin
collars onto her kimonos, affecting the suggestive nonchalance of the low-
city beauties, and dressed her hair in an elaborate coiffure high atop her head,
the way Ozaki liked it most.

Uno Chiyo made quite an impression on the literary world, though her
fame as "O-Chiyo-san, the classic beauty," greatly surpassed her fame as Uno
the writer. In fact, "critics," while only briefly commenting on her works,
have much to say about her devotion to Ozaki. They extol her as "Ozaki's
obedient wife, asking his permission before doing anything."[4] "She loved
Ozaki more than her art."[5] The rhetoric is always overblown, and the observations frequently incorrect. "I never put my husbands before my writing,"
Uno later said. "Never!"[6] Of course, not all the critical observations were
well intentioned. Uno had shocked many with her penchant for love, and
more than a few articles reproved her for her wanton behavior. Ozaki was
touted as her "young swallow," a term applied to men "kept" by older
women. Ozaki was barely half a year younger than Uno, and the label infuriated him. Whenever he heard someone call him this he would growl, "I'm
no swallow! I ran off with her like a wild dog!"[7]

The Great Kantō Earthquake of September 1, 1923, broke the quiet seclu-
sion the two enjoyed in Magome. The quake did not damage their property,
or affect them particularly, but it heralded a new age for the sleepy Magome.
Many writers and artists left homeless by the devastation began to migrate
toward Magome, drawn by friends there who could help them establish resi-
dences of their own. Between 1923 and 1929 over eighty writers and poets
moved into the area; among them were Hirotsu Kazuo (1891–1968), Hagi-

wara Sakutarō (1886–1942), Miyoshi Tatsuji (1900–1964), Murō Saisei (1889–1962), and Kawabata Yasunari (1899–1972). Before long the area was dubbed the "Magome Literati Village."

The members of the Magome Literati Village began to gravitate toward the Ozaki cottage. Ozaki was a dynamic and well-liked person, constantly in the company of admirers. Friends gathered nightly to discuss literature and leftist activities, to gossip, and, of course, to drink. Uno was always there to attend to them, serving treats she had whipped up in her kitchen under the eaves. Since most of the residents of the Literati Village were too poor to own a radio, the gatherings became a means to disseminate information— world events at times but mostly mundane gossip: the latest love suicide, the latest divorce—and the Uno-Ozaki cottage became known as the "Magome Broadcast Center."

In spite of all this activity and excitement, Uno still managed to write. She continued to be published in *Chūō Kōron* but was also receiving attention from other quarters. By 1924 her works were appearing in *Fujin Kōron,* a woman's magazine sponsored by Chūō Kōronsha, as well as in prominent literary journals such as *Shin Shōsetsu, Shinchō,* and *Bungei Shunjū.* By 1925, just five years after her debut, she had published five different collections of short stories. Biographer Kondō Tomie terms Uno's sudden success "Cinderella-like. . . . She was extremely lucky. She danced on ahead without a mentor, without a supporting coterie, and without having to struggle through a period of impoverished obscurity."[8]

Uno's works perhaps did not deserve the attention they received, but they were not being judged on their literary merits alone. As the "critics' " comments reveal, they were not being judged at all. Uno the wife, the pretty woman writer, was more the subject of consideration than what she wrote. She was a sensation.

Also important in helping Uno establish herself in the "literary world" was the fact that she entered the scene virtually unchallenged by other women writers. Since women were not generally judged alongside their male peers at the time, they were set aside from the literary mainstream and lumped together under the category of *joryū sakka* (women writers). All the women who would later become Uno's contemporaries and rivals—Hirabayashi Taiko (1905–1971), Hayashi Fumiko (1903–1951), Sata Ineko (b. 1904), and Enchi Fumiko (1905–1986)—were still in their "wandering years" and were not actively writing. Miyamoto (Chūjō) Yuriko (1899–1951), with her interest focused on her new and failing marriage, was not writing consistently. And Tamura Toshiko, earlier the recipient of attention for her bold depiction of feminine desire, had followed her lover to North America. The only other woman writer in any position to challenge Uno was Nogami Yaeko

(1885–1985), who had stunned the literary world in 1922 with "Kaijinmaru," a riveting story based on a true account of cannibalism aboard a ship lost at sea. Nogami was a talented writer with surprisingly broad vision, who had earlier secured the backing of the eminent Natsume Sōseki (1867–1916). She had all the credentials to make an outstanding writer. But, properly married to a university professor, she was the very epitome of the "good wife, wise mother" and hardly the material for a "celebrated woman." Uno Chiyo, on the other hand, "had appeared on the literary scene like a comet, a perfect target for journalism. Beautiful, young, and with a history of fiery love affairs, the talented Uno Chiyo had all the qualifications necessary to become a popular member of the 'literary world' in the late Taishō period, filling the void left by other women writers."[9]

Uno was a prolific writer during these early years. In fact, she wrote more at this time than she would ever write again. "I was happy, and I wrote all day long. . . . I meticulously described every detail of my life. My dog got sick and I wrote about it in a story; a new neighbor moved in next door and I wrote about *that*."[10] Later Uno was loath to look at anything she wrote prior to her early masterpiece *Irozange* (Confessions of Love, 1935), because she considered those works "worthless." Her self-assessment is not far from the mark. Her early works are hackneyed, melodramatic, and generally redundant. Almost all deal with naive young women who in a bold quest for freedom or financial success in the city (i.e., Tokyo), leave the confines of their country homes only to fall victim to poverty and abusive lovers. Despite the immaturity of these works, Uno did find her share of admirers. Critics praised her ability to delineate the subtle shades of a woman's emotions. Many commended her honesty in portraying women of simple, sometimes questionable, virtue. Kitagawa Chiyoko, for instance, preferred Uno's women to those of Nogami Yaeko or Miyamoto Yuriko.

> [Nogami and Miyamoto] may write of the most profound agonies, but I feel that they are on some high pedestal, and I am far beneath them looking up. . . .
>
> The greatest flaw in works by women is that they do not strip themselves completely bare. But Uno, I feel, is exceptional. The women she creates are slovenly and deceitful, but they do not make me feel the least bit uncomfortable, perhaps because I can sense behind them the author's own candor and honesty.[11]

While Uno was dashing off story after story about "slovenly and deceitful" women, her husband was suffering from bouts of writer's block. His career at the time was as low as hers was high; hardly any magazine would publish a work by him. Ozaki would eventually become one of the more successful, and thereby infamous, of government-sponsored wartime writers, a reputation for which he was to pay in the Occupation-era purges. During his student days at Waseda University he had been interested in Marxism, and, though his political views were vague, he associated with the Proletarian writers. After his debut in the *Jiji Shimpō*, he began to write about the Kōtoku Shūsei Grand Treason Incident of 1910, and, because his sympathies were supposedly with the alleged traitor, most of his works were banned or censored. One-third of the fifty-page "Gokushitsu no an'ei" (In the Shadow of the Prison Room, 1922), for example, was censored when it appeared in the politically liberal journal *Kaizō*. Critics ignored his works, therefore, since most appeared in "abbreviated" form, when they appeared at all. Publishers avoided him because they did not wish to take the time and incur the expense of publishing a work that would be censored, or worse, banned— meaning that all copies of the magazine or newspaper would be confiscated. Uno did her best to encourage her husband's efforts; at times she virtually bribed editors to accept his submissions. "It is certainly distressing," she was to say, "when the wife's works sell but the husband's don't."[12]

Ozaki apparently was of a high-strung disposition. It must have been torture for him to sit alongside Uno in their tiny "love nest," his nerves wound to the breaking point, while she dashed off story after story. Being a member of the Proletarian movement, even if only nominally, had its additional pressures; Ozaki was expected to conduct himself like an intellectual. Uno had earlier freed herself of any need to write under a particular political program, but Ozaki could not. The strain of literary incompatibility and professional jealousy began to tell on their marriage.

They would have to find an outlet, and in February of 1927 Kawabata Yasunari offered one when he invited them to join him at Yugashima, a lonely hot spring village at the foot of Mt. Amagi on the Izu Peninsula. They gratefully accepted his offer, both believing that the quiet hot spring would give their creativity the boost it had Kawabata's; he had just published his early masterpiece "Izu no odoriko" (The Izu Dancer, 1926). They set out for Yugashima with Hagiwara Sakutarō and Hirotsu Kazuo.

But the change in venue provided only temporary relief. Ozaki still could not accept the fact that he was competing with his wife. He admired Uno's talent and was grateful to her for the support she had given his career. In fact, he was so dependent on her financially and emotionally that friends often referred to Uno as his *neesan-nyōbō* (big sister-wife).[13] But Ozaki did not want a big sister; he wanted a wife, and he could not help but resent Uno for her success. "Two writers living together," he was to say, "was tantamount to having a thief and a detective under the same roof."[14]

Ozaki began to vent his frustrations in the fiction he was writing at the time, describing his difficulties with Uno in thinly veiled accounts, such as that in his story "Kajika" (River Deer, 1927):

> They had drained from each other's lives all that there was to be gotten from them. In loving, in hating, there was already no freshness or life left. It was as if they had fallen into identical traps. By the repeated, wearisome habit of putting each other off with minor emotions, of favoring each other with morsels of affection that were more like leavings, they barely managed to feel different from each other. It couldn't go on this way, . . . It was not that either of them was bad. It was just that the marriage itself was unnatural. Aside from the physiological distinction that he was a man and she a woman, they shared exactly the same temperament.[15]

As the story continues the narrator recounts a conversation he had with his wife in which he accuses her of always demanding her own way, of using him but never really needing him. He declares that he wants to live alone so as to restore his own self-esteem. As the story ends his wife is crying pathetically while he stands beside the river watching frogs (the river deer) mate.

Uno was horrified by the way Ozaki portrayed her in the story, and she was humiliated that he had described in print a personal argument they had actually had in Yugashima. Moreover, it hurt her to think that he could convey to his readers feelings he had not adequately communicated to her. Up until this time they had carefully avoided exposing their personal life in print. It had been their tacit understanding that, whereas they might write of people who resembled themselves, they would not write *about* themselves. But Ozaki had broken this trust with "River Deer"; and he had done it in a way that was extremely unflattering to Uno.

For a brief period Uno contemplated abandoning her writing for Ozaki. She wanted to live the life of a "normal" wife. "I'll leave the hot springs and go home. I'll do just as he says, whatever he says. I'll toss aside my own silly ego and set him free within the far-reaching boundaries of my love."[16] But Ozaki found her suggestions too ridiculous to consider. Having Uno Chiyo as a normal wife would not have been a panacea to his suffering. There was little that could be done. Uno began to spend more and more time at the hot springs alone, reasoning that her absence would give Ozaki the room he needed and would also release her own pent-up frustrations.

> I wonder now if my constant trips to Yugashima were not the cause for my break with Ozaki. But when I recall the feeling of liberation that I had when I first came to this inn nestled in the mountains and hung my towel, damp from

the bath, over the railing outside my room and looked out upon the river, I can well appreciate the strangeness of the things we humans do.[17]

It was not just the solitude of the sleepy mountain town that intrigued Uno, but the energetic and avant-garde college men who had also migrated to Yugashima—seeking the quiet warmth of the waters as well as the company of the other artistic souls sojourning there. A few, captivated by Uno, began to gather regularly in her room to discuss Baudelaire, Cocteau, and the latest Western fashions. Uno found the conversation fascinating, much more stimulating than the tiresome topics Ozaki was wont to discuss. Hirotsu Kazuo describes these conversations in his essay "Shōwa shonen no interi sakka" (Intelligentsia Writers in the First Years of Shōwa, 1930; Kitagawa is the fictionalized name for Hirotsu).

> No doubt the conversations with those college boys awakened in her a fresh interest, more so than her husband's discussions with Kitagawa. Surely she had grown bored with their never-ending diatribes on Rudin and Oblomov. The college boys spoke of Cocteau. . . . For every day that her husband and Kitagawa mulled over the same old arguments, she was growing younger and younger.[18]

Uno abandoned her beautifully old-fashioned kimono with its collar of black satin and began to wear Western dresses. Soon she was to bob her hair. This new haircut, known as the *mimi-kakushi* (ear-hiding style) for obvious reasons, featured flapper-style bangs, short hair in back, and longer hair angling along the sides into points at the chin. It is difficult now to imagine the outrage this hairstyle provoked, but in 1927 it was a scandal. In fact, only fifty years earlier short hair on women had been outlawed.[19] By Uno's day, women no longer needed to fear the law, but even so they were believed to be immoral, if not frightening, for their outlandish coiffures. Children on the back roads of Magome would run away shrieking when they saw Uno approach. But before long this strange species of woman, known as *modan gāru* (modern girl) or *mo ga* for short, began to arouse more curiosity than fear.

> Lately the word *modan gāru* can be heard at every turn. "I saw a *modan gāru* slip in front of the Maru Building," one will hear, for example. Or, "I saw one take a tumble in the Ginza." One slipped, one fell—the reporters seem to burst with glee. Oh, it may be rude, I suppose, but they mean no harm. It is just that *modan gāru* are cropping up everywhere like bamboo shoots after a rain.[20]

The author of the above essay, however, laments that these women are not truly "modern"; they are not even as radical as the "new woman" of the earlier era, who was at least "new."

> The *modan gāru* is just an ordinary woman who cuts her hair short and shaves the nape of her neck until it glistens blue. She may dress in a dangly fringe that displays her calves with more aplomb than a Nerima farmer hawking radishes; and, she may dab her lips and cheeks with imported rouge and stroll about with the latest parasol. But in the end the changes are only skin deep. Nothing is different inside. She is just like an old piece of furniture with a new coat of paint."[21]

For Uno Chiyo, the act was not political—not, that is, that she was aware. She cut her hair to look younger; everyone thought that a woman with short hair looked more youthful than her years. And Uno, well aware that Ozaki was younger than she (if only by half a year), thought that if she rejuvenated her appearance she would continue to attract him. When the barber cut her hair, she believed he cut seven years off her looks.

Bobbed hair was in keeping with the mood of daring and decadence that swept through Japan during the late Taishō and early Shōwa period. Jazz music and social dancing soon became the rage. In Magome, one of the most ardent hosts was the poet Hagiwara Sakutarō. He bought a phonograph, threw a rug over his tatami-matted floor, and held dance parties at regular intervals. Uno Chiyo was nearly always in attendance, gaily sashaying through a tango with a young admirer.

Legend has it that Sakutarō, in awe of Uno's unconventionality and profoundly attracted to her, asked her to instill his wife, Ineko, with just a touch of the flapper spirit. Only recently Tanizaki Jun'ichirō had promised his wife to his best friend, Satō Haruo, but Tanizaki reneged on the deal when he found that his rivalry with Satō had quickened his own affection for his wife. Sakutarō hoped that a little jealousy would revive his languishing marriage, too. He had contemplated divorce on several occasions, reasoning that Ineko "was stupid, she did not get along with his mother, and her skin was rough."[22] But he had changed his mind each time and was now spurred on by the erotic possibilities of envy.

Uno evidently undertook her task with earnestness. She dragged Ineko, and Mrs. Kawabata as well, to the barber shop and had their hair bobbed. This accomplished, she taught Ineko to dance, introducing her to a variety of young men. When Ineko ran off with one of them, leaving her two young daughters behind with Sakutarō, Uno was blamed.

Kondō Tomie has termed the Taishō and early Shōwa period "the era of adulterous women." Men had been indulging in extramarital affairs for centuries, of course, but now women—and highly placed women at that—indulged as well. "Modern girls," it seems, were particularly susceptible to this adulterous "fever." Almost by definition a "modern girl" was modern only after she had freed herself from the confines of marriage. Uno, attempting to attract Ozaki to her, instead turned him away when she cut off the old-fashioned coiffure he had prized. He despised her new look.

But there were those who found Uno's new look captivating, and central among them was Kajii Motojirō (1901–1932), an aspiring young writer and one of the college men constantly in attendance upon Uno at Yugashima. Kajii was in the English Department at Tokyo Imperial University but, suffering from tuberculosis, had been convalescing at the hot spring since November 1926.

Kajii was fiercely in love with Uno. He visited her room nightly and stayed for hours. Often he sneaked in to see her after midnight by climbing in through her second-floor window. Once, at a dance party in Magome, he even came to blows with Ozaki over the latter's treatment of Uno, and earlier at Yugashima he had engaged Miyoshi Tatsuji, another Uno admirer, in a fist fight. Given Uno's constant trips to Yugashima, and Kajii's obvious infatuation with her, it was not long before rumors about the two began to circulate, rumors that Uno emphatically denied.

Uno was clearly fond of Kajii. She took great delight in his impetuosity and brashness. She was equally impressed by his keen sensitivity and by the quiet somberness that she felt just beneath his show of bravado. She was aware of his passion for her and even admits leading him on rather cruelly—an act she was later to regret. Yet despite Uno's penchant for Kajii, she has consistently denied ever being in love with him; she describes her affection for him rather as that of a sister for a brother.

Few believed that she and Kajii were not intimately involved, and some still doubt her now. "Even my own people do not believe me. My secretary, who has been my closest companion for years, is certain that Kajii and I were lovers!"[23] If the majority opinion is believed, one has to ask why Uno, who had already made a reputation for herself as a writer who "strips (herself) completely bare," wished to conceal this affair. Was it because she was still unwilling to lose Ozaki, regardless of their barren relationship? Or perhaps her secrecy was encouraged because she knew Kajii was dying and would not be able to offer her the refuge she would need.

But whether or not Uno and Kajii were intimately involved is less significant than the fact that they appeared to be. Uno was spending most of her time in Yugashima and, to all outward appearances, had abandoned Ozaki; this was intolerable to most of the members of the Magome Literati Village. They urged Ozaki to seek a divorce. He was then, in early 1928, serializing a novel in the *Jiji Shimpō*, which, given Ozaki's previous success rate, was quite an achievement as well as a lucrative enterprise. He spent his earnings on entertainment in the Ginza, and there he met Koga Kiyoko, a seventeen-year-old waitress at the Café Lion. Spurred on by his friends' accusations and enchanted by Kiyoko's sweet naiveté, Ozaki asked her to marry him.

Uno did not know Ozaki was serializing a novel until she saw it in the paper. She rushed home to congratulate him, only to find that he had deserted their bungalow and was roving from one friend's house to another with Koga Kiyoko. Uno was furious with Ozaki's meddlesome friends, but mostly she was hurt. His friends had once been hers as well, and now she discovered they had all turned against her.

The ensuing separation was not easy for either of the two; it was especially cruel for Uno, who had no new lover to turn to. Kajii visited her briefly in the summer of 1928, but, when his condition continued to deteriorate, he returned to his family home in Osaka. To make matters worse, Ozaki, it seems, was unable to break with Uno completely. He continued to visit her from time to time, and occasionally they met at the homes of mutual friends, Ozaki often in the company of his young lover.

Uno was not yet ready to relinquish Ozaki either, and the emotional turmoil drove her to despair. She could not bear to remain behind in her Magome bungalow. For more than a year, from the early spring of 1928 to the fall of 1929, Uno drifted between hot spring inns and long-term hotels, where she entertained herself with the countless college students who happened along. In addition to these nameless paramours, she was rumored to have been involved with Makino Shin'ichi (1896–1936), a writer and a friend of Ozaki's who spent much of March and April of 1929 in Uno's Magome bungalow. Mah-jongg and drinking parties began to occupy Uno's time. She began to drink heavily and at one point acquired the barbiturate Vernol from a doctor she had met in Yugashima. Uno mixed the drug with alcohol, enjoying sometimes for days on end the dreamlike stupor it induced. Her friends feared she would resort to suicide.

Uno turned to writing instead. Earlier she had dashed off story after story on topics as inconsequential as her dog. Accompanying her break with Ozaki, her writing slowed and became decidedly personal, almost therapeutic. Ozaki had written of their marriage, and she would too. Uno began to turn the focus of her fiction inward, mining her own experiences and emotions for the material of her stories. Her fiction from this time onward began to conform more and more to the *watakushi shōsetsu* form—the mainstream of Japanese prose fiction.

The concept of *watakushi shōsetsu* is interpreted in many different ways by writers and critics. Generally translated as "I-novel," it is neither a novel, in the strictest Western sense, nor always a first-person narrative. The form claims to represent an author's lived experiences just as the author lived them, without any fictional mediation. Yet inevitably it allows for embellishment, alterations, and synthesis; thus, readers are left not with documented fact, but with an emotional, at times almost spiritual, re-creation of an author's experience. In short, the *watakushi shōsetsu* is a form "riddled with paradoxes."[24] For the purpose of this discussion, perhaps it can best be understood as a story about the "I," the self, the author, or, that is to say, the persona the author creates.

In "Shitsuraku no uta" (Song of Lost Happiness, 1929), for example, Uno makes no attempt to disguise herself with a fictionalized name or a temporal subterfuge but appears directly in the story, or so it is made to seem, and gives voice to the various emotions she experienced during her separation from Ozaki. In the following scene, the first-person narrator has gone to a friend's house uninvited. All of her old friends are there drinking and laughing. In the entry hall she sees her husband's shoes and next to them his young lover's colorful *geta* sandals. The narrator feels excluded and betrayed.

> "You traitors! Liars! Bastards!"
> Like an idiot I cursed those standing behind me. But it did not give me the slightest comfort.
> "There is nothing left," I told myself. "All has been destroyed!" I leaned against the wooden fence and began to cry. When I turned I found my husband standing by my shoulder. He seemed drunk. I stared at him. He seemed barely able to stand. His head lurched forward and his bare chest pressed against the fence. My eyes blurred and all I could see was a lump tumbling toward me.
> "You came to see me?"
> The lump spoke. I hid my head. It was not the same. Not the same at all. But a thread of happiness as slender as a spider's web came to console me. I smiled through my tears like a schoolgirl.
> "See how my hair has grown!"[25]

Writers of personal fiction frequently wrote of the same experience over and over, altering the particulars somewhat in an effort to grapple with the shifting ambiguity of memory. Uno was no exception; her break with Ozaki was a multidimensional event, not satisfied in one telling. Each story offered a new dimension, as if a new layer of memory had been stripped away to reveal a different reality. "Tanjōbi" (Birthday), for example, was written the same year as "Song of Lost Happiness," but it is more controlled and somewhat more detached. Masako, the third-person narrator, leaves her husband after a bitter quarrel and strolls through town with a male companion. She sees a copper teakettle in a shop window and impulsively dashes in to buy it.

"We have gone long enough without a teakettle. This will come in handy."
But suddenly it occurred to her that a teakettle was hardly an appropriate purchase for a wife who planned to run away from home. Blushing, she was quick to add, "Well, by buying this kettle I'll insure that the next woman to live in that house will have it that much easier."[26]

This scene, and the one quoted above, reveal more than just the details of Uno's break with Ozaki. They show subtly yet poignantly the pressures exerted on a woman newly aware of her own self: she longs to dash recklessly ahead in her exploration and celebration of this self, yet nonetheless she is held back by a desire for traditional domesticity—the long hair and the teakettle. It is these two conflicting forces that would continually pull at Uno, determining the direction of her life and generating the impetus for her creative expression.

4

CONFESSIONS

OF LOVE

By the summer of 1929 the heyday of the Magome Literati Village had passed. Hagiwara Sakutarō, having lost his wife to a younger man, was no longer hosting gala dance parties. Hirotsu Kazuo had left and Kawabata Yasunari was planning to do the same. Uno and Ozaki's house remained, but its chief inhabitants refused to return. Ozaki was staying with friends, and Uno continued to wander. In June she traveled to Ikaho hot springs with her close friend, the writer Miyake Yasuko (1890–1932), Yasuko's seventeen-year-old daughter, Tsuyako, Kawabata Yasunari, and several others. As accommodations were limited, Uno and Kawabata shared the same bed, though Uno stated later, somewhat amused, that there was no romantic attraction between them whatsoever. "I had known Kawabata for a long time, and I felt for him . . . well, what should I say? I did not think of him as a man; and he did not think of me as a woman. We were like two sexless beings sharing the same bed for the night, that was all."[1]

Uno was ready to convince herself that she had no further interest in men. "I shall live alone," she pledged. "Instead of loving a man I shall love my work. I shall love myself. In order to become a respected, independent person (no woman has ever achieved such) I shall take no man as my husband, no matter who he may be. I shall simply live alone."[2] Uno was so determined to live alone that she formed her own "singles club" (with a membership of one) and drew up a charter of independence:

Economic Independence
Emotional Independence
And a determination to follow my own will!!![3]

She tacked the charter to the wall of her room.

In the late summer of 1929 Uno spoke of traveling to Shanghai but instead moved to Kobe to gain inspiration for a novel she had been asked to serialize. Here she was able to see Kajii from time to time. By December she was back in Tokyo, staying again in the inns along the Ōmori coast. On December 21, 1929, she began serializing *Keshi wa naze akai* (Tell Me Why Poppies Are Red) in the *Hōchi Shimbun;* it was her first newspaper novel and an important achievement. Many in the literary world had expected Uno to fade away after her humiliating break with Ozaki, and for a time it seemed she was heading toward destruction. But "like a phoenix," as Kondō Tomie said, she rose from the ashes of her sorrow even stronger and more sensational. The daily serialization, in 150 installments, lasted until May 22, 1930. The title, it is said, is one Kajii had suggested.

Like most newspaper novels, *Tell Me Why Poppies Are Red* appeals to a popular audience. It is made up of an intricate weave of murders, suicides, and illicit love affairs that occur and reoccur in cycles, all connected by the ever predictable yet, in this case, highly implausible concept of "cause and effect." Uno proved that she had read well the gothic romances in her Iwakuni outhouse, for her story offers a showcase of suspense and drama, including not only the stereotypical wicked woman but foreign gunrunners as well. She propels her readers onward with tantalizing asides, hinting devilishly at the content of the next installment. The novel was so popular at the time that it was adapted for the stage in January 1931.

Tell Me Why Poppies Are Red is engaging reading but not great literature. Fifty years after publication Uno wrote: "This novel is so overly romantic and the series of coincidences so unbelievable that when I read it now I cannot but feel that certain twinge of pity an adult feels when reading what a child has written."[4] Today this novel is often referred to not because it merits critical attention, but because it served as the bridge that led Uno to Tōgō Seiji (1897–1978), the next important personal force in her life.

Tōgō Seiji was a well-known Western-style painter influenced by the Futurists and the early Cubists. Once an apprentice to the great Taishō master Takehisa Yumeji (1884–1934), he had attended Aoyama Gakuin, where he applied himself to literature and music. Upon graduation he returned to his art studies, traveling to France in 1921, where, according to most accounts, he spent his time in bars or in the boudoirs of wealthy Parisians, while allowing his wife, Nagano Haruyo, to fund his "studies." Haruyo lived with him briefly in Paris, where she gave birth to their son, Shima. When her money ran out, Tōgō sent her back to Japan; she had to fend for herself until his return in 1928. Once home, he found that he could not abide married life. He became involved with several young women, among them Nishizaki Mitsuko, the nineteen-year-old daughter of a rear admiral in the Japanese Imperial

Navy. Tōgō planned to marry Mitsuko, but her father would not consider his proposal and did what he could to keep the couple apart. In the meantime, Tōgō turned to another young woman, Nakamura Shūko, and "married" her in February 1929, despite the fact that he was not legally divorced from Haruyo. One month later Tōgō met Mitsuko again, and they resolved to die together. On March 30, 1929, they turned on the gas, cut their throats, and waited for death. But Tōgō's maid discovered them and summoned help; both Tōgō and Mitsuko survived.

Love suicides were not infrequent at the time. In fact, in the 1920s and 1930s hardly a day went by that a major newspaper did not report one. Stringent laws regulating marriage were thought responsible for the rash of suicides. The civil code prevented women under the age of twenty-five and men under thirty from marrying without parental consent, and, when that consent was not forthcoming, as was frequently the case, young couples often looked to the "other world" for happiness. This was the basis for Tōgō's attempted suicide with Mitsuko, and the tabloids were quick to capitalize on the incident, running bold-faced headlines: TŌGŌ SEIJI, ART WORLD PRODIGY, AND REAR ADMIRAL'S DAUGHTER IN GAS SUICIDE.

The suicide attempt was a sensation, and the furor it inspired was enough to pierce the cocoon of solitude Uno had spun about herself. The impact of the news was intensified by the fact that Uno knew Tōgō. She had met him years earlier at the Enrakuken, where he often dined with Kon Tōkō. More recently she had renewed her acquaintance with him at the Miyake house, where he frequently visited Tsuyako's husband, who was also a painter. In a 1930 essay Uno breathlessly describes her reaction to Tōgō's suicide attempt. "I knew this man! So, he was capable of something so spectacular! His blood was like a flower to me—like a red cluster of flowers."[5] As the essay continues, Uno relates that one day she found herself, quite by coincidence, in Tōgō's neighborhood. She walked past his house only to find the windows closed tight, and she imagined that "inside the flower was blooming." Rather than pursue the matter, however, Uno left Tokyo and did not make another attempt to meet Tōgō until she began writing *Tell Me Why Poppies Are Red*. "I was serializing a story in a newspaper at the time and decided to write of a violent death by gas poisoning. Why did I have to use gas in the scene? I am not sure. But wishing not to write anything implausible, I sent him a letter, asking him to meet me."[6]

Uno insisted that her intentions in contacting Tōgō were strictly "business"; she needed help with a scene and that was all. But apparently she and Tōgō did not waste words on the past. When Uno saw him walk through the door of the café where they had arranged to meet she was thrilled by the sense of danger he presented. "Deep within my heart I heard the sound of that heavy helmet (of resolve) breaking asunder."[7] Without further ado the two left the café for Tōgō's atelier.

In later accounts, such as in *Watashi no bungakuteki kaisōki* (My Literary Memoirs, 1971), Uno often describes this encounter as if it took place a mere month after the suicide attempt rather than at the time she was serializing *Tell Me Why Poppies Are Red*:

> Seiji had just returned from France. He had failed in a lovers' suicide with a certain young woman, and the newspapers had blown the event all out of proportion in a way I've never seen since. We met right after that. There was nothing between us to ignite such a burning passion, and yet that night we were brought together.
>
> The next morning when I awoke I noticed what apparently I had missed the night before. The bedding we had used was spattered with blood stains. When I saw it I did not say, "My god! Isn't this blood?" Nor did I say, "Is this the blood from *that* night!" Had I been a proper woman I would have fled in terror at the sight. But to the contrary, I felt all the more inclined to remain right where I was. . . . Perhaps, had I not seen those stains, I would not have stayed with Seiji as I did.[8]

Because Uno's accounts of her life seem so frank and genuine, it is tempting to take her at her word, and biographers frequently do. In interviews the author herself will impishly describe her meeting with Tōgō almost word for word as it appears in *My Literary Memoirs*. It is not that she means to misrepresent the truth, but it seems that now, in her nineties, her memory is informed more by her fiction than by the facts.

The particulars of Uno's encounter with Tōgō, the when and where, are really less important than the consequence. Uno found a force in Tōgō, a sense of direction and intensity that she had long lost with Ozaki. Tōgō, in 1930, was just as exciting and terrifying as the brash young Ozaki had been in 1922. Instead of trying to intimidate her with talk of prostitutes and the allure of adultery, as Ozaki had done, Tōgō dared to flaunt his failure at love suicide. He was not afraid of offending society, nor was he particularly afraid of offending Uno. There was a recklessness, a danger about him that thrilled and rejuvenated her. It is this delicious defiance of theirs that she reveals so brilliantly in her fictional records of their encounter.

Both Uno and Tōgō had been living on the edge of disaster; in joining their lives together they found a mutual, if temporary, respite. As Uno's literary persona recounts in "Kono oshiroi ire" (This Powder Box, 1967): "We were birds-of-a-feather in a way, a dangerous pair, neither knowing what to do. And so, we didn't do anything. Nothing happened. Once we began to live together we put an end to our lives of dissipation."⁹ Their lives settled into a quiet pattern, such as that noted in "Jidenteki ren'ai ron" (A Record of My Loves, 1959): "I got up in the morning and made toast for my husband. I sent his dirty shirts out to the cleaners. My solicitude for him, that of a normal woman, pacified my heart. Whether I loved him or not only the gods could say, but we had both been saved."¹⁰

In August 1930 Uno and Ozaki were formally divorced. Ozaki immediately married Koga Kiyoko. Uno and Tōgō "married" but not legally—Tōgō had still not divorced Haruyo. Even so, that fall the major newspapers ran articles on their union, and Uno had announcements drawn up on expensive gold-rimmed cards, which she sent around to her acquaintances. Kajii Motojirō was reportedly distressed to learn that Uno was newly united, especially to a notorious playboy like Tōgō. The last time he had seen Uno, while she was living in Kobe, he had made her promise to come to him when he was near death and hold his hand. But his family failed to send for her, and Kajii died without her on March 24, 1932.

Early in 1931 Uno and Tōgō rented one-third of an acre of land in the Awashima area of Setagaya and, though they had no funds, began to build an elaborate house, completely Westernized and in the stark, geometrical style of Le Corbusier. It was painted white and constructed at the far end of the lot, so that a large expanse of green lawn, devoid of bush or tree, stretched out in front—a very peculiar "garden" by Japanese standards.

Shortly after they moved into their new estate, Tōgō brought his seven-year-old son, Shima, home to live with them. Uno states that they had failed to include a single room for the child and had no choice but to tuck him away in a drab room at the back of the house. Haruyo, Tōgō's legal wife, contests Uno's assertion in a venomous article that appeared in the May 1931 issue of *Fujin Gahō*. Haruyo stated that not only had Uno prepared a room for Shima, but she had outfitted it so handsomely that Haruyo was advised to seek a refund for the paltry school desk she had just bought her son. Even if Uno had prepared a room for the boy in her estate, it is clear that she had made no place for him in her life. She did not dislike the boy; indeed, from Shima's accounts it seems she enjoyed dressing him like Little Lord Fauntleroy and parading him along the Ginza.¹¹ But she was not willing to mother him—that task she left to Haruyo.

Apparently, Tōgō took it upon himself to raise Shima. Haruyo was allowed to visit the boy from time to time, and she often stayed the night with him in the Uno-Tōgō estate. Although Uno and Haruyo had their differences, they were not great rivals. Uno, after all, was not the woman who had taken Tōgō away from his family. Nishizaki Mitsuko was the guilty one, and both women shared a resentment of her.

As unconventional as life with Tōgō Seiji may have appeared to others, it was something of a watershed for Uno; it offered her a chance to change. She has since stated that all her husbands transformed both her life and her writing. Much of this transformation came about because of her conscious effort to dress herself, at least temporarily, in the colors and costumes preferred by the men in her life. Many have compared her to Chekhov's character Darling, who changed her personality whenever she changed husbands. For Ozaki, Uno was the "virtuous wife"; for Tōgō, she became the fashionable Parisienne.

> I feel helpless even now, wondering how much longer I'll continue this imitating. When I think about it, I get terribly discouraged, even in my proudest moments. My Mr. Strindberg, my Mr. Chekhov, and my Mr. Schnitzler. . . . I am thirty-eight years old, I've been writing for twelve years and I don't know who I really am. Now I am the wife of a painter, Tōgō Seiji. These days I wear French-inspired, light-colored clothes instead of those somber Scandinavian outfits I wore a few years back. I don't remember when I made the switch, and when I spread my old clothes out to air, I can't help being amazed that I did, in fact, wear them once. Now I'm trying to become like Madame Nowaie, and so glamorous hotels and parties, horseracing, fickle wives and good-looking gentlemen abound in my stories. "What car should this woman be driven in?" I ask my husband. My stories smell of perfume worn by fancily dressed young women.[12]

Uno's appearance changed quite literally while she was with Tōgō. He took her to a tailor in Yokohama and had dresses fashioned for her in the latest styles. He even convinced her to abandon her usual mask of makeup for a light film of olive oil, thus allowing the natural luster of her dark skin to glow through. Tōgō's influence went well beyond dress and toiletry. His interests in French culture, painting, and literature were transferred directly to Uno. She began reading Cocteau, Molière, and the other writers that Tōgō recommended. Fifty years after her affair with him, she described her indebtedness as follows:

> My work was writing. I had thought that literature and art had absolutely nothing in common, but I was wrong. Before I even realized it, I had been changed as completely as black to white. My writing up to then had been, I suppose, "Naturalistic." I had floundered about in subject matter as dismal as a snail crawling over the ground. When I came in contact with Tōgō's paintings,

I do not know how to express this, but I was deeply impressed by the abstract Western world they evoked. . . . The abbreviated lines of his paintings opened my writer's eyes. It happened so swiftly. I, a woman, unconscious of it all, followed as though I were being swept along by a torrent. Had I not met Tōgō then, I would not be who I am today.[13]

Tōgō's influence on her writing was immediate. Her works became leaner, more condensed abstractions of her earlier stories. They are stark narratives, generated mainly by dialogue or by a sudden flash of color. "Danro" (The Hearth, 1932), for instance, opens as follows:

A cold winter night. An old woman wearing a red smock and a young woman wearing a black kimono are knitting and talking quietly before the old-fashioned hearth where twigs are burning.
Old woman: "And then what happened?"
Young woman: "I said, 'Well, I'll see you tomorrow.' But I had no intention of going to see him. From the very start I had not wanted to go. And then, when I made that telephone call. . . ."[14]

Uno's narratives during this period are perhaps too sparse, her canvases too bare. However, the experiments she made were important; they taught her to pare down the excesses of her earlier fiction and to concentrate more on the crafting of her stories.

Uno's new attention to her art meant that her production began to slow, and slower production meant less income. For a couple already living beyond their means this was a serious predicament. Soon police "red tagged" the furniture and other belongings in the newly built estate, threatening to repossess them if bills were not met. The building contractor hired thugs to terrorize the couple into paying what they owed. Tōgō began to paint commercially, turning out canvas after canvas in a scheme to raise money. Uno took the paintings to Kyoto and Osaka, where she entered them in exhibitions, loaned them to galleries, and otherwise tried to induce Tōgō's patrons to purchase them. But the days apart and the financial burden began to weigh on the couple, and before long Uno found herself in the arms of another man. Tōgō grew suspicious and, following Uno to Osaka, discovered the affair.

Uno and Tōgō returned to their house, which was now nearly paid for. The affair was not mentioned again, but their relationship never regained the exuberance it had had before Osaka. Tōgō had clearly tired of Uno, and Uno could not bear the malicious turn their relationship had taken. Just as earlier she had escaped to the inns of Yugashima, now she began slipping off to a small cottage not far from their house.

About five years had passed since I first moved in with Tōgō. Suddenly I began to feel desperate, unable to continue. One day I announced, quite out of the blue, "I have rented a little cottage just down the road." I carted a small desk and a cushion over, packed up lunch, paper, and pens and worked there during the day. At night I came home. What had I begun? I do not believe I was so engrossed in my work that I had no choice but to act as I did. Rather, I wonder if I did not feel that I had to flee somewhere, away from that stagnant house.[15]

Uno began to stay at her study for longer and longer periods. Eventually she moved to an apartment in Ōmori, and then finally, in the early months of 1934, to Yotsuya, a considerable distance from her Awashima home. She did not come home every day; sometimes she did not come home for weeks. In the spring of that year Nishizaki Mitsuko moved into the house Uno had built with Tōgō.

Tōgō claimed that he ran into Mitsuko by accident sometime after Uno had left him, but in fact he had been seeing her while Uno was in Osaka raising money. In an essay Mitsuko states that it was, ironically, *Irozange* (Confessions of Love, 1933), the story Uno was then serializing about Tōgō's many affairs, which rekindled her love for him. When Uno learned the truth she was devastated. Had it been any other woman, the sting would not have been as sharp; but by returning to Mitsuko, Tōgō was cancelling out the passion he had shared with Uno. "Could it not be said that, even though I lived with Tōgō for five years, I had been nothing more than an interlude in their affair?"[16] In a sense Uno was right. Mitsuko, who had married in 1931, left her husband and child in 1934 to live with Tōgō. Two years later she was granted a divorce. She and Tōgō married in 1939 when Mitsuko became pregnant, and they remained together until Tōgō's death in 1978.

What infuriated Uno most was that she had absolutely no room for complaint. She, it was made to seem, had left Tōgō and had willfully opened the door to Mitsuko. Uno realized that she had been very carefully manipulated.

> I had no right to complain, no matter how you looked at the situation, and that drove me into a frenzy! . . . It reached the point where I would not even allow myself a word of reproach. I hated Tōgō for returning to that woman. I forgot all the things I had done, and, for the first time, began to hate a person outright.[17]

In a way Uno seemed to savor the pain inflicted by the loss of Tōgō. She was now fairly adept at losing in love and even created what she called her "Broken Heart Exercises."

To say I keep the bitterness of a broken heart tucked away and suffer without telling a soul would be misleading. My heartbreaks are always big affairs. I give vent to them in the bluntest, most exaggerated way. I don't complain to anyone, but alone, where no one can see me, I wail and make a great stir, too pathetic to imagine.

While cursing my absent lover I cling to the futon. All night long I am in an uproar, squirming like a caterpillar, gripping the pillar like a cicada, sobbing. Sometimes I run through the dark alleys where no one else goes, calling out my lover's name. . . .

I know it sounds crazy, but after I have carried on like this for a while, I feel just like a baby who has cried its fill. "Now what on earth was I so upset about?"[18]

Uno turned to another outlet for relieving her anger. Just as earlier she had written story after story of her break with Ozaki, now she turned her attention to her separation from Tōgō. "Some day I would like to write a book about all this," she told an interviewer. "I will expose that man to the bone."[19] And write she did. Many years after the affair, Uno commented on this tendency to turn her failed romances into literary successes: "No one is as fortunate as a woman writer. No sooner does she break up with a man than she can write about it all without the slightest sense of shame."[20]

"Wakare mo tanoshi" (Parting Pleasure, 1935) and "Miren" (A Lingering Attachment, 1936) are the most frequently cited of the many stories Uno wrote of her break with Tōgō. As *watakushi shōsetsu*, each suggests a candid, frank portrayal of this emotionally devastating moment, and each was admired for this willingness to bare all "without the slightest sense of shame." "Parting Pleasure" is written in diary form, which enhances the feeling of intimacy between the diarist and the audience, for we feel we are being granted a privileged glimpse into the woman's private life.

Today we settled everything. Comparatively calm, I did not shed a single tear. How strange that I should feel so refreshed. He came by today dressed in a tailored, brown-checked suit with a white silk scarf. His face was cleanly shaven. I was reminded of the dashing man he had been so long ago. But, I have few memories of him like this, perhaps because my love for him was always shallow. Still, what a blessing it is to be able to leave him without a tangle of emotions. Tonight I will begin a new life.[21]

The diarist in "Parting Pleasure" finds that she is invigorated by the prospects of her new life alone; the heroine of "A Lingering Attachment" is not as confident. Kayoko is enslaved by her relationship to her husband,

Shinkichi. When they are together she describes herself as "a prisoner fearing the jailer's whip" or as "an animal longing to break free from its cage."[22] Her entrapment is further symbolized by the house she has struggled to build with her husband—a ludicrous structure that now fetters them financially. Though Kayoko is eventually able to leave the house and her husband, she cannot free herself entirely from lingering feelings of regret.

"Parting Pleasure" and "A Lingering Attachment" were admired as daring exposés of "truth," yet in them we cannot help but notice the mediation of a very selective and discriminating memory. Each story appears to offer a view of the affair from a different angle, either that of the calm, composed diarist or that of the near-hysterical woman. Yet both works tell essentially the same story—the same story we had earlier in "Birthday" and in "Song of Lost Happiness"—that of an intelligent, highly passionate woman caught in the contradiction between wife and writer. Each cycle of stories reveals the same pattern of creative development as well. "Birthday" and "Parting Pleasure," the earlier of the two stories in each cycle, depict women who rush headlong, almost gleefully, into their new life of independence; whereas "Song of Lost Happiness" and "A Lingering Attachment" go back and rewrite the story, describing the dark realities of separation—the betrayal and the uncertainty.

The more a writer writes about himself or herself, as Edward Fowler suggests in *The Rhetoric of Confession,* the more that writer becomes defined and delimited by this self-portrayal. "Once an author had fashioned a particular persona, however, he could alter it only at the risk of appearing to act out of character and perhaps offending or even losing his audience. In order to make his writing 'true to life,' then, he had to continue acting out the role dictated by this literary self-image. Tail began wagging dog; persona now on occasion shaped the person in real life."[23]

Some writers, it is suggested, lived lives of scandal simply to have material for confession—material in keeping with their literary personas. Although Uno states that she was fortunate to be a woman, since her life of scandal lent itself so easily to fiction, it would be an overstatement to conclude that she lived as she did to write. We might more accurately suggest that she lived as she did because she wrote.

Women writers, almost by definition, were outside the bounds of social acceptability. Women had long been enjoined to a world of silence. According to *Onna daigaku,* the feudal code of female virtue, "The only qualities that befit a woman are gentle obedience, chastity, mercy, and *quietness*" (emphasis mine).[24]

Uno and many other women writers found themselves caught in a contradiction. They could be silent and join the voiceless circle of respectability, or they could write and by so doing write themselves outside this circle; for, as Gilbert and Gubar note in their definitive study of nineteenth-century Anglo-American women writers, ". . . a life of feminine submission, of 'contemplative purity,' is a life of silence, a life that has no pen and story, while a life of female rebellion, of 'significant action,' is a life that must be silenced, a life whose monstrous pen tells a terrible story."[25] It is perhaps no coincidence, therefore, that many of the Japanese women who chose "significant action" over silence, who chose to write, found themselves unable to marry or marry well. Tamura Toshiko, Uno's great successor, blazed a trail for those to follow by divorcing her husband and running off with a married man younger than herself. Hayashi Fumiko, Hirabayashi Taiko, Sata Ineko, Setouchi Harumi and others drifted from man to man, often enduring physical and mental abuse from these men before finally freeing themselves. This pattern of marital inconstancy was not limited to women from the lower strata of society; Miyamoto Yuriko, born into wealth, also divorced her husband and embarked on a period of wandering that would see her to the Soviet Union and back. Not all women writers left their husbands of course. But those, like Enchi Fumiko, who chose to stay married regardless of the sterility of their lives, usually found themselves forced to masquerade as the submissive woman, while inside their spirits raged. The consequences of this duplicity can be found in their work in the depiction of characters who are trapped within their own charade.

Perhaps the greatest exception to this pattern was Nogami Yaeko, who was able to combine motherhood, married life, and writing with happy results. She was extremely lucky, however, in that she had a husband who appreciated her talent and who was wealthy enough to afford her the time to write. She had maids aplenty to tend the house and was thus free to indulge in her art. But to an extent Nogami also suffered from her husband's largesse. Because she did not lead a life of daring, devoting herself to writing at all costs, her works were often criticized as tepid and aloof from the vicissitudes of life.

It was almost imperative, therefore, that a woman writer be a woman who could not stay married, a woman given to extravagant bouts of passion. And it was generally expected that she would turn this life of passion into fiction —each, in a sense, thrived on the other. But a writing program like this was not without its pitfalls. As described above, once an author was locked into a certain persona, writing lost its fresh appeal and became not so much an expression of self as an expression of self-image, of persona. Many writers, overwhelmed by the need to preserve this self-image at the cost of their integrity, chose to give up writing altogether; others chose silence through death. But still others chose to diversify; and Uno was one of these.

Her brief liaison with Tōgō Seiji produced another important work, *Iro-zange* (Confessions of Love), which she serialized in *Chūō Kōron* from 1933 to 1935. Unlike "Parting Pleasure" and "A Lingering Attachment," however, this work is not based on Uno's romance with Tōgō, but on the series of affairs he had before he met her. In her memoirs of her life with Tōgō, "Aru otoko no dammen" (Profile of a Certain Man, 1984), she speaks of her inspiration for writing *Confessions of Love*. "Once Tōgō said to me, 'How about it? Would you be interested in writing about my love suicide?' *Confessions of Love* is almost word for word the story he told me."[26] Uno's claim is not as exaggerated as it may seem. Certain scenes in *Confessions of Love* resemble "almost word for word" Tōgō's essay on the suicide, "Jōshi misui-sha no shuki" (Notes from a Failed Suicide, 1929).

Later, when *Confessions of Love* was acclaimed as "the best love story in modern literature," Tōgō accused Uno of living with him for the sole purpose of gathering material for the novel.

> What Tōgō said was not true. Yet, because I had poured all my effort into writing this long work, it seemed as if he were right. This novel was more interesting than anything I had written before, and it was a better seller. But this was no source of pride for me. The success of the work and most of its charm lay in Tōgō's skill as a storyteller and not in my ability as a writer.[27]

Confessions of Love was extremely popular. In an era of vapid personal accounts and drab proletarian pieces, it was a breath of fresh air—full of romance, suspense, and adventure. "This story surges," critic Kamei Katsuichirō said, "with the attitude of 'freedom' as well as the peculiar notion of epicureanism that permeated the period from the end of Taishō to the beginning of Shōwa."[28] Uno writes of the dance halls and the milk bars; the young women who gleefully defy convention in their pursuit of sexual freedom; the confusion, the decadence, and the intellectual malaise of the age. Everything about the book coalesces to elicit the sense of heady modernity that suffused the late 1920s.

By the time her work appeared, this era of *ero-guro-nansensu* (eroticism, grotesquerie, and nonsense) had passed. Japan had invaded Manchuria in 1931 and was teetering on the brink of an extended war in the Asian continent; the world had grown dark and was growing darker still. Japan was now mounting a campaign to purge itself of the dangerous voices of dissent and of just the sort of "Western-inspired" decadence Uno celebrated in *Confessions of Love*. Although the work was a popular success, many critics were outspoken in their disapproval of its excessive and indulgent sexual promiscuity. Uno was soon labeled "a writer obsessed with illicit love," a distinction she bore for nearly a decade after the work.

It was mostly in retrospect that critics began to recognize the narrative significance of *Confessions of Love*. They were especially impressed by the fact that a woman writer had so successfully told a "man's story" and from his voice. Saeki Shōichi has called Uno's male protagonist, Yuasa Jōji, "a man reeking of manliness," "a Japanese Don Juan."²⁹ Yamamoto Kenkichi, comparing Uno to such English greats as Emily Brontë, described her as the only woman in Japan to write from a male perspective. The importance of Uno's achievement with Yuasa is not so much that he is male, but that she is able to narrate the story in his voice, using his persona. For a *watakushi shōsetsu* author to write from the viewpoint of someone other than herself was revolutionary. The opening lines of the work are important to appreciate the narrative accomplishment Uno made. " 'I wonder where I should start,' he said, reflecting for some time before slowly starting to speak."³⁰ As the story opens we have a third-person narrator reporting an event. With the next sentence, the third-person narrative vanishes, and Yuasa takes the stage for the remainder of the work, speaking directly, intimately of his own experiences. Saeki says of this evolution in style, "By effacing herself from the narrative and attuning herself to the rhythm and breathing of a man, another person, she has opened the road to an Uno-style narration, a style separate from her personal 'I.' "³¹

Uno has termed this style of hers *kikigaki* (hear-write tale). She wrote Tōgō's story just as she heard it told; at least that is the impression she gives her readers. What emerges in *Confessions of Love* is a narrative monologue. This style is by no means unique to Uno but, indeed, conforms to the classical *monogatari* tradition. *Monogatari* (the telling of things) was frequently distinguished by a sense of orality. Early *monogatari*, we know, were often shared by means of an orator who read the story aloud to a small and intimate audience. Even when the story was read silently, there was in the story's narrative presentation a sense of communion between audience and narrator. Uno establishes just this sort of narrative relationship in her story. "I wonder where I should start?" She opens with a question, thus immediately drawing the reader into the narrative process—into a relationship with the narrator paralleling that between the storytellers of old and their audiences.

The orality of the tale and this mood of intimacy evoke as well the time when *zange* (confessions) were a form of entertainment. Friends would while away an evening sharing confidences, often about romantic trysts, as in the "rainy night discussion" in *The Tale of Genji* (ca. A.D. 1000). In medieval times priests or nuns, with little to do at their monasteries on dreary winter evenings, would confess their reasons for taking the orders—reasons often rooted in failed romances. But the best-known example of a confession for diversion is Ihara Saikaku's *Kōshoku ichidai onna* (The Life of an Amorous Woman, 1686), in which an old woman, a self-styled nun, confesses to a life of licentious pleasure in what seems to be a parody of the earlier religious-inspired confessions.

The medieval confessions, particularly those told in the voice of a nun or priest, were often cloaked in Buddhist morals, yet the underlying aim in all these works was entertainment. *Confessions of Love* is no exception. Although the entire story anticipates the final suicide attempt, there is nothing gloomy or even particularly tragic about the work.

Certain scenes do seem reminiscent of those in standard romances or tragedies. Yuasa's desperate efforts to find Tsuyuko, their futile flight, and, finally, their suicide attempt are all familiar romantic situations. But in each scene, just as the melodrama is reaching its peak, Uno interjects a ludicrous detail that turns the potential pathos into something approaching comedy. The suicide scene is a case in point.

> The sun went down and although we couldn't see each other's faces clearly in the faint light seeping through the curtains, Tsuyuko was apparently staring at the scalpel she held in her hand. "Maybe now's the time . . . ?" I said and just at that moment what seemed like a burst of hot water came fountaining out, soaking through my thin shirt. Tsuyuko had cut her throat first and I could see the blood gushing from the wound as I called out to her. Thoroughly agitated, I gathered up her limp body and laid her down on the bed. I had wanted to remain calm but a frenzy shook through me. "I can't die in a shirt that's soiled like this," I told myself in all seriousness. I got out of bed and took a fresh shirt from the bureau, removing the shirt that had been drenched in Tsuyuko's blood. I was so flustered that I didn't stop to think that if I was going to do the same to myself, the new shirt would become even more bloody. I carefully fastened the buttons and rushed to Tsuyuko's side where I took up the other scalpel.[32]

Here we do not have the sublime poetry of playwright Chikamatsu Monzaemon (1653–1725), whose characters gain dignity on the road to death. Rather we have a narrator who describes with scientific detail his foolish antics in the face of death.

Yuasa is an ineffectual lover at best. Yet for all his bungling he is somehow endearing. This is perhaps Uno's greatest achievement in *Confessions of Love.*

While she was serializing the story, she and Tōgō were undergoing a very painful separation, one that would leave her hating Tōgō outright. A less objective writer might have turned the story into a forum for airing her many grievances against the man who had jilted her. Yet there is nothing about the narration of *Confessions* that indicates such violent emotions. Perhaps Tōgō would have depicted himself in a more favorable light, as translator Phyllis Birnbaum suggests, but it is a significant testament to Uno's maturity as an artist that she did not render him even less attractive than she did. For a writer heretofore primarily dependent on the representation of lived experience this was indeed revolutionary. By removing herself from the narrative and writing essentially an objective account of someone else's experiences, Uno proved that she was not just a "woman writer" turning her scandals to profit, but a significant storyteller as well.

5

STYLE

In June 1936, encouraged by her friend Miyake Tsuyako, Uno founded *Sutairu* (Style), Japan's first fashion magazine. As its name implies, the project was not a serious undertaking. "Sutairu" (style) was a takeoff on the popular eye medicine "Sumairu" (smile), which is still marketed today. Regardless of its origins, *Style* was a surprising success. The well-known painter Fujita Tsuguharu (1886–1968) illustrated the cover of each issue; Tsuyako, and later Setouchi Harumi (b. 1922), contributed monthly articles and stories to the magazine. But above all *Style* was devoted to fashion, particularly Western fashion. Typical articles were "How to Wear a Summer Frock," "Proper Underwear—A Must with Western Dresses," and "The Beauty of a Suntan and How It Can Be Yours."

In April of 1936 Kitahara Takeo (1907–1973), a writer for the *Miyako Shimbun* (later the *Tokyo Shimbun*), visited Uno to interview her for an article to run on the women's page. Prior to the interview, Uno had read a story by Kitahara in a small coterie magazine. Moved by his work, she had impulsively dashed off a note to him. "I read your story and think you have impressive talent—a blend of Tanizaki Jun'ichirō and Balzac!"[1] When Uno finally met Kitahara, reputed to be an exceptionally handsome man, she fell madly in love. Soon she was calling on him daily at his office, and often sent her car around to fetch him after work. Kitahara's colleagues advised him to avoid the notorious Miss Uno, but Kitahara was not deterred. Before long Uno persuaded him to leave the *Miyako* and to join her staff at *Style*, sweetening the offer by promising to let him concentrate on serious writing, rather than the hack journalism expected of him by the newspaper. She saw to it that his second story, "Tsuma" (My Wife), was published in the November 1938 issue of the prominent literary magazine *Bungei*. She is also credited with engineering Kitahara's nomination for the Akutagawa Prize that year. Although he did not win the award, being nominated was an honor in itself.

In November 1938 Uno began publication, at Kitahara's suggestion, of the literary magazine *Buntai* (Literary Style) under the auspices of the Style Company. This magazine was, as Donald Keene has suggested, an apology for the frivolity of *Style*. It was dedicated to serious, "pure" literature and was sponsored by Miyoshi Tatsuji and Ibuse Masuji (b. 1898), among others. Kitahara and his colleagues were deeply involved with French literature and philosophy at the time, and the table of contents of *Buntai* attests to these interests, with essays on Proust and Gide and translations of Valery.

Soon after Kitahara met Uno he proposed to her, but Uno was not at all certain that she wanted to lock herself into another relationship. She had established herself as a successful entrepreneur, and she was proud of her hard-won independence. What would marriage do but return her to the tiresome patterns of confinement? Besides, Kitahara had a young daughter, Miki, from a former marriage, and Uno half-suspected that Kitahara had tendered his proposal out of a need to provide Miki with a nursemaid. Uno was not at all confident that she could be a mother at this late date. Plus, she was now forty-one; Kitahara was ten years younger. But perhaps the most important reason keeping Uno from marriage was that she so enjoyed the lovely romance she and Kitahara shared. They took long strolls together on summer evenings, often with Miki in tow. At times they would go to see foreign films, though Uno claims she spent the whole time gazing at Kitahara's handsome profile. She feared marriage would end their romance and relegate their relationship to mere habit—it had happened before.

Kitahara was insistent, however, and they were married on April Fool's Day (an irony not lost on Uno), 1939, in an elaborate ceremony at the Imperial Hotel. *Style* illustrator Fujita Tsuguharu and novelist Yoshiya Nobuko (1896–1973) served as the go-betweens, and scores of well-wishers attended, along with curiosity-seekers and photographers. The following morning the major newspapers carried announcements—all, of course, prominently printing Uno's age as well as Kitahara's.

After the ceremony the couple moved to a newly constructed house in Hayashi-chō, Koishikawa. They had a garden for Miki, but she never played there. She suffered from a congenital spinal disease, which shortly after the marriage developed into meningitis. Her suffering was acute, and Uno did her best to nurse the little girl. In Kitahara's *watakushi shōsetsu* "Mon" (The Gate, 1939) he records how one night Uno was awakened by cries. She rushed downstairs to Miki's bedside only to find the girl resting quietly; she had heard the sobs of a neighbor's child. Kitahara was shocked; a real mother, he observed, would never have made such a mistake. Miki died in July, on the morning of her seventh birthday.

By 1941 the war in the Pacific was under way. Government restrictions on publications had always existed, but now, under the banner of war, they grew into an extensive and insidious web of censorship. Dissident writers were imprisoned, murdered, or otherwise silenced; all other writers were made to understand that they would either cooperate with the government or write nothing at all. Most writers had little choice but to comply. Even Miyamoto Yuriko, a staunch Communist, reluctantly joined the *Nihon Bungaku Hōkoku Kai* (Japanese Literature Patriotic Association), founded in 1942. She could not have withstood, she later said, the isolation engendered by failure to join.

The literary scene was now dominated by those writers willing to cooperate with the military campaigns. Uno's former husband Ozaki Shirō heeded the call and became one of the most enthusiastic members of the *Pen Butai* (Pen Unit), a propaganda organization formed in 1938. Many of Uno's associates and fellow writers volunteered to serve as war correspondents for several of the major newspapers. Hayashi Fumiko traveled to China in the winter of 1937 as a correspondent for the *Mainichi Shimbun.* Yoshiya Nobuko went to the front for the same paper. In 1941 Hayashi Fumiko returned to China, this time under the sponsorship of the *Asahi Shimbun.* She was accompanied by Sata Ineko, a writer who only a few years earlier had been an active member of the Communist party.

Not all writers joined the propaganda units voluntarily. Many, like Uno's *Buntai* associate Ibuse Masuji, were conscripted to serve for the *Rikugun Hōdō-han* (Military Information Corps). Kitahara Takeo received his orders in mid-November 1941 and was sent to base camp in Akasaka. Uno was not allowed to visit him, and much of the time she did not know where he was. But in March of the following year she learned that he had been dispatched to the island of Java in Indonesia; he did not return until December.

Prior to the outbreak of the Greater East Asian War in 1941 Uno had been able to publish her "love-obsessed" stories largely unhindered by the increasing austerity campaigns. During the lean years of 1941–1945, however, the military censors began to close in on any work—no matter how politically vacuous—that did not portray an attitude befitting a country at war. Tanizaki Jun'ichirō's *Sasameyuki* (The Makioka Sisters) is now famous for the rage it provoked among the censors when it was first serialized in *Chūō Kōron* in 1943. One of the military examiners explained:

> This novel goes on and on detailing the very thing we are most supposed to be on our guard against during this period of wartime emergency: the soft, effeminate, and grossly individualistic lives of women. . . . What are we to make of the attitude of a magazine that prints such a novel? This is more than a

simple case of poor judgment: it is the rankest indifference to the war effort, the attitude of a detached observer.[2]

Uno's particular brand of fiction was, if anything, "soft, effeminate, and grossly individualistic." She had to take precautions if she meant to publish; a magazine with a title like *Style* was doomed. In 1941 she changed the name to the slightly more innocuous *Josei Seikatsu* (Woman's Life) and, as Western fashions were clearly taboo, she began to celebrate the kimono. She was able to keep the magazine afloat until January 1944, when it was closed by a government regulation to conserve paper. Her other journal *Buntai* had ceased publication in 1939 because of financial infeasibility.

Uno was able to publish only a handful of stories during the war. One such work, "Tsuma no tegami" (A Wife's Letters, 1942), was written in the form of letters from a wife to her husband away at the front. It accorded so well with the sentiments of the day that it was sold as a letter manual. Many a wife packed the slim book—handsomely bound in a black cover with white cherry blossoms—off with her war-bound husband as a reminder of her love.

Uno, however, denies having any interest in propaganda or in the war. "Hayashi Fumiko went off to the front," she said. "Kitahara went off to the front. Everyone went off and I was left behind. I did not stay behind because I was against the war. I was neither for nor against it. It simply was not in my nature to do such things."[3]

Uno was not interested in the political battles that raged outside her world of passion. She did become a founding member of the women's chapter of the Japanese Literature Patriotic Association, which after the war evolved into the influential *Nihon Joryū Bungakusha Kai* (Association of Japanese Women Writers). But any writer who wanted to write had to join the Patriotic Association in some fashion. Uno was hardly concerned with the latest governmental regulations or the developments in China; she was too busy scouring the nearly depleted markets for enough material to make all the members of the women's chapter the matching *mompe* (farmer's trousers) women were expected to wear at that time. She, like the wife in her story, involved herself in the war only to the extent that it affected her relationship with her husband. "For a woman like me, this great war, which has been going on for I do not know how many years, began in my mind only last autumn, the day you left."[4] The war for her was only "a woman's war," a war of emotions; it began when her husband left and ended when he returned.

By far the most significant work Uno wrote during the war was "Ningyōshi Tenguya Kyūkichi" (The Puppet Maker Tenguya Kyūkichi, 1942). In the spring of 1942, Uno saw a *jōruri* puppet at the home of *Chūō Kōron* editor

Shimanaka Yūsaku. Shimanaka's wife manipulated the puppet for Uno, turning its head and opening and closing its eyes. Uno was impressed by the intensity of emotion the puppet was able to express. "The depth of sorrow visible in her eyes, closed into a thread, could never be expressed in the closed eyes of a living woman."[5]

Bored in her empty house, Uno conceived the idea of interviewing the man who had carved the puppet. Shimanaka introduced her to Kume Sōshichi, a journalist in Tokushima, Shikoku, who had earlier written an article on the puppet maker for *Chūō Kōron*. Uno sent a long and impassioned letter to Kume, describing her "burning desire" to meet the puppet maker. When Kume offered to introduce her, she set off immediately for Tokushima.

Tenguya Kyūkichi, the same puppet maker Tanizaki Jun'ichirō had referred to in his work *Tade kuu mushi* (Some Prefer Nettles, 1929), lived on the outskirts of Tokushima in the little village of Wada, and though he was already eighty-six when Uno met him, he was still hard at work carving puppets.[6] Uno was profoundly moved by the old man's diligence and by the simplicity of his life. For the past sixty years he had sat in the same room, facing the same dusty road, breathing life into his puppets. For a woman who could hardly manage to stay in the same house or with the same man for more than five years, this was a revelation. Uno took advantage of Kitahara's absence and remained in Shikoku for half a month interviewing Tenguya Kyūkichi and writing down what he said. Her story of the encounter, "The Puppet Maker," was serialized in *Chūō Kōron* from November to December 1942.

This work, a *kikigaki* ("hear-write tale"), has two narrators, the interviewer and the puppet maker; but the focus is on Kyūkichi. "Well, come on in and make yourself at home," he says. "If I'm to tell you my story I can't be thinking of you as some guest come down from Tokyo."[7] And so his story unfolds, moving here and there through time as one recollection calls forth another. He describes his boyhood and his early days as an apprentice. He reflects on his marriage and on the joys and hardships of his calling. At times his tale is rich with folksy humor and simple wisdom; at times it is sad.

"The Puppet Maker" marks an important advance in Uno's narrative art. Donald Keene notes that this work is "Uno's second debut as a writer" (*Confessions of Love* being the first), "this time not as a daring, liberated woman, but as the painstaking chronicler of a way of life that still lurked beneath the modern surface of Japan."[8] In *Confessions* Uno concentrated on the creation of a carefully delineated plot and on evoking the heady excitement of the modern age. But in "The Puppet Maker" she forgoes her insistence on plot and applies herself to "the telling of the tale." *How* the tale is

told is just as important as *what* is told. Kyūkichi speaks entirely in the rustic
Awa dialect of Tokushima. Miyao Tomiko writes of his speech: "In the
work, the Awa dialect is lovely and refined. Today everyone says rustic dialects are 'uncouth.' But the utterances set down in this work are far superior
to and much more elegant than the Tokyo dialect. They please the ear as well
as the eye."[9] The dialect gives Kyūkichi's voice depth and the richness of life.
As Kawamori Yoshizō notes: "From time to time I can hear him pause for
breath. The reader suddenly feels he is sitting with old Kyūkichi, face to
face."[10] Kyūkichi's quiet, venerable voice casts a spell over his audience,
drawing them into his world—the world of the past.

As Miyao observes, the words are a pleasure to hear as well as to read. And
yet there is sorrow implicit in Kyūkichi's speech; he speaks the language of
yesteryear, and he tells the story of a bygone era. The puppet theater, he
fears, is on the brink of destruction. Tanizaki had predicted twenty years earlier that "When this puppet maker dies, the art will be lost forever."[11] In
Kyūkichi's voice as well we can detect a quiet lament, and it is this ever-
present note of sorrow that imparts a solemn dignity to "The Puppet
Maker," and renders the work an outstanding achievement.

Prior to "The Puppet Maker" Uno had never shown an interest in *bunraku*
(puppet drama). But shortly after meeting Kyūkichi she began attending per-
formances as often as possible. "I felt just like a foreigner going to see
bunraku for the first time," she admitted.[12] It was perhaps surprising to some
that Miss Uno, arbiter of modern fashions, was suddenly interested in a relic
like the puppet theater. But Uno's encounter with the puppet maker had
made her aware of the beauty and fragility of Japanese traditions. In the last
paragraph of "The Puppet Maker," Uno gives voice to her concern as well as
to her hope that the art will survive. The interviewer has returned to Tokyo
and has just received an Oyumi puppet from Kyūkichi:

> I dressed the puppet in a kimono and searched about for a comb to fix in her
> hair. While I busied myself I was overcome by a strange feeling. By doing what
> I was doing, that is, by dressing the puppet and looking for a comb for her hair,
> was I not offering proof, if but slight, that the puppet would not perish? I was
> certain that the old man, too, had known this all along.[13]

Kamei Katsuichirō writes that "The Puppet Maker" marked a turning
point not only in Uno's art but in her attitude toward art. Her meeting with
Kyūkichi, he says, was "an eye-opening experience."[14] Through this experience Uno learned the value of art and the importance of single-mindedness.
She writes of her first meeting with the artist:

Tenguya's house was in a section of Wada known as Nakamura. The road before his house was always crowded with horse carts and wagons traveling to and fro. The dust poured into his workshop, covering everything. It was so bad that you could hardly open your eyes. And yet, there he sat. From the time that he was sixteen until his eighty-sixth year he had sat there motionless on a small cotton striped cushion. He had worked like this for more than seventy years without ever taking a day off.

That's it! I thought. I, too, would sit in my studio without missing a day, and I would work. Anybody can write. But few are those who can sit at the same desk day after day.[15]

Uno gathered up her pencils and prepared to work, but it was some time before she could apply herself to the task as diligently as she had hoped. She would first have to wait for the excitement and confusion of the war years to abate.

In January 1943 Kitahara returned to Tokyo and was released from service. Uno had tried to keep him up-to-date on her many activities while he was overseas. She had written to him frequently, describing the vegetable garden she had planted and the new projects she was planning. Whenever she rearranged the furniture in the house she sent him a photograph, so the new arrangement would not seem unfamiliar to him when he returned. She often included photographs of herself as well, in seductive poses. (Evidently this was a great source of joy for the military mail censors!) Of course, Uno went on and on about her meeting with the puppet maker, much to Kitahara's annoyance. "Puppets! Puppets! I'm sick to death of your puppets!" he complained upon his return.[16]

In March 1944 Uno and Kitahara left Tokyo and sought shelter in Atami, a hot-spring village on the Izu Peninsula where other writers had gone to wait out the war. A year later, fearing Atami was in danger of an air raid, they moved to the little town of Mibu in Tochigi Prefecture, where they lived with Kitahara's parents until the end of the war.

Shortly after the Emperor made his fateful announcement over the radio declaring Japan's surrender on August 15, 1945, Uno and Kitahara gathered up a few belongings—a change of clothing, a light futon, and a rosewood desk—and boarded a train for Tokyo. "Everyone everywhere was heading for Tokyo. We were packed in the train like sardines. But not a soul laughed at the curious figure Kitahara cut, carrying the desk on his back as if it were a child. We would need the desk tomorrow when we began to write. That rosewood desk was precious."[17]

The Style office in Yotsuya had burned down. The couple stayed with Uno's younger sister Katsuko for several nights in her cramped three-mat room before moving to Magome, where they took a room in the house Uno had built with Ozaki Shirō twenty years earlier. In January 1946 Uno received a message from Maeda Hisakichi, the president of the *Sankei Shimbun,* an Osaka-based newspaper company. He would supply her with the capital and paper if she would reopen *Style.* Uno accepted the offer and found a temporary office in a bomb-scarred building in Yurakuchō. That February she named Kitahara company president, assembled several members of the former staff, and ran a three-line advertisement in the newspapers announcing the revival of *Style.* Within days money orders began to pour in, so abundantly, in fact, that they were able to pay the paper and printing bills before publication began and never had to draw on the capital Maeda offered. The first issue, published February 1946, was sold out before it ever reached the stands. The morning the issue was to be released people came from miles around and waited outside the office in a line that circled the building twice; some were armed with radishes or leeks that they had gathered from their gardens with the hope of trading them in exchange for a copy of *Style.*

People were starved for fashion, and the magazine offered a glimpse of a world long denied. The covers of the magazine featured glamorous Western women, and, though the focus was on fashion, there was a plethora of essays and articles introducing American manners and customs. Courtship and marriage were favorite topics, along with the novel notion of "ladies first."

Style was so prosperous Uno was able to build a new office in the Ginza that included living accommodations for herself and Kitahara. They enjoyed nightly excursions to cabarets, often with the entire Style staff. In 1948 they bought a villa in Atami, and in 1950 they built a luxurious house next to the estate of the famous Kabuki actor Onoe Kikugorō VI. In 1951 Uno flew to Paris, where she dazzled the Parisians with her gorgeous kimonos. While she was there she met the philosopher Alain (Emile Auguste Chartier, 1868–1951), to whose works Kitahara had introduced her before the war.

In those grim years when most Japanese were struggling to survive, Uno and Kitahara were immensely wealthy, but they did not abandon literature entirely. In December of 1947 they revived *Buntai,* again to atone for the frivolity of *Style.* The postwar *Buntai,* with the support of Kobayashi Hideo (1902–1983), Aoyama Jirō (1901–1979), Kawakami Tetsutarō (1902–1980), Miyoshi Tatsuji, and Ōoka Shōhei (b. 1909), was impressive. Kobayashi's "Gohho no tegami" (The Letters of Van Gogh, 1952) and Ōoka's *Nobi* (Fires on the Plain, 1951) were first serialized in *Buntai* in 1948. But like the prewar version, *Buntai* was not a profitable enterprise and was abandoned after July 1949.

Style, too, had begun to encounter troubles. Copycat magazines had inspired competition, driving sales down. In an attempt to augment their income Uno opened *Sutairu no mise* (Style Boutique) in 1950. Located on the first floor of her Ginza building, the store sold, among other garments, kimonos of her design. The cover and opening pages of *Style* now featured glossy photographs of models wearing her kimonos in bold patterns of contrasting black and white. A year earlier Uno had embarked on a second fashion magazine, *Sutairu Yomimonoban* (A Style Reader), which was meant to appeal to a more popular element, but the project had failed miserably and left a sizable debt.

In 1952 *Sutairu sha* (Style Company) was investigated for tax fraud. Uno claims to have been caught completely unaware by the audit. According to her, fifteen or sixteen men burst into the office unannounced and began to confiscate files and papers, and even the scraps in the wastebasket and the personal notes in the women's handbags. No one was quite certain who these men were or what had happened. But later, when Uno tried to sort through the incident, she learned that a disgruntled Style employee had alerted officials to financial mismanagement. The investigators found that the company had been remiss in 60 percent of its taxes. Penalty and interest charges approached one hundred million yen. Kitahara, as president of the company, barely escaped imprisonment.

Uno has since admitted to lazy bookkeeping practices. They left the financial matters entirely to their underlings and were so busy spending *Style* proceeds that they had little concept of its income. In fact, Uno explains that they did not even bother to separate their personal accounts from their business accounts. When *Style* faltered Uno and Kitahara lost everything in an effort to keep it afloat. They sold their villa in Atami and Kitahara's family home in Mibu. They moved Style into their Kobikichō house and sold their Ginza office. In 1956 they moved Style back to the Ginza, into a little office across from the Kabukiza, and sold their Kobikichō house. They sold the many art items that they had accumulated over the years. "One by one we lost everything," Uno wrote, "as if we were stripping off our skin."[18] And, later she reflected, "People usually hang themselves in times like these. But we did not die."[19] Instead she and Kitahara struggled to meet their enormous debts. He wrote potboilers, and she began to concentrate on her kimono designs. She met with enough success to maintain the Style Boutique, and she even managed a tour of America with a company of models in April 1957, where she exhibited her kimonos in Seattle and New York. Despite these successes, Uno's magazine business continued to flag, and she was forced to close the doors to Style in April of 1959.

Understandably, Uno did not write much during this period. But the one significant work she did produce, *Ohan*, would become her masterpiece. The opening sections of *Ohan* were first serialized in *Buntai* from December 1947 to July 1949. When *Buntai* folded Uno moved the serialization to *Chūō Kōron*, where she published sections year by year, finally completing the work in May of 1957.

"I had always wanted to write a novel like this," Uno said, "and I began laying plans."[20] She had been inspired to write *Ohan* when in Shikoku interviewing the puppet maker. While rummaging through a local secondhand shop she struck up a conversation with the shopkeeper; before long he told her his life story. *Ohan*, she says, grew from this meeting. The shopkeeper planted the seed, perhaps, but the story is entirely Uno's.

Ohan is a *kikigaki*, and, as in Uno's earlier *kikigaki*, the narrator is a man. Here the narrator has no name; he is known only as the heir to the Kanōya dye shop.

> It's kind of you to ask. Yes, I grew up as the son and heir of a dyer's shop in Kawara Street, the Kanōya it was called. But my family lost its money long ago, and now I run this small business, a second-hand shop. It's only a rented room in the front of somebody else's house, as you can see. Sometimes I wonder what makes me put myself to this trouble when I have all the money I need. I really can't help smiling at my own foolishness.[21]

The story the man has to tell is simple yet dramatic. His wife, Ohan, several months pregnant at the time, was taken away from him after her family discovered that he was squandering his money on a geisha. Rather than pursuing Ohan, the man moves in with the geisha Okayo and allows her to support him. Seven years later he happens to see Ohan again and tries to persuade her to visit him at his shop. As Ohan is a profoundly timid woman, and hesitant to interfere in the man's new life with Okayo, it takes time before she can muster the courage to go to him. But soon they begin to see one another as often as they dare, while taking care not to let Okayo find out. Eventually, almost accidentally, the man promises to move back to Ohan and their son. Ohan is ecstatic, but before the man spends one night with her in their new house, he loses heart and flees back to his geisha. That same night his son dies in a freak accident. Following the forty-ninth day observance of the boy's death, Ohan departs for a distant province, leaving the man a brief letter:

> I realize now that no one has been as lucky as I. I did not live in the same house with you, it is true, but we were in fact husband and wife, and I wonder if you didn't love me more than if we had been together.
>
> . . . The one thing that still bothers me is my inexcusable behavior to Okayo. After I have gone, please give her my share of your love. There are

many more things I would like to say, but something inside is hurrying me on, and I will put down my brush. Please dress warmly so you won't catch cold.[22]

The man tries to find Ohan but she has left no clues to her whereabouts. He must content himself with Okayo, with the new room she has built for him, and with Osen, the niece she has adopted as their daughter.

> All day long now, more even than before, I hear Osen's voice calling, "Father! Father!" and at night I feel the warmth of Okayo's body as she nestles to me and shamelessly says, "Let her go to some other province if she doesn't need a man. I need a man. I want my man." I feel as if I have understood at last that this is my punishment for my brazen crimes in the face of Heaven.[23]

Summarizing *Ohan* in this way hardly does the work justice, for it is not the story itself that is so appealing but the way it is told and the atmosphere Uno evokes. Uno uses dialect in *Ohan,* as she had in "The Puppet Maker," but here she creates her own by combining the Iwakuni, Tokushima, and Kamigata dialects. What emerges, therefore, is "in a sense an artificial language," as she has said, but also one that is imbued with the colors and cadences of the past. The dialect becomes something of a living entity itself, surpassing the limits of the printed word. Like "The Puppet Maker," *Ohan* is best appreciated when read aloud.

> If a single actor were to read this work aloud, as the blind minstrels did in the past, then I believe he could best convey its charms. Here and there you might insert the chords of the *biwa* or the twang of the *shamisen.* Even when read silently, this work possesses the ability to make you feel as if you were hearing it spoken aloud. In short, *Ohan* is music, a lyric.[24]

When *Ohan* was first published in book form by Chūō Kōronsha in 1957, the jacket carried the following testimonial by critic Kobayashi Hideo: "I found this work interesting in that it offers the essence of Chikamatsu. . . . With a compelling use of words that outlive their power as mere words, the author invents a storybook world of fantasy, rare among contemporary novels which have surrendered completely to fact."[25]

Much has been made of the resemblance of *Ohan* to the puppet plays of the great dramatist Chikamatsu Monzaemon (1653–1725). The *kikigaki* style gives the sense of a direct recitation, and the dialect has the rich nuances of a Chikamatsu script. "If one strains one's ears," Takahashi Hideo writes, "one can hear the chanter. One can see the puppets moving this way and that on the stage."[26] The setting of *Ohan* as well—a sleepy castle town—recalls the world of the puppet plays. The old wooden houses, with their broad eaves and latticed windows, are dark even at day, and the temple groves are full of shrill insects. The narrow streets ring with the clatter of *geta* sandals and with the twang of the *shamisen*. Everything coalesces to create the world of yesteryear, familiar yet somehow mysterious.

Most important, however, it is the characters who offer the "essence" of Chikamatsu. Ohan, in her quiet suffering, is clearly in the tradition of a *sewamono* (domestic play) wife. She has been compared with Osan in *Shinjū Ten no Amijima* (The Love Suicides at Amijima, 1721).[27] Both wives selflessly endure their husbands' infidelity. Okayo is a Saikaku "amorous woman"; her lustful demands for a man stand in sharp contrast to Ohan's gentle submissiveness. "Any woman who lets her man be taken away by another woman is a fool," she snaps. "She's got to take precautions if she doesn't want to lose him."[28]

Uno has admitted to being rather bewildered by all the attention to the *jōruri* elements in *Ohan*. "Mr. Kobayashi was very kind to say those nice things, but quite frankly it took me by surprise."[29] She insists that she was influenced by Madame de Lafayette's *La Princesse de Clèves,* a work Kitahara had introduced her to that she had read over and over. Yet there is little similarity between *Ohan* and the seventeenth-century French novel she so admired. What is interesting, therefore, is the traditional literature and drama that crept into *Ohan*. "I would not have thought they had influenced me at all. But I wonder if subconsciously I remembered the verses popular in the puppet plays that traveled to my town when I was a girl."[30]

Indeed, much in *Ohan* seems to have been culled from Uno's memories. Although she has said the story was based on what a shopkeeper in Shikoku told her, the events she describes vaguely resemble what happened to Uno's birth-mother, Tomo, who, like Ohan, was taken away from her first husband when her family discovered he was a failure. The castle town that emerges from the pages of *Ohan* is drawn from Uno's home town. The place names Daimyō Koji, Kajiyachō, Hangetsu-an, and Garyō Bridge are those of Iwakuni. Yet what we find in *Ohan* is not contemporary Iwakuni. "It is the image of Iwakuni," Uno says, "that was reflected in my eyes when I was a child."[31]

Uno's sleepy castle town of yesteryear apparently hit a responsive chord among readers just emerging from the darkness of postwar Japan. Readers were charmed by her old-fashioned tale—all the more because it was so unexpected from a writer of such modern tastes. *Ohan* garnered Uno several impressive accolades, among them the Noma Prize for Literature in 1957, an award she shared with Enchi Fumiko for her *Onnazaka* (The Waiting Years); and the Association of Japanese Women Writers' Award in 1958.

6

BOTTICELLI'S
VENUS

Uno was fifty when she began *Ohan,* and sixty when she finished. Donald Keene notes in *Dawn to the West* that many, if not most, women writers of the modern period wrote their best works after the war and thus at an advanced age. "Even women who had established themselves before the war felt inspired to write in a different and generally more effective vein after the reforms promulgated by the Occupation, such as giving women the vote, opening all governmental universities to women, and making women equals of men before the law."[1]

It is certainly true that the postwar constitution engendered a new sense of independence among women. Perhaps equally significant in the sudden flowering of female-authored works after the war was the common age of the women who were writing and the milestone this age represented in their lives as women. Many, like Hirabayashi Taiko and Hayashi Fumiko, were in their late forties. Others, like Uno Chiyo and Nogami Yaeko, were older still. In other words, they had reached a point where they were freed from the day-to-day chores of mothering, if they had children, and they were more or less freed from the demands of sexual love or from the need to locate their own identities in the men with whom they associated. As Uno notes, once she reached an age where she could no longer indulge in love with the same fierce passion she had shown earlier, she began to change her view of both life and art.

Strangely my attitude changed after I turned sixty, as if I had been freed from some demonic curse. I could see the world clearly. I felt I had put on an entirely new pair of glasses. Why was this? To put it succinctly it was because I could no longer involve myself in romantic affairs, no matter how I clamored and fumed. As soon as I realized this, the world, which earlier I could barely see through the swirling fogs of romance, became perfectly clear, as if the fog had melted away to blue sky.

This phenomenon is sad but also rather interesting. Now I see all that I have done up to this point as clearly and indifferently as if I were beholding the life of a stranger. When I was there in the whirlpool I could not think at all, but now I have developed a sort of spectator's stance.[2]

Uno's passage to this "spectator's stance" began shortly after the war, when she and Kitahara found themselves drifting apart. Kitahara had other women, and he made no secret of his affairs. While Uno had faithfully awaited his return from Southeast Asia, he had been cohabiting with a Dutch-Indonesian woman. Once back in Japan he took up with another woman, a former *Style* employee, with whom he had a child. Apparently he had other affairs as well for he bared the details of his relations with these women in the *watakushi shōsetsu* he was writing at the time. Uno could not help but know, and yet, unlike the Uno of a younger age, she did not protest. By 1950 they were living virtually separate lives; Kitahara spent more and more time at their villa in Atami and then in a house he built in Aoyama. During the last years of their marriage Uno lived with Kitahara in the Aoyama house, but she occupied a separate wing. They rarely saw one another. Once the Style enterprise was dissolved there was nothing left to hold them together, and, in 1964, Kitahara asked Uno for a divorce. She had expected it of course, and she did not protest. "I did not tell him that I did not want the divorce. But I cried a little once I was alone. I did not cry because divorce was painful. I suppose my tears were brought on by a different emotion. It's just that we'd been together so long!"[3]

Uno's break with Kitahara, as had her breaks with Ozaki and Tōgō, soon became the subject of her fiction. As she notes in "This Powder Box," "I could never write until something like this had happened. Could you say then that writing was not work for me but rather a form of withdrawal?"[4] Therapy, perhaps, would be a comparable description. In *Sasu* (To Sting), which she serialized from 1963 to 1966, Uno carefully chronicles her marriage to and subsequent divorce from Kitahara. The heroine of the story, while fully aware of her husband's infidelities, refuses to confront him with the facts or even to acknowledge that he had hurt her. "I felt then that my heart was riddled with bullets. Yet I pretended that I had not received a single scratch. . . . In the eyes of others who knew nothing of his affairs, I must have appeared a fulfilled and fortunate woman. It is strange, but I saw myself as they saw me. There are no scars. It is best to think that there are no scars."[5] Midway through the work the woman confronts the facade she has struggled to create. "I stood before the mirror in a ladies' clothing store downtown, staring at myself in an evening gown of gorgeous imported fabric. Was it witches' work? A momentary illusion? Compared to my husband's lover, a woman I had never seen, I looked like a pathetic woman in some sort of disguise."[6]

The heroine of To Sting sees a stranger in the mirror, an old and bewildered woman who has forced upon herself the disguise of a "fulfilled and fortunate wife." Just behind her disguise, she knows, is the horror and the hurt of her true condition. Almost in protest against this pain, Uno creates in the pages of To Sting a wife who submissively accepts her husband's infidelities, or rather, who effectively denies that they wound her. She convinces herself in her silence that she is happy.

While in the midst of serializing To Sting, Uno became a member of the Tempū Society. Master Nakamura Tempū (1876–1959), founder of the society, was a doctor and psychologist famed for his holistic, positive approach to mental and physical health. He taught that one could preserve one's well-being through concentration and the cultivation of a positive self-image. Instead of wasting precious mental and physical energy worrying over stressful situations, patients were encouraged to "look on the bright side of life" and to treat themselves only to positive reinforcements.[7] The influence of Tempū's philosophy is reflected in the way Uno was able to say good-bye to Kitahara, or, at least, in the way she says she said good-bye. "After Kitahara asked me for a divorce I busied myself helping him pack so that I would not dwell on the pain. This is one of the lessons I have learned from my many experiences. If there is pain in my life, I immerse my whole self in it."[8] In a later work she explains why: "After I have immersed myself, my body becomes accustomed to whatever it was I found so painful. It is strange, but once I am accustomed to it, it does not seem to hurt anymore."[9]

The heroine of To Sting similarly throws herself into the pain of parting as she sends her husband off. She does not allow herself to feel resentment. Rather, her last words to him are the casual, formulaic "See you later." Her last glimpse of him as he walks away is not one of anger but of an emotion akin to happiness. "This is what he wanted," she says. "And because he wanted it, I found myself wanting it, too."[10] Moreover, when her friends, finding that she is not "a fortunate woman" after all, try to commiserate with her, she counters by telling herself "Their words had nothing to do with me. My husband stayed with me for a long time—out of consideration for my feelings—and knowing this calmed my heart."[11]

Many were impressed by the new persona Uno had created in To Sting, by

her ability to accept her husband's departure with quiet equilibrium. Hagiwara Yōko writes:

> I know of no other author who can describe the separation between a man
> and a woman with such freshness, with such a store of love. Women writers in
> particular write of the hatred they feel toward their men. To purge their hearts
> of any lingering affection, they spew a profusion of rancorous words through-
> out their works. . . . There is none of that in *To Sting*.[12]

Uno was soon deluged with letters from women who wanted advice on
how best to deal with the problems they confronted. One woman wrote that
her husband had left her and that she wanted to die. Uno telephoned the
woman immediately and told her, "Put on your best kimono and stroll down
the street. But first, go to the beauty parlor and have your hair done."[13]

Not all of Uno's readers, however, found the quietness of *To Sting* com-
forting. Setouchi Harumi, a writer with passions not unlike Uno's, remarked
that the very control demonstrated in the work was to her a mark of sorrow:
"Between the carefully controlled lines there is a lament."[14] The controlled
lines of the work become, metaphorically, the bars that trap the heroine in
her deceit. Indeed, the more she claims to be happy, the more one feels she is
hiding her true feelings, and foisting a disguise upon herself.

In 1969 Uno wrote another work which addressed the subject of female
self-denial, *Kaze no oto* (The Sound of the Wind). Though not as finely
crafted as *Ohan, The Sound of the Wind* resembles the earlier work in many
respects. It is a *kikigaki,* narrated in Iwakuni dialect and set at some point
around the turn of the century. Moreover, the story itself is familiar; again
we have a man cast between two very different women, one the submissive
wife, the other the brash and brazen "other woman." Yet the differences
between this work and *Ohan* are as striking as the similarities. *The Sound of
the Wind* attempts to tell a story of greater consequence and as a result lacks
the masterful simplicity of *Ohan*. It is not based on a specific account told
Uno by a specific person, as were *Ohan* and the other *kikigaki,* but rather it is
modeled on the life of Uno's father. From his well-placed birth to his spectacular death, Seikichi, the male character in *The Sound of the Wind,* is drawn in
Toshitsugu's image. The tale, then, is one pieced together from fragments of
memories, and from rumors, moods, and feelings.

A second and significant distinction between *Ohan* and *The Sound of the
Wind* is that of narrative voice. *Ohan* is narrated by a man, and we are permitted to view Ohan and Okayo as a man might. Okayo is all flesh and drive
and passion, whereas Ohan is inarticulate at best; she clings to the shadows,

silently, breathlessly. She is more a wraith, more a ghost of goodness, than she is a woman. The narrator of *The Sound of the Wind,* however, is a woman —the neglected wife Osen. She gives voice to the story Ohan could not tell, or was not allowed to tell. And yet, like Patmore's Honoria, as Gilbert and Gubar note in their study of Victorian writers, she "has no story except a sort of anti-story of selfless innocence based on the notion that 'Man must be pleased; but him to please/Is woman's pleasure.' "[15] Hers is a story of silence, a story of watching and waiting and retelling other people's stories. She tells the story of Seikichi and his mistress Oyuki, and between the lines of their story we find her own "anti-story," her story of non-self.

Osen's ability, indeed, her eagerness to deny herself may seem highly improbable to readers today, but it was not so long ago that Japanese women were judged by their willingness to suffer and to submit to others. Jealousy, in particular, inhibited a proper submissive attitude and was to be avoided. The *Onna daigaku* of the eighteenth century cautioned:

> "Let her never even dream of jealousy. If her husband be dissolute, she must expostulate with him, but never either nurse or vent her anger. If her jealousy be extreme, it will render her countenance frightful and her accents repulsive, and can only result in completely alienating her husband from her, and making her intolerable in his eyes."[16]

Raised on such teachings, Osen is horrified by the glimmer of jealousy lodged in her own heart. She fights to control it and does so, like the heroine of *To Sting,* by denying that it is there.

Oyuki, the "other woman," is equally a victim of a patriarchal society that defines women as either inside or outside the family system. For Osen, though, Oyuki represents freedom. Riding horses and scampering over balcony railings like an acrobat, Oyuki is everything that Osen wants to be yet denies—passionate, courageous, self-assured, sensual. Like her counterpart Okayo in the earlier story, Oyuki stands very nearly as Seikichi's equal. Whereas she does not hold financial leverage over him, as Okayo did over her man, she is able to control him sexually.

To borrow terminology put forth by Gilbert and Gubar, Osen is the "angel in the house." Like Ohan she is more a silent, selfless specter than a human being. She must be ever vigilant in her efforts to keep herself pure and to quell the serpentine nature of her jealousy. In contrast to her angelic nature, however, there is another woman, bold and daring to the point of madness. She is Osen's other self—her inner self—"the madwoman in the attic." This "madwoman," Gilbert and Gubar note, is not merely presented as a foil for the subdued and angelic heroine. That is, she is not to be read as the bad woman to the other's good; rather, she is more accurately understood as the author's double, and both she and Osen signify the author's expression of a life of fragmentation—a life divided between angel and madwoman, between what she is expected to be and what she is.

Osen and Oyuki are equally reflections of Uno Chiyo. Indeed, Uno has indicated more than once that both *Ohan* and *The Sound of the Wind* are autobiographies. In the contrasting characters she creates, we can see the two distinct forces that have been constantly at work in the author's life—one a desire to settle properly, the other a desire to rebel against the strictures of marriage in an effort to be true to her own inner nature.

All her life Uno seemed to feel a need to define her self in terms of the men with whom she associated. As a child she had played the role of obedient daughter, answering her father's demands with bright-eyed eagerness. She did not care, she tells us, that she suffered in the process. She was doing his bidding and that made her proud; it gave her definition. When her father failed to fulfill her need for love and approval, she sought to duplicate him in her lovers, playing for them the role of femme fatale or "good wife," depending on their expectations. For them she changed her hair, her clothes, even her personality at times. In the process of winning a man's love, she inevitably lost her "self." To be the woman her man would have, she was compelled to deny the woman she was; the feelings of inauthenticity and stagnation this engendered were enough to send her out on her own once again. As she had asked in her 1936 essay, "A Genius of Imitation":

> Someday, when I am older, will I be able to get rid of this impulse, this wanting to be a "good wife," without feeling lost? Would I then be able to write my own story? I don't wish not to be a woman, but I'd certainly like to be a woman whose sense of purpose comes from within.[17]

Perhaps *Ohan* and *The Sound of the Wind* are Uno's attempts to write her own story, for it is in the contrastive pairing she creates that she gives voice to the zigzag pattern of her life. Ohan and Osen, ideal women as perpetuated by the patriarchy, are silent, submissive, and selfless. They are the "good wife/wise mother" that Uno could never be—that no woman could ever be. Yet this is the woman Uno thought from time to time she should become. She tried to be this woman for Fujimura Tadashi, and for Ozaki Shirō—to the point of considering abandoning her literary aspirations for the latter in an effort to save their marriage.

Okayo and Oyuki, on the other hand, seem to signify Uno's rebellion against the impossible demands of society. Bold and capricious, these women are in control of their lives and their men, and they will not be easily challenged. The same might be said of Uno herself; more often than not she was the dominant partner in her relationships. She was older than most of her spouses, or was perceived as such, and in general was the financial superior. She supported Fujimura Tadashi in Kyoto and Tokyo and saw him settled in Hokkaido before moving on. She was described as "keeping" Ozaki, her "young swallow," and was instrumental in helping him launch his career. She was completely undaunted by Tōgō's many challenges and was indeed able to match his outrageous behavior, blow for blow. And Kitahara, ten years her junior, was initially dependent on her not only for his financial well-being but for the modicum of literary success he enjoyed. What Ozaki suggests in "River Deer" was probably true for all Uno's partners: "Aside from the physiological distinction that he was a man and she was a woman, they shared exactly the same temperament." They were equals—at times rivals— and it was this strength of hers that Uno felt was responsible for driving her husbands away from her and her from them.

> I never acted babyish with my mother. This is strange, I suppose, because I was a girl. But even so I responded to her much as a son would have. Perhaps this is why in my later marriages, my feelings as a woman were quite unlike those of other women. . . . I cannot recall, in any of my marriages, ever begging or wheedling my husband for anything. I do not remember ever flinging my arms around his knees and collapsing in tears. I handled everything related to our livelihood without consulting him. And most of it I was able to manage fairly well. It was always for the best if he just stood by silently and let me take care of things. But could you say a man finds such a woman sweet and lovable? I suppose I knew all along that the kind of woman a man really loves is one who will burst into tears for him over the silliest little thing.
>
> Perhaps I needn't even say that after my husbands left me, they all turned to this sort of sweet little woman. All of them. I, too, was a woman, but my mother had graced me with a man's spirit, a spirit which, try as I might, I could not shake loose.[18]

After Kitahara left her in 1964, Uno stopped fretting over her "man's spirit." She no longer felt compelled to have a man in her life. Perhaps the change came because she believed "no matter how [she] clamored and fumed" romantic relationships were no longer possible. Or perhaps she began to recognize that they were no longer necessary. Uno's transition from celebrated femme fatale to single older woman was superficially simple; it seemed to be the natural course of events, after all. But at a deeper, emotional level it required a significant adjustment. The decade or so following her break with Kitahara marked a period of intense self-evaluation, the outcome of which was charted in her fiction.

Annis Pratt, writing about British and American women authors, notes that in the fiction of older writers, the purpose of the work is not so much to integrate the individual into society (as that has all been done before) but to integrate the heroine with herself. Quite often she returns to nature in her effort to relocate and reaffirm her sense of self. A similar pattern can be detected in Uno's life. In 1967, having tired of the hectic pace of life in Tokyo and still suffering the sting of her most recent divorce, she traveled to the mountains of Nasu and there bought a parcel of land. Before long she built a small, prefabricated house on the site—"a shack," as she was to call it, but hers nevertheless.

> After a woman has grown old, do you suppose she no longer falls in love? Perhaps she does not love in the romantic sense of the word. But there are times when she thinks, "Isn't this the same as romantic love? Yes, it is exactly the same." After I moved to Nasu, my feelings for the mountains were thus. I carried things to my mountain home in the spirit with which I brought presents to a man.[19]

Uno turned away from society and sought instead to integrate her self with herself. Nature is "less threatening to her selfhood than love," Pratt observes. It "becomes an ally . . . keeping her in touch with her selfhood, a kind of talisman that enables her to make her way through the alienations of male society."[20] For Uno nature helped ameliorate the pain that lingered from the past. "From time to time the past disappears and then reappears," she says. "But the memories that flit across my mind are sweet, not painful. I wonder if this, too, is a product of age. What I thought were wounds have instantly disappeared into my natural surroundings."[21] In her Nasu refuge Uno enjoyed, almost for the first time, the wonders and tranquillity of nature and of herself in nature.

> I am moved by the sound of the insects, the sound of the stream, the sound of the wind in the trees. It is as if I am hearing these all for the first time. The beauty of the starlight splashed across the night sky is not something of this world. And in the forest, which stretches as far as the eye can see, the light from this house seeps out from under the narrow eaves and spreads faintly over the bamboo grass.[22]

In her mountain retreat, Uno was able to examine herself as dispassionately as she examined her garden. She began to take stock of her life, her many loves, and she describes this process in the memoirs and personal vignettes she wrote during the early 1970s. In *Story of a Certain Woman Alone,* which she wrote in 1971, she traces the life of Kazue, the Uno persona, from birth to her encounter with Tanabe (Tōgō Seiji). She does not analyze or justify her actions but merely presents them. As a consequence she renders Kazue as little more than a young animal of passion, going where desire leads her, with no grand motives and few regrets. Happy moments, sad moments, celebration and despair—all are narrated with the same level tone, a tone Setouchi Harumi has likened to "a bug crawling over the ground."[23] "Kazue looks at even the rawest scenes from her past battles," Setouchi observes, "with the philosophical gaze of a disinterested bystander, as if she were recalling the scenery that slipped past on some pleasant journey."[24]

Time allows for distance, and distance in turn gives the author the wherewithal to reshape the past. "Is it really natural to forget the past?" Uno asks. "Perhaps then what I remember now is not the truth. Perhaps I remember only what is pleasant. No, I remember by reshaping the past into something pleasant."[25] Yet, as Fukuda Hirotoshi observes, "She does not reshape the past to flatter, but to enable her to look back over it as one pure stream."[26] In Uno's selective process, therefore, we can detect a need to recreate a simplified, purified version of her life. There is an effort to bring cohesion to her fragmented life, almost as if the author were sifting through her past in search of an answer or a legitimacy for her unconventional life.

Uno continues this process in *The Sound of Rain* (1974). This memoir includes instances from the entire spectrum of her life, past to present, but focuses on her relationship with Kitahara (named Yoshimura in the story), who died September 29, 1973, after a long illness. In recording her reaction to his death, Uno imparts to *The Sound of Rain* the somber mood of a farewell, a farewell she could not bring herself to deliver while Kitahara was alive. Because of this quiet, almost mournful tone, some have termed the work a requiem.

Before Uno's first-person narrator can bring herself to accept Yoshimura's death, she must first accept her past with him and the person she has since become. Thus, in *The Sound of Rain* the narrator once again dredges up those moments from the past—moments that gave her the greatest pleasure and the sharpest pain. As in the earlier Kazue story, the past no longer engages the narrator and she can view it all with the detached equanimity of a spectator.

Critics often suggest a comparison between the Uno persona of these memoirs and the poet Ono no Komachi. Indeed, the image Uno creates of an old woman staring vacantly at the falling rain while she ponders her youth recalls Komachi's famous poem:

> The cherry blossoms
> Have passed away, their color lost,
> While to no avail
> Age takes my beauty as it falls
> In the long rain of my regrets.[27]

Yet Komachi is depicted in legends and dramas as bitterly yearning for the past. At times her longings are so rancorous that priests must be called in to placate her raging spirit. Moreover, she is generally presented as a hag, mortified by her aged condition. White-haired and clothed in rags, she is decrepit and lost.

Uno's self-portrait is quite different. She feels no dark regret over the passage of time, nor does she feel shame at her present condition. She has grown old, this is true. But she finds beauty in her aged self just as one might find beauty in the gnarled trunk of an ancient tree. She is alone and she is old, but she feels that is best.

Nowhere is Uno's appreciation of self more wonderfully rendered than in her *watakushi shōsetsu* "Kōfuku" (Happiness, 1970).

> Every time Kazue gets out of the bath, she stands in front of the mirror and examines her naked body for a moment. She uses the towel in front for modesty and turns her hips slightly, standing at an angle. Her skin has turned slightly pink.
>
> "I look like her," she thinks.
>
> She thus notes her resemblance to Botticelli's Venus. There is the similarity in the way she is standing, although no seashell supports her. She also has the same feet and the slightly rounded stomach. This description might imply that Kazue enjoys staring at herself at length, but in fact this is not the case. She just notes the resemblance and soon gets dressed.
>
> In fact, Kazue does not very deeply believe that her naked body resembles Venus. A body with more than seventy years behind it is hardly likely to come close to Venus's. Perhaps Kazue's skin bears blemishes in places and occasionally sags. But her eyesight is failing and the steam from the bath makes the objects before her even more obscure. Kazue includes these shortcomings when she enumerates the happy aspects of her life. In this manner, Kazue collects fragments of happiness one after another, and so lives, spreading them throughout her environment. Even what seems odd to other people, she considers happiness.[28]

The image Kazue finds in her mirror sharply contrasts with that the heroine of *To Sting* sees in hers; the latter looks in horror at "a pathetic woman in some disguise," while the former playfully sees a vision of Botticelli's beauty. Kazue's reflection is one of optimism and of happiness. Most likely Uno discovered this vision in the teachings of the Tempū Society. One of Tempū's methods for inducing a healthy self-image was to have patients look at themselves in a mirror every morning, while thinking only positive thoughts.

It is this positive acceptance of self and life that has so attracted Uno's readers. When Nogami Yaeko finished reading *The Sound of Rain*, she is reported to have said, "Though Uno wrote over and over of her love for Kitahara, the one Uno really loves is Uno herself."[28] This self-love, however, is not to be understood in a narcissistic sense but rather as a very healthy self-esteem, denoting an inner strength not unlike that which Kazue feels when she gazes in her bathroom mirror. The seventy-year-old Uno can celebrate herself as a fully accomplished individual. She can laugh at herself and at the same time revel in the fact that she has been "reborn" from the waters of the past as a new woman, a whole woman.

7

I WILL

GO ON

LIVING

In the mid-1970s Uno began to receive recognition for her accomplishments as a writer and a "celebrated" woman. In April of 1972 she was accorded the Twenty-eighth *Geijutsuin shō* (Academy of Arts Award) for her long service and outstanding contributions to Japanese arts and literature. Two years later she received the *Kun santō zuihō shō* (Third Order of the Sacred Treasure), an imperially sanctioned title traditionally conferred only on men whose lives and works embellished the nation. The awards brought with them handsome stipends, but more than that they gave Uno the recognition she had long merited. Upon receipt of the Third Order of the Sacred Treasure she traveled to her old home in Iwakuni and presented the certificate bearing her name before the family altar.

Uno did not rest then, of course; she continued to write. Soon it became clear, however, that she could not stay with her literary memoirs forever, and, since she was no longer involved in romantic entanglements, she was unable to write about new affairs. She decided to write of something outside her realm of lived experience.

> I thought that there would be an endless store of other subjects, but there was not. I am quite lazy, and when I finally decided to write of something other than myself, I knew of nothing to write. I had no idea what I ought to write. I knew that when other writers set about writing a novel, they gather materials. I had never once gathered materials. . . . But in the end, I decided to go in search of a story.[1]

Actually, Uno had "gathered materials" before; she had sought out Tōgō
Seiji when she wanted to write of suicide, and she had visited Tenguya
Kyūkichi when she wanted to write of puppets. Perhaps, because the ideas
for these works occurred so spontaneously, she did not believe that she was
consciously creating stories outside the realm of her own personal experience.
She now wanted to seek an appropriate subject, and it is this deliberate search
that offered a new departure for her. But unlike "other writers"—Akutagawa Ryūnosuke, Tanizaki Jun'ichirō, Nogami Yaeko, and Enchi Fumiko,
for example—she did not gather her materials from history or from scholarly
tomes. Rather, she sought them within the margins of everyday life.

Uno began traveling to out-of-the-way villages, poking through forgotten
places, and interviewing those from the highest to the lowest levels of society. While she was in Iwakuni, for example, she became acquainted with a
prostitute who catered to U.S. servicemen. Uno accompanied the woman to
her home town in Matsue, where she learned of the woman's unfortunate
love affair with a British soldier during the Occupation. Inspired by what she
heard, she wrote "Yaeyama no yuki" (The Snows of Yaeyama, 1975), a
charming, fairy-tale account of the romance between a naive Japanese village
girl and the gentle-spirited British soldier who loved her. A year later Uno
wrote "Cheri ga shinda" (Cherry Is Dead), which continues the story,
bringing the heroine from Yaeyama to Iwakuni, where she supports herself as
a prostitute until she is killed by a drunken soldier. "She was really just a normal woman," Uno said of the model for these stories. "But it is often in the
usual that we find the unusual."[2]

Of the many "discovered stories" Uno wrote during this time, the most
impressive is *Usuzumi no sakura* (The Gray Cherry Tree, 1974). Kobayashi
Hideo told Uno of an ancient cherry tree in Gifu Prefecture that had allegedly
been planted in the sixth century by Emperor Keitai. The tree had broad
boughs and blossoms so delicately pale they seemed almost gray. Knowing of
Uno's fondness for cherry trees, he urged her to go see it. With typical
impulsiveness Uno dashed off to Neo in Gifu Prefecture. She was dismayed to
find the tree on the verge of death and immediately began a campaign to save
it, raising funds and eliciting the support of the prefectural government.
New grafts were eventually performed, and the tree was revived. Thanks to
the publicity, the huge tree, its gnarled branches supported by bamboo
staves, became a tourist attraction; people poured into the sleepy mountain
village every April during the blossom season. The citizens of Neo, greatly
benefiting from the extra income, have dubbed Uno their patron saint.

Claiming to have been bewitched by the beauty of the tree, Uno began to
write of her experiences in Neo. The work she created, *The Gray Cherry*

Tree, opens as a typical Uno *watakushi shōsetsu,* but then, perhaps as the author was moved by the spirit of the tree, evolves into a story of mystery and imagination that transcends the limits of lived experience.

The story revolves around three women: Yoshino Kazue, Makida Takao, and Makida Yoshino. Kazue is the typical Uno surrogate; she is aloof, observing all with calculated poise. Makida Takao, arrogant and slightly eccentric, owns the rice fields next to the cherry tree. Kazue believes that the water from these fields is rotting the roots of the ancient tree, and she asks Takao to convert to dry fields, but Takao refuses. On the surface the story concerns Kazue's battle with Takao over the welfare of the tree. As the story unfolds, however, it becomes increasingly clear that more is at stake in this struggle than simply the tree's life; the tree becomes a symbol of immortality for Kazue. "For an old woman like me," Kazue says, "the fact that a tree twelve centuries old was rejuvenated by grafts from younger roots was fascinating."[3] To prolong the life of the tree, and by extension her own, she must confront Takao, the force of death. Takao is a persuasive opponent—she hides her great age beneath swathes of lamé and velvet and bedecks herself with diamonds. But stripped of her trappings, she is a skeleton.

> She takes off her dress and immediately drapes it over a hanger. Once she is down to a single chemise she sits on the tatami and slowly removes her false teeth, first the upper set and then the lower. Her tiny body grows tinier still. Sitting there with no teeth in her mouth, she is not her usual witch-like self. I do not know whether she is eighty or ninety. She is not human. She seems more like an object.[4]

Behind Takao's mask of youth and beauty is emptiness. Kazue observes Takao in terrified silence; she recognizes in Takao an image of herself, the self she may become. As in Uno's earlier works, we again have two female characters who function as separate poles in a single individual. Takao is Kazue's other self, the ghost of her future—and Kazue is in constant battle with her future. She fights for life and beauty, while Takao fights for death. The tree becomes the fulcrum of their struggle, eventually taking on human proportions in the person of the pale, mysterious Yoshino, the spirit of the tree.

As a child Yoshino was given to the Makida family to atone for a crime her father had committed. "No matter how you treat my daughter, I won't protest," her father said when he handed Yoshino to Takao. "Boil her and eat her; fry her and eat her. I don't care."[5] Indeed, Takao feeds on Yoshino's beauty, selling her body to the aging, wealthy men who patronize the restaurant Takao owns. She seeks to consume Yoshino as certainly as the water in her fields devours the roots of the gray cherry.

Yoshino must die, and when she does, Kazue finds her even more beautiful, more mysterious in death. The next time Kazue visits the gray cherry tree, she realizes what she had known intuitively all along: "I felt as though Yoshino were here. . . . as if her beauty were here in the life of the tree."[6] The cherry tree has been restored, its blooms more glorious than ever.

In *The Gray Cherry Tree* one can appreciate for the first time in Uno's works an attempt to come to grips with something stronger, something deeper than personal experience. Uno states that she was trying to create a "Dostoevsky world" with *The Gray Cherry Tree*. Her comment reveals that she had hoped to imbue her work with a sense of profound urgency, with something that more closely approached, as she said, "the issue of human existence."[7] To that end *The Gray Cherry Tree* stands as a singular achievement.

The Gray Cherry Tree was not an easy work to write. Uno states that it was the most difficult story she had ever written, and also the most satisfying. "I kept shaping the characters to suit my own liking, as if I were hammering them out of stone."[8]

Perhaps because of the energy required to write such a work, Uno soon found herself returning to the comfortable medium of personal reflections. The 1980s marked a new period of activity for her. From February 1982 to July 1983 she serialized *I Will Go On Living* in the *Mainichi* newspaper. Shortly after serialization the work was published in book form, becoming an overnight best-seller. Uno had written of her life in countless other works, so *I Will Go On Living* is hardly unique. She even includes passages taken directly from her earlier memoirs, *Story of a Certain Woman Alone* and *The Sound of Rain*. Yet, *I Will Go On Living* has a completely different flavor. The earlier works were clearly fictional re-creations of certain moments from the author's life, but *I Will Go On Living* appears to have little conscious artistic manipulation; it reads more like a warm, gossipy chat between old friends. Uno describes her many love affairs and her successes and failures with the same easy indifference she uses to discuss her daily habits of walking ten thousand paces or eating tofu.

Readers were impressed by Uno's tongue-in-cheek humor, by her optimism, and by her practical approach to life. The serialization of the work provoked an outpouring of letters to the *Mainichi*. The newspaper printed the letters along with Uno's responses and soon she was cast as the "Ann Landers of Japan." For several months the newspaper ran a weekly advice column, with Uno answering queries with her typical quick sagacity. Many of the problems she dealt with were marital or amorous, but more than a few involved child-rearing, career changes, and etiquette.

Uno's sudden popularity did not stop there; soon she was invited to appear on TV talk shows, and women's pulp magazines clamored to interview her. She had been rediscovered by a generation of modern readers who had not known her as a daring femme fatale, but who now saw her as a delightful, if slightly eccentric, old woman who had had a taste for adventure. Uno was not one to hesitate when it came to revealing the intimate moments in her past. She told of her many love affairs with candor and amusement, disclosing her mistakes along with her successes. Seeing how her young audiences hung on every word, however, she always concluded with a note of caution. "It was one thing for me to do what I did. But I do not advise any of you to follow my example!"

In the spring of 1984, the TBS (Tokyo Broadcasting System) TV station dramatized *I Will Go On Living* in a splashy thirteen-part series with Toaki Yukiyo in the starring role. In November of that year Obata Kinji staged the work at the Imperial Theater with the infamous Yamamoto Yōko playing the part of Uno Chiyo.[9] In October 1985 Ichikawa Kon adapted *Ohan* for the screen with Ishizaka Kōji, Ōhara Reiko, and Yoshinaga Sayuri. This new interest in Uno brought about a resurgence in publications of her writing. Her old works were reprinted and displayed prominently in bookstores along with collections of her contemporary essays, each bound attractively in a cover bearing her kimono trademark, a delicate cherry-petal motif.

On the evening of November 30, 1985, Uno celebrated her eighty-eighth birthday, a particularly important milestone in Japan, with an elaborate party at the Tokyo Imperial Hotel. As the popular tune "We are the World" blared out over the audience, Uno was led onto the stage by the writer Setouchi Harumi, who, having taken Buddhist vows years earlier, was dressed in a nun's habit, her head completely shorn. Uno wore a girlish kimono with flowing sleeves and had festooned her hair with flowers. During the course of the festivities, she changed two times, like a young bride, into other kimonos of her design. With each new kimono she paraded across the stage with a new escort—Hagiwara Sakutarō's young grandson and Morimoto Takerō, a handsome TV personality. The list of guests included a wealth of celebrities—the designer Issei Miyake, the actress Yamamoto Yōko, and the writer Maruya Saiichi.

The celebration took some by surprise. It hardly seemed appropriate for a woman Uno's age to cavort about like a schoolgirl, but then Uno had never concerned herself with what others deemed "appropriate." She had lived her life on the edge of respectability, racing madly into the whirlwinds of romance and following her heart wherever it led. With her past in mind, therefore, her eighty-eighth birthday party seemed a very appropriate tribute to a life of unconventionality and insuppressible passion. As one guest put it, "Only Uno Chiyo could get away with something like this."

Uno did not stop living once she reached a venerable age. She did not stop writing or exploring or loving. Rather, she came to understand what Tenguya Kyūkichi had meant when he told her back in 1942,

> Every time I finish a puppet I'll always be thinking to myself that the next'll be even better. That's right. 'You can do better,' I'll tell myself. I guess death'll be my first and final stopping place—can't very well be making anything better after that, now can I? Even Hida no Takumi and Hidari Jingorō didn't go and say, 'Yes, this's my masterpiece, now I can die.' No, they kept on working, and if they'd lived any longer there's no telling how many great works they'd have made. But death is, after all, the final stop. It puts an end to your art.[10]

Uno, too, had always set her sights ahead. Once she crossed her eighty-eighth year she began a new writing project, a sequel to her memoir *I Will Go On Living*. Yet unpublished, she intends to title the work "Watashi no bannen" (My Twilight Years). "I suppose it's safe to say I'm in the twilight of my life now. Or perhaps I'm being a bit hasty?" Like Tenguya Kyūkichi, she expects to continue working on this and similar projects until the day she dies.

In December 1987, at the grand age of ninety, Uno published "Ippen ni harukaze ga fuite kita" (Suddenly a Spring Wind), her first work of fiction in over a decade. The story itself is slight—a fairy-tale-type romance in the *kikigaki* style. But critics were impressed by the optimism of the work and by the fact that a ninety-year-old writer had so delightfully captured the fresh passion of youth.

Uno has always been something of a slow writer, and now in her "twilight years" she is even slower. But she is also more disciplined. She keeps a notebook handy by her bed so she can jot down whatever inspiration comes to her as she rests. Until the summer of 1990, when she began to suffer from a slipped disk, she rose every morning before dawn and made a light breakfast for herself, proud of the fact that she was able to do most of her own marketing and cooking. After breakfast she would spend her time at her low writing desk, her papers spread out before her and a tray heaped high with meticulously sharpened pencils within easy reach.

Poor health has now made writing difficult for Uno. Because of back problems she can no longer sit at her low desk but must use a table and chair. With the firm but affectionate assistance of her secretary and constant companion, Fujie Atsuko, Uno is able to continue working on "My Twilight Years," and she still manages an occasional brief essay.

Writing is not Uno's only concern; she still maintains her kimono boutique, though most of the business is handled by others. In the late 1980s she established a "village," known as Bansei-mura (Village of Ten Thousand Generations), near Tōno City in Iwate Prefecture, where she hopes to preserve the architecture, traditions, and fables of the past. And her impishly smiling, bespectacled face is still found with frequency on magazine covers and in newspapers. Cajoled by interviewers to reveal her longevity secrets, Uno has offered:

> Water. Drink plenty of water. It's good for health as well as beauty. . . . Don't worry. Don't get all worked up over things. And walk. I walk five thousand paces a day now. When I go outside people call my name. They say, "Let me shake your hand—I want to live long, too."
> . . . Well it's better than if they ignored me!
> You see, I never forced myself to do anything I didn't want to do. I've lived my life just the way I wanted to.[11]

This, Uno concludes, is her secret to long life. The same may be said for her writing; she never forced herself to write. At first she undertook projects for extra income. "It did not matter what the subject was," she has stated. "As long as I wrote about something that would interest others I would profit."[12] But later, when she derived her finances from other enterprises, she wrote because she wanted to. Or, as she has said elsewhere, because she had to.

> I am possessed of a relentless desire to write. Writing brings me great joy. But it also brings me sorrow because I can never write more than a few lines a day.
> I have another occupation, one that is not as constraining. It is easier, perhaps more enjoyable—kimono designing. . . . If I did not design kimonos, perhaps my energy for writing would wither.[13]

Uno's other occupations allowed perspective, and, more important, permitted her the freedom to pursue her art unencumbered by financial considerations. And so, aside from all her other accomplishments—kimono designer, magazine editor, and village head—her writing will be her legacy. "What I write today I want to be better than what I wrote yesterday. I'll do what I can to go on living, and while I'm alive I'll work with all my might. Death'll be the final stop."[14]

That final stop will invite a new assessment of Uno's art and contributions. She will most likely not be counted among the major writers in the literary pantheon; she lacks the breadth of a Natsume Sōseki, or the poetry of a Kawabata Yasunari. But then, Uno never really intended to be a literary heavyweight. Dreams of such magnitude were beyond the realm of imagination for women of her generation. Even those who did approach writing with more apparent seriousness will have a difficult time finding a place alongside the likes of Sōseki and Kawabata. Women's writing at the time was simply not accorded the same value as men's. Women who did "attempt the pen" were regarded more as anomalies than as serious writers, and more often than not they were thought to be slightly scandalous.

But Uno very cleverly manipulated the prejudice and suspicion that surrounded intelligent, outspoken women during the early twentieth century. She subverted the status quo and used her femaleness to her advantage by turning what the world saw as scandal into personal profit. "No one is as fortunate as a woman writer!" she could exclaim with little hesitancy. And of her propitious debut in the literary world she acknowledged: "I now feel lucky, being born a woman." In part Uno's disclaimers are traditional modesty. She worked hard and often under less than encouraging conditions to achieve recognition. Moreover, she surprised her peers, and perhaps herself as well, by becoming in later years a significant writer and one extremely proud of her craft. Once she lost the aura of femme fatale and gained an appreciation of herself as "a woman whose sense of purpose comes from within," the works she produced were beyond compare. "The Puppet Maker," *Ohan*, "Happiness," *Story of a Certain Woman Alone*, and many others will remain as lasting testaments to her talent. These stories are artfully told and beautifully crafted and will remind all who read them of the resiliency and subtlety of Japanese literature. And Uno Chiyo will long be remembered for her zestful optimism and for her unfailing passion for life and love and art.

Chronology of

Important Dates

1897	Uno Chiyo born in Iwakuni.
1899	Her mother dies.
1900	Her father marries Saeki Ryū.
1904	Uno enters Iwakuni Elementary School.
1910	Graduates from elementary school; enters Iwakuni Higher School for Girls.
1911	Sent to marry cousin; returns after ten days.
1913	Her father dies.
1914	Graduates from Iwakuni Higher School for Girls; begins teaching at Kawashimo Elementary School.
1915	Resigns; travels briefly to Korea.
1916	Moves to Kyoto with her cousin, Fujimura Tadashi; moves to Tokyo; works at the Enrakuken.
1919	Marries Fujimura Tadashi.
1920	Moves to Sapporo.
1921	Wins first place for "Shifun no Kao" (Painted Face) in *Jiji Shimpō* short-story contest.
1922	Returns to Tokyo; meets Ozaki Shirō.
1924	Divorced from Fujimura Tadashi; marries Ozaki Shirō.
1930	Moves in with Tōgō Seiji; divorced from Ozaki Shirō.
1934	Leaves Tōgō Seiji.
1936	Founds *Style* magazine.
1938	Inaugurates *Buntai* magazine with Kitahara Takeo.
1939	Marries Kitahara Takeo.
1942	Joins the women writers' chapter of the Japanese Literature Patriotic Association. Travels to Shikoku to interview Tenguya Kyūkichi.
1944	*Style* is closed by government order.
1946	Revives *Style*.

1947   Uno and Kitahara revive *Buntai* with Kobayashi Hideo, Aoyama Jirō, Miyoshi Tatsuji, and others.

1951   Travels to Europe with Miyata Fumiko for two months; her stepmother, Ryū, dies.

1957   Travels to the United States, where she displays her kimonos at the International Exhibition in Seattle, Washington, and at B. Altman's Department Store in New York; awarded the Fifth Noma Prize in Literature for *Ohan*.

1958   Awarded the Ninth Association of Japanese Women Writers' Award for *Ohan*.

1959   *Style* goes out of business.

1964   Divorced from Kitahara.

1967   Buys land in Nasu and builds a small cabin.

1971   Awarded the Tenth Association of Japanese Women Writers' Award for "Kōfuku."

1972   Accorded the Twenty-eighth Academy of Arts Award.

1974   Awarded the title of Third Order of the Sacred Treasure.

1982   Awarded the Thirtieth Kikuchi Kan Prize for Literature.

1985   Celebrates her eighty-eighth birthday at the Tokyo Imperial Hotel.

1990   Named a "Person of Cultural Merit."

Bibliography of Significant Works by Uno Chiyo

1921 "Shifun no kao" (Painted Face) (*Jiji Shimpō*, January 2).

1922 "Haka wo abaku" (Opening the Grave) (*Chūō Kōron*, May).

1929 *Keshi wa naze akai* (Tell Me Why Poppies Are Red) (serialized in *Chūō Kōron* from December 1929 to May 1930). Chūō Kōronsha published the work in book form in November 1930.

1933 *Irozange* (Confessions of Love) (serialized in *Chūō Kōron* from September 1933 to March 1935). Chūō Kōronsha published the novel in April 1935. An English translation was published in 1989 (Honolulu: University of Hawaii Press).

1934 "Mohō no tensai" (A Genius of Imitation) (*Shinchō*, July). An English translation can be found in *To Live and to Write* (Seattle: Seal Press, 1987).

1935 "Wakare mo tanoshi" (Parting Pleasure) (*Kaizō*, June).

1936 "Miren" (A Lingering Attachment) (*Chūō Kōron*, October).

1942 "Tsuma no tegami" (A Wife's Letters) (*Bungakkai*, July and September). "Ningyōshi Tenguya Kyūkichi" (The Puppet Maker Tenguya Kyūkichi) (*Chūō Kōron*, November–December). Later brought out in book form by Buntai-sha, 1943.

1943 "Nichiro no tataki kikigaki" (Narrative of the Russo-Japanese War) (Buntai-sha).

1947 *Ohan* (serialization began in *Buntai*, December 1947, June 1948, and July 1949; and then was moved to *Chūō Kōron*, finally ending in May 1957. In July of 1958, Chūō Kōronsha brought the work out in a single volume. An English translation can be found in *The Old Woman, the Wife, and the Archer* (New York: Viking, 1961).

"Watashi no seishun monogatari" (Tales of My Youth) (serialized in *Style* from May to October).

1959   "Jidenteki ren'ai ron" (A Record of My Loves) (serialized in *Fujin Kōron* from January 1959 to January 1960).

1963   *Sasu* (To Sting) (serialized in *Shinchō* from January 1963 to January 1966). An English translation entitled "To Stab," can be found in *Stories By Contemporary Japanese Women Writers* (New York: Sharpe, 1982). (Translation is of the third chapter only.)

1967   "Kono oshiroi ire" (This Powder Box) (*Shinchō*, January).

1969   *Kaze no oto* (The Sound of the Wind) (*Umi*, July). Issued in book form that same year by Chūō Kōronsha.

1970   "Kōfuku" (Happiness) (*Shinchō*, April). English translation in *Rabbits, Crabs, Etc.* (Honolulu: University of Hawaii Press, 1982).

1971   *Aru hitori no onna no hanashi* (Story of a Certain Woman Alone) (serialized in *Bungakkai*, January–December). Published in book form by Bungei shunjū-sha, 1972).

        Watashi no bungakuteki kaisōki (My Literary Memoirs) (serialized in *Tokyo Shimbun* from January 1971 to February 1972).

        Usuzumi no sakura (The Gray Cherry Tree) (serialized in *Shinchō* from January 1971 to November 1974). Published in book form by Shinchō-sha in 1975.

1974   *Ame no oto* (The Sound of Rain), Bungei shunjū.

1975   "Yaeyama no yuki" (The Snows of Yaeyama) (*Bungakkai*, July).

1976   *Mama no hanashi* (Mama-san's Story) (*Umi*, March).

        Suisei shoin no musume (The Daughter of Westshore Hall) (*Umi*, May).

        "Cheri ga shinda" (Cherry Is Dead) (*Bungakkai*, September).

1977–   *Uno Chiyo zenshū* (The Complete Works of Uno Chiyo) issued in
1978   twelve volumes by Chūō Kōronsha.

1980   "Nokotte iru hanashi" (The Story That Remains), Shūeisha.

1982   *Ikite yuku Watashi* (I Will Go On Living) (serialized in *Mainichi Shimbun* from February 1982 to July 1983). Published in book form by Mainichi Shimbunsha, 1983.

1987   "Ippen ni harukaze ga fuite kita" (Suddenly a Spring Wind) (*Shinchō*, December). An English translation was published in *WINDS* (December 1989).

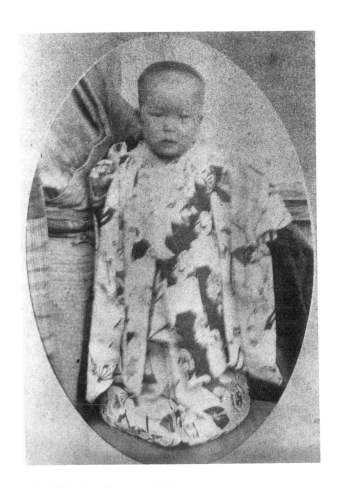

Uno Chiyo in infancy, ca. 1898.

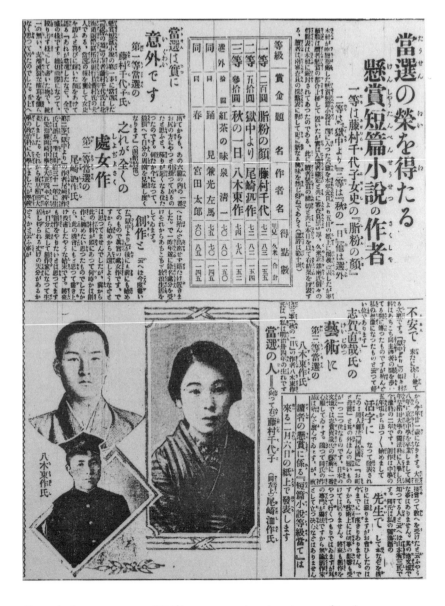

From the January 21, 1921, *Jiji Shimpō* announcing the winners of its short-story contest. *Right,* first-place winner Fujimura Chiyoko (Uno Chiyo); *above left,* second-place winner Ozaki Shisaku (Ozaki Shirō, Uno's second husband); *below left,* third-place winner Yagi Tōsaku. (Courtesy of Kindai Bungakkan)

At Yugashima Hot Springs in Itō, 1927. Uno, age thirty, is second from the right. Standing next to her with a walking stick is the poet Miyoshi Tatsuji. (Courtesy of Kindai Bungakkan)

Uno's second husband, Ozaki Shirō, 1938. She was married to him from 1924 to 1930.

With the artist Tōgō Seiji behind his Yamazaki house in 1931.

Uno Chiyo, 1932.

At the writer Yoshiya Nobuko's house in 1936. *Seated from the left:* Hayashi Fumiko, Uno Chiyo (age thirty-nine), Yoshiya Nobuko, and Sata Ineko. (Courtesy of Kindai Bungakkan)

The January 1, 1937, issue of *Style,* the fashion magazine Uno edited. (Courtesy of Kindai Bungakkan)

Uno Chiyo on the patio of her Awashima house, ca. 1933.

With Kitahara Takeo, her third husband, on their wedding day, April 1, 1939. Uno is forty-two and Kitahara is thirty-two.

With the puppet maker Tenguya Kyūkichi in his Tokushima shop, 1942.

A meeting of the Women Writers' Association at Uno's Kobikichō house, ca. 1952. *Seated from left:* Masugi Shizue, Itagaki Naoko, Nakazato Tsuneko, Yoshiya Nobuko, Miyake Tsuyako, Ōhara Tomie, Abe Mitsuko, and Ōtani Fujiko. *Standing from left:* Uno Chiyo (in her mid-fifties), Tsuboi Sakae, and Amino Kiku. (Courtesy of Kindai Bungakkan)

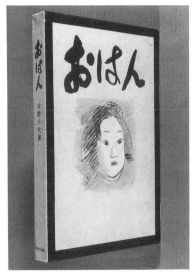

At a party following the Fifth Noma Prize for Literature Award Ceremony. Uno, sixty years old, received the prize in 1957 for *Ohan.*

The book box for *Ohan,* designed by Kimura Shōhachi and published by Chūō Kōronsha in 1957. (Courtesy of Kindai Bungakkan)

With the Oyumi puppet head Tenguya Kyūkichi carved for her before his death. Uno is in her late sixties.

With Morimoto Takerō at her eighty-eighth birthday party held at the Imperial Hotel, November 30, 1985. The kimono she is wearing with gold and silver overlay is of her own design and inspired by the "Gray Cherry Tree" of Gifu Prefecture.

On the veranda of her Iwakuni house, 1987. Uno had the house restored in 1973.

With the "Gray Cherry Tree" in Neo-machi, Gifu Prefecture, spring 1988. (Courtesy of *Croissant*)

PART TWO

The Works

THE PUPPET

MAKER

I first saw one of his puppets last spring when I was visiting a friend. It was an Oyumi puppet from the play *Awa no Naruto*.[1] She was dressed in a simple kimono of coarsely woven, striped cloth, yet I found the sorrow in her face compelling. My friend's wife took the puppet in her arms and, slipping her hand up under the sash, began to move her for me. Being a female puppet, her eyes were the only movable features on her face, and they should have opened when the appropriate toggles were pulled. But for some reason, this puppet's eyes remained tightly shut. I heard myself gasp. In the puppet's eyes, eyes that refused to open, I could sense an emotion so profound it could never be expressed in the face of a living woman.

The puppet I saw that day was not one of his better works, and yet those eyes, held shut as they were for some unknown reason, startled me. Perhaps that is why I gasped, and perhaps that is why, days later, I still could not forget the beautiful sorrow that had been etched so deeply in her face. To tell the truth, I know very little of the old arts, of *jōruri* and the like, and knowing nothing of the play that features the character Oyumi, I did not understand why she should be so sad. Yet as I gazed at the puppet I felt implicit in her face the very depths of a woman's sorrow, and I grew curious about the person who had carved her.

After some inquiry I learned that the puppet maker lives in Tokushima of Awa in the neighborhood of Wada. His name is Yoshioka Kyūkichi, though he is more popularly known as Tenguya Kyūkichi; and very often this is abbreviated to Tengu Kyū. He is in his eighty-sixth year. I rather impulsively decided that I would pay him a visit. Even I was surprised at myself. After all, we are in this state of emergency, and it hardly seemed appropriate for me to be dashing off to Shikoku to meet a man for no better reason than that his puppet impressed me.

I

"Well, come on in and make yourself at home. If I'm to tell you my story I can't be thinking of you as some guest come down from Tokyo.

"I was born eighty-five years ago, the Fifth Year of Ansei, in Nakamura of Myōdōgōri, little over half a mile west of here.[2] When I was a boy, folks in a village like ours didn't have such a thing as a surname, but being of samurai stock my family bore the name Kasai. I was born the third son of Kasai Iwazō. My mother died when I was three.

"My father made his living as an indigo pattern-dyer. Nowadays they're just called 'dyers.' They made pictures with their dyes, too, called 'dye-shop prints.' I expect you've seen the banners set up at a boy's first Boy's Day celebration in May. Some'll be of the great Benkei surrendering to the young Ushiwakamaru, or sometimes they'll have Yoichi of Nasu piercing the fan target with his arrow. Well, those were the sort of pictures my father made.

"My father raised me single-handedly. He was a pattern-dyer, but even so didn't have a workshop of his own. He and my brothers worked at the master-dyer's place and weren't often home. I was left to run wild until, at the age of seven, they put me in the local temple school.

"I went to school there for eight years. Now that might not sound like much to you, but in a country town like ours it was something of a long time. Back in those days about all we did in school was work in our primer, the *Teikin Ōrai*, reading and copying.[3] We had none of the high-minded learning children have today!

"Now as I look back on it, I can see that I enjoyed working with my hands even as a boy. I was clever at it too, if I do say so myself. I wasn't much when it came to writing out my lessons, but I did like to paint. Perhaps I was thinking of following in my father's footsteps, I'm not too clear on it now. But then I began making puppets. Some I fashioned from paper stiff with mud, and others I whittled out of paulownia wood. I had a friend at the temple school named Fujimoto Benkichi. He was a bit touched when it came to making puppets. Around here we call folks 'touched' when they carry on about something with such fever they seem near crazy. Well, Benkichi was touched on puppets. He'd make them out of balled up paper, right there at school. We'd stretch a cloth over the little desk where we studied, as our curtain, you see, and then one of us would crouch down low and move the puppets about while the other one watched from across the way.

"Oh, now let me think . . . would have been back when Tokushima was under the rule of the Hachisuka family. Puppet shows were allowed within three leagues of their castle lands, but only puppet shows, mind you. Kabuki and the like were strictly forbidden. And so, you see, the puppet shows caught on like wild fire. Why, traveling troupes would come out as far as this village nearly every day. Folks took to calling them 'box puppeteers' on account of they kept their puppets in the box they carried along with them. Usually had around six—a youth and a maiden, a mother and child, an everyday man and a buffoon. With six puppets they were able to put on a decent enough show. They'd carry their boxes strapped to their backs, and then, sounding the wooden clappers 'ka-chi! ka-chi!' would march right in the front gate of some estate. They operated their puppets themselves, you see, reciting the story as they went along. Sometimes there'd be one among them to play the *shamisen*.

"Well, Benkichi and I couldn't think of anything more exciting than pretending to be box puppeteers. Every chance we got we played our puppet game under the school desk. But now if the school master caught us at it, he'd have us stand at attention atop the desk for half an hour, sometimes a whole hour.

"So, you see, even as a child I gave myself over to this sort of tomfoolery. I never lifted a finger around the house. When it came time to weed the back field I wouldn't so much as pluck a stalk. I was in school from dawn to dusk, and when I got home there usually wasn't anyone around to tell me what to do, so I'd set in to playing my puppet game again all by myself. Oh, I didn't need much to make my puppets, but if I ever found myself wanting a piece of cloth or such, there was always someone in the neighborhood kind enough to give me an old scrap or two. I'd sew costumes—kimonos and undergarments and such—and then I'd dress my puppets up and set about playing theater. Now I expect this'll sound strange, but do you know there were some who'd come along to see my plays, even though the only puppets I had were those childish paper-made ones? I had my share of patrons, too. Yes, back in those days you had to have 'patronage,' as they called it, to get along in the theater world. Well, I counted as my patrons the young wife next door and her daughter and all the other children in the neighborhood. They were all likely to bring me something, a cloth for a curtain, say; or something I could use in my plays.

"Around that time, I believe it was, there was a man named Abe Kamekichi who ran a sword dōjō on the grounds of the Hachiman shrine back in Nakamura. Times being changeable though, before long sword practice fell out of fashion, and Mr. Abe began teaching the Chinese classics there instead.

My father was in charge of helping with the school. I don't quite know what you'd call his position nowadays, but he was responsible for opening the school and locking up afterward and for preparing tea and such. But as my father was generally too busy with pattern dying to see to his tasks, he passed the job along to me when I turned thirteen. You can't really say I got much of an education there, but in my spare time I was able to ask questions about this and that. I couldn't read the whole of *The Four Classics,* mind you, but I did manage to get through *The Great Learning* and *The Analects of Confucius.* Yes, I suppose you could say I was left to grow up wild. But I wonder now if that wasn't the way my father intended it.''

2

"Back then there were about three men in the region known as puppet makers. There was Deko-Chū, Tsunezō of Ōe, and then there was Tomigorō, sometimes known as Deko-Tomi, the man who would later become my master. I often wonder why I took it into my head to become a puppet maker. I was just a boy of fifteen or sixteen, after all, still wet behind the ears. How could I have been so certain I was to follow the puppet trade?

"Well, let me tell you . . . off in the countryside around here there was such a thing as the cotton exchange. In Akui, the town just down the road, there were quite a few cotton dealers. They'd store up cotton brought in from Sanuki, and the womenfolk here would go to town, buy up some of that cotton and cart it home where they'd run it through a gin to remove the seeds. Oh, I expect a city person like yourself hasn't had occasion to see such a contraption, nor a spinning wheel for that matter, but the women would spin the cotton into thread on a spinning wheel. Oh my, they'd make those wheels whir. And when they were through they'd lash the thread onto a loom and weave out bolts of cloth. It doesn't take much time at all when you consider how it's done now, but back then, well, it took a long while. Once they'd finished a bolt of cloth they'd take it back to the same store and trade it in for more cotton. From the profit they turned, they were able to make a little extra for their purses. Most of the womenfolk in my village gave themselves over to this sort of sidework. The young wife next door was no different. That woman, I tell you, all she had to do was see my face and she was off telling me to learn puppet making. Oh yes, every time she saw me that's just what she said.

"Truth be told, the theater was thriving right about then. By theater, now, I mean the puppet theater. When autumn rolled around, what with the festivals and such, there'd be a good many puppeteers out on the road. One day they'd set up a performance in Wada, and the next they'd come around to Nakamura. Yes, they traveled round all the villages in the area, from the hundred-family villages to those of a hundred and fifty or so. The young fellows would hire on a master chanter and practice *jōruri* chanting. There wasn't a man or woman around who hadn't had at least a taste of *jōruri*. My, things were different then, no denying it. Nowadays folks won't take part in anything, no matter what, unless you first hand them a nice sum of money. But back then, you did work because you enjoyed it, and that was pay enough. Far as meals were concerned, there'd always be someone to feed you. In a sense, yes, it was like playing, but it was one way to set yourself up in an occupation. And, when the puppet theater was in its heyday, there were more than thirty theaters in Awa alone. About all the villages around here had the kind of theaters farmers operated in their spare time—not a proper building, mind you, but just one in the fields. They'd spread straw matting down along the ground and put up a roof of thatch. Long as the weather lasted, that was good enough. But sometimes the local squire would stage plays on his property—for three days running.

"As a boy I was sickly, coughing and wheezing all the time. Folks said I had asthma. Seeing as how I was so weak, everyone thought it best for me to find a job that would have me seated most the day. The young wife next door came out and told my father what she'd been saying all along, that I ought to become a puppet maker, and so he finally took me to see Master Tomigorō. I was sixteen. I don't recall if it was spring or summer. Anyhow, folks had been after me so long to learn the trade, I soon found myself believing it was the job for me. If anyone asked me, 'Will you become a puppet maker, boy?' I answered right away, 'Yes, I will!' And so, you see, I didn't feel any regrets being sent off to an apprenticeship.

"My master was a tight-lipped man, and somewhat of a stickler for details. When you're to serve a master—and I suppose it'd be the same no matter what kind of trade you're in—you've got to prove yourself worthy before you can set about learning your master's craft. You do this by giving yourself over to his demands. Well now, I was an ornery boy by nature, but I soon found myself answering to disciplines I'd never had at home. I got up at five o'clock every morning, and I worked until ten at night. That's right, I had night duties to see to until ten o'clock. But as soon as they were done, I'd head out for my nightly entertainment. What's that? Oh heavens no, by nightly entertainment I mean the sumō matches held on the grounds of the nearby shrine. That's right, there were matches there every night, and I'd go to wrestle a bout or two. I suppose you couldn't expect someone as slight as me to be much at sumō, and let me tell you there were more than a few who had a laugh at my expense. 'Look there!' they'd holler, 'He can't be but four foot tall! Little fellow like you got no business wrestling!' And then they'd break into great guffaws of laughter.

"Yes, that's right. I did receive a salary, but can't say I'd know how much it would be at today's count. I suppose it was around twenty sen. As I recall, I was paid on Obon and New Year's Day. But other than that I can't remember ever receiving anything else from my master—be it money or praise. It wasn't like it is now. Why, the master might say something like, 'You're a hard worker, boy!' But that was as close as you'd ever get to a compliment. He'd never praise the puppet you'd carved, or tell you you'd done a good job. But now I guess that was just the master's way of disciplining his students. Yes, I believe it was as much as three years after I'd become an apprentice before someone came upon me at my work and praised me for it, saying I looked like I'd turn into a fine puppet maker someday.

"I've told this story to any number of folks, but there was a time in my life that I knew I'd be heading down the wrong path if I didn't watch my step. Back then, on the north side of the village, there was a man by the name of Tamaki Toyosō who was touched on kendō. He wanted a sword partner. Oh, not that he was interested in teaching swordsmanship. He was a wealthy man, you see, and didn't need to be teaching; he just wanted someone to spar with. Anyone would do, so long as he liked the sword. Well, being a boy, I figured a little kendō practice would help me with my wrestling, so as soon as the hour struck ten I was off to Mr. Tamaki's for lessons. He was kind enough to wait up for me. Yes, I went every night—never missed a night—and I soon found that I was throwing myself into my lessons, heart and soul. Even Mr. Tamaki said to me, 'Boy, you show real promise. You ought to devote yourself to the sword.'

"All the while my master knew none of this. But then one day a customer, one who'd come to place an order for a puppet, mentioned on his way out, 'I hear you do fine work with the sword.' I guess someone had told him of my kendō lessons.

"About three years or so passed, and I saw a customer who used to come to our shop earlier, one who always had a word of praise for me before he left. But this time as he was leaving he looked down at me and said, 'Your carving hasn't improved one bit, now has it?' His remark cut into my heart. Man can't give himself but to one occupation. I'd already promised myself to the puppet master for ten years. Didn't matter how long I studied the sword,

I'd never be able to feed myself by it. I realized what I was doing was wrong.
Well, I continued to go off to my lessons every night just as I'd been doing;
after all, Mr. Tamaki was a wealthy man, and he wanted a partner. Wouldn't
do for a boy like me to anger him. I continued to go, though I did so with
only half a heart, and before long I had Mr. Tamaki telling me that my kendō
skills weren't getting one bit better. But now as a consequence my carving
had improved. I suppose it makes a difference when you put your heart into
what you do. I gave myself over to carving puppets. The sword was nothing
more to me than a hobby. Oh, I was so devoted to my puppets now that I
was improved five years' worth in a single year. When that customer came
around again, he took one look at my work and said with a sigh, 'Well, well,
next time I come with an order, I'll place it with you instead of the master.' I
don't mean to boast now, I'm just telling you what he said. But, I guess if
you give yourself over to your work, really put your heart into it, then folks
are bound to notice.

"Yes, when I think back on how it was to be young, on how I poured
myself into my work, well, I guess you could say I'm somewhat jealous of
my youth. If only I could work that way now.

"I stayed on at the master's place for nearly ten years. Let's see . . . yes, I
was twenty-six when he finally released me. Guess it doesn't sound right for
me to be judging my master; after all, he was kind enough to see to my training. But I must say he was keen on perfecting the smallest detail of a puppet's
inner mechanisms. Yes, he was a real stickler for details, he was. And, as a
consequence, he was known far and wide for making puppets that never
fouled up during a performance. Why, you could ask any puppeteer, in any
theater, and he'd tell you Tomigorō's puppets were the easiest to handle.
Tomigorō poured everything he had into making certain the puppet's inner
workings were done just right—just the way they'd been done for centuries.
But you see, no matter how close his puppets kept to tradition, no matter
how smoothly they turned even the trickiest of stunts—when it came to the
power in the puppet's face, well, I'd say his weren't any better than ordinary.
And, I suppose that's why folks often said his puppets failed to come to life
on stage. Now here I am talking in a big way like this—but it's because I've
only just come to understand it myself, now that I've reached this old age of
mine.

"You see, art is tradition. It's the same for carving puppets, too. If you're
going to carve Lord Hangan, you carve him the way tradition tells you he's
got to look.[4] And, if you're going to carve the hero Yuranosuke, you carve
him in keeping with the Yuranosuke tradition, the way he's been carved for
centuries.[5] But what happens to art when it's done the same way over and

over for hundreds of years? Back in the old days folks did things a certain way because it seemed natural to them. But now we've reached the point where we're just copying the way things were done long ago without really understanding why, and so long as we're just copying, it doesn't have much meaning for us. Years ago folks lived with one goal in mind, and once they reached that goal, well, they were ready to die. But now, if you don't set your sights higher and higher and aim to get beyond whatever goal's been set, you might as well go ahead and die, and you sure don't have any business talking about art. But, you see, I didn't come to figure this out till four or five years ago—and it dawned on me when I finally noticed folks weren't coming to the puppet plays much anymore. They were turning up their noses at it. How I wish I'd realized this sooner!''

3

"If this story were a play, then I suppose you could say we've come to the third act. If we do the third act today, the rest of the play won't last another week.

"Won't you have a cigarette?

"Yes, I suppose about all I ever did was work. No, that's not exactly it either. All I ever did was carve. Puppet heads, that is. This may be the third act—but let me tell you a thing or two about art. There're folks who set their sights on one level in art—and once they've reached that level, they figure they're finished for life. Then we've got craftsmen like Hidari Jingorō who keep right on perfecting their skills until the day they die.[6] You see, there are those who always push for better, who are always struggling and trying so long as they've got breath in their bodies. And, I wonder if this isn't where art is said to live. Once you've decided that you've gone far enough—you can't do better—well, then that'll be the end for you. I don't know how much longer I'll live. Maybe two more years, maybe three, but this that I'm telling you is what is closest to my heart.

"That's right, I was twenty-six when I was let go from my apprenticeship to the master. I don't remember exactly how it was I got my release. But Heaven must have been looking out for me. I was adopted by the noodle-seller Yoshioka Utarō to be a husband to his daughter, and before long we had a daughter of our own. We moved into a house not but a stone's throw from the master's place. That's right, this very house. Oh, I was young then. I don't quite remember if she fell for me, or maybe I was the one to fall for her. Her name was Oryō. I'm not sure how old she was then, just can't remember unless I sit here and count up the years; it was so long ago. She was a girl from these parts, of course. And she was able to eke out a living on the cotton exchange I spoke of earlier. That's right. I've lived in this house ever since I left the master's place. Now it's such a tattered old place, all black with soot. When I moved in, it had a heavy thatched roof, but we replaced that a while back with this tile roof here. That's about the only change we ever made on the house, though. Otherwise it's just as it was when we moved in.

"Well then, to make a long story short, soon after we married my wife had the child. I still had two, maybe three months to serve on my contract, but the master let me go anyway. I got to take the chisel I had used over the years and a few tools—but that was all I was given. I was a craftsman, after all. When my term was up I didn't need to be hauling about bundles of belongings like some hired servant. Instead, I carried off a few of my master's customers. But that's the way things were done back then—it didn't anger the master.

"No, he never uttered one word of praise for anyone, and he didn't criticize either. That was just his way. When I think back on it now, I was a busy fellow in my youth. You might find this hard to believe, seeing as how my calling in life was to make puppets, but do you know I couldn't recite one line from a puppet play? That's right. Not one line. I didn't have time to be learning lines. That's just the way it was when you had to serve a master!

"What's that you say? The puppets? Well now, when you look at a puppet here, right up under your nose like this, and when you look at that very same puppet up there on the stage, you'd think they were two different puppets. Here's what I find most interesting about carving. If you compare the eyes, nose, and mouth on a puppet's face to those on a person's face, you'll find the puppet's much larger in scale, too large, really. But, if they weren't, you'd never be able to see them up there on the stage. The puppet you see living and breathing up there, and the one I see here in my hands while I'm carving, are different puppets in different worlds. I had to learn to focus my mind on how the puppet would look on stage. I had to learn that if I carved one way, it'd show up well, but if I did it another way, it wouldn't. No, I never got to feeling satisfied with myself for a puppet well made. But now and then I'd see one up there on the stage and I'd think to myself, 'My, doesn't it show up nice!'

"Everyone's said to do some things better than they do others—and the same holds true for carving. Now, you'll find some who'd rather carve female puppets, while others are better at males. Me, I can't force myself to choose between the two. But I do prefer to carve main character puppets, male or female. If I carve a minor character, say a scoundrel like Bannai, folks'll look at my work and say I've done a fine job.[7] But when I carve a character like Yuranosuke, I want people to look at that puppet and feel right down to their bones that this indeed is Yuranosuke and that he couldn't be carved any other way. Now that's no easy task, let me tell you.

"The difference between carving a male and female puppet, I think, is that a woman's face seems easier to carve. It's smooth, you see, and mostly blank. But a man's face has to have clear-cut features, and character. You know how it ought to look before you set to carving. So, you cut out the mouth, and, as you commence to fasten the toggles to the eyes and brows, you realize that the puppet you've carved looks nothing like the one you had in mind before you got started. That's why they say it's so much more difficult to carve a male puppet. But, when you get right down to it—whether you're carving a male or a female—it doesn't matter how well you've made the toggles. No, whether they work all that well doesn't have much to do with the success of the puppet. It's the spirit in the face that matters, and that is decided the moment you take up the block of wood and make your first cut.

"Well now, just a minute. This's the strange part about it. I said that the toggles don't have much to do with the success of the head; but, now, I guess that's not exactly true. You see, it just won't do to have somebody else make the toggles for you. I don't understand it quite myself, but for some reason you've got to make those toggles yourself. Otherwise, well, it just wouldn't be right. So, I guess when all is said and done those toggles really do have something to do with bringing out the spirit in the puppet.

"There are a lot of things about my work that I understand with my heart but can't put into words. Yes, there're a lot of things I can't explain. Now, say you've got two puppets here: one's a nice-looking fellow and the other looks mean. Both of them are forty years old, and both are highborn. But there's something that sets them apart from one another, you see, something about their spirit. And that difference is made, that spirit flows into them, the minute you take up the block of wood and make the first cut.

"Or now take a farmer. All his life he's worked the fields. But one day he up and travels to the city. He stays just a month doing business with the townfolk there, and all of a sudden he's a different man. Doesn't even look like a farmer any more. That's how it is with all the classes, don't you see. Men are born a samurai, a farmer, a craftsman, or a merchant, and they ought to be going about the work they were born to do. But there're always those who'd rather try their hand at something not theirs by birth. That's the way it is with the world, and it makes it hard to carve. To confound it further, there's a shadow to every ray of light, a backside to every front. Man may seem hard and cold on the outside, but if he's like that at home—well, he's going to have a hard time getting himself a son, let me tell you!''

The old puppet maker is in his eighty-sixth year. He's been in the puppet-making business for close to seventy years, from the time he first began his apprenticeship at the age of sixteen to the present. As I listened to him describe how he spent these years devoting himself to his puppets, I was moved beyond words. During the course of those seventy years he has been sick but once. He had, in his words, a touch of stomach catarrh (paratyphoid fever, actually) and the illness forced him to stay in bed for twenty-seven days. But other than that he has not missed a day of work. "During those twenty-seven days," he said, "I lay my head down." I am not certain exactly what he meant by "lay my head down." He may have meant that, since he was ill, he stayed in bed with his head on the pillow. But for someone like the old man, who has worked continuously his whole life through, the words "lay my head down" must have a special resonance.

Whenever I saw the old man at his work he was always in the same position—almost as if he were a statue—his hands frozen in motion. What must he be thinking, I wondered, as he plied his chisel back and forth, pouring heart and soul into his work—the very same work he has been doing for seventy years! Just trying to imagine it left me struck by an emotion I could not describe.

The old man married when he was twenty-six. Almost sixty years have passed since then, and over those sixty years he has lived in the same house. Well, that might be common enough here in the country. But the old man has sat on the same tatami mat, surrounded by the same weather-beaten shōji screens, facing the same old road. Yet the world outside, the people who have passed along that road, have changed more than I could ever imagine.

I had never thought anyone could actually sit in the same place for sixty or seventy years doing the same thing day in and day out. If the person were performing a religious austerity, like those who practice zazen, perhaps I could understand it. And yet here was this old man, doing just what I had thought impossible.

"I don't know how it looks to others," he told me, "but I've a reason for sitting right here all day long, never going out. You see, if someone came on business while I was away—well, wouldn't be anybody else here who'd know what to do. No, I decided it was for the best if I stayed in as much as possible. Look, I've got my tools and things all laid out around me so I can sit right where I am with everything at hand's reach."

The sort of life the old man has led may not seem all that strange in a country town like this. No, he has lived just as a tree or flower might live, completely natural. When I looked around, I noticed the house across the road, and wondered if, in the old days, it hadn't been a gathering place for the young women in the cotton exchange. Out front there was a sign that read "Paper-Rope Factory," and every now and then, when the reed screens hanging down over the storefront swayed, I caught a glimpse of the young girls inside busily at work. I could hear the whir of wheels and the high, clear voices of the girls singing "China Nights," "Oh Woman Your Fickle Heart," and other ballads. Their voices were so close I couldn't believe they were being wafted across the road by an errant wind. No, it seemed the girls were sitting right beside me. I wondered if the old man heard them, too.

"You know what I think?" he said. "I think the puppet theater has seen its last days."

Indeed, the old man believes that it is now only a matter of time before the puppet theater perishes completely. And yet he continues to devote himself all the more to this dying art. If those in my line of work ever heard that the alphabet we use—that is, the alphabet I am using now—was shortly to go out of existence, I doubt they would continue to write, hoping against hope that by doing so they could perpetuate their art. No, we would give up immediately, and that is why I sense in the old man an extraordinary depth of passion.

"That's right. When I was young I wanted to carve puppets just as fast as I could. But now I don't much care about the money. If I can just make a good puppet, I'll be satisfied. You see, when you're carving a puppet, if you're worried about all kinds of things, you'll end up making one that's not at all like the one you would've made if you'd just gone about your business with a peaceful state of mind. I like thinking over my work as I go along. I'll say to myself, 'Now if I'm to cut here I'll get a wise face, but here'll give me a cantankerous one. And then again, if I was to do it this way, why I'd get a sorrow-stricken face.' Sometimes I'll be so caught up in my thoughts—wondering how the face'll turn out—I can't sleep at night. I don't know the words to describe the way you ought to carve a puppet. I don't know how to tell you that if you cut this way it'll make for a wise face, but if you cut here the puppet'll come out looking mean. All I can say is, while I'm sitting here carving, my hands know just what to do. Oh now, I'm not the only puppet maker around with hands that can carve and chisel. I expect it's the same for all of us.

"I've been making puppets for a long time now and passing them along to other people. Even so, I don't recollect feeling they were especially good. And, if I was to make a particularly good puppet, I certainly wouldn't regret parting with it. No, every time I finish a puppet I'll always be thinking to myself that the next'll be even better. That's right. 'You can do better,' I'll tell myself. I guess death'll be my first and final stopping place—can't very well be making anything better after that, now can I? Even Hida no Takumi and Hidari Jingorō didn't go and say 'Yes, this's my masterpiece, now I can die.'[8] No, they kept on working, and if they'd lived any longer there's no telling how many great works they'd have been able to make. But death is, after all, the final stop. It puts an end to your art."

4

"You say you want to know how I came about the professional name 'Tenguya?' My master Tomigorō was known as 'Wakamatsuya.' He had a Tengu mask painted on the shōji screen out in front of his shop, you see, and when it came time for me to leave him and start up a shop of my own, well, I decided I'd go and name my place 'Tenguya.'[9] I could have taken over his shop name 'Wakamatsuya,' but I thought 'Tenguya' would be a bit more interesting. Now when folks pass by my sign they'll say, 'You can wager that fellow's a braggart!' But I suppose there's not a soul works with *jōruri*—reciting and such—who isn't something of a braggart!

"What's that you say? Oh, about the 'Best in the World' that's written on the sign out front. I imagine there are those who'll tell you it's an exaggeration, but I figure if you're going to write anything at all you might as well exaggerate. Now, some'll swear there never was any such thing as a Tengu—not even in the old days. Most will tell you a Tengu is just someone who talks nonsense and goes about proud and puffed up telling lies. But then when they look at my shop, you see, they say 'Well now that Tengu's a real serious sort.' Least that's what I've heard. Yes, they say there isn't a lot of sense to my name, because I'm too honest to be a Tengu. Then they're all the time going by and calling me a 'master artist.' Oh yes 'master artist' is what they say. Now I may put on like a mighty artist, but of all the things to be saying! I'm no master. I'm just the only puppet maker around! But if folks are going to have to remark on my talent—well, I guess there's just not much I can do to stop them.

"Yes, yes. Folks call this little patch behind the house the 'Tengu Garden.'

I don't remember when it was they gave it the name. I take real pleasure in growing chrysanthemums, you see, and before I even knew what had happened, why my garden here was overrun with the flowers. I doubt you'll find anyone else who'd grow such a common old flower on the same patch of earth for forty or fifty years on end.

"But listen, my heart was never divided. No, I was devoted to my puppet carving just the same, and I didn't go about my gardening with the same spirit I gave to my puppets—I didn't ever try to either. But whenever folks saw me tending my flowers, why they'd say I was completely given over to gardening. That's just the way I am. Once I set my mind to something, I'll chase at it with a fever. Let's say I'm to go net fishing down by the river. I'll be likely to fish there until my net breaks, and if that should happen, I'll run off to have it mended so I can fish some more, and, if the net breaks again, well then I'll go have it mended again. You see, I'm just the kind of person to get carried away over any old thing.

"But my whims and my carving are two separate things, completely separate. Back when I was young, I had an interest in wrestling and swordsmanship, but I never ran off to practice my sports until well after ten o'clock at night, and up till that time I was hard at work in the master's house. Even after I got my own place and set myself up in business . . . well, I suppose I would allow myself to step out into the garden now and again after I'd finished up my work. But that's about all. Never a day went by that I was too busy in the garden to work on my puppets.

"No, I might take a liking to just about anything I chance to see, but I never once thought I'd turn my full attention to any trade but carving. I'm just the sort of fellow who can do most anything he sets his mind to, that's all. I suppose I might have thought once or twice about taking up the sword —getting me a group of students and teaching them the skill. Oh, I suppose there was a time I was even half serious—I was just that taken with the sport. But, now listen, times weren't like they are now. I wasn't of the right kind of family to be teaching the sword, and it wasn't long before I gave up the idea.

"My wife, you say? Well now once we got married she took to helping me with my work. Why yes, she made puppets too, of a sort. I mean, after I carved a puppet she'd cover it with paper and paint it and such. She was my assistant with the puppets, and she also made papier mâché dolls for children. Yes, she did all sorts of things. She died seven or eight years ago. When was it now? Well, I won't know unless I look it up. The month and day are written out on her Buddhist name tablet, you see. Her age'll be there, too.

She was a year older than me. Or now maybe it was a year younger. Well, to make a long story short, she didn't die of any illness—seems it was just old age that took her. We lived together in this very house for years and years. It's sad, yes. But, after all, old age being what it is—you've just got to learn to live with loss.

"Once people leave this world they don't come back. Being left behind, well . . . it's not the best thing that could happen to you. She was such a help to me all those years. Yes, I'd have to say 'Old Grandma' took care of me best. I tell you, my old wife and me, we went through some hard times together—mighty hard times. But I don't want to burden you with all that now. Let me just say that when you surmount your sorrows, you'll find joy on the other side. It's the same for everyone, I expect.

"Now as a rule I don't like bawling others out. I make it a point never to get angry with anyone no matter what, and I don't recall ever getting into a fight. There are some who are always thumping others on the head, but I just wonder what good it does to be hitting people in the head? Now when you get to the relations between husband and wife, they're the same for everyone, in all walks of life. Difference lies only in the depth of feeling between the couple. Well, I don't know how it looked to others, but I don't believe anyone could say that the feelings between my wife and me were shallow. No, I tell you—if anyone with eyes in his head came into this house, he'd see right away that that old wife of mine was the one who ruled the roost. Goodness! I was always getting into trouble with that woman! She'd fume over something and then there I'd be bowing and scraping and doing my best to beg her pardon. But no matter what I say now, she certainly did help me with my work. Why, if I'd ever step out back and lose track of time tinkering in the garden, she'd be there railing at me. I suppose you could say she was something of a nag!

"Well now let me see. . . . What was it she'd do for me that I appreciated most of all? Sometimes I'd work late into the night, you see, and when I did she'd always wait up so she could lay my bed out for me. Well now I suppose just about anyone would have done the same. Laying out bedding is no great task. But once I'd crawled into bed and started off to sleep, I'd sometimes feel my old wife go around behind me and pat the quilt down soft around my shoulders. That's all. But no one else would have done it.

"When she died I was grief stricken. Oh, I suppose anyone would have felt the same. But now quite a few men'll take a second wife. I suppose their feelings for the second'll be different than those for the first. When my wife died I couldn't forget her right away. And I found it hard to mention my

pain to others. Reciting the sutras was one way to find release. But if someone asked me just what kind of pain I felt, well, I could go on and exaggerate, but now how was I to describe the fine threads of feeling in my heart?''

Except for the vivid recollections of his boyhood, the old man's memories
came back to him in hazy wisps. He was not even certain when his wife died
—the woman who shared his life for more than fifty years. "My children
were all girls," he told me. "There're three: Shigeri, Yoshie, and . . . well
now, there's one more. What is her name? Looks like I've clean forgot."
Then after a pause he added, "It's Katsuno," and having finally recalled his
daughter's name he continued with his story.

From what the old man told me, I found it hard to imagine him as a
youth, riding the angry waves of the floating world and making his name as
a new master craftsman. But that is to be expected, I suppose. He is such an
old man now. In fact, it seemed to me that the Tenguya Kyūkichi I saw
before me had left far behind him the young Tenguya Kyūkichi of his stories.
And this was not simply because the old man's memories had grown dim.
Rather there was something about him now, something in his presence and
spirit that reminded me of a stately old tree stripped of leaves. And he was
more reluctant than most (even among the typically reticent country people)
to talk about his past; he meant to speak of art.

"There's one thing that sets me apart from others," he told me. "Most
folks'll guard their trade secrets, won't tell them to another for the world.
They figure that if they can keep them to themselves they can profit. But not
me. As soon as I learn something new I'm eager to share it. I'll tell one or
two fellows and before I know it five or six have heard. Yes, others are much
better at keeping secrets—and turning them to their advantage. And I suppose that is where we differ most."

5

"Looking back on it now I'd say the
puppet theater peaked around 1880 or 1890 and has been going downhill ever
since. Yes, that would mean the theater was at its height when I was in my
thirtieth or fortieth year.

"There were theaters in Kyoto and Osaka, all through the Central Region
and on down toward Kyushu—always livelier in the west than up toward

Tokyo—and all of it born right here in Shikoku. Not but twenty leagues from Tokushima is the birthplace of those first traveling box puppeteers. Four villages claim the honor—Hiruma-machi, Ikeda, Kamomura, and Nakanoshō. Among the four they always had about a hundred puppeteers out on the road. The area around here is mountainous, as you see, not enough flat land to go around. Not everyone could make his way as a farmer, planting fields and such. That's why, I imagine, so many fellows set out with their boxes. Well now, nothing's changed the land since then. This place is still all mountains, but you hardly see a traveling puppeteer anymore. Why, they've become such a rare sight along these roads that when one was spotted the other day there was a newspaper man right behind him asking to take pictures. But, you know, the puppeteer begged him not to do it and said, 'If you take my picture and run it in that paper of yours, even if folks mightn't recognize my face, they're bound to recognize the puppets I've got here in my hand, and if they do, then before long the whole village'll know that I'm back on the road.' That's just what he said. Now in the old days you'd never hear of it, but nowadays when a fellow sets out on the road he's ashamed of it and the fact he's got to make his living traveling about from place to place. Well, they can say what they will, but I tell you, the only reason they head out there in the first place is because they like it. They liked doing it back in the old days, and they like doing it now. Wouldn't be out there otherwise.

"Now, when was it? There came a time when my wife and I and our oldest girl Shigeri—yes, the one who lives with me now—went off to Osaka to make those life-size puppets, the kind they use in those old sideshows. You know the ones, don't you? 'Have a Glimpse at Heaven—Have a Peek at Hell.' But, just saying we had to go all the way to Osaka to make them ought to tell you how the world had changed. At the time life was full of hardship. The war with the Russians had just drawn to a close and my wife and I set out alone for Iyo, where we worked for nearly half a year. The theater in Yawatahama had burnt down, you see. They'd built a brand new one right after the war and were using real gunpowder for stage effects when one day they didn't mix the shot just right and it exploded in a raging fire. Burnt the place to the ground with not so much as a puppet saved. That's why someone came around asking me to go there and help out.

"After Yawatahama we went back around by Sanuki. Goodness! If I'd known I was to talk about all this someday I would have kept a record of dates and such. Yes, when I was a youngster folks said my memory was keen. But now they're saying I'm downright forgetful. I suppose being able to forget is something of a blessing though. When I look back on those days—no matter how painful they were at the time—they're just like a dream to me now.

"I was busy with the shop here, so my wife and daughter went off to work with a traveling puppet-show troupe. They went as far as Sakushū, as I recall. Well, you see, when you're starting out to make a puppet head—starting out clean with just a block of wood—we say that you're 'chopping out' a new puppet. And now a woman just isn't up to a task like that. They're good at repainting the faces and repairing the wigs for the puppets—and that's just what my wife and daughter did when they worked for that traveling theater. And now listen here, in the old days the theaters would set their stage down along the dry river beds and that's where they'd hold their shows. But sometimes it would rain while they were there and would keep right on pouring, and nobody'd be able to eat. That's where the saying 'No food when it rains' comes from. Now, if you had yourself an easygoing, generous sort of patron, you could expect a little money even when the rains forced you to close your shows. But if your luck ran out, well, wasn't long before you'd pawned off nearly all your puppets for your daily fare. Oh, admission fees would have been around two sen for adults, I believe, and one for children.

"Well, once things took a turn for the worse, everything started going wrong. I'll be damned if I could figure it out—everywhere I turned there'd be a new problem. Speaking for myself, I suppose it wasn't so bad. I had my work, and if I'd only had myself to worry about it wouldn't have been much trouble at all. But soon after the war all manner of new amusements came flooding into the area. There were the *naniwabushi* ballads, the reformed plays, and the new-style drama. Of course, the movie pictures hadn't made it out this far yet, but even so, the puppet plays were being squeezed so bad you hardly chanced to see them anymore. Since I was living in my old hometown, we didn't need to worry about going hungry, and I'm grateful for that. But the years were lean, and we had children to raise, old folks to tend, and rice to buy. That's right, we had to buy rice, and it went for about one yen a bushel, if I recall. I lived in the country, that much is true, but I didn't own one patch of rice land. Had to buy my own rice.

"My goodness, if that's all I'd done in times like those I doubt I would've lived to see this day. There came a time when I set out with the traveling troupes myself. Now I just told you theater folks don't eat on days of rain, but I was different. I was the puppet carver and I got paid right away, show or not. Sometimes I'd even get paid before my work was finished. So I guess you could say I had it a good bit better than the chanters and the puppeteers.

Anyway, no matter how difficult life became, I always told myself that I'd never do anything but carve puppets.

"Over my long life I've seen lean years and rich years. During those lean years though, I can't honestly say I never wished for a different sort of occupation. But then I figured if a fellow fails to make a living at one kind of job, he isn't likely to succeed at another. When times were bad it often happened that I'd be commissioned to make a puppet, and then the person who'd placed the order wouldn't show up when the job was done. Oh, I'd try to sell the puppet off, but I'd have a time finding someone to buy it. It's not like selling food or such that anybody'd want. Then, just when I was about to give up, why times would change and someone would come along with the money for the puppet.

"Strange, isn't it?—the ways of the world. I'd be thinking as much as I went about my work. I decided that whether I made fistfuls of money, whether it rained or shined, I was going to keep on working. I figured that was the only way to keep from suffering when times got rough. Now there were days when I didn't get any work from the theaters. But I never sat idle. If I wasn't carving *jōruri* puppets, I'd make masks, ornamental dolls, or children's toy dolls, and somehow or another I'd make enough for a day's wage. Oh, I wasn't disappointed with the kind of life I led, but I don't know how I looked to others. My eldest grandson works for the Osaka Railroad. Once I remember saying to him, 'Boy, you ought to take over the puppet trade.' He's the heir to the family business, after all. Well, times were rough then and he looked at me and said, 'Grandpa, how much you make a day?' 'Oh, I told him, 'I make as much as fifty to sixty sen.' I suppose that's what decided him. As soon as he graduated middle school he signed on with the railroad. Well, since that time I've become this famous puppet maker folks are always talking about. I wonder what he thinks of me now? No way for me to know, of course, I haven't seen the boy in twenty, thirty years. But I have to say, I'm quite proud of that grandson of mine. The way I see it, once you've made up your mind to do something, you ought to give yourself over to it body and soul. I've heard that over these last twenty or thirty years my grandson has been at his work without taking off a single day, not a single day. Yes, the boy turned to me and said, 'How much you make a day?' all worried about money. But for that very reason, see, I think he's a fine fellow. He has my praise.

" 'Do whatever you want,' I always tell the young folk around here. 'Just don't quit halfway.' "

6

"My religion? Well, what would you say it is? Three days out of the month I go to the family shrine to pray. That'll be on the first, the fifteenth, and the twenty-eighth. Even so I couldn't point to any one thing and say this is what I believe. And yet, as I'm making my puppets, I feel as if I'm praying to the gods. Don't you see, where my skill stops—when it doesn't go any further—that's where you'll find the gods. Yes, they're there just beyond human understanding.

"If you hurt somewhere you call in a doctor, and you're probably grateful for his services, but I imagine you'll be looking to some power even higher than the doctor, praying and making all kinds of promises. Now I'm not saying that's what I'm about when I'm carving puppets. But let me just say that if you don't reach out to the gods first—make some kind of effort—then they sure aren't going to go out of their way to help you. If I was to tell you what I thought about the gods and the buddhas, then I'd have to explain it like this: Before I start to carve a puppet I have it all clear in my mind how that puppet ought to look. But there's always one part I just can't get no matter how I try—yes, there's always something missing, and it's in that part, that missing part, where the gods reside.

"What's difficult about carving a *jōruri* puppet is first of all making one that'll come to life on the stage, and second of all making one that'll be in keeping with the story of the play. Puppet makers always have to keep these two facts in mind. Well now I've lived a long life, and I've been at this business quite some time, so I can say a thing or two about it, and I'll tell you right now that most of the puppets I've seen in my day are just ordinary.

"They say that when you're fixing to carve a young girl puppet you should make your heart like a young girl's—all meek and mild. But when you're to carve a samurai you should pull yourself up proud and proper. Now it'll sometimes happen that when I set out fully intending to carve a manly looking fellow like a samurai, by some accident I end up with a puppet that looks downright mean. This's the mystery.

"To make a long story short, before you start to carve you should make yourself humble, the way you are when you pray to the gods. When I'm to carve Yuranosuke, I try to imagine what he must have felt. There he was a masterless samurai, yet he was bent on slaying the man who wronged his lord. While I'm thinking on it I start to carve, and while I carve I think about which way I ought to cut to bring out the face I want.

"In a puppet play they'll sometimes use a different puppet head for the same character, depending on the scene. Take the play featuring the warrior Kumagai, for instance.[10] The Kumagai head they use in the second act won't do at all for the third. In the third act his face has got to be full of the sorrow he feels as he trudges back to camp after slaying the handsome young Atsumori. A Yuranosuke puppet looks a good deal like the third act Kumagai, and that's why the same head is used for each character. But I suppose Kumagai looks more courageous. He's a bit fierce, truth be told. You see, in the puppet theater there are two types of chief retainers. There are the Great Retainers and there are the Yuranosuke Retainers. In the old days, those who were puppet connoisseurs would tell you which type they wanted when they placed an order.

"After you've set yourself up as a full-fledged puppet maker you can't have any difference in the spirits of the puppets you made early on in your career and the ones you made later. Yuranosuke is Yuranosuke, and there's no reason to ever stray from tradition in carving him. You carve your puppets according to the type of role they're to perform and you cut each one differently to account for their spirit, their age, and whether they're male or female. Now you can carve a houseboy and a lord out of the same block of wood, but they'll still come out different because the way you cut the wood determines the puppet's age, rank, and even the way the puppet seems to feel. I don't really know how to explain it. I suppose most anyone could carve a rough outline of a puppet's face. Most anyone could do it, but now if you don't carve each puppet differently according to age and rank and such, and if you don't follow the traditions for carving that've been passed down over the ages—well, nobody's going to buy your puppet.

"The way to carve's been determined long ago. If a fellow comes up to me and remarks that a puppet's spirit differs with the mood of the puppet maker when he sits down to carve, then I'd have to say that man's a liar.

"You see, not too long ago one of those moving picture fellows came around and asked to make a movie of my work. He filmed me making a new puppet—got me making the first cut in the wood. Well, months passed and I finally finished the puppet about the time the Gennojō, one of the puppet theater troupes still left in these parts, came to town. The movie picture man said he wanted to film my new puppet on the stage in a real drama. He talked it over with the theater folks, and they said it'd be no problem filming them with my puppet, no problem at all except they didn't want to use the brand new puppet—said they'd much prefer to use the puppet I'd made some twenty years ago. It was the same puppet as the one I'd just carved. Now you might already know this, but once a puppeteer's been using a puppet for a number of years he becomes attached to it, and he's going to find it difficult to all of a sudden start using a different one. Anyway, they explained all this to the fellow, but he said no, said it had to be the new one. He wanted to show how I'd taken a block of wood and turned it into a puppet that could hold its own on stage. He went on about it, real insistent fellow, until finally the theater folks pulled out the Kumagai puppet I had made some twenty years ago and stood him up alongside the one I'd just made. 'Take a look at this,' they told him, and sure enough there wasn't one splinter of difference between the two, not one splinter of difference. I can tell you that fellow sure was surprised.

"It's a fact. The puppets I carved over twenty years ago and the ones I make today are exactly the same. They're exactly the same and yet there's a difference. How are they different? They're different in my heart, that's all. There's nothing you can see with your eye, but I know there's a difference. I just don't know quite how to explain it. Guess it's something only the gods can know.

"Now, as I told you earlier, the way a puppet's to be carved was decided long, long ago, and no puppet maker, no matter how famous he may be, ought to break with tradition. Not only does a puppet maker have to follow tradition, he has to be sure that his heart accords with it too, and that his puppets come to life. You can turn puppets out clean and even, as if you were stamping them out with a mold, but they'll never draw a single breath. I don't know how to tell you to give life to a puppet, and even if I was to take up a block of wood right here and carve it for you, I doubt that I could show you what it is that gives a puppet life. But I suppose that's just the way it is with any art.

"I can't even say that I understand puppets that well myself, but what I don't know with my mind I feel with my heart. It's like judo. In judo you want to throw your opponent but you can't do it with your own strength alone. You have to wait until you sense your partner getting ready to make his move and then, when he comes at you, you twist him down. Or, if you've got a timid partner you wait until you feel him draw back and then you sweep him down. It's all a matter of reading the other's mind.

"Mr. Tamaki, the man I took sword lessons from when I was a boy, only used frontal attacks when he sparred with me. He wanted me to learn to face my opponents so I could see into their hearts.

"Now I imagine this won't seem to have much to do with what I've been saying, but when I meet people, I always study their faces to see what kind of puppets they resemble. Most of the time I don't even realize I'm doing it. 'Are they the flirty type?' I ask myself. 'Or grimly serious?' I try to figure out what kind of people they'll be by examining their faces. You could say it's stood me in good stead with my puppet carving. At one point I went so far as to study fortune-telling, the kind that's based on the reading of a person's face. But like they say, a fortune-teller can't tell his own fortune. If he was to seek his customers only among the wealthy—because they're the ones likely to pay the most—then what kind of fortune-teller would he be?

"Well now, I'd say it's the ears that hold the key to a puppet maker's style. You see, when you come across a stranger you can't tell just by looking at his ears whether he's good or bad—and the same holds true for puppets. There's no set pattern for carving ears. We don't carve them one way for a righteous man like Yuranosuke and then another for the wily scamp Gonta.[11] No . . . whether old or young, man or woman . . . whether the puppet's role is big or small or his character good or bad . . . the ears are always going to be the same. And, because they are, I'd say here is where a puppet maker's own character shines through. Yes, it's all in the touch of the fine-bladed knife and, mind you, the difference is slight, indeed!"

7

"That's right, I had three children, each one of them a girl. The oldest, Shigeri, lives with me here. We adopted the son of the rice dealer across the way as her husband and the heir to my name. My father was an adopted heir, I was too, and then my daughter's husband came to us the same way. That's three generations of adoptions, you know.

"Katsuno's still living. The second girl, Yoshie, she was the best of the three I thought, but she died young. From the outside I guess it must have seemed that I'd done all right by my girls. Shigeri had her husband, and I had my heir. Yoshie was the type who could do just fine for herself, so we sent her out to marry. And then Katsuno took off some place, I don't recall where.

"Kaname was my adopted son. His family ran a rice shop and worked the fields and such. Oh, now, I'd have to ask Shigeri when it was he came into our family. She'd know. I'd planned to train him in the ways of puppet carving myself, and did manage to set him up as a full-fledged puppet maker. Took the name Tengu Kaname. But wouldn't you know, just around that time we were so tied up with orders to repair old puppets that he never did have a chance to test his mettle. He died before he could make a puppet worthy of his name. It broke my heart to lose him. He wasn't just a son-in-law, he was my heir.

"Whenever I get set to teach someone a thing or two about carving, I tell him right from the start that I'm not going to sit there and explain every little thing. I show him one of the puppet heads I've carved and tell him to try and carve one like it. Then, as he goes along, I tell him 'that looks fine,' or 'that's no good.' But what I can't ever tell him is how he should make the final strokes, the finishing touches. For a long time I'll ponder over those finishing touches myself. I think on them so hard I become completely swallowed up in my thoughts, and then I proceed to carve. But even if I can't come right out and explain to my students all they should do, I show them with my hands. I guess it amounts to the same thing. When I do try to tell them a thing or two about their carving, I usually end up saying more than they want to hear. Someone's feelings get hurt, and I wish I'd never said a thing. Yes, I tell you, when you're trying to teach students to carve, best thing to do is say nothing at all, least that's what I believe . . . and yet it's hard to know exactly what to do. Every master's going to find something he doesn't like about his student's work. There'll be something. But what good does it do blurting it out? No, my father told me long ago, he said, 'Don't ever say anything to anyone about their work,' and he lived to be ninety-three. I suppose it was this advice of his that kept him alive so long.

"Well now, let me see, the only apprentices I ever had were Kaname and my nephew Benkichi. Owing to certain reasons, Benkichi and I don't speak anymore. A while ago it was decided that Kaname's boy Osamu would follow in the puppet trade. Now there's a story here I'd like to tell, though I do feel a bit sheepish mentioning it since it concerns His Royal Highness the Prince. Oh, now when was it? Prince Nashimoto paid a visit to our city of Tokushima. I was asked to call on him at his lodgings, on account of him wanting to see a puppet. So I went to him with one of my puppets. Not one that had been used yet, but one I'd just made—a Kusunoki Masatsura puppet.[12] He seemed rather taken with it. 'How splendid,' he said. Yes, that's what he said, and he beckoned me to come close so I could show him how the puppet moved. Now can you just imagine it? There I was a humble old puppet maker, yet I was being treated better than the governor himself, who had to watch it all from a distance. I sat right up beside His Imperial Highness and showed him what my puppet could do. I was up there with him for some time, too. Yes, it was the honor of a lifetime!

"When I was summoned to the prince's lodgings I went along with the governor, now let's see, that would've been a gentleman by the name of Kanamori Tarō. When he saw how pleased the prince was with my puppet, he remarked, 'It'd be a real shame if the art ends with you. Hurry up and name an heir!' As soon as Osamu got wind of that he began to work at puppet carving for all he was worth! Yes, up to then I'd just about given up. I figured I'd die and take my art with me; and Osamu, for his part, hadn't much felt like carrying on the business.

"Nowadays the only other puppet maker in these parts is that Benkichi I mentioned earlier. Used to be there was Deko-Chū of the Fukuya Shop and Deko-Tsune to the west; we knew him as Tsune-han. He had a boy named Junjirō. They're all dead now. What with all the other fellows dying off you'd think my life would be that much easier. I guess folks believed we were all rivals, seeing as how we were in the same line of work. But that wasn't the case. Each of us worked for a different theater and didn't need to bother about the others. And since we all carved puppets—which take quite some time to finish—we couldn't exactly be competing over the numbers turned out. But, of course, in our heart of hearts each one of us wanted to be the best.

"Now when was it Deko-Chū passed on? I don't remember just now. His work was well known in these parts, and there was a reason for it. You see, his father got himself in some kind of trouble. Nowadays I doubt his crime would have seemed that bad, but at the time it was serious and he was exiled on account of it. Had to go to Osakagoe [the boundary between Awa and Sanuki]. Once his sentence was up he came on back to his old home, but having been branded a criminal, he wasn't allowed to use his own name anymore. Well, since he couldn't use his own name, he used his son's. Every time he made a puppet he signed it 'Chū,' or 'Made by Chū.' Bequeathed everything to that boy, even though he wasn't but an infant at the time. And so, you see, ever since Chū was just a little fellow his name'd been spread far and wide.

"Now Umanose Komazō was a puppet maker years and years ago. There's never been another who could carve brave and dignified puppets as well as he —least not so far as I can tell. He was best at main character puppets. His female puppets were said to be sweetly girlish, but I don't suppose they were his strongest point."

While the old man and I sat and talked, people stopped by from time to time to see him—all sorts of people. Some would come on business and others just to sit at the doorway and gossip. Occasionally they would come inside for a cup of tea. The old man never went out of his way to receive his guests. He simply went on with his work—a tranquil look on his face.

Next to the old man there was an ancient-looking brazier with a pot of glue on top of it lightly simmering. The old man always had a teakettle there, too, warming over the coals. Now and then he would stop long enough to pour himself a cup of tea. When guests stopped by he would offer them a cup and would drink along with them. In fact, the old man drank constantly. "Now you be sure to write this down," he told me with a laugh. "Some say tea is poison, but that just isn't so. If it were, do you suppose I'd have lived as long as I have drinking the way I do? And then there're those who never drink tea and still die young! Oh, I don't touch liquor; never smoke. But I couldn't very well just drink water, now could I?" Yes, the old man certainly is fond of his tea. He uses high quality leaves and brews his tea until it is as strong as possible.

The old man is not particularly fond of socializing. Perhaps it would be more accurate to say he is somewhat withdrawn. And yet there is something about him that puts others at ease. I guess someone who has lived as long as he has does not worry over little things the way others do. For instance, once while I was there someone called to the old man from the road out front and asked if they might cut a few of the chrysanthemums that were blooming behind the house in his garden. The old man glanced up long enough to call out in a loud voice, "Go help yourself!" But then he was back hard at work.

Kyūkichi always wears a smile when he is talking with one of his guests. Well, it is not a smile actually, but he makes one feel that he is smiling. His face is gentle and kind. He told me that he had made up his mind long ago never to get angry with anyone no matter what happened, and that is why his expression is always quiet. But when he was engrossed in his work his face took on an entirely different cast. He began to look irritated, adamant, as if his features were set in stone. This face of his is neither young nor old; it is timeless and beautiful. I imagine when he was young he was very handsome. Once, while we were talking, he did happen to mention something of the sort. "Years back I was a good-looking fellow," he told me. "They say that pine trees have their prime, and all living things their bloom. Well, human beings, too, have their moment to flower. Now when I look back on when I was young, I'm struck by the truth of it. Oh yes, there was a time when I was right handsome, falling in love with the girls and breaking a few hearts, too."

8

"Oh, it puts me in a bad mood, let me tell you. And when I'm angry I can't do a bit of work. Well, to make a long story short, sometimes my wife would come and tell me, 'I'm off to such-and-such a place.' Now I'd tell her that on account of me being so busy that day she'd have to put it off, go some other time. But then she'd set in to telling me why she had to be going that very minute, and before I knew it she was gone, and I was fuming. Oh, the madder I was the madder I'd get at myself for being all fired up over something as piddling as that. I suppose it's my own fault. I'm just not the sort to argue. Well, let me tell you, I do the best I can to steer clear of that sort of business.

"No, I can't exactly say I do it for my health, but around noontime I'll walk about a half mile down the road and then turn around and walk back. Never once had a massage, but it's become my habit to stretch out all the joints in my body—once in the morning and once at night—just to be sure they're in good working order. Yes, while I'm still lying in my bed in the morning I do these exercises before getting up. I stretch my arms out over my head as high as they'll go, and then I lift them up and down, up and down—just to see how well they move. Do the same thing at night after I crawl in bed. Sometimes I'll be so stiff I can hardly lift a finger. Happens more frequently now that I'm getting on in years. But I'll keep trying to lift my arm, and as I'm working on it these old muscles'll finally loosen up and let me move. I guess you could call this a lazy man's sport, seeing as how I do it in bed. But my father used to do the same thing, and I can remember watching him when I was a boy. He'd say, 'Oh it hurts me here today—when I go like this. Looks like I won't be able to move at all.' Now I know just what he meant by it.

"My father was fit as a fiddle up until the day he died at ninety-three. He'd walk over here from Nakamura and then walk back the same day. He only worked at the dye shop till he was sixty or so, but he always had his wits about him. Age didn't muddle his mind. What's most precious to me now is the fact that I was able to be with him when he died. I walked into the room where he was and said, 'How you doing, Pa?' I guess he'd been waiting for me because he looked up at me and said, 'I'm so glad you came.' Two hours later he died. I was fifty-two or fifty-three at the time. When it suddenly came to me that a father could love his child that much, well, my heart was filled with joy. So this is what it means for parent and child to part? . . . My father was ninety-three, after all, yet he could still answer clearly when spoken to."

I was startled to find that the old man was crying. We had talked about all kinds of things and he had hardly registered any emotion. But now here he was in tears. Old people, it is said, are easily reduced to tears, but there was only one other time that I chanced to see Kyūkichi cry. His tears poured down his cheeks in a torrent too swift to wipe away.

"The other day I heard Kōtsubo-han on the radio reciting the *Chūshingura*.[13] If I ever were to meet him face-to-face I'd certainly like to congratulate him on the fine job he did. He came to the part where Lord Hangan cries out in despair, 'Has Yuranosuke still not come?' Oh, I can hear those words even now, just like they were inside my ears. I'll never forget them. Yes, and then of course Lord Hangan must thrust the sword into his belly and kill himself even though he's not said good-bye to his beloved retainer." As he spoke the old man's eyes filled with tears that spilt down over his face. I watched silently, overwhelmed.

From time to time Kyūkichi would receive distinguished guests. While I was with him a banker from Tokyo stopped in, and on another occasion the school inspector came by from the prefectural office. I do not know what they thought of the old puppet maker, but they asked him all sorts of questions. "Whom do you admire most?" for example, or, "What was the most interesting moment in your life?" To these questions the old man answered:

"Person most admired? Well, let me think. Folks in my line of work don't know anything other than their trade. But I'd say I admire those who set their mind to something and are always striving to do better. Whether a carpenter or a farmer makes no difference, so long as they spend their life questing after knowledge. Yes, I think that sort of person's worthy to be admired.

"Now about that most interesting moment. . . . I guess it'd have to be back when I was fifteen years old or so. That was right when the age of the Daimyō was giving way to the Meiji Restoration, you know, and everyone was up and celebrating the changes taking place. Men and women, grandpas and grandmas . . . didn't matter who . . . everyone was up and shouting 'Well, why not! Anything goes!' They'd burst into a stranger's house shouting and carrying on—didn't much care if the owner cursed them or laughed at them. Some of the merrymakers hid their faces behind masks and some painted theirs up, but others just went with the face they were born with. They'd eat all the rice cakes they could lay their hands on, and they'd drink their fill of liquor, too. But as soon as they'd be full, why someone'd shout 'Let's dance a bit till we're hungry again!' and they'd all set in to dancing. 'Well, why not! Anything goes!'[14]

"A group of fellows set out like that, dressed only in their loincloths. Didn't have a penny to their name, but they made it all the way to Ise Shrine feasting and dancing. I wasn't but a little fellow at the time so I could only follow after them as far as the neighboring village. Oh my, it was some celebration—the likes of which I've never seen. Yes, I'd have to say that was the most interesting moment in my life.

"Now I suppose there was a reason for it all, but seeing as how it happened when I was just a boy, well, I didn't really understand it. It's just that everything was undergoing changes. The next-door neighbors'd be at their spring cleaning—when along would come a gust of wind and carry off their prized paper charm. It'd land down the road aways, and then someone'd come along and pick it up. The next thing you know, he'd be carrying on like it was a blessing from heaven. Yes indeed, thought that charm had just fallen out of the sky! Why even when folks came across an old Daikoku charm lying in the road, they'd set into dancing, shouting all the while, 'Look! Oh look! A blessing from Heaven!'[15] Happened so often the little dance they did came to be known as the 'Blessing from Heaven Jig.' Oh, I suppose a blessing from heaven was reason enough to celebrate, because soon the whole household'd be up and dancing. 'Well, why not! Anything goes!' they'd holler, and they'd dance on down to their neighbor's house, shouting and carrying on. And when they were done there, they'd march right on to the next house. 'Well, why not! Anything goes!' It got to be that for a whole half a year or so no one could do a lick of work. And then the Fushimi Battle put an end to it all."[16]

The old man had a faraway look in his eyes as he described the past. It seemed that these events of long ago—events we could not truly understand —were still very much alive in his memory.

Once when I came to visit the old man and called to him where he sat at his work, he did not answer. After a minute he raised his head slightly, but he still did not say anything to greet me. Instead I overheard him mutter to himself, "Not worth a damn today." Someone came and led him off to bed. I sat by myself in the old man's workshop for close to an hour wondering what would become of him. Was this the way he would die? Other members of the family, though, told me that he was put to bed like that from time to time. But they added that after he had slept nearly half the day he would return to work refreshed. As I waited for him to awaken, I found myself caught in a tangle of feelings.

Before long the old man returned, wearing his usual gentle smile. He looked straight at me, greeted me politely, and then began to talk as he always did, as though nothing had happened. He soon settled in to telling me the following account. Now I am not certain that I learned this story that day, perhaps it was the next. At any rate, he spoke clearly and buoyantly, and this is what he said:

"When I pause to think, I realize that all people, no matter who they are or what they do, ought to work with all their might up to the moment they die so as to leave behind something worthy. For myself, you see, I hope to leave something that folks'll praise, instead of something that'll make them laugh. I'll be working on it up to the day I die. Don't you see, if you can leave behind something that you've poured all your energy into, well, you won't mind dying much. Now, I've outlived the span of life alotted to most folks, and I don't know how I'll have to suffer come my time to die, but I do know that whatever falls my way I want to be able to face it. Twice now I've had these fainting spells where I've blacked out, and I've worried that my time might come while I'm in the midst of one. Now that would be just too easy, don't you think?—slipping away like that unawares. There are those who'll say that a fellow like me'll have an easy death, seeing as how I've lived so long. Oh, I suppose my time to go is drawing near, but I figure I'll hold out for another year or so.

"Well, years back I'd hear folks remark on 'heaven and hell.' I'm not sure there are such places. Long time ago there was a song that went 'You can say there's a heaven, but no one really knows. The path there is long, and no one's yet come back. Even Shaka and Miroku are still on their way.' [By that the old man means that the path is so long the buddhas still have not reached heaven.] I expect it's true. I'm figuring I ought to go ahead and set out on that road, see what it looks like up there. If it looks good, I'll holler back down to my girl here and tell her to hurry up. But now I just wonder if my message'll get through! Yes, that's the way things stand with me."

9

The day before I was to return to Tokyo I went to visit Kyūkichi again. It just so happened that the Gennojō Puppet Troupe had come to town that day, and I thought I should see one of their plays before I left. I also thought it would be nice if the old man would accompany me, and that is why I paid him this last visit.

"A play, you see, used to be an event everyone enjoyed—something to look forward to, and you wouldn't find anyone complaining of being tired after a day at the theater. It was something of a treat back then. Yes, that's the way it was, but, truth be told, I don't much want to go these days. The theater has changed—why, it's changed more than you could imagine.

"Now, in the old days when you went to see a play, the theater was always full of young people. There'd be ground-blessing celebrations in the autumn, you know, time to give thanks to the gods of the earth for their bountiful gift of rice. Oh, now I suppose it's not just the earth that produced that rice, but anyway, that's the sort of celebrations there'd be. Folks would use the occasion to stage plays and such. The chanters and puppeteers would all be young and only thing the old folks did was go and watch. Lots of young girls would come around, too.

"But look here, now you've got these movie picture shows that everybody's so crazy about. All you've got to do at a movie is sit back and watch the screen, and you can follow the story without much trouble. Young girls nowadays are so used to the movies, they have a real time trying to make sense of the old-fashioned language used in the puppet plays.

"Was it summer before last? Yes, I believe it was then that I had occasion to go and see a play. But if I was to go to the theater now, I expect I'd find that the folks I knew in the old days, old folks like myself, are all dead and buried. And, if one or two of them are still living, well, I don't imagine they get out much. Yes, you see, once you've lived to be seventy or so—well, that's just about as far as you can go. You'll find only a sprinkling as old as that at the theater. Isn't that right, Shigeri? Wouldn't you say Old Man Ino and his wife are about the only ones left who still go? That old Mrs. Ino, she must be close to ninety, maybe even ninety-one, but she certainly does love the theater. She still gets out to the plays.

"No, I don't really recognize the puppets they're using nowadays. In this region there're still a number of theater troupes but none any better than the Gennojō and the Rokunojō. Both of them mostly use the puppets I made. Now when I see my own puppets up on stage, I don't start into grumbling to myself like I used to about how I ought to have carved them—wishing I'd cut a little more here or made the face rounder there. Folks know that puppets are my life, and I imagine when they see me at the theater they think I'm going to be criticizing every little slipup there on stage. But I'm not that way anymore. I just go to the theater and watch the play like any other fellow. I don't pay attention to any one thing. Most of the puppets there are mine. But I guess that's just the way it should be, and I don't think much of it.

"In the old days they'd stage plays in a field somewhere. They'd start around seven o'clock in the morning and would go till nightfall. Once the sun went down they'd take split logs and pile them up one on top of the other to make a bonfire. Often times the faces of the puppeteers would turn black with soot because of it. And, oh my, the village girls would scamper noisily over the meadow paths with groups of young men on their way to see the play."

That was the last I heard of the old man's stories. Exactly ten days had passed since I had paid my first visit. As I bade him farewell, the old man stopped what he was doing and turned to me. "You and I . . . there's more difference in our ages than I can even figure. But every day we've shared tea and stories just like two old friends. Well, I don't know that we'll ever meet again."

I went to the village play by myself, unable to convince Kyūkichi to join me. And yet, I felt that he was there beside me just the same. The theater was a typical country one. When I went inside I found it very quaint. The old man had told me what to expect, and yet I was still surprised to see that almost all the people sitting there on the floor watching the play were old. There was even an old nun among them, and several old gentlemen who seemed to be retired town officials. But most of the audience was composed of simple men and women from the neighboring villages. They had come dressed in kimonos of homespun cloth. Alongside them were oil-paper umbrellas, stacks of lunch boxes, and other bundles. The people were interested in the drama, of course, but instead of sitting quietly and watching the events on stage they talked to one another, ate, and seemed truly to enjoy themselves. Perhaps, being as old as they were, they knew the plays so well they could talk and carry on like that and still follow what was happening on stage. I suppose all they had to do was sit there.

"Do you like it?" I overheard an old man ask the woman beside him.

"Oh, yes, whenever I hear the *jōruri* ballads I feel all calm inside."

"Certainly was a wealth of passion in the words of old!"

The puppets I knew so little about were performing on a darkened stage. They were large, and the puppeteers, I could see, had to put a great deal of energy into the roles their puppets performed. At first I was at a loss as to what I should feel, but before long I ceased to notice the puppeteers, and at that point I was pulled into the drama. We came to the scene where Kumagai, having captured Atsumori, looks down to see that his foe is a handsome boy. I found that I was in tears when the chanter sang the line, "He brandishes his sword. But behold, beneath the armor a jewel-like face." What power must this art possess, I thought, if it can move to tears even someone like myself, someone who knows so little of its secrets.

It was raining. In the country they call this sort of day "a rain holiday," as there is nothing left to do once the fields have been planted. The countryfolk set out for the theater early in the morning, holding aloft their oil-paper umbrellas and hoisting their big picnic bundles upon their backs. They brought rice balls with them stuffed with pickled plums, and loquats, which they peeled before eating. They brought tea, too, in old bottles. When I first entered the theater, all the munching I heard reminded me of silkworms chewing away at their mulberry leaves. I was enveloped in a nameless mood. As I sat there amidst it all, I felt that I was beholding the death of the puppet theater. This was the way it would go, would it not? It would simply fade away. I felt all about me an undercurrent of sorrow. The other spectators, unaware of the fate awaiting their beloved theater, were talking among themselves in loud, cheerful voices. I wondered if this were not what the old man had noticed when he came to the plays. Perhaps this was why he had refused to come with me. On the train back to Tokyo I thought about it all for a long time.

Half a year has passed since my trip to Shikoku. Yesterday I received the Oyumi puppet I asked the old man to make. Unable to forget the puppet I had seen at my friend's house the spring before, I had asked Kyūkichi to make me one like it. Perhaps it was just my imagination, but I felt that the puppet I now held in my arms was much, much better than the one I had seen earlier. To borrow the old man's words, the puppets might have been exactly the same in form, "without a splinter of difference," and yet they were different. The difference lay, I knew, in the heart of the old puppet maker.

I dressed the puppet in a kimono and searched about for an antique comb to fix in her hair. While I busied myself I was overcome by a strange feeling. By doing what I was doing, that is, by dressing the puppet and looking for a comb for her hair, was I not offering proof, if but slight, that the puppet would not perish? I was certain that the old man, too, had known this all along.

THE SOUND
OF THE
WIND

I

The Yoshinos of Takamori . . . now they were my husband's real family. But he left his home there and was adopted into my family as my husband and the heir. His name was Seikichi.

My, yes, the Yoshinos of Takamori were a wealthy family, well respected in these parts. They owned land in Kuka, Hongō, Tabuse, Shigino, Fujiu . . . goodness, the list could go on and on, for no one really knew how much they had. The rice they harvested from those fields came to nearly five thousand bushels a year, or so I'd been told. They were sake brewers, you see, had been for generations, and were so prominent around here that all you need say was "the Takamori Yoshinos" and everyone would know just who you meant. That's why on the day Seikichi came to marry into my family, the whole town turned out with a great to-do. It was all on account of him being a son of the Yoshinos.

No, I didn't see it myself, but later heard others say that horse after horse made the four-league journey here from Takamori, each animal hauling great oblong chests wrapped in green swirl-pattern oil cloths. But, in truth, even that mountain of possessions was but a slight affair, considering they were the only belongings of a Yoshino son sent off to wed. All the same, the townsfolk carried on as though they'd never seen such a sight.

It was in the springtime. I had only just turned sixteen, and, oh, I was bashful! During the ceremony I wouldn't lift my eyes, not even when I heard them declare us man and wife. It wasn't until the next morning when we were sitting in the Clock Room with our breakfast trays set out before us, that I began to think of him as my husband.

I had awoken early that morning, as was my wont, but before I could slip out of bed he grabbed me roughly and said, "Where do you think you're going! Get back in here awhile." He wouldn't let me up. Our bedroom was in the back of the house, and from the light streaming in through the cracks of the rain doors, I could tell the sun was rising higher and higher. Still, he would not let me go.

Okaka was living then.[1] She did everything for us—everything save dress us—and that morning she prepared a special breakfast of bamboo shoots, boiled codfish, whale meat in vinegared bean paste, and *wakame* soup. Seikichi picked a sliver of the white whale meat up with his chopsticks, and, holding it out before him all a-dangle, growled, "You tell your Okaka I don't eat whale meat!"

"Yes sir," I barely managed the whisper.

I suppose you could say it was the morning's sake having its effect on him that made him behave so mean, at least that's what I told myself. But when I looked up into his face, I found not so much as a dewdrop worth of anger there. Really, the mouth that uttered those hateful words was smiling. Seikichi was smiling at me. I suppose he was teasing me; I was such a silly young thing, and he, well, I imagined he was somewhere over thirty. No one had told me about his age, but he seemed much older than I. And there he was teasing. Oh yes . . . but more than his playfulness, it was that smile of his that caught me unawares and tore its way deep into my heart. When I raised my eyes and looked at him, really looked into his face for the first time in my life, he won me completely. Now the memory is a painful one.

What's that? How did he get along with Okaka? Oh, just fine, so fine in fact that there were those who said she had him marry me because she was in love with him herself!

It was Seikichi's habit to come right out and say whatever was on his mind, but no one faulted him for it. I suppose they realized he meant no harm. Once he turned to Okaka and said, "Look here at the thongs on my rain clogs. See that I get a new pair." Then again, there was the time he announced. "I'm off to Kudamatsu to buy a horse. Give me money." He didn't come to me with his requests but went straight to Okaka and told her whatever he had to say. She never once protested. "We took our bridegroom from a fine family," she'd tell me laughing, "now we've got to take care not to lose him." Oh, but she liked to tease!

After he married into my family Seikichi never had anything you could call an occupation. It did seem, though, that he had some scheme in mind and was just waiting for the right moment before getting started. At least that's what we thought, Okaka and I, and we tried not to be partial. When he was still a boy Seikichi left home and worked all sorts of jobs around Kyoto,

Osaka, and Tamashima, so if he had wanted to work here he would have had little trouble finding something. There just wasn't anything he was willing to do. And, of course, he received such a handsome allowance from Takamori, he never lacked for money.

Horses laden with packages made the trip between Takamori and our town nearly every day, and we were always hearing the cries of the packhorse drivers ringing through the streets. "Tōkaiya here! Tōkaiya Delivery!" On the first and fifteenth of every month, Seikichi's older brother made certain a messenger came around on horseback with Seikichi's allowance in a stongbox, a red-lacquered strongbox as I recall, with a big padlock on the side. Seikichi's brother always put a letter in with the money, but Seikichi never so much as wrote out a receipt note, much less a thank-you.

I suppose it was just our habit not to pay any mind to Seikichi's behavior. Once Okaka told me, "There's a reason for Sei's high-minded ways, you know. Ever since he was little the Yoshinos had his future all decided, but he didn't cater to their ideas and took to rambling around Kyoto and Osaka while still just a boy."

Seikichi's older brother was crippled from birth, but even so it didn't keep him from seeing to the family business. He sat every day, all day long, on the straw-matted dais at the back of the shop. He propped himself proud and proper against the *kotatsu*. I heard he sat there at the heated table even during the summer months. He ran the brewery, big as it was, without a hitch; so, I suppose Seikichi thought it only fitting for the heir of such a fine establishment to send his younger brother a bit of money now and then.

It was in the autumn of the year following our marriage that Seikichi went to Kudamatsu and bought that first horse of his. Our boy Naokichi had only just been born. No, I'll never forget that day.

"Okaka! Osen! Get out here and take a look at my horse!" Seikichi hollered from the post road.

I ran out clutching Naokichi. Okaka and the maids came stumbling out behind me. It was in the chill of the evening, and I could see Seikichi sitting atop the horse as it pranced toward us, raising its forelegs high, tossing its mane, and snorting. Okaka and I had no notion of how to judge the horse, but I thought the way the white dapples on its chestnut coat glistened in the dark was lovely.

"Okaka, I'll spread straw out by the well and bed the horse there tonight. Fine horse, don't you say? From tonight on this horse'll be master of our house!" Seikichi shouted excitedly as he rode around to the back of the house.

In the darkness all I could see was the horse's white breath. I could hear a scraping sound—the bucket on the wall of the well. Seikichi must have been drawing water. It was then I felt a shudder brush through my heart like a sudden gust of wind. What had brought on this shudder? Was it the unexpected appearance of the horse? I didn't know. I didn't understand it at all.

2

Our household was turned inside out with the arrival of that horse. Seikichi set in immediately to clearing away a patch of land by the tangerine orchard out back, and before ten days had passed he had built himself a little stable there, so pretty, really, it was hard to imagine he meant it for the horse.

Every morning Seikichi would lead the horse out of the stable and along the path through the bamboo grove to the place where the Omizo River ran deep. The Omizo flowed down from the peak of Mount Odaishi, and, though we called it a river, it was nothing but a stream, really—ten feet wide and water so clear you could see the pebbles along the bottom. Seikichi would wash the horse in the sparkling cold water, scrubbing away at him from head to hoof with a handful of straw. All the while he'd speak to the horse soft and low, "Whoa boy, here, here." Sometimes he'd sing packhorse driver songs in a voice so loud it echoed all the way to Mount Odaishi.

"Master Nambu's out washing his horse!" Word would get around and before you knew it a crowd had gathered to watch. "Nambu" was my family name, you see. My grandfather had been the village squire years back, and ever since his time it had been the custom in Kawanishi to call our menfolk Master Nambu.

Seikichi named his horse Seiryū, using a character with the same sound "sei" as was in his own name. He hired on Nakamura Gohei from Hirata Village as his groom. Every other day they'd lead Seiryū out for his "drills," as they called them, along the moat by the old Kikkō Castle grounds. On those days Seikichi rode the horse himself. And, goodness, if he didn't put on a show—galloping though town with Gohei close behind!

"Nambu's at it again!" some would say scornfully. Others had only words of praise for Seikichi. And then there were those who'd gaze after him full of envy as he sauntered by. It seems there wasn't a soul around ever thought to rebuke him for his behavior. Seikichi was the second son of the Takamori Yoshinos, after all. He could do just about anything and the world would look the other way. Besides, I suppose they thought he looked about as grand as the great lord himself, sitting atop his horse like that, and with a groom in a blue satin jacket fast by his side!

Let me see now, it would've been in the spring of the following year—the day of the Equinox Festival. In a southern town like ours the cherries bloom early, and that year the streets were full of noisy crowds pushing this way and that as they went about flower-viewing. The noisiest place by far was the grounds around the old Kikkō Castle—there along the moat where the Spring Races are held. Yes, horse owners had come from all the towns and villages hereabouts, and some had even come from as far away as Kudamatsu, Tamashima, Tokuyama, and Yanai.

Before Seikichi married into my family, horse racing had meant nothing more to me than seeing the red and white curtains strung up along the moat. I'd passed those curtains any number of times, but never once had I drawn close enough to peer inside. And then that year Okaka and I both rose early and had our hair dressed. We bundled up lacquered boxes full of treats and got set to head out to the castle grounds.

"Take Naokichi with you," Seikichi called out to us. "He's my boy so he's bound to love horses!" Yes, that's what he said. Well, Naokichi was still only a little thing, and just beginning to crawl. But I pulled out his special baby clothes, the ones the Yoshinos had sent for his thirty-third day ceremony, and I dressed him in the yellow silk underkimono with black and red stripes. Over that I layered a lavender silk kimono with long, dangling sleeves. Once Okaka and I had finished all our preparations, we set out with the nursemaid Oaki and several of the housewomen as well.

No, I tell you, until the moment it happened I never even dreamed I was destined for such sorrow.

It was a clear, sunny day. The cherry trees stretched as far as the castle ruins. Branches heavy with blooms spread out over our seat like a parasol. Pretty as they were, I must confess, I found the blossoms something of a nuisance, drooping down all over us as they did. And then there were the flower-viewers drinking and singing and making such a fuss I was afraid they'd pull the red and white curtains down. The race patrons' seat wasn't but a stone's throw from where we were, and Seikichi was right in the middle of them, sitting proudly on a stool covered in blue velvet. He must have held more than half of the race shares, I imagined, to be acting the way he was. Of course, he was seeing to the needs of his own horse, but he also seemed to be directing the rest of the race as well, for he was shouting out orders and waving a baton. All the while there was a stream of men servants going back and forth to his seat carrying reed-wrapped casks of sake.

"Congratulations, Master Nambu," they murmured as they set the casks down at his feet. There was a young geisha in attendance on him as well, sent over from the Mikkazukirō House, or so I'd been told. I remember her hair was done up high in a fancy Shimada and knotted with a white paper cord. She must have been charged with collecting all the gift announcements. My yes, those announcements, and gifts, too, were piling up around Seikichi's seat like mountains, and the girl kept such a careful eye out over them all you would have thought she was guarding her own belongings.

Let me see now, our horse Seiryū was entered in the ninth race, the next to the last race. "One more to go, one more to go," those around me muttered to themselves as they counted off the races. People ought to have been restless by then, but I was told everyone was saying they had come "to see the Nambu horse run," and not a soul left early.

Seiryū's greatest rival was Tatsumaki, a horse owned by the Nōtoya Dry Goods Store in Kudamatsu. He had the same character *ryū*, for dragon, in his name as was in our Seiryū's—only his was pronounced *tatsu* . . . "Dragon Wind." He and our "Blue Dragon" were led out to the track. The race track? Well yes, I've been calling it a "race track," but it was just the every-day footpath along the moat. Only today it had been decked out with those red and white curtains I told you about. With seven horses lined up across it, though, the path was crowded. Seiryū was on the outside and Tatsumaki on the inside—all set to challenge one another.

"Bang!" The signal gun sounded. All seven horses leaped out at once and came thundering toward our seat. As I recall, Okaka and I were still fairly calm at the moment, not having yet befuddled ourselves with the excitement. The horses's legs were in front of me all a-tangle. The tall green grass along the moat began to quiver as if brushed by the wind. Oh my, but I can see it so vividly even now!

Our jockey's blue jacket and the red jacket of the Nōtoya jockey began to blend as the two raced side by side. They were so close you couldn't tell which was in the lead. Those around me were shouting for their favorites. "Go Seiryū!" "Go Tatsumaki!" Their cries swelled throughout the track. Suddenly, up ahead of the horses, I saw a pale blue scarf, or something similar, begin to unfurl in the breeze, and then a woman's shrill voice rose up above the rest, "Seiryū! Give it heart! Run!" A young woman dashed out onto the track, her scarlet underskirt fanning open as she ran. And then, as if it had been some sort of signal, our jockey's blue jacket began to surge ahead. Seiryū was two yards in front of Tatsumaki, and then three.

"Look out!"

"What're you doing?"

Everyone was shouting and screaming. There was a man on the field now, and he swooped the woman up in his arms, pulling her out of the way. My head started swimming and I couldn't be sure what I saw after that. When I asked later, though, someone told me that a woman had taken the pale blue shawl from around her shoulders and had flung it out at Seiryū. The suddenness of it had jolted the poor horse so, he tore off in a panic, outstripping Tatsumaki.

I didn't understand it well myself. Was Seiryū the kind of horse to bolt out wildly like that on account of a sudden shock? Or was he just moving into his stride when that woman threw her shawl out at him, making it look as if she had set him off? Whichever it was, I didn't think Seikichi himself knew he had a horse with such spirit. And if Seikichi hadn't known, well, there's no reason in the world to suspect that woman could have been any better judge of Seiryū's nature. Later I overheard others saying that they'd never heard of a horse being scared into winning a race. Yet no matter what was said, I believed our horse won because that woman threw her pale blue shawl out at him. And, I believe even now that this was what triggered the curse that was to haunt my life ever after.

Yes—you see, Seiryū opened up three yards between himself and Tatsumaki, and then five. Wasn't any doubt that he had won, and as he galloped across the finish line, all at the track leaped to their feet.

When I looked around I saw the man who had rescued the woman still standing in the middle of the field with her in his arms. He was shouting and screaming for all the world like a crazy man. Was no mistaking it now, the man was my husband . . . it was Seikichi.

"That, that girl. She's Oyuki." I heard Okaka whisper at my ear. "She's Oyuki alright. Miss Oyuki of the Tanokura." I could hear Okaka as plain as day, and yet I was so confused that at first I didn't know whom she meant.

3

Try as I might, I could never describe with pen and paper what happened in just the half year that followed.

The mountain of prizes Seikichi received from the Spring Races lay piled up about the Clock Room for several weeks. Amongst them were seven reed-wrapped casks of sake, and for days on end Seikichi was in a fine mood drinking with his friends. He'd call them over early in the morning, and they'd sit there all day with their cups. Seikichi said our groom Nakamura Gohei was the one who'd won the race, and he'd call him in from Hirata Village almost every day. No, he didn't send for him to train the horse. Gohei was there to drink.

"Go to the Tanokura, Gohei, and fetch Miss Oyuki!"

Seikichi often began shouting for Miss Oyuki when he'd had his round of drinks. She was there to share a cup or two with him, but even so I wonder if anyone felt the least bit hesitant about inviting her into this house.

The Tanokura was only sixty yards or so down the post road from here. Earlier Miss Oyuki's family had operated a bathhouse there. She was their only daughter, and I believe she was about three or four years older than me. She was a big-boned girl, her skin as white as snow.

"Now there's a girl I'd love to sink my teeth into!"

I often heard men say this sort of thing about her. Yes, people around here had all sorts of things to say about Miss Oyuki.

Her mama and papa went off to Hawaii and left her behind with her grandma. But then in no time at all, as I recall, Miss Oyuki, too, disappeared. Some said she had gone off to Himeji and was staying on such-and-such a street, and others said she'd gotten herself settled as the mistress of a stockbroker in Osaka. Before long it seemed everyone around here just forgot her. I could hardly believe my own eyes then when I saw her at the racetrack that day.

Miss Oyuki began coming to our house every day or so after that.

"Look here what I've brought!" she'd call out gaily as she breezed into the house. She always brought something nice with her—fish or boiled pepper leaf. She'd bound over the entrance step, without even waiting to be asked inside, and head straight for the Clock Room, where she'd plop down alongside Seikichi. She'd fill his sake cup, leaning up soft against him all the while, looking for the world like one of the women in those Kabuki plays that come down this way ever so often from the Kamigata. She was so lovely, really, I couldn't take my eyes off her myself—woman though I was.

"What a wicked hussy—to be taking advantage of the mistress's kindness like that! She's trouble, that one." The maids cursed Miss Oyuki behind her back, but whenever she came over, let me tell you, they scrambled out to greet her like she was our most honored guest.

"Okaka! Bring some omelets, will you. And make 'em thick now. That's the way Miss Oyuki likes hers."

"Yes sir!" Okaka would shout as she bustled off to the kitchen. She never complained, or made it seem she did any of it just because Seikichi had asked her to. No, she truly enjoyed doing whatever she could to make Miss Oyuki happy—at least, that's the way it looked to me. Miss Oyuki was somehow able to win her way into your heart. I suppose you could say she had some

kind of power over people. Or perhaps, folks just tried to please her because
they wanted to see Seikichi happy. And it wasn't just Okaka and the maids
either. I guess in my heart of hearts I wanted to please Miss Oyuki, too.

Yes. I believe it was after the rainy season, in the heat of the summer, that
Seikichi first began talking about tearing down the tangerine orchard behind
the house and building riding grounds there.

"Riding to the old Kikkō Castle every day isn't bad. But look here,
Gohei, how'd it be to build a training ring behind the house? That'd be better, wouldn't you say?"

"Yes, sir, right there where the tangerine orchard is'd be fine."

"The tangerine orchard? Why, that's just the place."

Seikichi turned to Okaka with that smile of his. "Listen, I'm thinking of
turning the orchard into a riding ground. We'd be able to train there as
much as we pleased, and by the next Spring Races we could go up against
Tatsumaki, or any damn horse for that matter, and be assured of victory!"

"By all means, help yourself to any of the land here. If you can use that old
orchard, then you're welcome to it. You probably know it's a lot of bother
to grow tangerines, and then they're not even that good for all the effort."

Okaka put on her brightest face. The way she spoke made it sound as if she
were truly taken with the idea. I found myself swept up in her happy mood.
Looking back now, it seems so hard to believe.

The tangerine orchard had been in our family since my great-grandfather's
time and even before. It stretched for several acres behind the house—all the
way to the Omizo river pool. Yet, when Seikichi proposed tearing it down,
no one breathed a word against him. Later I learned that the townsfolk had
chided us behind our backs. "Did you hear? They're going to tear down the
Nambu orchard so he can build a riding ring!" They spoke as if we were
doing something sinful.

When the trees bloomed in the spring, the fragrance from the white blossoms filled the air, drifting all the way to Okinomachi. And, in the autumn,
when the trees were in fruit, brokers would come from as far away as
Ōshima County to purchase our Nambu tangerines. And, oh my, the
branches would be so heavy with the beautiful fruit, they'd seem likely to
snap in two. I must sound boastful, going on about my own property like
this, but it was just such a lovely orchard. And then we tore it down without
so much as a sigh. I expect the world around us thought we'd taken leave of
our senses.

"Don't ever let on you care. Just close your eyes and pretend not to
know." Okaka said this over and over. How can I ever forget her words?
Whenever Seikichi told me what he was planning to do—do you suppose I

acted like I minded? No, I acted as though it didn't bother me in the slightest, and Okaka surely knew this. But, for her to have spoken to me as she did, repeating herself over and over, I wonder if—in her heart of hearts—she wasn't apologizing to our ancestors for destroying their beautiful orchard.

Yes, workmen came from Waki and Imazu. There were so many, you see, that in less than half a month they had cleared the land. They worked with such a bustle and flurry, felling the trees, digging out the roots, and leveling the land, that it was almost pleasant to watch. When they'd finished, the ground spread out smooth and wide as far as the eye could see. The first thing I noticed was the red *torii* of Myōgen Shrine. I remembered how earlier I'd just barely been able to make out the bright red gate among the tangle of trees. But now here it was standing stark before my eyes. I finally understood what a dreadful thing we'd done.

It was toward the end of the summer that year when they finished the riding grounds. Seikichi had never been happier. He'd rise early every morning, long before Gohei had even arrived, and would head out to ride. And, oh, but he'd gallop around the new riding grounds like a wild man! It was around that time, as I recall, that he took to dressing like a jockey—wearing the kind of white muslin shirt they wore. He'd run the horse up and down the field until his shirt was soaked through with sweat. Once his ride was over, he'd lead Seiryū back to the stable, where he'd tether him; and then, stripping to the waist, he'd stand there swinging his arms all about in big, wide circles. Looked like he just wanted to show the world how pleased he was with himself.

One evening Seikichi said, "Why don't you jump up here on the horse, Oyuki?" He said it out of the blue like that.

When Miss Oyuki first started coming around, everyone took care to call her "Miss," even Seikichi. But at some point, I'm not certain when, Seikichi began calling her Oyuki. Oh, that was just his way. He wasn't one to stand on ceremony, and it didn't matter to whom he was talking either. So, I guess it should have come as no surprise that he was casual around Miss Oyuki.

"Could I?" she answered slyly, tilting her head back as she looked up at Seikichi on the horse. Then, before I could even be certain what she was doing, she scrambled up behind him. "Oh dear, how scary!" she squealed, and she threw her arms around his shoulders. At that moment she didn't look to be any older than thirteen. Where, I wondered, had she learned such wonderful tricks—tricks only a circus girl could do?

"Hold tight!" Seikichi yelled, and he gave the reins a snap. Okaka and I gazed after them as they galloped through the twilight. "Look at them go!"

we called out to one another. "See, there they are!" All we could see were
Miss Oyuki's calves glowing white under the fluttering red hem of her
underskirt. We trained our eyes on them, watching spellbound until they,
too, faded into the darkness.

From that time on Miss Oyuki was at our house every day. If Seikichi
went somewhere, she went with him. If he stayed out the night, she stayed
out with him and came back with him in the morning. I heard that most
everyone called her "Nambu's mistress." Maybe they were right . . . but
even if they were, I didn't feel a great hardship had befallen me. All I knew
was that I didn't want to stand in Seikichi's way. Whatever he wanted, I
wanted for him. Whatever.

"Thanks to Miss Oyuki our Seiryū won the race," Okaka would tell me.
And then she'd be likely to counsel, "Osen, look but pretend not to see. A
man, such as he is, will do this sort of thing three, maybe five times in his
life. If you make a fuss each time, you're bound to wind up the town laugh-
ingstock."

I suppose I'd be lying to say I never felt so much as a dewdrop worth of
jealousy. But even so, I never dreamed of going to Seikichi with my com-
plaints. Never.

I'd see them to the door as they set out together. "Hurry home!" I'd call
out after them. But to say I didn't feel the slightest twinge at such moments,
well, it startles even me.

4

"Have a listen to this!"

Whenever Miss Oyuki got back she liked to call us around, so she could
tell us what had happened the night before. Her stories always made us
laugh. Once she told us about the Mikkazukirō—the inn in town where she
and Seikichi often went. Oh yes, Seikichi enjoyed entertaining other horse
owners. He'd invite them in from near and far and treat them to drinks and
feasting. But now according to what Miss Oyuki told us, one night, after
they'd been at their drinking, Seikichi slipped down to the kitchen to look
over the dinner they were to serve his guests. The soup that evening was sea
bream. Well, Seikichi took up an empty bowl and, instead of having it filled
with the broth, placed a live chick in it. That's right, a live chick. Then he
put the lid back on tight and had the tray set out before Master Sōmura of
Yanai. Well now, Master Sōmura looked over his tray of food and mumbled

out politely, "My, my, yet another bountiful feast." He reached for the soup bowl, pulled off the lid—and out popped the baby chick. Such a little thing, its feathers hadn't even grown in full, but, oh my, there it was flapping its puny wings and peeping with all its might!

When Miss Oyuki told the story she threw her hands up in surprise—imitating Master Sōmura. The way she told it, I felt I could see everything right before my eyes. I could hear Master Sōmura sputter and spew, and I could see the geishas tumbling over each other in fits of laughter.

Seikichi loved jokes. Why, he was able to pull off wilder stunts than I could ever imagine. And Miss Oyuki always hurried home to tell us of his latest prank. After one of her stories I would sometimes find the maids grumbling behind her back. "Just listen to the way she goes on!" they'd mutter. "Makes me sick to see her all puffed up like that, bragging on her own lover!"

If Okaka ever caught them, though, she'd give them a sound scolding. "And, what are you so uppity about?" she'd demand. "Don't you think the master's just the funniest man there is? Putting a chick in a soup bowl—now who would've been so clever!" And then Okaka would go over the whole story herself, getting so excited as she told it, she even outdid Miss Oyuki! She certainly enjoyed those pranks of Seikichi's!

Yes, that's right. Okaka never once uttered a word against Seikichi. She wouldn't, no matter what he did; and I suppose her attitude was passed along to me. Oh no, it's true, all of it. Okaka and I never felt inclined to oppose him. But, I don't really understand it myself—about the fact that I wasn't even jealous of Miss Oyuki. Oh, I suppose I did feel a touch of envy toward her, but that was only on account of her riding lessons. They started back on that summer evening, as I believe I told you, when Seikichi took it into his head to put her up there on the horse behind him. I suppose you could say the sight of Miss Oyuki sitting astride that horse made him all the more inclined to ride. And he began seeing to Seiryū's training himself. Now, I don't mean to say he planned to let Miss Oyuki take the place of his groom. I just think he enjoyed watching her ride. Miss Oyuki liked to wear her long hair swept up high atop her head in the "butterfly" knot that was all the fashion. She tied it loosely in place with a white paper cord—the way the geishas did. And, oh yes, she would often wear a yellow silk kimono with woven stripes of red and black. The same kind of kimono the heroine Okoma wore in the play "Shirokiya"—you know of it, do you? Such a sad, lovely play. The kimono certainly became Miss Oyuki, and she always wore it with an undercollar of fawn-dappled lavender.

It wasn't so very long before I saw her in that yellow silk kimono sitting all by herself astride Seiryū. She was tearing through the field behind the house and screaming in such a high-pitched shrill her voice cut clear across Myōgen Shrine and echoed all the way to the streets of Okinomachi; at least that's what someone told me later.

"Pull back on the reins! Sit tight in the saddle!" Seikichi chased after her shouting out instructions till his voice grew hoarse.

Miss Oyuki's butterfly knot fluttered up and down with each bounce. I couldn't take my eyes off her. She was beautiful. My goodness, I imagine I was even more taken with her than Seikichi himself.

It was around this time that Seikichi began talking of buying another horse. You see, Miss Oyuki had become such a skillfull rider, she always wanted the horse to herself. This meant she and Seikichi had to take turns. He'd go out for a while, but then he'd have to hurry back to let Miss Oyuki have her ride. Well now, Seikichi just couldn't abide waiting his turn for long, and I suppose that was why he took it into his head to get another horse.

"Okaka," I was to hear him say before long, "when the Tōkaiya fellow comes by this way, see to it that he takes this message box off with him."

Seikichi had written his brother a letter. I think I told you that since he moved into our house, he hadn't sent so much as a note to his brother in Takamori. To be sending a letter off to him now . . . well, couldn't be any doubt he was asking for money. Okaka and I both felt embarrassed by it. Looking back on it now, I suppose you could say this feeling of ours was a premonition.

"If it's money for the horse you want, why don't you let us give it to you?" Okaka asked. "I won the community draw not too long ago, and I do believe the money's still lying around here somewhere." But Seikichi wouldn't hear of it. He flashed one of those smiles of his—that magic smile —and told Okaka, "Now what're you going on about? I'm just having some fun asking that gimp-legged brother of mine to buy me a horse. Ha! Don't give it a second thought."

Seikichi enjoyed nettling others. It was just his way of having fun; so we imagined he was only teasing his brother with that letter and didn't pay it much mind.

It was toward the end of autumn—one beautifully clear morning. Gohei had come early to begin work, and, as usual, Seikichi was in the back field with Seiryū. Seikichi was in a fine mood, and—as was his habit when he was feeling good—he was seeing to Miss Oyuki's riding lesson.

"What do you say to entering that exhibition event at the Spring Races next year?" I heard Seikichi call after her. "You could tie a light green headband round your head and gallop back and forth like a circus girl on the new horse I'm looking to buy you! Damn! Just thinking of you out there starts my blood racing!"

Seikichi never missed a chance to talk about the new horse. Oh yes, Gohei had introduced him to a horse trainer in Kudamatsu, and Seikichi had struck a deal. He set about fixing up the stable—making it larger—and everything was ready for the horse, whenever it was to come.

"I'm not nearly as excited about those races next spring as I am about riding through town with you," Miss Oyuki replied. "There we'll be, side by side, and everyone'll gaze after us just bursting with envy!" She threw her head back and laughed so hard I expect she'd forgotten Okaka and I were standing right there.

That was when it happened. We heard the clanging of a horse bell out along the post road and with it the low husky voice of the packhorse driver. "Morning! Tōkaiya here. Message from Takamori."

"The money's come!" Miss Oyuki squealed, and she leaped down from the horse.

"Wait here," Seikichi hollered after her. "I'll go see." But they both ran off toward the front of the house clutching at each other all the while.

Was money for a horse really such a cause for joy? I'd had no idea. Okaka, Gohei, and I hurried after them, just as if we were being reeled along on a string. But when we got there . . . I didn't know what had happened. The lattice door was wide open and Seikichi was standing there bolt upright gripping the message box in one hand and the lid in the other. His face was as white as ash.

"That bastard! Thinks he'll show me? . . . Well, you just watch!"

He hurled the message box to the ground—the letter flying—and charged off behind the house.

5

What on earth could've happened? For the briefest second none of us knew. The letter lay on the earthen floor of the doorway where Seikichi had flung it. His brother's letters always contained money—always! Why, you could depend on it! But was Seikichi's anger now on account of the fact that he'd received just a letter this time and nothing more?

Okaka told me about it later. She said that Seikichi's brother had refused

him the money out of respect for our feelings. In his letter, she told me, he'd
written with great care and formality: While I do not wish to begrudge you
the paltry sum needed for a horse, I do feel it best to pursue even hobbies in
moderation.

You see, from what I could gather there wasn't a soul around who didn't
know by now about Miss Oyuki. It's likely then that those at Takamori
knew the only reason Seikichi wanted the horse was so he and Miss Oyuki
could go out riding together.

Oh, now I don't imagine Seikichi's intentions were as well planned as others made them out to be. But somehow or another rumors went the rounds,
and once they were out there wasn't a thing Seikichi could do to quiet them.

It all happened so fast I couldn't be certain of what I'd seen—but there was
Seikichi, still in his white muslin shirt, sitting astride Seiryū. He tore off over
the field—didn't even bother to open the back wicket but leaped over it and
raced off down the post road like the God of Lightning himself. We stared
after him as he rounded the bend, heading off toward the teahouse by the
mountain pass. He didn't stop.

"Where are you off to? Please don't go! Come back!" Okaka cried after
him, and then turned to Gohei. "Quick, now! Go after him! Stop him!"

But before Gohei could move Miss Oyuki fixed her cool gaze on Okaka
and said, "Now you don't really suppose he could stop him, do you? There's
not a thing you can do, so you might as well just hush." And she plopped
down on the entrance step as if nothing had happened. Miss Oyuki was
right, of course. No one could stop Seikichi now. But even so, Okaka stood
there in the road gazing off toward the teahouse.

The house was still that night. Oh my, but it was quiet. Okaka and I huddled close to Miss Oyuki as if she were somehow our only source of strength,
and we waited in the Clock Room for Seikichi to return. There was a full
moon that night, its reflection mirrored in the garden pond. Outside it was
as bright as day, dazzling, dreamlike.

Seikichi hadn't been back to Takamori since the day he married into my
family. Not since that spring two years ago. It didn't matter what the occasion, he had refused to go back even once, and so I couldn't imagine he'd
stay the night there now. The three of us waited, hardly daring to breathe.

Suddenly, softly, we heard the tall grass in the back field swish and then
the sound of hooves. Seikichi was coming—not down the post road out front
but along the dark path by the river. Soon I heard a thud as he swung himself
down from the saddle—and I knew he had reached the stable.

"I'm back."

Was I imagining it? His voice seemed to waver—thin and colorless—and his face was as pale as a wraith's. Or was it just that the moon was so very bright?

"I showed that bastard!" he muttered as he strode toward the house. "Thought he'd fix me, did he!" He untied his black silk vest and shook out a handful of silver coins. They clattered down over the wooden floorboards of the veranda.

Earlier I believe I told you that Seikichi was wearing a white muslin shirt —the one he always wore when he rode—but he had tied the black silk vest on over it.

Well now, when we saw that heap of silver coins glittering there in the light of the moon, we all let out a gasp, even Miss Oyuki, and not one of us uttered a word.

"You should have seen it!" Seikichi laughed. "I rode Seiryū straight off the highway and right up to that bastard's table. 'Give me my money!' I hollered. 'I've come for what's mine by rights—don't try to stop me!' Well, let me tell you, the shop clerks and the maids came charging in from every direction, my brother's wife right behind them. Damn, if she hadn't stopped me I'd have wrung that gimp's neck!"

Seikichi grew all the more excited as he told his story, waving his arms about and imitating his poor brother's frightened struggle as if it were the funniest thing he'd ever seen.

"I've come for what's mine by rights!" This was a fine statement for Seikichi to be making, but in all truth it was an exaggeration. His brother was born lame—as I've told you—and under the circumstances it was only fitting for the family to make Seikichi their heir, second son though he was. But now he was a willful boy—did only as he pleased. He turned his back on them all and wandered off to some distant province. I don't think he ever intended to come back for his share of the inheritance. No, I don't think he planned on it even in his wildest dreams. But then, dream or not, there he was threatening his older brother. It was all a game for Seikichi. I knew this, and so did Okaka.

Seikichi's sister-in-law was a just and gentle woman. She was able to sympathize with him, and she also understood her husband's anger. It was she who stood between the two and tried to reason with them. I imagine she was the one who finally convinced her husband to give Seikichi the money. Yes, I knew this for a fact the minute I saw Seikichi's ashen face.

As the night wore on, Seikichi's mood began to brighten, until he was in fine spirits. "Call Gohei over!" he demanded. "Why the hell did he go home while I was out drumming up money!" And, though Gohei had only just gone back that morning, someone went out to Hirata Village to call him.

Seikichi spread the money out before us. It looked like he was counting it out, but I think he just enjoyed taking the coins up in his hands one after the other. "This is the price of the horse," he told us. "And this'll go to the trainer in Kudamatsu. Now Gohei, I want you to use this to cover whatever expenses you have getting the horse back here. You're to stay over tonight, but I want you to set out first thing tomorrow morning, hear?" As I watched Seikichi I could tell he was already picturing that new horse of his prancing up the road to the house.

It really wasn't such an unusual event—this buying of a horse—but the whole household sprang to life. It was as if we'd all been bewitched by Seikichi's boyish glee. Miss Oyuki pulled the *shamisen* out and set in to playing. Gohei knotted a kerchief around his head and began to dance. We carried on like that until the break of day—dancing and celebrating.

When I look back on it now, I realize that this night marked the point where we lost the will to reason.

6

Just after the New Year had begun, around the time of the Seven Herbs Celebration, a terrible influenza swept through our town. Some were calling it the Spanish flu and others a worldwide plague. It spread through every street, down every alley in the villages and towns hereabouts. Not a household was left untouched. Doctors did all they could, but there weren't enough to go around—so many had been stricken. People began dying one right after the other.

The maid Otome was the first to fall ill in our household. My boy Naokichi took sick after her and barely escaped with his life, poor child. And then, just when we were rejoicing his recovery, why the illness caught up to Okaka. Now, this sort of influenza didn't pose much threat to children and young people, at least that's what we heard, but it preyed on the elderly— those who had reached the prime of life without knowing so much as a day of sickness. Five days after Okaka was stricken she breathed her last.

It had come on so suddenly. I looked at Okaka's face as she lay in death. The stray hairs at her temples were tangled somewhat, but other than that there wasn't a thing to suggest she was no longer living.

"I wonder what she left by way of parting words. She worried so for the young mistress I doubt she'll be resting easy now!"

When I learned that this was what the neighbors were saying among themselves I couldn't believe my ears. Surely they were talking of someone else—not me. But, of course, by now the whole town knew what was between Seikichi and Miss Oyuki, and I suppose most thought this would have weighed heavily on Okaka as she lay dying. But now, here's where fact is contrary to rumor.

You see, what Okaka wanted to tell me was nothing like others imagined. I understood her feelings—so well, in fact, I felt I could take them up and cradle them in my hands. She didn't waste time worrying over Seikichi and Miss Oyuki. No, she never felt it was anything to fret about. Okaka believed that if you were patient, you could weather just about anything with a spirit as peaceful as the quiet that settles in after a violent storm. Oh, I suppose you could say she saw this whole business with Miss Oyuki as just one small step in Seikichi's never-ending quest for pleasure. According to Okaka, a woman wasn't to stand in the way of a man's pleasure. Not ever. And she didn't just mean his pleasure with women, either. No, whatever Seikichi wanted— whatever—she never denied him. But it was even more than that, you see. Okaka always made it seem that what Seikichi wanted, she wanted, too. She made it seem that it had all been her idea from the start.

Well now, if Okaka had wanted to leave me any last testament, she would have bid me do just as she had done. I'm certain of it. Wasn't any reason for her to spend her final rest fretting over Seikichi and me—for all I had to do was treat him just as she would have. That was all.

"Don't you worry, Okaka," I whispered in my heart as I sat at her bed-side. "I understand." In the flicker of the votive candles her lips seemed to move, and I thought she was trying to speak to me. I felt myself slipping into a trance.

"Osen, I hear you and Oyuki slept together when you were girls," Seikichi said one night two months or so after the forty-ninth-day observance of Okaka's death. Miss Oyuki had moved in to stay right after Okaka died and had begun to act like a member of the family. That's when Seikichi said what he did. I had put Naokichi to bed, as I recall, and was in the Clock Room having a late supper with Seikichi and Miss Oyuki. That had become our custom.

"Yes," I whispered.

"Remember?" Miss Oyuki laughed. "We'd stretch out on the dressing room floor, side by side, and drop off to sleep."

I was only five or six at the time, as I recall. Miss Oyuki would have been eight or nine. I don't remember why we did what we did, but nearly every day I'd go over to the Tanokura Bathhouse to lie on the dark wooden floor of the dressing room with Miss Oyuki. Just thinking back on it is enough to make my cheeks flush scarlet.

Miss Oyuki had been coming over to our house for close to a year now, or more. Why hadn't I remembered our childhood games before? But no, it's not that I hadn't remembered.

They closed the bathhouse right after Miss Oyuki's papa went off to Hawaii. They closed it down, you see, but the empty dressing room made for a fine playroom. The wooden doors were locked and the shop curtains had been taken down by then. Miss Oyuki and I would stretch out side by side on the wooden floor, just like she said. It was dark, but streaks of sunshine seeped in through the cracks in the doors. In the dim light I could just make out Miss Oyuki's plump body glowing faintly white. Oh, I can see her floating before my eyes even now.

But this was just a game we played as children, and I had never given it much thought. I expect all my memories of those days just faded into the distant past. But Seikichi took it into his head to drag them back again. It was just another of his pranks. I suppose he enjoyed watching me fidget with embarrassment.

If Okaka had been alive . . . if only she had been there by my side! For the first time since she'd passed on I came to know how lonely I was.

"Shame on you! Telling lies! Now that your Okaka's dead I think you and Oyuki ought to sleep together like you did when you were girls. How about it? Oyuki and Osen—side by side. We'll start tonight."

I nodded silently, unable to deny him.

For the first several months after that, I felt I was living in a dream. And then, one night, something horrible happened. You see, I wasn't able to sleep with my baby anymore, but had to let his nurse, Oaki, keep him in the inner room. He'd cry now and then and every time I heard him—oh, but I'd be torn by misery. Well then, that night I just could stand it no longer. Without really thinking, I rose to go to him, but before I could get out of bed I felt Miss Oyuki wrap her warm, moist hands around my shoulders. She held me back.

No one else seemed to care at all for poor Oaki and the baby—left all alone in that big inner room. But I, how can I find the words for it? It only reminded me of how lonely I'd become since Okaka left me, and I wasn't able to think of anything else.

"Miss Oyuki, how would you have us prepare the fish tonight?" The housemaids began turning to Miss Oyuki for their instructions. Oh yes, they'd go to her for matters high and low, and she began to do most everything Okaka had done before her.

Her house, the Tanokura, wasn't but a stone's throw away, and she could have stepped over for a visit anytime. But, unless there was an important piece of business to see to, she never went home.

"She left her poor old grandma there by herself years ago. Wouldn't make sense for her to worry over her now!" Some secretly criticized Miss Oyuki. But by now no one thought it strange for her to be staying on at our house.

Yes. That's right. By this time I, too, had begun to depend on Miss Oyuki. She took care of things for me now that Okaka was gone, and it never occurred to me to begrudge her for it. I can't imagine how I must have looked to others though.

7

One evening toward the middle of February we had a heavy snowfall—a rare event in these southern parts. Seikichi was beside himself with joy. He said he wanted to drink his sake while looking out on the snow, so he had the shōji screens opened in the Clock Room. He sat there eating a late supper, watching the snow glide softly into the garden pond.

"Miss Oyuki, your grandma's come. . . ." Oaki called out from the corridor; her voice sounded heavy with worry.

Miss Oyuki's grandma was a kind old woman. She never came calling unless she had an important reason. But it seemed to me that Miss Oyuki took delight in worrying her. She always had some excuse for not rushing to her side—at least that was her usual way. But tonight was different. She jumped right up when she heard Oaki call, just as though she'd been expecting her grandma to come for her.

"I'll be right there!" she called out. She sounded nervous. "I'll just be going home for a bit," she said. "But I'll be back before long."

I peered through the crack left between the heavy paper doors of the Clock Room and watched her setting out with her grandma. Her hair knot, high atop her head, seemed to droop under her umbrella. She'd hitched her scarlet underskirt up high, tucking the hem in her sash. No, I'll never forget the way my heart pounded as I watched her walk off into the snow.

Seemed about half an hour had passed when Seikichi suddenly said,

"Oyuki's late," as if he'd only just remembered she was gone. And then suddenly she stumbled in through the front door. She was barefoot—hadn't even bothered to put up her umbrella. She clung to the lattice door and sank to her knees in the doorway.

"He's . . . he's there."

Before she could finish a man with an Inverness cape slung down low across his shoulders rushed up behind her. He'd come out in the snow without his shoes, too. "Beg your pardon," he called to us. "I'll just have a word with Oyuki." I thought he was fixing to march right in, but he hesitated, seemed afraid to push his way in past the lattice door. Instead he stood where he was and, clinging to the doorway, called to Miss Oyuki. "Do you think . . . think you can . . . you can just leave like that!" His words came out in gasps.

Oh yes. That would be the first time I saw the man. He looked to be a good year or two older than Seikichi, and he was thin. Yes, thin and fine boned. Didn't have much by way of eyebrows, but his eyes were sharp, so sharp I felt they could pierce a person's heart.

He took hold of Miss Oyuki's skirt with his long, bony hand, and just as he did Seikichi stepped out in front of him. "You'd like a word with Oyuki, would you?" Seikichi bellowed. "Sorry fellow, but Oyuki's my woman now. You got something to say to her, you tell me!"

Seikichi's voice was as cold as ice. I'd never seen him so calm, so composed. He was wearing a thick kimono of striped indigo and a Hakata sash. And, on account of the heavy padding in his kimono, he seemed larger than usual. Standing where he was up on the entrance step, he loomed over the man. I don't know what got into me, but when I saw Seikichi there like that, I dashed out in front of him and clung to the hem of his kimono. "Don't go out, please," I begged. "Come back in."

I don't know what I could've been thinking to do such a thing. Seikichi shook himself loose and stepped down heavily into the earthen doorway— just as though I wasn't even there. He stood right up against the man, almost brushing his cape he was so close, and said, "You got something to say to Oyuki—you tell me! Tell me, I said!"

"I want to talk to Oyuki—I've nothing to say to you!"

Just then Miss Oyuki worked her way free of the man, and scrambled up into the house—didn't even stop to clean her feet.

"No! Oyuki wait, please! I just want to talk to you. Please!" He was so busy trying to follow her, he seemed to forget Seikichi standing right there in front of him.

"Are you blind! You son-of-a-bitch!" Seikichi hollered. He yanked the man up by that cape of his, hoisted him under his arm and flung him out onto the road.

"Gohei! Close the front door. Bolt it!"

The man banged on the door, calling out for Miss Oyuki. He kept it up for some time. A large crowd of people began to gather on the snowy road in front of our house. I couldn't see them, but I knew they were there. I could feel their presence.

"The police've hauled him off," I heard one of the serving girls say. Closing my eyes, I could see him as he was being led away.

I had thought Seikichi would let loose with a fit of rage once the man had finally been taken off. After all, he was given to violent tempers. But he just acted like nothing had happened. And I found that strange. Nobody from the police station came to question us, and the night and all its horror melted away with the snow—leaving no trace, or so it seemed. But that was where I was wrong.

8

Is there anything as strange as a man's heart?

Seikichi never once blamed Miss Oyuki for what happened that night. Far from it—ever since that man came after her, Seikichi did all he could to please her. At night, when they had gone to bed, you might have expected him to ask her a thing or two about the man, but he never did—and it wasn't because I was lying there beside them, either. No, I don't think they minded a bit whether I was there or not. I told you earlier, didn't I, that I slept next to Miss Oyuki? Well, being so close I couldn't help but overhear them—no matter how they whispered. But they never said one word about the man, and I found that strange.

Well, now that I think of it, I do remember one night. Seikichi never put out all the lights in the bedroom, you see. He always kept the paper lantern lit, with the wick trimmed low. In that dim, flickering light I couldn't be certain what I saw—but that night Seikichi took Miss Oyuki up in his arms and embraced her with such a passion I was afraid he'd taken leave of his senses.

"On account of that fool," he cried, "I love you twice as much as I did— no, ten times as much!"

And then, in a voice I'd never heard before he called out to me.

"Osen! Watch! Watch there from your bed and you'll see just how much I love Oyuki!"

Before my eyes he began to make love to Miss Oyuki with a frenzy close to madness. And she, too, began to cry out—in a voice loud so I could hear— "Yes! Oh yes . . . do whatever you want with me!" She held his head between her hands and pressed it to her breast, burying her face in that thick, short-cropped hair of his.

I don't know how many years have passed since that night, but whenever I think back on it I still feel a chill creep down my spine. Yes, I suppose the fact that I was lying right there beside them only fanned the fires within them, causing them to act as they did. I understand that now, but at the time I was just a girl, a silly little girl, and I was scared half to death. All I could think of was my Okaka, and how pitiful I was now that she was gone.

Seikichi and Miss Oyuki soon began to turn all their attention to their riding practice. The Spring Races were fast approaching, and I imagine that was one reason for their sudden interest in training. But I wonder, too, if it wasn't a sign that Seikichi's affection for Miss Oyuki had quickened.

Shirayuki, that was the name they had given the horse Seikichi bought for Miss Oyuki—the one he'd bought the autumn before with his brother's money. They'd named the horse after Miss Oyuki, you see, and true to his name he was as white as snow. Shirayuki was fine boned and willowy alongside the stocky Seiryū. And, oh my, Seikichi and Miss Oyuki must have been a sight as they pranced through town together, their horses side by side.

Seikichi hardly ever used the riding grounds he'd built behind the house. No, he said it made better sense for them to train on the racetrack—and so nearly every day he and Miss Oyuki rode out along the moat by the castle grounds.

"Woman's got no business parading around on a horse like that!" Oh, some spoke out against Miss Oyuki in secret. But no one, not a single soul, dared to breathe a word against her in public—not against the mistress of a Yoshino.

And then there was that day around the beginning of March—a warm, sunny day, as I recall. I had seen Seikichi and Miss Oyuki off on their ride, as I was wont to do, and had gone back to the Clock Room to play with Naokichi.

"What a sweet boy you are, such a sweet boy!" Oaki cooed as she cupped his little chin between her hands. "Just look at him, ma'am." And she rocked his tiny head back and forth. "Now give us a smile, a pretty smile!"

Not even two years had passed since his birth, and already he was showing a resemblance to his father. Really, the likeness around his nose and mouth was striking. When he was happy, his laughter would pull his eyes into a thread. Oh my, that smile could win its way into anyone's heart, but, I tell you, every time I saw it, my own baby's smile, why, my heart would freeze with fear.

I no longer felt the jealousy I'd felt earlier when I watched Miss Oyuki ride off with Seikichi, leaving me behind. I suppose this was on account of Naokichi. I had Naokichi. I lifted the baby out of Oaki's arms and cradled him in my own, walking with him out the front door. I didn't have any reason for doing what I did, I just strolled out to the road. That's when I saw them. Seikichi and Miss Oyuki were not but sixty yards away—there in front of the Atarashi-ya, where the road turns off toward Okinomachi. It was them alright. They were on their horses and there was a man, or someone, crouching down in the road before them.

"Oaki, come take a look at this—see, down there by the Atarashi-ya?"

"It's, it's that man—the one who was here the other night," she said. "But now, has he been in town all this time? Look! He's trying to grab hold of Seiryū!"

Oaki was right. It was the same man, and he was wearing the black Inverness cape he had worn the other day. We were too far away to see what was happening, but it looked like he'd thrown himself down on the ground before Seiryū. Now and then his arms would shoot up as if he were speaking to Seikichi.

"Oh no, don't!"

As Oaki screamed I saw Seikichi bring his whip down on Seiryū. The horse leaped forward, bounding over the man as if he were nothing more than a hurdle in a steeplechase. Shirayuki followed.

A crowd of people spilled out into the road, and we lost sight of the man. Oaki and I ran into the house, hurrying to get inside before Seikichi got back. I could hear Gohei leading the horses into the stable and mingled with these sounds was Seikichi's voice, loud and spirited. Miss Oyuki was there, too, chattering gaily.

It didn't seem there was anything to worry about. I felt myself relax. And still, what I had seen haunted me. Even to this day I can remember the way that man looked as he crouched at the horse's feet. Poor man. The spring sun was shining down so warm and bright, and there he was wrapped in that heavy cape.

9

According to the rumors going around, the man in the Inverness cape was the one who had taken care of Miss Oyuki when she was in Osaka. He had been a clerk in a stockbrokerage house at the time, but he'd grown up in Shigino, a village not far from here. Seems he struck out for the city while still young. He and Miss Oyuki were attracted to one another right from the start, since they were both from the same region. For a time they lived in luxury, but then the man made some foolish bids on the rice market and was ruined. It wasn't long before he was nothing but a shadow of what he'd been. Miss Oyuki left him without so much as a word of farewell.

I learned there wasn't a soul in town who hadn't already heard of this. But, you see, somehow the news never reached me. And then, when the man disappeared after that snowy night, I had thought he was gone for good. At least I saw no more of him. But it seems he'd left his home in Shigino and was staying somewhere in town. Perhaps he'd taken up lodging in one of the nearby inns, I don't know. But I was told he would lie in wait for Miss Oyuki and when she'd pass by on her horse, why he'd do anything he could to get her to stop. "Wait! Please wait," he'd cry, waving his arms out wide to the side.

He didn't do this just once or twice, either—but every day. Some said privately that Seikichi went out of his way to meet the man in the streets. "Why does he have to go riding through town all the time?" they'd grumble. "Doesn't he have his own riding grounds? No, I'd say he takes pleasure in provoking the man."

The master of the Yamashiro-ya, the geisha house in Sashimono-chō, came by one afternoon. Let me think, yes, that would have been three or four days after that incident down at the Atarashi-ya. Master Yamashiro had brought a man servant with him carrying a cask of sake. As they stepped into the Clock Room I heard him say to Seikichi, "Now let's stop all this nonsense, sir. Things are bound to get out of hand if we let them go." He was laughing.

Seikichi liked to send for geishas from the Yamashiro-ya, and he and the master often drank together.

"Why don't we just call that fellow over, give him some money, and settle this thing once and for all," Master Yamashiro continued. "After all, won't do for someone as fine as yourself to be stealing another man's woman."

"What's that you say? Stealing?" Seikichi flashed him a grin.

I sat nearby as they spoke, holding my breath in fear of what Seikichi might do next. I had expected him to fly off in a temper over what Master Yamashiro had said, but he just listened to it all like some obedient child. I was thrown completely off-guard. But then, I suppose hearing his old drinking companion tell him he was stealing another man's woman did have some sort of power over him.

"All right then. I'll meet him," Seikichi answered unexpectedly. "But do you think he'd come if *we* invited him?"

They decided to ask a geisha from the Yamashiro-ya to act on their behalf. She was also from Shigino Village. And then, before anyone could change their minds, they set the meeting for the evening of March 13th—the Eve of Shiinō-sama, a festival in these parts. They arranged to meet the man at the Mikkazukirō in the Daimyō Koji, and they planned to seal their talks over a cup of sake.

There were five or six days left before the meeting. Master Yamashiro came over to our house several times to see to the arrangements. Everything was left to him—even the sum of money to be paid the man. To the outside world, I suppose, it must have seemed that all the fuss was on account of the upcoming Shiinō-sama celebration. Inviting that man, too, was made to seem just a part of the festivities.

IO

I will never forget it. No, never. It was the 13th of March, the eve of the Shiinō-sama festival. The doors of every household were decorated with large paper lanterns and branches of paper blossoms. From dawn the pounding of the festival drums echoed throughout the streets.

Early that morning Miss Oyuki sent for the hairdresser, the one in Shinmachi. She had her hair done up high in a butterfly knot, so loose it looked like it might tumble free at any minute. She dressed in a fine-patterned kimono of lavender crepe and stood before the mirror holding first a fawn-dappled sash with a satin lining across her breast and then a one-piece brocade. Unable to decide between the two, she asked Seikichi to choose.

It was a warm, lazy day. The cherries would soon be in bloom. Seikichi had been in a fine mood since morning. He opened the shōji screens in the back room and gazed drowsily at the maids as they went about their chores.

"Well, I suppose I'll have to be on my best behavior with that fellow. But then, this is the last time I'll ever see him anyway. When all's said and done, I'll throw a big celebration.''

"I can't wait to show him!" Miss Oyuki cooed. "There you'll be scattering money right and left like the great lord himself. Oh, it'll be fun. But, I tell you what I'm really looking forward to is parading before those Mikkazukirō geishas. Once they see me all dressed up, they're going to think even more of you!"

Seikichi and Miss Oyuki teased one another as they dressed for the evening. When they finished they were prettier than a prince and princess in a picturebook. Seikichi had dressed in an indigo-striped kimono with a matching *haori* jacket. His sash was light blue and dotted with an iron-arrow design. Oh, I don't suppose you could say he was elegant, but to my eyes, so accustomed to his white muslin riding shirt and black vest, he was especially handsome. Just before sunset the two of them set out in rickshaws.

I didn't know all the details of the arrangements they were to make with the man, but I knew if Master Yamashiro was in charge, everything would turn out for the best. The man would agree to all the terms, I was certain of it. He'd leave our town and would never be seen again . . . and then, everyone would stop talking about the whole affair! Yes, I was able to calm myself with such thoughts. Truly, nothing's as pathetic as the human heart.

As I watched them set out in all their finery, I hadn't the slightest inkling that this night would mark the beginning of my nightmare. To the contrary, I felt that the fear that had gripped my heart these last few weeks was certain now to fade. How can I explain my relief? Later that evening I sat quietly with Oaki listening to the cries of the street peddlers hawking their wares and to the voices of the neighbors pounding out rice cakes for tomorrow's festival. Our house was perfectly still.

Yes, you see, since our family was still mourning Okaka's death, we hadn't decorated our door with paper flowers. This should have stood as a warning to the festival dancers, but even so a group of young revelers ran up to the house carrying lion masks and shouting gaily, "Here come the shrine lions—blessed Eve of Shiinō-sama!" I guess they just didn't know better.

As the night wore on the celebrations grew more and more lively. I suddenly remembered the talks at the Mikkazukirō and wondered how they were faring. For some reason my heart began to pound.

"Please don't take offense, ma'am, but how do you suppose that man'll react when he sees the master and Miss Oyuki dressed so fine and acting so friendly with one another?" Oaki had read my mind.

"Oh I know he won't be pleased. But Master Yamashiro will be there, and, as experienced as he is in the ways of the world, well, I'm certain he'll take care of everything." I tried to convince myself, yet in my heart I prayed over and over to Lord Shiinō and to Okaka.

That night the moon was as bright as the noonday sun. After I tucked Naokichi in bed I walked out to the veranda, and before I was even aware of where I was, I had wandered into the Clock Room. Seikichi and Miss Oyuki had been spending a great deal of time in the Clock Room of late, and it had come to seem their private domain. I didn't really mean to burst in on their room, but I hadn't entered by accident either. They'd left all sorts of gift announcements strewn about. Perhaps they'd been reading them over just before they set out because seven or eight were still unrolled and spread out on the floor.

The Spring Races weren't but ten days away. But even so, I couldn't understand why there were so many gift announcements here. I looked over the large sheets of soft white paper, a celebratory red ribbon painted across each one. The names of the honored and a description of the gift were written in bold strokes on each sheet. "One keg of refined sake for Master Nambu" several read, or "one basket of seabream." Most of the sheets bore the same sort of message, but then I came upon one that was different. Instead of "Master Nambu" the one honored was "Miss Oyuki."

The only person ever named as the bestower on all the sheets was the master of the Mikawa-ya. I had heard his name before. Yes, he was a horse breeder from Kudamatsu, the one who had once owned Shirayuki, Miss Oyuki's horse. Well then, I wondered, did this mean Miss Oyuki was really thinking to enter that exhibition race this spring? Had all that talk been more than just chatter? If it were true, then had she already been given a rank?

Tell me, is there anything as frightful as a woman's heart? There I'd been, fretting over those two as they set out for the Mikkazukirō. But now, looking at all those gift announcements, I felt my worries had been little more than a lie. In their place I saw Miss Oyuki in her light green headband sitting astride Shirayuki just like a circus girl—her red underskirt fluttering about her calves as she galloped back and forth. She was real—so real I felt I could touch her.

I hated it. Yes, I hated watching Miss Oyuki on her horse galloping off to the shrine grounds. I hated it, but, how do I explain this heart of mine? The more I hated her, the more I hated myself for feeling as I did. Truly my heart was cold—more barren than that of even the most jealous woman. Just thinking of it sent a chill of terror over me, and I believed that it was all on account of my own horrible self that Seikichi had done those terrible things.

Later that night, long past midnight, I saw Gohei running, half stumbling to the house. He had come up along the river path by the stable. Not fully aware of what I was doing, I hurried out to the veranda—there where it faces the pond.

"Please don't be upset, ma'am. Just stay calm and hear me out. The master . . . he and that man. . . ." Before Gohei could finish he sank to his knees and collapsed on the earth and gravel. The moon was out, bathing the garden in a light as bright as day. I saw Gohei's thin legs, wrapped in blue breeches, tremble slightly, and in that second I suddenly understood everything that had taken place at the Mikkazukirō. I could see the grisly scene unfold before my eyes. Seikichi waved a knife in the air. He lunged at the man, and then. . . . Yes, it is so clear to me, after all these years . . . everything, even the expression on Seikichi's face.

"Where is the master now?" I asked.

"The police took him away. Master Yamashiro sent me round for a change of clothes. Yes, well you see, he's got blood on his clothes. He needs clean ones, and I'm to take them to him at the jailhouse, at least that's what I was told."

"Oaki! Come with me, please." I hurried off to the storeroom.

That day of snow suddenly flashed before my eyes. It was the first time I'd ever seen that man. Yes . . . he'd come right up to our front door chasing after Miss Oyuki, and Seikichi had stepped down in front of him. "Are you blind!" he had yelled. "You son-of-a-bitch!" And then he yanked the man up, cape and all, and hurled him down on the road. Seikichi was laughing. Yes, he stood there laughing at the man. I could never forget the way he looked then, and I was certain he was laughing just like that when he stabbed the man.

Oaki's hands trembled as she helped me gather up a set of clothing for Seikichi. But I was calm. I carefully picked out a kimono, a jacket, and a sash. I chose the ones that Okaka had sewn for Seikichi when he first married into our family—oh, how long ago it was! She had meant Seikichi to use this striped kimono of heavy cotton twill as an everyday garment, but since taking up horseback riding, Seikichi hadn't so much as touched it. If he would just wear it now, I thought, wouldn't he be fulfilling Okaka's long-cherished wish? And, if he pleased her at least . . . well, I found myself given over to such notions.

"Put Naokichi to bed, Oaki. Well, shall we go then?" As I stood to leave Gohei came flying after me.

"Oh no, ma'am! You can't go. You can't. It'll only make things worse; Master Yamashiro said so. He told me over and over that you weren't to go."

How can I possibly describe the way I felt at that moment? I stood there watching Gohei run off along the river toward the Okinomachi levee carrying that bundle of clothes. Thinking back on it now, I realize it was then—in that very instant—that something took hold of my heart.

Oh well, to all eyes I suppose I was still an innocent girl, and I wonder if they weren't just trying to protect me from the horror of it all. Or perhaps they thought they could set everything straight before I even understood what had happened. I don't know. But I do know that I couldn't have stood there as I did if I hadn't felt so strong at that moment. In a voice so sure of itself I hardly recognized it as my own I said, "Oaki, go over to the Mikka-zukirō and have a word with the mistress there. Find out what happened, but let her think you've come of your own accord."

II

Oaki told me that once she reached the Mikkazukirō it was in an uproar with people streaming in and out. Most of them were there to celebrate the Eve of Shiinō-sama. They were shoving this way and that, she said, and crowding together like an avalanche ready to give way. Oaki hid for a time in the shadow of the cistern. Then she crept into the garden behind the inn. "I'm from the Nambu house," she called as loud as she dared. "Please let me speak to the mistress!" But she was told the mistress had been taken along with the others to the jailhouse.

Well, Oaki didn't leave right away. She came across the old man in charge of the footwear and persuaded him to tell her what had happened. Being so old he rambled on a bit, but this is what he had to say:

"They were in the upstairs parlor—Master Nambu always has his parties there, you know. Oh, they were having a lively time, they were. Seems to me they'd just sat down to feasting. Master Nambu always has himself a fine feast! Well now, it was getting on toward half past ten in the evening, as I recall, and all of a sudden the plucking of the *shamisen* stopped—just stopped. One of the serving girls let out a scream, and then I heard the thud of footsteps on the main stairway here. Seems that fellow was trying to run down the stairs. Oh my, he was in a hurry. His sash was undone and his underclothes were hanging wide open. Poor fellow, he was turning first one way and then another, trying to get away. And then your master came charging down the stairs right behind him like he was fixing to run him over. 'Coward!' He shouted out something like that. 'How far you think you'll get?' And then he started stabbing away at the fellow like he was going to tear him to bits.

"Now, I didn't see it myself, but one of the serving girls told me that while they were up there in the parlor, the man drew out a knife. That's right, he was the first to draw his knife, and he started after your master. Oh, can't be any doubt your master meant to kill that man, but folks's saying he did it to protect himself. And, if that's the case, well it doesn't seem to be such a serious crime, least that's what I heard someone say—someone who knows what happened."

Master Yamashiro burst in on us while Oaki was in the midst of her story. "Please forgive me, ma'am. I've made a mess of things, a terrible mess. I tell you, I've never met a bigger fool than that man there!" Master Yamashiro paused for breath and then continued, "Truly, ma'am, I don't know what to say. Who would've thought this would happen? No, he agreed to our terms. He'd settle with money, he said. So how could we have known he'd come sneaking into our meeting with a knife in his coat? The master flew into a rage, let me tell you. But who could blame him? And then that fellow took a swipe at him. Oh yes, he's the one who struck first—and the one who strikes first is in the wrong. So, you see, your husband didn't commit such a serious crime—why even the chief of police said as much.

"What's that? Well, yes, your husband was stabbed. But it's just a scratch really, nothing to worry over. So long as the other fellow doesn't die, your husband'll be home in no time. So please don't worry. Just wait here for him —quietly."

"But how is the other man?" I asked.

"Well now, that's not easy to say. I don't really know myself. The old man at the Mikkazukirō's the one who took him to the doctor, so I suppose we'll be hearing how he is by and by. I was told his left arm looked like it'd nearly been wrenched off and that it dangled down about his side. But no one dies from that, you know. That's just what I heard someone say."

"But if he dies? . . ." I couldn't get the thought out of my mind. I felt a shudder sweep through my body. "Please, please spare his life!" I prayed deep in my heart. I knew if he lived, Seikichi's crime would be slight. But I wasn't thinking of Seikichi alone. No, I couldn't forget that night over a month and a half ago . . . the night of the snow. That poor man looked so helpless as he lay crumbled in the road by our house, wrapped in his Inverness cape. And then there was that afternoon not so long ago when I'd caught sight of him in front of the Atarashi-ya, cowering on the ground beneath Seikichi's horse. Maybe it was my imagination, but in my memories the man seemed to be pleading, yes, begging Seikichi for mercy.

"Please don't let him die."

I prayed for Seikichi's sake, but I also prayed for the man—for my husband's enemy. Oh, how shall I explain this heart of mine?

"And what about Miss Oyuki?" I suddenly remembered her. Had she been hurt, too, I wondered, and for the first time that evening I began to worry for her. But thinking of Miss Oyuki only made my heart freeze as if it had turned to ice in my breast.

"That woman . . . she! . . ." Master Yamashiro spit the words out, and then continued with a grimace as if the very mention of my husband's mistress filled him with scorn.

"That woman leaped over the window rail and scrambled out on the roof like a damn circus girl. She didn't get so much as a scratch. I tell you, that one has the devil's luck, she has. I can't understand how she gets away with it!"

I don't think I've ever been so struck by the look on a person's face as I was then. No one had ever come right out and spoken so angrily against Miss Oyuki, at least not in my presence, and I hadn't supposed anyone could.

Don't you see, Miss Oyuki was my husband's mistress—even if it was just for the time being. And, I suppose most people were hesitant to say too much about her to me and all the trouble she'd caused in the past.

Not but a while ago I'd sat waiting in the Clock Room, horrified by the empty heaviness of my own heart. But now, hearing that Miss Oyuki hadn't been harmed, I was relieved; really, I can't describe how happy I was.

Miss Oyuki returned just as day was breaking. "Otoki! Oyoshi!" she called out for the maids, her voice strained. "Hurry up and lay my bedding out. Oh, I've just got to sleep a bit, ma'am, I feel like my whole body has turned to cotton." And no sooner had she loosened her sash than she flung herself across the bed.

We slept in the room at the back of the house, as I've mentioned before, and there was no need for Miss Oyuki to call for her bed. All three had been laid out from the night before—Seikichi's placed between Miss Oyuki's and mine—and they were still out that morning. Well, Miss Oyuki fell asleep as soon as her head touched the pillow—just as though nothing had happened. She had managed to slip out of her fine-patterned crepe kimono and had spread it out over her as a cover. I was used to seeing Miss Oyuki sleeping in the dim glow of the lamp. Yes, I saw her every night. But seeing her bare white legs lying tangled in the kimono now was somehow very eerie.

"Ma'am," I heard Oaki calling to me softly from the other side of the door. Her voice was tense. "Did she say anything about the master?"

"No. Not yet. She's sleeping now."

"Oh." I could hear Oaki softly swallow.

12

The Shiinō-sama Festival began the next day—just as it did every year. From early morning I could hear the festival drums, each beat pounding deeper and deeper into my heart the misfortune that had befallen my family.

Gohei came by. I knew he would. He was soon followed by Master Yamashiro and then the mistress of the Mikkazukirō. My goodness, each visitor came so close upon the other, I wondered if they hadn't brushed shoulders on the way. They told me that the Mikkazukirō mistress would see to all Seikichi's needs while he was in the jailhouse—his meals, his laundry, everything. I knew he was in good hands, but even so I was all the more anxious to go to him myself. Yes, I decided that, come what may, I was going to take Oaki with me and go to the jailhouse that very day!

I knew what Master Yamashiro had said—that seeing how all this trouble was caused by Miss Oyuki, I'd only confound the investigation if I were to show my face now, and might even make it worse for Seikichi. I knew what he'd said, but I wasn't sure that I agreed. No, I felt that if I didn't go to my husband, if I didn't at least try, well, tongues were going to wag, and then there'd be all manner of things said against Seikichi and me.

Oh, but it was times like these that I longed for Okaka and wished she were here by my side!

"Be my guest! If you want to go! . . . And, if anybody else wants to go, they can go right ahead for all I care! We've got mistress and wife living in this house side by side, why try to hide it!" Miss Oyuki's laugh was full of scorn. "But listen here," she continued. "Before we do anything else we ought to send someone to Takamori to get some money out of the folks there. That's right. First thing we need to do is pay off those police officials. Don't you see, if that fellow doesn't die, there won't be anything to hold on Seikichi . . . why, he'll be home before ten days' time. Least that's what that policeman said—oh, what's his name? You heard him, too, didn't you, Master Yamashiro—the bald-headed one?" And then, turning to face him, Miss Oyuki added sweetly, "Oh, I do hate to trouble you, but won't you go off to Takamori for us?"

"I'll go. So help me, I'll go. But it won't do a bit of good, you know. Money's not going to solve a thing!"

"It might not, and then again it just might. It doesn't hurt to try, now does it? Or maybe you have a better idea?"

Miss Oyuki's voice was full of power. I'd never heard her talk like that before, and it frightened me. But it also made me feel I had something to rely on. I knew she'd been kept over at the jailhouse the night before and that she'd been pressed till the break of day to answer all manner of questions. But I doubt she flinched even once, and now here she was ordering Master Yamashiro about—worldly man that he was! Oh, I found it strange the way people jumped whenever Miss Oyuki spoke. Very strange indeed.

"Oaki—be quick now and get Master Yamashiro a rickshaw—a two-man rickshaw."

"Now just a minute!" Master Yamashiro roared. "I've got to get back to my business before I can set out. Today's the Shiinō-sama Festival, for heaven's sake—or have you forgotten?"

"Well of course it is—and all the more reason for you to hurry home as quick as you can! So now take the rickshaw, do whatever needs to be done, and set out for Takamori from there." Her voice was so sweet it could've melted your heart. Oh my, but Miss Oyuki was clever!

No, I didn't get off to the jailhouse with Oaki until well after sundown that day. News of Seikichi's troubles had spread through town, you see. We bolted the front door, but even so revelers stopped on their way to and from the festival and tried to peek in through the latticework. Why sometimes there'd be so many of them out there stretching and straining, it looked like there was a wall of faces just beyond our door.

I pulled a scarf around my head and face and set out quietly with Oaki. She was carrying Naokichi. We didn't go out the front, but around back by the stable. As we pushed our way through the bamboo thicket, I could hear the horses stamping in their stalls. I suppose it was just my imagination, but somehow the sound of their footfalls was sad, pitifully sad.

We walked on toward the Omizo. It was deathly quiet . . . not a soul in sight.

"What was Gohei about today?" I asked.

"He was down at the old castle grounds from noon, ma'am, exercising the horse."

"Seiryū, you mean?"

"No ma'am, Shirayuki. He said that even if the master was gone, he'd at least enter Shirayuki in the Spring Races for him."

"Just Shirayuki? . . ." I couldn't bring myself to say anything else. Did Miss Oyuki mean to enter Shirayuki in the race, I wondered. Did she plan to have Gohei ride for her? I had thought they'd race Seiryū whether Seikichi was there or not. But now it seemed they would enter Shirayuki instead—no mention of Seiryū—and somehow I didn't believe Miss Oyuki meant Gohei to race for her. No, I expected she was planning on riding the horse herself.

Yes, she'd tie on that light green headband and ride the horse in that special sideshow, or whatever it was.

Here she'd already gotten Seikichi in enough trouble, could she really be planning something so foolish—just on a whim like that—no heed to what others might think? Was she thinking she'd be able to sail right into the races on account of Seikichi being one of the most powerful patrons around? I had no idea. "Oaki," I said. "This might be foolish, but let's not say any of this to the master. Let's just talk of whatever'll please him. And not a word about the horse, hear?"

"Yes ma'am."

When we'd gotten as far as the little lane behind Okinomachi, we suddenly heard the strains of the festival parade off in the distance. The pounding of the drums rang through the night, drawing closer and closer. Just then the moon glided out from behind a cloud and shone over Garyō Bridge—big, round, and pretty as a picture. I could see the wooden whitewashed stockade surrounding the jailhouse across the river. How strange, I thought, that my heart didn't leap in terror at the sight. Seikichi was somewhere deep within those palings. I knew that. I had known it since the night before. But, you see, I just hadn't had the time to worry over it. No, before I even knew what I was doing, or where I was, or why, I was standing there before the jailhouse.

"Oaki, where do you suppose we go now?"

"You just wait here, ma'am. I know the handyman here. Yes, he's the one who married the daughter of the owner of the Sakazuki-ya Liquor Shop—the one on that street there. He told me to call for him when we got here, said he'd help us."

Oaki slipped in through the back gate, leaving me alone. I hid in the shadow of a tree and waited for what seemed forever. I'd never once set foot within that white fence, not once in all my life. Yet, as I stood there waiting, I felt as if I were being drawn inside.

"You idiot! What the hell are you doing bringing a baby into a place like this. Stupid idiot! Get out of here and don't ever bring that boy back again. Get out, I said!" Seikichi's voice was coming from the room next to the back door. When I turned to look, I saw Oaki stumbling toward me.

"He's in that room there, ma'am. The police chief says you can go in and see him." As soon as she'd finished she hurried off, clutching Naokichi.

I was led straight to Seikichi's room. It was dark but for the light of a single lantern, and Seikichi was sitting there in the middle of the room.

"Won't you forgive me? I should've come sooner," I said.

"Thanks for coming."

I couldn't believe this was the same man who'd shouted so angrily not but a minute before. How gentle he was now!

"Oh, don't go looking like this is the last time you're ever going to see me! I'll be out of here in ten days—ten days! Just in time for the Spring Races. But now if I'm not . . . well, we'll just have to wait and see. Take good care of Naokichi, hear?"

He looked straight into my eyes as he spoke, wearing that smile of his that could melt your heart. Who would've guessed this would be the last time I'd see that smile?

Not ten minutes had passed when the guard came and led me away.

"Oh ma'am," Oaki cried as she drew up alongside me. "The master loves his little boy. He loves the little boy—that's why he said what he did!"

The minute I heard her the tears began to pour down my cheeks. We stepped out on Garyō Bridge, but just as we did, floats full of festival dancers started to cross from the other side. Oaki and I clung to the shadows of the railing and wove our way through the crowds. The pounding of the drums grew louder and louder, swallowing up the joys and sorrows of my own small life. Oh, no matter how many years have passed, I still remember the way I felt at that moment!

13

Master Yamashiro returned from Takamori early the next morning. He wasn't sure how, but everyone at Takamori already knew what had happened at the Mikkazukirō. They knew it all so well, he said, it was just as though they'd been there themselves.

"The master of the main house certainly is a strange one. I hardly had a chance to say even half of what I'd planned to say, when he handed me this handsome sum."

"Well, what did you expect!" Miss Oyuki snorted. "If they're ever going to dole out that money of theirs, now's the time to do it!"

"But, you see, that's where you're wrong. The whole time I was there he didn't say one word about our master, or the fix he's in. No, all he'd say was that he wanted me to be sure to tell Mistress Nambu here just how sorry he was for the whole mess. I was so busy thanking him at one turn and apologizing the next, I hardly had time to lift my head!"

"You must have been some sight, Master Yamashiro!" Miss Oyuki laughed like she'd never heard of anything so funny—seems she'd forgotten how the money was to be spent.

Miss Oyuki and Master Yamashiro had come to some kind of understanding over the money and how they would use it, but I hadn't the slightest notion what they had in mind. There were a lot of things in this house that I didn't know about! Really, everything was just the way it had been when Okaka was alive. I was treated like a child, like a silly little girl, while those around me took care of everything, not bothering to tell me any of it. Oh, sometimes they'd try to tell me a thing or two—but, I never knew what to make of it. I just didn't understand.

Miss Oyuki started making preparations all a-flurry. She didn't even pause long enough to finish her breakfast, and then she was off for the jailhouse. It was well after dark before she returned, and do you know she had the rickshaw driver pull her right up to the front door—to the front door like she was the Grand Mistress of the house!

"Come around to the back room, ma'am. I've some good news for you." And, before I could get to my feet she half dragged me with her into the bedroom.

Seikichi's bed had not been laid out that night, but Miss Oyuki's and mine were there—one right next to the other—each with their matching coverlets of Gunnai-checked silk. The lamp was trimmed low, as usual, and the two of us lay down together in the dim light. Suddenly I noticed the scent of Miss Oyuki's hair oil.

"I want you to listen carefully to what I have to say. I went to the hospital in the Daimyō Koji today."

"Oh?"

"You've heard about that fellow, I suppose, about his wounds? But now look, the stab wound he gave the master is far more important, don't you see. To be truthful, ma'am, it's nothing more than a scratch—really, it looks like he knicked himself with a fruit knife. But since he was stabbed first, it'd be better if that wound of his went clear to the bone. And so, I paid the young doctor there to say as much! There's not a thing in the world to worry about now. I've taken care of everything—the police and the doctors. Oh, the master'll be home most anytime now, I expect."

Whether Seikichi's wound was serious or slight had little to do with that poor man lying there in the hospital, I thought. But then, Miss Oyuki had contrived to make Seikichi's injury seem serious, thinking if it was, he'd be home all the sooner. And, I suppose I had to be grateful to her for that.

"Really, you've done so. . . ."

I was just beginning to thank her when she brought her face right up alongside mine and said, "Maybe, just maybe the master will get his pardon, or whatever you call it, by the day of the Spring Races, and, if he does, then maybe, just maybe he'll let me enter the race for him!"

She grabbed my shoulders and held them tightly in her warm hands. "No!" I thought. "Please, no!" I hated the very idea of her riding through the Kikkō Castle grounds. How I wanted to take my hands and pry my shoulders free from her damp grip!

I suppose I should have been rejoicing over the act of grace that was soon to befall my husband, but instead, there I was with those dark thoughts. I tell you, even I found my own heart frightful.

14

I'll never forget it. Five or six days passed, and each day we waited, fully expecting Seikichi to return at any minute. I suppose we should have behaved with a touch more shame, and I imagine others found it hard to believe our house had really met such a misfortune. We were anything but contrite. Why, every day Miss Oyuki would set out to see Seikichi. Nothing unusual about that, I suppose, but she'd get up early and have her hair dressed. Then she'd pull on her kimono and stand in front of the mirror holding up one sash after another until she'd finally decide which to wear. "Any messages you want me to pass along?" she'd say on her way out.

The cherry blossoms would soon be blooming. One morning I stood in the warm, clear sunlight to see Miss Oyuki on her way. She had draped a light blue shawl around her shoulders—the same shawl she had worn at the races last spring—the one she had flung out at Seiryū when she dashed out on the field.

"Time flies, doesn't it? Can you believe it's already time for this shawl again!" Her face was wreathed in smiles. Devilish, beautiful smiles!

Perhaps she smiled so because she realized, as she pulled the shawl up around her shoulders, that it was this shawl, this light blue shawl of hers that had bound Seikichi so tightly to her. In all truth though, when I saw the shawl I couldn't help feel that it was the cause of all the trouble that had befallen my family, and yet . . . and yet, there was no one among us willing to speak ill of Miss Oyuki now. Not now. After all, Seikichi'd be coming home soon, thanks to her, and I suppose we all felt grateful. But even so, how could I have stood there and not borne her even the slightest grudge?

Gohei had been in such high spirits he seemed like a changed man. I suppose Miss Oyuki had told him most everything. Oh my, but he had his heart set on racing this spring, and he'd been training harder than ever. "I heard the Nōtoya is entering a new horse this spring!" he'd announce, or, "I'll just wager all the horse trainers across the country have their sights on Seiryū. Yes, he's the horse to beat!" Why, he was so busy with the horse and all that most nights he wouldn't go back to his home in Hirata Village but would stay in our front room here. We were all so taken up in our everyday lives that we hardly thought of Seikichi being off in jail. It seemed more that he'd just gone off on a journey somewhere and was soon to return.

And then the evening of March 16th rolled around, Seikichi's fourth day away from home.

"Anybody home? Mistress Nambu! Miss Oyuki!"

It was Master Yamashiro. I could hear him by the veranda outside the Clock Room. Why was he calling for us there, I wondered, and not at the front?

"I'm here," I called out softly as I slid the shōji screen open. "I'm here but I'm afraid Miss Oyuki hasn't returned yet."

How can I describe what happened next? I took one look at Master Yamashiro's face—as white as ash—and sank weakly to my knees.

"Did he? . . ."

"Yes. Just a while ago—the bastard! The old woman at my place went by the hospital today to check on him and found he'd died." He paced back and forth before the garden pond as he spoke. "Where's Miss Oyuki? I've got to tell her."

You might have expected that at such a time Master Yamashiro would come by looking for me. But no, he wanted Miss Oyuki. I had no way of knowing what he had in mind.

The man had died. Did that mean Seikichi was a murderer? Just thinking of it gripped my heart with such a fear I couldn't even speak.

"I'll be going now. I've got to find Miss Oyuki."

Master Yamashiro was gone before I knew it. For close to half an hour, I suppose it was, I sat there on the veranda in a daze like some kind of simpleton.

A late moon had risen over the mountain ridge. So, had I let that much time pass? I imagined that Oaki and the maids and Gohei as well were already fast asleep. The house was as quiet as a grave. They had all been so certain Seikichi would be back, and their certainty had let them sleep. But the man had died. We'd gotten money from Takamori, and Miss Oyuki had scurried here and there trying to patch things up, and still it seemed it had all been to no avail! Oh yes, Miss Oyuki had bribed the chief of police, and she had paid the young doctor, but all had ended miserably. Do you suppose it made me happy to see Miss Oyuki fail? Then do you believe I was happy to learn that in one swift second my husband had become a murderer? For that is what he was now. He might have to spend the rest of his years in darkness, or worse, meet the same fate that poor man met and be put to death. Do you believe that made me happy?

All of a sudden I felt I could see Seikichi's face smiling just as he had that evening two days ago when I had seen him in the flickering lantern light of the jail cell. I could see him so clearly I could swear he was standing right there in front of me. And I could hear him as plainly as I had that night in the jailhouse. "Oh, don't go looking like this is the last time you're ever going to see me!" Yes, that's what he'd said.

The man had died. I couldn't get him out of my mind. Unreasonable as it may sound, I found myself hating him for not living. Why couldn't he have held out? But then I'd see him, the way he looked as he cowered at Seiryū's feet. Perhaps dying was his only revenge. Perhaps it was the only way he could get back at Seikichi. As I sat on the veranda, I felt as if my body were being swallowed up into the silence of the night.

15

What would Miss Oyuki have done if she'd been here? Seikichi was a murderer now. Would she have run off to help him, even so? Or would she have struck out in a different direction? Perhaps she already had.

"Oaki!" I shouted from where I sat on the veranda. "I must go to the master. Wake Gohei." What on earth was I planning? I wasn't certain myself. All I knew was that I wanted to go to the jailhouse, and I wanted to take Gohei along with me. That's all. And then it happened.

"Creeeak!"

I heard the back gate open—there by the path to the Omizo—and then I heard the tall grass swish and the sound of footsteps heading toward the stable. Yes, I was certain of it.

"Gohei! Come at once, the master's back."

"Yes ma'am," he called out drowsily and stumbled off to the stable.

In the pale moonlight I could see Seikichi running barefoot through the grass. He was wearing the indigo striped kimono Okaka had sewn for him, his sash hanging limply at his hips. And right behind him, yes, it was Miss Oyuki, wasn't it? Her butterfly hairknot looked as though it would spill loose at any minute.

"Don't make a fuss now—and don't be telling anyone we were here. Osen, I've got to go, but I'll be back. Take good care of the boy, hear!"

Those were his parting words. And then, as soon as Gohei led Seiryū out to him, he leaped into the saddle and tore off along the path by the river. He cut down the road through the Norimoto graveyard and headed toward the teahouse by the mountain pass, racing through the night like the God of Lightning.

"Mistress Nambu, I'm going with him," Miss Oyuki said as she climbed onto Shirayuki. She, too, set out, not but a step behind Seiryū.

It was all so sudden. One minute they were here—I had heard them, hadn't I? And the next they were gone, and I was left with only the swish the horses made as they raced through the grass. The sound grew more and more faint until finally it faded away. They slipped into the dark woods of the graveyard and disappeared from sight.

"Once they pass the teahouse, will they take the shortcut over Kuga Mountain and head off for Takamori?" I forgot that I was the one being left behind, and I prayed in my heart that they would go quickly, as quickly as possible.

"There'll be someone after them any minute now, ma'am. You'd better come inside."

"Yes, yes of course. Please shut the stable door and cover all the tracks with straw. Mustn't let anyone know they've gone by horse." I rambled on, not knowing where I was or what I was doing as I hurried into the bedroom.

That night! How many years have passed since that night, and still I have not forgotten it! Not any of it.

"Go! Go quickly." I prayed, and in my heart I could see them on their horses racing side by side along the moonlit road. Oh, how the sound of the wind tore through my breast!

"They should have reached the Kuga Mountain Pass by now, don't you think, Oaki, don't you? And, why . . . why do you suppose it's taking so long for the police to come after them?"

"Well, ma'am, I suspect they haven't found he's missing yet. Miss Oyuki didn't part with all that money, you understand. She had enough left over to pay off that handyman, the one married to the Sakazuki-ya girl. Yes, I imagine she paid him to help Seikichi escape, and the police don't yet know he's gone."

Oaki, Gohei, and I huddled together in the back room. Even after dawn broke, we hardly dared to breathe.

I could never put down on paper all that happened that night. Never. I didn't feel that my own husband, my Seikichi, had been stolen away from me by Miss Oyuki. No, the thought never even crossed my mind. All I could think to do was pray for their safety. They had slipped away in the middle of the night, down the back road through the graveyard, while the rest of the town slept. Even so, I was worried lest someone had seen them, had noticed them fleeing in the night.

An inspector came around after daybreak. He headed straight for the stable and saw right away that Seikichi had fled on horseback. When he left he took Gohei with him to the jailhouse.

16

Yes, now let me see, ten days passed before a messenger was sent around from Takamori. I can never forget it. A man named Yashichi, who had worked in the Yoshino brewery for years and years, came by after dark. He had crossed the mountain pass in straw sandals.

"Master Yoshino of Takamori has instructed me to tell you that every month, on the first and the fifteenth, he will send money for Master Nambu, just as he did when the master was here. He'll also send an allowance for the boy, Nao. He knows money can't right the wrong done you, ma'am, or calm your fears. But it is the least he can do. That's the end of his message."

I was touched by my brother-in-law's kindness, really, so touched I could not keep the tears from spilling down my cheeks.

"Please don't worry about us," I managed to say. "We have the rice from our rented fields and the income from the house we lease out. It's not much, but we'll get by."

"Yes, I understand, but Master Yoshino has told me to tell you that, seeing as how we don't know where your husband is, we can't possibly send the money to him now. We hate to burden you, but couldn't we leave his portion with you?"

My brother-in-law had seen into my heart of hearts. I hadn't thought it possible. True, Seikichi was gone, and I had no idea where to find him. I knew I couldn't possibly send him the money, but after listening to his brother's message . . . well, I just don't know how to explain my feelings. I was determined to get that money to Seikichi somehow, some way, wherever he was. Yes, so determined it made me tremble to the depths of my very being.

Later that evening Yashichi told us how Seikichi and Miss Oyuki had reached Takamori in the early morning dark. They took money from Seikichi's sister-in-law and then headed off toward Kudamatsu. That's all he knew, he said, and then later they learned of the master of the Mikawa-ya in Kudamatsu, the one who had sold Shirayuki to Seikichi. Well, Seikichi and Miss Oyuki rode as far as Master Mikawa's place and had him buy their horses. Then they boarded a train. "We'll just be going off to the Kamigata for a little sightseeing," Seikichi said as he left. "Take good care of my horse now. I won't be long." And then he smiled that smile of his. He acted like he wasn't going all that far.

Oh, when I think on it now, I find it so strange. I don't suppose Seikichi let on he'd killed a man and was running for his life, but even so, news travels fast. The horse owners hereabouts were bound to know the trouble he was in. I suspect Master Mikawa had heard all about it, there's no reason to believe he hadn't. And yet he put on like he didn't know a thing.

My yes, it wasn't long before the police found out that Seikichi'd gone to the Mikawa-ya and then on to Kudamatsu Station. And they heard that he'd bought two tickets to Osaka. But that's all anybody knew. No one knew if he'd gone all the way to Osaka, or if he'd gotten off somewhere in between. Yes, it was just as his older brother had said, "Seeing as how we don't know where your husband is, we can't possibly send the money to him now."

I took the packet of money from Yashichi and placed it on the family altar. Seikichi had the money his sister-in-law had given him, along with what he'd gotten for the sale of the horses. But even so, how long would that last? Neither Seikichi nor Miss Oyuki were much when it came to saving money! I was sure they would soon be needing more. Oh, I tell you, for all those years that they were away not a day went by that I didn't worry over their well-being!

17

The cherry blossoms came and went, and young green leaves began to fill the trees—with them the gossip gradually faded. Gohei returned to his home in Hirata Village. But one day I called him back.

"I have something to ask you, Gohei, something very important. I don't know what you'll think of this, but I'd like to buy that horse back, my husband's horse; I want to bring him back here. And I want you to train him."

I had thought of only two things in the days that had passed—of buying back the horse and sending Seikichi his money. That was all I could think about, awake or asleep. Gohei had never been one to say no, and now he was only too willing to see to my request.

"Do you mean you want me to train Seiryū? Just as I did before?"

"Yes. Oh, I know we've missed the Spring Races this year, but won't you work with Seiryū, train him till he's fit to win again—just like he did last year? And, if you do, well, I imagine it'll make the master very happy."

"Not once, not even in my dreams, did I ever hope to race for the master again! I don't know what to say, ma'am." Gohei looked up at me, his narrow eyes sparkling. "Well then, I'd best be hurrying off to Kudamatsu, tomorrow at the latest. But, tell me, ma'am," and then he looked staight into my face. "Would you have me buy Shirayuki, too?"

How do you suppose I felt hearing those words? I'd never once even dreamed of bringing Shirayuki back—not that horse. And yet, without so much as batting an eye I said, "By all means. Buy Shirayuki, too."

Shirayuki had done no wrong. And yet the memory of Miss Oyuki sitting astride that horse was burned deep into my heart. I certainly didn't want to buy that horse. No, I'd had no intention of doing so. And then I answered as I did. Why? Oh, I suppose in the briefest second it took me to answer, I realized that if I brought that horse back here and kept it as before, I'd be able to turn a bright face to Seikichi, off in his distant land, a face unclouded by shame. And Seikichi would be pleased. But even more than this, you see, I suppose I suddenly saw that it was jealousy that had turned my heart against the horse, and I was ashamed. After all, Miss Oyuki had stayed with my husband, as selfish as he was, and had followed him off to heaven knows where —not knowing if she'd ever come home again. How she must be suffering now! I had no right to think ill of her.

It wasn't long before Seiryū and Shirayuki were once again in our stable. Early every morning Gohei led them out, side by side, for their training.

"You'd have thought she'd at least let the horses go! Couldn't you say they were the real cause of that trouble after all! And here she's brought them back!"

Oh yes, I heard the gossip, and it didn't stop at that. I was told there were those who said, "Now what on earth would possess a woman to get into the horse business!" And then there'd be others who'd declare that it was Miss Oyuki that possessed me and made me act as I did. Yes, I heard the gossip, but I paid it no mind. Besides, I decided that if any spirit had possession of my heart it was Seikichi's and not Miss Oyuki's. But there wasn't a soul around who knew how I felt.

I could hardly believe the person I'd become. Why every morning I'd pull on a pair of striped cotton leggings—the likes of which I'd never even dreamed of touching before—and I'd go out to tend the horses. Can you just imagine! There I'd be alongside Gohei bathing the horses, and then I'd give them their feed. After sundown, once I'd put Seiryū in his stall, I'd sometimes hear the back gate creak and I'd think Seikichi was coming home. No, I knew it couldn't be him—but, oh, how my heart would leap at the thought! I guess I believed that by doing my best to care for Seiryū I was building a road to Seikichi—a road that would lead him back to me.

Well yes, Seikichi had gone off with Miss Oyuki and had left me far behind. Even so I never once doubted he'd return. That's right, no matter how he might travel, no matter how distant his heart might grow, I knew he'd never abandon his old home—not completely.

"It's such a shame about the young mistress!" I'd hear the neighbors say. "How many years has it been now since her husband ran off?"

"And do you know that every morning she still has the breakfast trays set out for those two! Now I've heard of a faithful wife setting out a tray for her husband when he's gone. But to do so for his mistress, too! Oh, a woman as selfless as all that just sets my teeth to itching!"

I heard what was said, but I couldn't believe it was me they were talking about. Surely they meant someone else. It was true, Seikichi had taken Miss Oyuki off with him to some unknown province. He had taken her, not me. But that was because he knew she'd be of more use to him. Really, who else could have possibly gone with him on such a dangerous journey? I had no way of knowing how they were faring in their distant land, but I did know one thing. If Miss Oyuki was with him, Seikichi was well cared for. Yes, while they were off so far away, I was safe in my own house with my boy Naokichi here at my side. Together, quietly, we were able to wait out the years and months for their return. I was lucky. And it was all thanks to Miss Oyuki.

18

Two years after Seikichi left, Seiryū beat the Tomita horse of Yanai and the Kawasaki horse of Tokuyama to win the Kikkō Cup at the Spring Races. The former lord of the town presented the award.

"What's the world coming to when His Lordship grants the Kikkō Cup to a murderer's horse!" There were those, I heard, who spoke out against us. But others rose to our defense.

"Why, that horse belongs to Mistress Nambu now!" they said. "And she's continued to tend to him out of respect for her husband—even though he went and left her. She's a good wife, and the Lord has recognized this."

No matter what was said, words alone could not describe the way I felt then. Seiryū, the horse I had cared for day and night, had won the Kikkō Cup. I felt I could understand for the first time all the hopes and dreams Seikichi had cherished for this horse—and my joy was all the dearer because I had cared for Seiryū with my very own hands.

When Seikichi had lived here, I had never once thought of seeing to the horses. Oh no, I had left those duties all to Gohei and Miss Oyuki. Looking back over it now, I can't but feel ashamed of myself. There I was, acting like a helpless little girl, knowing nothing of my own husband's feelings but treating him like some kind of stranger. What a fool I had been!

"Ma'am," Gohei called to me one day—it must have been just after the races. "I expect the master will have heard something of the Kikkō Cup. No matter how far away he may be, I'll wager he's heard of it."

"Yes, I think so, too," I said. "Surely he's heard."

Oh, I suppose it sounds farfetched, but I felt certain Seikichi knew everything that went on in this house. Yes, he knew even the smallest details of our life here as clearly as if he could see them.

His brother sent the money just as he had before without missing a day. I placed each envelope on the family altar until finally, when there wasn't room for even one more, I gathered them all up in a strongbox, which I tucked away in the Chinese chest in the storeroom. I was certain Seikichi knew of this, too. Morning and night Gohei and I talked of nothing else.

You wouldn't have thought the police would overlook a crime like Seikichi's; after all, he'd killed a man and then escaped from jail! But in two years' time the police hardly came around, and they surely didn't seem to be putting up any kind of investigation. I suppose I sound boastful, being such a simple woman myself, but, don't you see, it was all on account of Seikichi being the second son of the Takamori Yoshinos. That's just how well respected they were.

And then one warm day toward the end of spring, someone came by asking for me.

"Begging your pardon, but is this the Nambu house?"

I found an old man at the door dressed in the type of clothes day laborers from Kuga and Shigino Village wore. I didn't recall ever having seen him before.

"Yes, this is the Nambu residence," I said.

"Well then, you'd be the lady of the house. I've a message for you from Master Nambu." And he pulled a letter out from deep within the folds of his garment. I took it in my hands, still warm from where it had pressed against the old man's chest, and opened it, my fingers trembling.

At a glance I knew it was from Seikichi. There was no mistaking his thick brush strokes. He never rubbed the ink out properly, you see.

Osen, send the money with this old man.
Don't worry about me.
I heard about Seiryū.

That was all—just those three lines. When I came to Seiryū's name, tears filled my eyes, spilling over onto my cheeks. I called out to Gohei—my voice thick with emotion. "Look—look at this letter!" It was just as we'd discussed, just as I'd dreamed. The Kikkō Cup, the money I had saved—Seikichi knew about it all. I had been so certain he would, and learning now that I was right was somehow frightening.

"I'll take the money to him, ma'am," Gohei said. "It's a lot of money, old man, better let me go along." And with that he set about getting ready to leave.

The old man told us that Seikichi was hiding out with a theater troupe of sorts, along the shores of Ono Bay. He was staying in one of their makeshift cabins.

"Then he's only thirty leagues from here," I thought to myself. But I never once considered going to him. I knew I couldn't.

"Tell anyone who asks that I've gone off to Tabuse to look at a horse," Gohei said as he left. "And be sure to tell the womenfolk here the same."

As soon as Gohei and the old man had gone, I called for Oaki, and we walked down to the riding grounds behind the house. I took Naokichi in my arms—all he could think of then was flying kites—and I said to him,

"Naokichi, show your okaka how high you can make your kite fly. Go ahead. Oh my, just look at it!" The tail of the kite danced in the wind. As I watched it sail higher and higher over Myōgen Shrine, my eyes filled with tears.

19

It was evening when Gohei returned. He closed the heavy paper doors in the Clock Room and turned to me. "He hasn't changed a bit, ma'am. Not a bit. But then, I guess you could say he's even livelier now than before!" Gohei's narrow eyes sparkled as he spoke. He told me that Seikichi had let his short-cropped hair grow long and that he dressed it with a pomade of sorts. He also told me that Seikichi had taken to wearing European clothes of a type he'd never seen before. At a glance, he said, Seikichi looked like a completely different person. At any rate, no one would've guessed he'd killed a man and run away from jail, for he certainly didn't appear to be someone on the run.

Seikichi's cabin—there among the theater troupe shanties—was big, bigger than most. When Gohei arrived a crowd of men were gathered around playing cards on the wide wooden floor. It seemed they met there often, for Seikichi called them all by first name—didn't ever bother to be polite. I don't imagine he offended anyone though. It was just as it was when he had lived here.

As Gohei told it, Seikichi let out a big laugh and held his cards out for all to see. "Well, well, will you take a look at this! Just look at the hand I've got!" His face was beaming for all the world like a boy's.

"Master, won't you please check on the money here?" That's what Gohei said as he handed the strongbox over. But Seikichi just kept on playing without so much as glancing at the box.

When at last it came time for the theater to open for the evening, Gohei made ready to leave. Seikichi followed him out to the road. He threw a cape over his shoulders, one with a bright, shimmery lining, and led Gohei to a small tavern in the middle of town, where they had an early supper.

"So Seiryū beat that Tomita horse from Yanai! He's a strong horse, my Seiryū, a strong horse. But he's got even more to give. Run him in the Tamajima race this fall."

All they talked about was Seiryū it seems. Even when they parted, out in front of the tavern, Seikichi's last words to Gohei were about that horse.

"Keep an eye on Seiryū's legs, will you? Can't let him hurt those legs!" He didn't say anything else.

Miss Oyuki must have been off on an errand that day. Gohei didn't see her. But he did see a silk waterfall-pattern kimono hanging in Seikichi's cabin, there in the room with the wooden floor, and he was certain it was one Miss Oyuki used to wear.

"He certainly has luck on his side," Gohei said. "He might be far away, but there's not a thing for us to worry about. Not a thing."

I can still see Gohei, the way he looked when he said those words, his face set hard with hope.

The Seikichi Gohei described to me and the one I had pictured were completely different—really, as different as charcoal and snow. Why, I'd always thought that anybody running from the law would live a life of fear, frightened even by the sound of the wind. But here was Seikichi, without a care in the world, living all flash and show. I couldn't believe it. And yet, when I stopped to reflect, I realized that Seikichi had always lived a flashy life. Why should he change now? Even if he was in hiding, why shouldn't he live as he always had? It was the only way he knew. The more I thought of Seikichi and his wild, fearless nature, the more I found myself drawn to him.

"But he's bound to attract attention behaving that way, don't you think?" I heard myself say.

"Oh no, ma'am," Gohei answered with a laugh. "Don't you see, no one there knows who he is, and those European clothes he wears look so right, you'd think he was born with them on!"

Of course, we tried to hide the fact that we had heard from Seikichi, but Gohei and I were so excited afterward we nearly gave ourselves away. I told no one about it, not even Oaki, my closest companion. I spoke of him only to Gohei, and then only when no one else was around. I know this must sound strange, but I believed that when it came to Seikichi, Gohei and I were of completely the same mind. Really, it seemed that whatever I felt about Seikichi, he felt, too. And because of this, I wanted Gohei to be here with me in the house as much as possible.

With Master Yamashiro serving as go-between, I had Gohei marry Otoki, one of my maids. That would have been in the fall of the same year, I believe. Gohei used to spend the night here from time to time, and we always put him in the front room—the one set off from the entryway by a lattice rail. Yes, in these parts we call it the "shop-room." As soon as he and Otoki married, we set them up in the shop-room—gave them enough furniture to get them started on their married life.

Oh, I don't know . . . as I look back on it now, I wonder if I were wrong to bring Gohei into this house of women. He was a slender man, as fair as a woman, and had eyes that sparkled. Yes, altogether handsome, I'd say. Before I knew it Oyoshi was bickering with Otoki right and left. She'd been with us for a long, long time and had never been any trouble. But now here she was. She and Otoki were the same age, I guess . . . well. Even Oaki, who was much older, began complaining about Gohei. "Really ma'am! What do you suppose he finds so amusing in teasing our poor Oyoshi!"

But there was another way Gohei made his presence felt in this house without men. You see, we always put the horses first, no matter what happened. Even little Naokichi, not but four years old, would slip away from Oaki and come tagging along after Gohei and me while we saw to the horses. He followed us out to the stable, little thing that he was, and even down to the Omizo, where we'd wash the horses. He watched everything we did, and then he'd take to copying us—grabbing up a clump of straw in his tiny hands to rub along the horses' legs.

"Well I'll be! Looks like the boy here loves horses even more than the master!"

I suppose I should have been alarmed by what Gohei said. After all, if it were true we'd be in for trouble. But I couldn't help but be pleased by the idea.

I can't forget what happened next! The summer rains had just let up, and we were enjoying a clear, sunny day. Gohei was working with Seiryū in the back field while Naokichi watched.

"Little Master, shall I give you a ride?"

As soon as the words were out of his mouth, he snatched Naokichi up in his arms, leaped on the horse, and galloped off before I could stop them. Naokichi's yellow silk kimono snapped back and forth in the wind. I stared after them until they disappeared down the road to the Okinomachi levee.

"Oh no, ma'am," Gohei explained later, "I figured that if I galloped off like that, I'd scare him so bad he'd never want to ride again. But, you know, he wasn't scared a bit. Sat there snug against my thigh, he did . . . and him as little as he is. I must say I was impressed!"

From that day on Naokichi wouldn't even think of playing with his kites.

20

Naokichi began riding all by himself around the time he was seven, I believe. It had become our custom, as I've

said, to drop everything at the mere mention of the horses. Naokichi hardly
had to say a word before Gohei was up getting the boy set to ride. Yes, he
saw to everything. Naokichi wouldn't wear his kimono when he rode, but
had to have a pair of blue breeches, the kind that clung tight to his thighs. It
seems he wanted to dress like a jockey. Whenever I saw him like that, I never
paused to consider what the future might hold for him. No, all I could think
of then, in my heart of hearts, was how I wished Seikichi could see this boy
of his, all suited up in his riding attire. That's all.

Seikichi sent the messenger from time to time—usually once a year. But
sometimes he wouldn't come for two years running and then sometimes he'd
come four or five times a year. The old man always came, the one who
looked like a day laborer, and each time Gohei, carrying the money, would
go back with him. For the first five or six years, Seikichi hid out with that
theater troupe on Ono Bay. While he was there, I heard, he became the manager of sorts, seeing to all the theater business.

I didn't hear from Seikichi often, but I imagined he was still hiding out
with the theater troupe as he always had. And then, eight or nine years after
his escape, the old man came around again, and, as usual, Gohei, carrying the
money, headed off with him. They didn't go to the theater though. No, the
old man led Gohei to a tradehouse of sorts—humming with people—and
took him to a building out back where Seikichi was living on the second
floor. The tradehouse was a large one near the Kobe Port, I heard, and Miss
Oyuki had gotten herself a job nearby.

"Now you be sure to tell the mistress this," Miss Oyuki told Gohei with a
laugh. "She needn't fret over the master—not at all. No one here's so much
as pointed a finger at us."

Nearly ten years had passed since Miss Oyuki left, yet from what Gohei
said, she was just as plump as ever. She still wore her hair in that butterfly
knot she was so fond of, tying her heavy tresses up with a white paper cord.

I suppose when something happens over and over for a long, long time it
becomes a habit, and once it becomes a habit, well, it loses its power to
aggravate a person. That's the way it was with whatever Miss Oyuki said.
Hearing her tell me I needn't fret over my own husband ought to have made
me jealous, I suppose. But far from feeling jealous, I was grateful to her.
That's right, when I heard those words of hers I felt relieved. This is truly
the way I felt—but I don't imagine anyone else can understand it.

Seikichi had killed a man—a horrible crime—and yet he'd been able to hide
from the law for close to ten years. It was hard to believe. And the places he
chose to hide—a theater and a tradehouse—were busy places with people

coming and going, milling around with no one really knowing the other. In a crowd everyone's a stranger, I suppose. I wonder if this hadn't been one of Miss Oyuki's tricks for throwing the police off their trail. It certainly was about the only way Seikichi could've hidden—what with his love of show. Even so, ten years was a long time. I wondered if the authorities hadn't decided they'd just let him go—so long as he kept out of sight.

I was perplexed by it all, let me tell you, but what I found stranger still was Naokichi's love of horses. In the spring of his eighth year he began attending the school in town. But he refused to go if Gohei didn't see him there and back on the horse. One day I was summoned by the principal. "What's the meaning of allowing your boy to come to school on horseback! Nambu son though he is, I certainly don't think you should encourage such behavior."

It wasn't long before the whole town was humming with gossip. "Young Master Nambu's treading in his father's footsteps!" they'd say with a sneer. "Won't be long now before he'll be out there on that racetrack, too."

I asked the boy not to ride the horse, at least not to school. But he wouldn't listen to a thing I said.

"What's so bad about horses?" he demanded. "What difference does it make whether I walk to school on my own two feet, or ride there with my own two legs!"

My goodness—when he talked like that I could hardly believe he was a mere child of eight! But I did finally have him agree to ride only halfway to school, tie his horse just the other side of Garyō Bridge—there by the jailhouse—and then walk the rest of the way.

What's that? What did he wear to school? Well, you see, in a small country town like this children are supposed to wear a narrow-sleeved cotton kimono in a striped or splashed pattern with a three-length cotton sash dyed a dark blue. But now Naokichi would have none of it. He wanted some sort of European outfit in a check-patterned cloth. I certainly don't know where he ever laid eyes on such a thing, but all he talked about was this European garment. I had no idea what it was called, but it looked a good deal, he said, like those tight blue breeches he wore while riding.

"Gohei, you haven't been telling Naokichi stories about his father, now have you?" I tried to ascertain. But that Naokichi, my heavens, once he took a notion into his head, he would talk of nothing else. It wasn't long before I had the Kintoki, a little shop in town, order just such a suit of clothes from a tailor in Hiroshima.

When that box of clothes finally came, Naokichi was filled with such joy there's nothing to liken it to. His eyes narrowed as he laughed. That laughing face! Seikichi had laughed the same way that summer over ten years ago, when we had torn down the tangerine orchard for his riding grounds.

"It gives me a start, you know ma'am, but when the young master puts on that suit of his, he's the spitting image of his father! Sure do wish the master could catch a glimpse of him."

I glared sharply at Gohei. "Don't say such things! If I ever catch you so much as breathing a word of this to Naokichi, I'm afraid I'll have to let you go!"

I was alarmed. Gohei took care never to mention Seikichi to anyone—not even to his own wife. But then when he was with Naokichi, with this mere child, he'd let slip all kinds of things. "Your father'd never do that!" he'd say, or, "Your father always did it this way." If he'd say as much in front of me, I could only imagine what he'd say when he was alone with the boy. "Your father's got himself a suit of European clothes just like your little checked one," he might have said. And then, couldn't he have told the boy about his father's crime just as easily? Oh, I imagine Gohei hadn't meant to give the secret away. Perhaps he only wanted to explain the gossip Naokichi must have heard about town. I was certain something of the sort had happened, and oh, I worried how all those stories weighed on the boy's heart!

21

I first learned the news from Master Yamashiro; yes, it would have been the summer twelve years after Seikichi had left. That's right, the Obon dances were being held along the banks of the river. All my women set out to watch the festivities with Naokichi and Gohei, leaving me behind to tend the house. I was there alone when Master Yamashiro stopped by to call on me. He began talking about Seikichi's return.

"It won't be long before he'll be home, now. Just three more years. Why, I imagine he'll come back the Eve of Shiinō-sama. Yes, the Eve of Shiinō-sama three years from now you can expect to see him riding right up to the front door in a two-man rickshaw. 'I'm back!' he'll holler as loud as he can, and, oh my, won't there be a celebration!"

As I listened to Master Yamashiro, my heart . . . oh, what can I liken my feelings to then? It was as if a wave of hot water suddenly washed through my breast, filling me with warmth.

"Is it true? Is it really true?"

That's all I could manage to say and then the words caught in my throat.

That night when Naokichi returned from the riverbank with Gohei, I called him into the Clock Room. He'd been attending the Yokoyama Middle School since the spring. I gazed at him as he sat before me in his white, arrow-pattern kimono. His face was still sweet and boyish, but he held his shoulders square and his hands rested upon his knees in tight-clenched fists. Seikichi! Yes, he resembled his father so closely that for a minute I believed Seikichi was sitting before me!

"Naokichi, please listen to what I have to say. Your father . . . well, one spring twelve years ago—you were just three years old at the time—your father was in a fight and because of that fight, he stabbed a man, you see, and ever since he's been away on a long, long journey."

"I know. He killed the fellow."

"Oh no, Naokichi, he didn't kill the man. He didn't kill him. He stabbed the man, do you see? And later the man died on account of his wound. That's the way it happened."

"I already know all about it. He killed the man in a fight over Miss Oyuki. And if it ever happened to me, I'd do the same thing my father did, I'd kill the man!"

"What in heaven's name are you saying! Your father did not stab that man because he wanted to. He had no choice! The man came after him with a knife."

"Well, I'd have killed him whether he stabbed at me first or not."

His words sent a chill of terror through my heart—a terror so sharp I can still feel it.

When I told Naokichi that in three years his father's crime would be pardoned and that he would be able to come home, the boy just said, "I know. I've known it for some time now, Mother. Okamura told me—said it's written up in a law book somewhere."

Okamura was Naokichi's closest friend. I'd heard his older brother went to some fancy university up in Tokyo—I don't recall the name. But why, I wondered, had Naokichi not breathed a word of this to me—something as important as this! It broke my heart.

I looked into his face, which was drawn and solemn. "Darling, the reason I never mentioned any of this to you until today. . . ."

"You needn't bother now," Naokichi interrupted. "But listen. By the time Father gets home, I'm going to be a jockey—a real race jockey. Gohei's said so himself. Says I'm the fastest around, except for him, that is."

As Naokichi spoke he grew more and more excited until he seemed ready to burst with joy. I gazed into his face. He was laughing, and his eyes were narrowed into tiny lines. My heart froze at the sight.

Yes, as I reflect on it now, I see that it had been wrong to bring Gohei into this house. But then, Gohei wasn't the one to blame. It had been me, hadn't it? I had been the one who turned all my attention to the horses and to them alone. I was the one to blame.

But oh, for the two or three years that followed, it seemed we'd all taken leave of our senses—every member of the household. Naokichi had never been one to study at home—though I heard he did well in school. But as soon as he was home, he'd fling his satchel of books down on the entry step and race straight away to the riding field out back.

"Gohei! Gohei!"

Day in and day out I could hear him calling out to Gohei. Once in a while they'd ride together to the old castle moat. I was told that it was during one of those rides that Naokichi turned to Gohei and asked, "How about letting me ride for you in the Spring Races next year? Come on, how about it?"

Gohei met Seikichi once every two years or so. Couldn't he have mentioned Naokichi to him on one of his trips? He wouldn't have done so purposely, I imagine, but mightn't he have remarked on the boy's love of horses?

Gohei never thought of Seikichi as a murderer hiding out from the law. Heavens! I don't imagine the thought ever crossed his mind. No, Seikichi was his master, and I suppose Gohei thought of him as a truly remarkable man, born under a lucky star. And Gohei was not the only one to feel this way. Every member of this household thought of Seikichi as a wonderful hero. Okaka had passed these feelings along to me, and now Gohei, I suppose, was passing them down to my son.

22

Oh yes, the horses. . . . Well, Seikichi was gone for fifteen years or so—a long time anyway—and during that time we traded Seiryū and Shirayuki in on other horses. Oh, we traded horses any number of times. But each time we'd give the horse a name with either "sei" or "shira" in it. No, not the same names exactly, but Seidama—"Blue Jewel," you see, or Seiko—"Blue Tiger." Or now if the horse was white we'd call it Shiraume—"White Plum," or Shirabikari—"White Light." Once we had as many as three or four horses. My goodness but the stable was full! Those nights I'd drift off to sleep to the tune of hooves stamping softly. Really, I don't recall ever feeling as content as I did then.

"Looks like Mistress Nambu has turned into a real horsewoman!"

I knew this is what others were saying now, but I didn't think they meant any harm by it. To tell the truth, the only reason I did what I did was because I believed Gohei would tell Seikichi about it one day.

I won't forget it—that fourteenth spring after Seikichi's disappearance. Gohei had been in the habit of rising early every morning to exercise the horses. He'd been doing this for the last several years. But now he refused to enter any of the races hereabouts. The autumn before Seiko, the horse he was riding at the Tenjin Festival Race in Kudamatsu, had lost to the Kishino horse from Tamajima. Well, Gohei blamed himself. "Never thought it'd happen to me!" he said, and later he confided that his strength had failed, that he was now just too old to race. "Really ma'am," he said, "you've got to find yourself a younger jockey. The Nambu name is at stake!"

I might as well tell you I was suspicious of his motives. Hadn't Gohei cooked all this up just so I'd have to make my son his replacement? But Naokichi was my only son; he was the heir to the Nambu name. What's more, he was still just a schoolboy. Could I possibly allow him to play the role of a race jockey? How the gossip would swirl if I did! And yet, and yet . . . I suddenly found myself thinking of how happy this would make Seikichi, and, foolish as it was, I could think of nothing else.

I guess it was toward the end of February when we finally decided to let Naokichi enter the Spring Races. Most schools in these parts had just begun the examination period, but Naokichi didn't much care. He'd get up early every morning for a quick ride, and, as soon as he'd gotten home from school, he'd be on the horse again, galloping madly through the back field until the sun went down.

Gohei would run after him. "You're going to ride that horse to death, Master Nao. Why don't you give him a rest?" He'd plead as he tried to catch his breath.

"Oh? Well don't forget who lost the race last year!" Naokichi would snarl. "But this year we have us a different jockey, don't we!" And with that he'd spur his horse off toward the moat, leaving Gohei far behind. No one could stop Naokichi now, not when he was like that.

On the day of the Spring Races Gohei went with Naokichi to the castle grounds. I stayed behind in the house with the maids. It was spring vacation, I knew, and the schools were closed—but even so, it didn't seem right to be making too big a fuss over the race. I expect it was around two in the afternoon when a messenger from the Mikkazukirō came bursting into the house all out of breath. "He won!" he exclaimed between gasps. "Young Master Nao beat the Hatakeyama horse of Shigino Village!"

"Oh dear, we're in for it now!" I murmured. But even as I spoke, a picture of Naokichi sitting astride his horse floated before my eyes and my heart was bathed in a rush of warmth.

The Hatakeyama horse was not that strong, Gohei told me later, and beating it wasn't much of a win. But this was Naokichi's first race, after all. Wasn't any reason for him to be setting his sights too high.

Naokichi knew nothing of this, of course, and for him the victory was sweet. Long after he came back from the race grounds, he kept his face pressed to Seiko's neck. I thought perhaps he was crying.

Well, of course, I tried to keep the celebrations from getting out of hand. Master Yamashiro was the first to come around with his congratulations. "Well, well, looks like we've got us something to boast about until the master comes back! Good work, boy!" He was soon followed by that mountain of prizes and all those gift announcements. And then into the midst of it all came the lacquer sake cask from the Mikkazukirō. That very same cask. Suddenly I was reminded of that first horse race fifteen years ago when our Seiryū beat the Nōtoya horse, Tatsumaki. All the confusion and excitement flashed before my eyes.

Naokichi's school began again in April. On the second day his teacher, Mr. Kajimura, sent for me. "We had a meeting yesterday," he began. "Your son was brought up for discussion, and we all agreed that we simply cannot permit any student of ours to take part in horse racing. See that it doesn't happen again."

The next day when Naokichi came home from school he was red with anger. "I quit school, Mother!" he told me. "Who the hell thinks he can tell me not to race!" Well, I went straight to Master Yamashiro and asked him to go to the school for me, to try to set things right. But nothing came of it, and soon the whole town knew what had happened.

"Did you hear? Young Master Nambu's quit school and is bent on becoming a real race jockey!"

And while the gossip swirled, I hadn't the slightest idea what I should do.

23

Yes, when Naokichi quit school he was in the spring of his sixteenth year. He set out every morning with Gohei to train. When I looked at my son—at this boy of mine so determined to be a race jockey—my heart was gripped by a tangle of feelings. On the one hand, I was proud of Naokichi, and I wished for the world that Seikichi could see him. But on the other, I was terrified, yes terrified lest he was heading down the wrong path to a future no one could know. I was so troubled I could not sleep at night.

It's just that the boy so resembled his father. Really, it was frightening. Listening to him in the back field calling out to Gohei, I could swear it was Seikichi. Everything about him was just like his father—his size, the way he dressed, everything. Well, of course, Naokichi purposely tried to imitate race jockeys and wore whatever they would wear. But even his hands, as he tied the cords to his black silk vest, moved just as his father's had.

I tell you, every time I caught sight of Naokichi, I'd find myself thanking the gods. "It's to calm this pitiful heart of mine that you have blessed me with this glimpse of Seikichi," I'd say. Over those fifteen long years, whenever I heard the town gossip, or began to feel jealous of Miss Oyuki, I would remind myself, "Oh, but you have Naokichi!" And my sorrow would fade away like foam on the waves.

Oh yes! There wasn't a soul around who didn't believe Seikichi'd come home on the Eve of Shiinō-sama next spring. But even so, we set about preparing for the day in secret. I knew that Seikichi had taken to wearing European clothes, but I thought he might like to change into a Japanese kimono when he wanted to relax at home. So I pulled out his old kimono, the one he'd always worn when he was here, and began to restitch it. We changed the tatami mats in every room and did all kinds of chores. Seeing as how it was the end of the year, it looked as if we were just getting the house ready for the New Year's celebrations. Why, we fixed the bath, trimmed the trees and bushes in the garden, and, when we repaired the riding grounds, even Naokichi did what he could to help.

I didn't say a word to anyone but went to the storeroom and took out those three bedding sets of matching Gunnai-silk. I changed the covers and restuffed the quilts, and then, day after day I stretched them out on the drying boards to air. Every time I saw them there—those brightly colored check-pattern quilts—glittering, glittering in the sun, I would catch myself thinking that soon, yes, they would be laid out together again, the three of them side by side. . . . But I was too busy to linger over these thoughts. I would be off to another chore, my heart pounding with excitement. I didn't know to be afraid.

That morning it was warm and hazy. The whole household was busy with what would seem to be festival preparations. Master Yamashiro was here, too. Yes, he came by around sunset with a cask of sake. And the Mikkazu-kirō sent around a three-tiered lacquer box full of treats. Everything seemed to be in perfect order—but there was one last thing that weighed on my heart. No word had come from Takamori. The Tōkai Delivery had come by that morning, but they hadn't brought any special messages, or congratulatory gift. I suppose Seikichi's brother—as staunch as he was—wouldn't think it proper to celebrate the return of a criminal. Well, he might have his doubts, but it seemed even the townsfolk were convinced Seikichi'd be back before the night was over. As I waited I listened to the sound of the wind blowing over the Omizo. How it made my heart tremble!

"Mark my word, ma'am. He'll come back just as I said he would." Master Yamashiro assured me. "Yes, he'll come riding in a two-man rickshaw—right up to the front door—and he'll be shouting all the way down the road!"

"Oh, I hope not." I replied. "I'm afraid of what might happen if he were to create such a stir. I hope he'll wait until deep in the night and then slip back quietly."

"Oh now, don't you worry, he's too clever to go and do something foolish!" Master Yamashiro laughed.

Later, when I reflected on it, I realized that the man we awaited was not a murderer returned from exile, but a hero—yes, a hero coming home in triumph. At least that's the way we all seemed to feel.

I had done my very best to keep the house just as it had been when Seikichi left fifteen years ago. Nothing had changed. Everything was as it had been that night. The festival drums were pounding as they had then. And, oh yes, as I recall the lion dancers had been hesitant to come to our house that night —seeing as how we were still mourning Okaka's death. But tonight they came and went one right after the other in such a tumble I was certain they too knew of Seikichi's return.

"He's back."

Master Yamashiro got to his feet, and we all followed. He opened the shōji screens in the Clock Room. I couldn't see anything, but I could hear the sound of someone softly opening the back gate by the path along the river. And then I heard him call. "Gohei! Gohei!" he cried. "Bring a candle. Hey, I've come back, Gohei!"

A candle! He wants a candle! We all scrambled about for a candle before dashing out to meet him. In the dim, flickering light I could see Seikichi and Miss Oyuki standing in the doorway of the stable.

"Well, well, this must be Seiko!" Seikichi laughed. "For a minute there I mistook him for Seiryū!" He brought his face up alongside the horse's head, and Seiko twitched his ears and nudged Seikichi fondly, as if he had known him all his life.

It seemed to me that Seikichi was more impressed with the greeting this horse had given him than he was with the people who had turned out to see him home. He didn't have so much as a word of thanks for those who had waited half the night to welcome him. But now, you know, I couldn't bring myself to resent him for it. Instead I felt a joy welling up inside me. It was just as if all those months and years had disappeared in one brief second.

"Looks like you've been able to get on without me, ma'am."

"Welcome back, Miss Oyuki," I said, and then I turned to the boy. "Greet your father, Naokichi."

I hadn't meant to say that, not really. But then I saw Naokichi standing right before Miss Oyuki and staring at her like he was being drawn into her.

Miss Oyuki was wearing her yellow silk kimono with the lavender-dappled undercollar. Her hair looked as though it had just been dressed. Really, she looked like she always had—as if she had never left. No, neither of them looked like travelers come back from a long and distant journey.

"Hello, Naokichi," Seikichi said. "I hear you beat the Hatakeyama horse last year. Well, that's just fine, but how would you like your old man to teach you a thing or two about riding?"

Naokichi continued to stare at Miss Oyuki like he was in a trance. Oh, I don't know. I suppose he didn't really stare at her that long. It was probably no more than the briefest glance, and yet it troubled me.

"Come along now. Into the bath with you both! And let's get you out of those awful clothes!" Master Yamashiro spoke playfully, but Seikichi looked him straight in the eye. "You mean these?" he said. "Thanks to these 'awful clothes' I was able to hide as I did, I'll have you know. And, I'm just as grateful to this worn-out tote bag, too!"

I still remember the way we carried on that night. The feasting and drinking in the Clock Room lasted until dawn—and all of it made to look like a party for the Eve of Shiinō-sama. No one thought to ask whether this was the proper way to greet a man who'd killed another and had only just returned from years of hiding. No one, that is, who belonged to this household.

24

And then the next day, after Seikichi and Miss Oyuki had finished a late breakfast, they hired two rickshaws and set out to pay their respects to various people. Earlier that morning Miss

Oyuki had called in a hairdresser—not the one she used to call but a woman named Okome from Sashimono-chō. While the woman dressed her hair, Miss Oyuki gave her all kinds of instructions on how it was to be done, telling her this and that about the latest fashions in the Kamigata.

The Shiinō-sama Festival was well underway now, and the streets were full of floats pushing this way and that, carrying drum players and geisha dancers. I was certain Seikichi and Miss Oyuki would attract attention if they were to ride out right in the midst of it, but they set out together just the same.

Miss Oyuki told me about it later. She said that they stopped first at the jailhouse. That's right, they had their rickshaws pull up out front, and they marched in and greeted all the officers—even went right up to the chief of police! After that they spent the rest of the day going around to all the geisha houses and taverns where they used to spend time. They stopped by the shops of those who supported the races, and they visited all the other horse owners hereabouts.

Oh yes . . . in the days following the festival, word got out that Seikichi was back and all sorts of people came by to celebrate. Why, I hardly saw Miss Oyuki when she didn't have her hands full of gifts.

"Miss Oyuki! Miss Oyuki!" The house rang with her name. Up until the very day before, it had been my name they'd called. I thought I was dreaming. Oh, I don't expect anyone did it on purpose. And then I found that Naokichi, too, had taken to following Miss Oyuki around.

But . . . I didn't mind. I had managed the household for fifteen years, and now, suddenly, everything was just as it had been before Seikichi left. Really, when I stopped to reflect, I realized that I had been a servant who tends house during the master's absence. Yes, that had been my role, hadn't it? But I didn't feel the least bit angry. Miss Oyuki was here now, and that meant I could once again be that helpless little girl. I felt as if a heavy burden had been lifted from my shoulders.

It may have been my fancy, but it seemed that the Spring Races this year were attracting even more attention than usual. Oh, of course, by then the gossip of Seikichi's return, and rumors of the training he was giving his own son had spread throughout the town and well beyond.

Not even ten days were left before the races. The house was in an uproar. Seikichi and the boy worked furiously. They didn't train in the field behind the house, but raced off along the castle moat. Naokichi would strike out first on Seiko, and Seikichi would follow on Shiraume. Gohei ran along behind them, trying hard to keep up. On their way they'd pass right in front of the Yokoyama Middle School, often just as the students were heading

home. But Naokichi never once acted like a boy expelled from school. Far
from it, he'd sit astride his horse, proud as could be in his blue silk jacket.
Why, from the way he behaved, you'd think no one else in the world mattered! And what was worse, his own father acted like he'd never even heard
of Naokichi's trouble.

That's right. You see, there weren't but twenty paces between the racetrack and the school. Every spring when the races were held the area was
always full of people. But I'd never seen as many as I saw then. And all
around me I could see the black uniforms of the middle school students scattered in among the other spectators like so many parched beans.

"Listen, Nao, dear, you just be calm." Leaning in close to the boy, Miss
Oyuki said what she could to encourage him. "You've got to set your sights
on the Nonomiya horse of Otake, and now, he's nothing like that Hatakeyama horse you beat last year. But you just keep telling yourself you
can win!"

Naokichi had been expelled from school the year before, and now all his
old classmates were here to watch him race. I was afraid they'd make him
nervous, but not Naokichi—no, he hardly noticed them at all. Truly, I
couldn't understand what Miss Oyuki saw in a boy like Naokichi—as willful
as he was—but there she was fussing over him just the same, like he was her
own flesh and blood. I suppose she did it to catch Seikichi's attention.

The Nonomiyas of Ōtake were so wealthy they were said to be second
only to the Takamori Yoshinos. Hachiman Kabuto, their horse, had won the
championships for three years running—last year, the year before, and the
year before that. Oh, he was famous, and I felt just placing second or even
third to a horse like that was honor enough.

It was already two o'clock in the afternoon when they finally got around
to the seventh race. Seiko and Hachiman Kabuto had barely lined up bit to
bit when the gun sounded and they leaped forward. "Go Seiko!" "Go
Hachiman!" People began calling out for their favorites. Seiko was on the
outside the first time around the track, and he slowly began to slip back.
Naokichi leaned down low on the horse's neck. Just as he did the sky opened
up in a thundershower. Rain poured down in huge round drops. Naokichi's
classmates couldn't have remembered what had happened here sixteen years
ago, but there were plenty of others who could. The sky had been blue, they
would recall; and it was blue this time, too, just as blue as a picture, when all
of a sudden those dark clouds gathered, sending rain streaking down like
blades of bamboo grass. Panic took those along the track. And those outside
the curtains as well, the flower-viewers. They all began to throw scarves over
their heads as they dashed for cover. And then a shout went up among the

crowd, but it wasn't on account of the rain. No, when I turned to look I saw the horses coming around the track for the final stretch and . . . could it be? Seiko was in the lead!

If it hadn't been for the rain and all the excitement it caused would Seiko have won? But no, it wasn't the rain that had earned the victory—it was the jockey, Naokichi.

Naokichi slid down off the horse's back and stood there in the rain, his hands over his face. Was he crying? Seikichi leaped up from his seat in the race-master's box and Miss Oyuki dashed out from her place among the spectators. They both reached Naokichi at the same time. Miss Oyuki threw her arms around the boy's neck, and they clutched one another tightly—their hair and clothing drenched with rain. I watched them, but in my mind I saw Seikichi taking Miss Oyuki in his arms as he had done sixteen years ago— when she had thrown herself out on the racetrack.

"Oyuki's gone and fallen for Naokichi!" Seikichi teased later. We were all home then, celebrating.

"That's right. I'm in love. But who couldn't help but love the man who beat the Nonomiya horse!" Miss Oyuki flung her arms around Naokichi for all to see—just as she had at the racetrack. Perhaps it was the sake, I told myself.

"Well, well, Oyuki, you've got yourself two men now!" Seikichi laughed. "Come here, Naokichi. You're a grown man now, so have a drink. Here, I'll pour it."

And so, you see, from that night on Naokichi learned to drink as well.

25

It happened one evening ten days or more after the races. Master Yamashiro arranged a party for Seikichi at the Mikkazukirō to celebrate his return. He invited all kinds of people; all the horse owners hereabouts, everyone. The man from Kudamatsu—the one who had helped Seikichi escape—was there, I heard. Miss Oyuki asked that they celebrate Naokichi's victory, and he was invited as well.

That evening Seikichi was in a fine mood. He dressed in an indigo silk kimono with a sash of an iron-arrow design, and, while the maids fussed over him, he climbed into his rickshaw. "Hurry home!" I called after them as I saw them out the door. I would never have dreamed this would be the last time I'd see his face so full of life.

The party at the Mikkazukirō was merrier than words could describe, from what I heard. Oh, I don't suppose it was right to host a party for a man just out of hiding, but even so I was nearly giddy with the joy of it all.

Seikichi and Miss Oyuki had set out in a festive mood, and I was told they were already well into the midst of the party when someone called out, "Master Nambu! Join in the dance—you, too, Miss Oyuki!" Yes, you see, a good many geishas had gathered in the room to dance. Well, Seikichi got up and joined the group. They danced out of the room and down the hall, but when they got to the main staircase, the one that leads to the front door, Seikichi's legs gave way and he tumbled to the floor, coughing blood as he fell.

"Master!"

"Call a doctor!" someone shouted.

Upstairs and below everyone clamored to help. They lifted Seikichi up and carried him to the hospital in the Daimyō Koji, not but a quarter mile away.

By the time I heard the news and reached the hospital myself it was well past midnight. Master Yamashiro was standing in the hallway arguing with a young doctor. "Now look here! You have to move him to another room! He's in the room that man was in—why, it's the very same room!" The minute Master Yamashiro caught sight of me, he hurried to my side.

"And that's not all. I'll have you know that he coughed blood in the exact same spot where he stabbed that man fifteen years ago and spilt his blood. That's right, there on the stairway of the Mikkazukirō! And listen, folks are saying all kinds of things. They're saying it's the wrath of that man come back to haunt him. 'Yes, a vengeful spirit is something to fear,' they say, and I don't think I'll put up with another word!"

Seikichi was sleeping, his face pale. So this was the room where that man had lain fifteen years ago. Could there really be anyone left who remembered? The hospital director was no longer here. He'd been replaced by a younger doctor. No, no one here knew anything of those events so long ago. They put Seikichi in this room, they said, because it was the only empty one. The doctor told me Seikichi should be left to rest quietly for several days, but that he ought to be moved to a hospital in Hiroshima before long. The doctor there would know what kind of surgery to perform, he said. But, whatever I did, I was not to delay.

"Osen is here," I whispered. Seikichi opened his eyes slightly and smiled. The lamp at his bedside glowed dimly. Perhaps that was why . . . he looked like a completely different person. I gazed at his head on the pillow and discovered for the first time white strands scattered through his tousled hair.

While I was there Miss Oyuki and Master Yamashiro continued to argue with the doctor. At last they got their way and a patient across the hall was asked to move.

"We've got a new room for you! A nice big room!" Miss Oyuki announced.

"No," Seikichi said. "This room's fine." And he wouldn't move.

I wondered if the man who died here fifteen years ago had left behind his vengeful spirit, but I didn't believe it. No, I felt that if I turned to that man now and prayed to him with all my heart to help Seikichi, yes, to make him better, I was sure he'd hear my prayer.

Seikichi stayed the night in the room, and then dawn broke. Miss Oyuki was furious. She said people were going to be coming by to call on him. They'd see him in that very room, and they'd start poking around for some new gossip about what happened so long ago. I didn't think there was need to worry, though. After all, weren't we the only ones left who knew what had taken place in that room fifteen years ago? Soon after daybreak, geishas dressed in their everyday kimonos began to stream noisily into Seikichi's room with their pretty little attendants. All was so lively and bright, whatever had happened the night before seemed like a faraway dream.

It was agreed two days later that Seikichi would go to a hospital in Hiroshima. "I'm going, too, Mother," Naokichi announced out of the blue. We had already decided that Miss Oyuki would accompany Seikichi to Hiroshima, to look after him, you see. But why shouldn't his own son be with him as well? Oh, there was nothing wrong with it, of course, and yet I felt a shadow fall over my heart. How can I possibly explain it? He would be alone with her, morning and night—just the two of them looking after Seikichi. The thought weighed on me.

The day Seikichi was to leave for Hiroshima I was busy from early morning getting his things ready. I folded his kimonos one by one and placed them in his traveling case. I packed a dress kimono, one he could wear home on the train once he'd been cured. And I chose an everyday kimono for him, too. "Yes, this is the one I restitched for him," I thought to myself, "hoping he'd wear it once he returned from hiding." And then I remembered that it was the very one Okaka had sewn for him, pouring her heart into every stitch.

Seikichi had only just returned! How was it he'd be leaving again so soon? I opened the shōji in the Clock Room and peered outside. Everything was just as it had been when I had waited here alone for him. Everything was just as it was, and yet it was different. Somehow it was all empty now. The stable, the riding grounds, even the levee down at Okinomachi that he had only just crossed—they were all the same, and yet they were empty.

It was clear that morning and already as warm as summer. Seikichi said that the pains in his stomach had lessened somewhat. We all went by rick-shaw from the hospital to the station, even though it wasn't that far.

"Well, don't we look like a traveling show!" Seikichi joked. He seemed his old self again.

The train came. Naokichi and Miss Oyuki stood on either side of Seikichi and, putting their arms around him, helped him climb the station stairs. It was all as if they'd planned it in advance. Suddenly my heart was stabbed with the memory of those two in each other's arms at the racetrack, the rain streaking down like bamboo grass.

Miss Oyuki had always seen to Seikichi's needs. There wasn't anything unusual about her doing so now. And, of course, it was only natural for a son to want to help his father. Then why was it that the sight of them walking off together threw my heart into such a flutter?

"I'll bring you something nice to eat when I visit," I called to them as I clung to the window of the train. "And I'll see to it that Seiko gets plenty of exercise while you're away."

26

The house fell silent after Seikichi left—like a flame that's suddenly snuffed out. I looked after the horses with Gohei, just as before. But I was only going through the motions—hardly aware of what I was doing.

Master Yamashiro went to Hiroshima now and again to look in on Seikichi. The old woman from the Mikkazukirō went, too, from time to time. I didn't need to go but once or twice every ten days or so to bring Seikichi a change of clothes or whatever he might be needing. Sometimes he'd be feeling fine, but other times he wouldn't. With the rainy season he took a turn for the worse.

"Naokichi, why don't you come home for a bit?" I asked on one of my visits. "It gives Miss Oyuki more work to have you around like this."

But Seikichi wouldn't hear of it. "No. Naokichi needs to be here with Oyuki. Don't you, boy?"

"But really, how can you? . . ." I began, and then Miss Oyuki inter-rupted.

"His father's gone and said as much, ma'am. Looks as though the boy's got permission!" She laughed slyly, like a girl playing tricks.

The room was sweltering. Seikichi was lying on his back, and I could see a smile spread slowly over his wasted cheeks. I'll never forget that smile. He was a father! Shouldn't he have scolded his son for disobeying me? And, as a man, shouldn't he have rebuked Miss Oyuki for her arrogance? But no, not Seikichi. No, he loved to nettle others. I wonder now if he didn't say what he said on purpose—just to tease me.

And so, Naokichi stayed on in the hospital with Miss Oyuki. He didn't leave until Seikichi was sent home in February of the following year—his illness still not cured. Oh, I suppose it would seem only natural for a son to want to stay on with his father—especially when he was so sick. But Naokichi had loved those horses to the point of madness. How was it, I wondered, that he could forget them now so completely—not even coming home once in half a year's time?

"Young Master Nao certainly is devoted to his father, staying with him as he does," Master Yamashiro remarked once. "But then I guess it's to be expected, seeing as how the boy never knew his papa up to now." Had he meant to attack me with these words? The thought left me chilled to the bone.

It was a cold winter morning around the first of February when Seikichi returned from Hiroshima. Later I learned that the doctors had advised him to wait for the cold spell to pass. Seikichi's cheeks were hollow, and he was wasted to skin and bones. I could hardly believe he was the same man I had seen only shortly before—freshly returned from his long rambles and bursting with life. We put him straight to bed—no, not in the back room where the three of us had always slept, but in the Clock Room. Here he could look out over the garden pond. When night fell Miss Oyuki and Naokichi stretched out on either side of him to sleep. He rarely called out for Miss Oyuki anymore, but he would turn his head slowly and search the room for her, his sunken eyes glittering.

Where was my place in all of this? The question haunted me. "Darling, Osen is here." I whispered in my heart as I knelt at his feet. And, as I massaged his legs—oh, but the tears would stream down my cheeks, big round tears. I wondered what he was thinking, now that his life was at its end, and I wanted to ask him. I didn't care how it might rend my heart, I wanted to do whatever I could to help him see his final wish. No, I didn't care how wrong it might have seemed.

"Oh my heavens, the master's gone!" I heard Oaki scream.

That morning a heavy snow had fallen. Perhaps that was why, I don't know, but no one was in the Clock Room with Seikichi. The last time I had looked in on him he had been resting quietly, but then, without saying a word, he must have crawled out to the road, for that is where we found him, still in his night clothes.

"Look! The master!" People were shouting all around me, stumbling through the snow to reach him. He struggled to the middle of the road and then, too tired to go further, glared back at us. "Don't come any closer!" he shouted.

Where on earth had he found the strength to crawl as far as he had! His sash was loose, his nightclothes nearly open, and his bare legs, as thin as withered tree limbs, lay stretched out over the snow. There was no one else to be seen on the road.

"Come back inside!" I pleaded as I ran after him. "Please, come in the house!"

"What the hell are you doing!" Miss Oyuki screamed at him. "You get in here this minute. Gohei, go out there and get the master. Pick him up and carry him back in."

"Don't come any closer! I'll cut anyone who tries!"

Seikichi was waving something now—something shiny. A knife! Where he'd gotten it I don't know.

"Look out!" someone cried.

Seikichi began to cough blood, large bursts of blood, there in the snow. "I'll cut you!" he cried again, but as he tried to pull himself up, Naokichi sprang on him, wresting the knife away.

It was over in an instant. I watched Gohei carry Seikichi back into the Clock Room. Seikichi dangled limply from his arms.

"Oaki! Get a rake quick and smooth over the snow there in the road," Miss Oyuki cried. "Cover it up!"

I threw myself over Seikichi's body. "Tell me!" I begged over and over. "Tell me what you would have me do!"

27

Two days later Seikichi died without uttering a word. It was just as if his life had been sucked away.

It was still snowing the day of the funeral. All morning long I sat by Seikichi's bed, and then it was past noon.

"Mistress Yoshino of Takamori is approaching, ma'am," Gohei stepped in to tell me. Yes, Seikichi's sister-in-law had come down for the funeral with a press of servants. But as soon as word got out that the Mistress of the Yoshino House was in sight, people spilled out onto the road to catch a glimpse. I heard the shouts go up outside, "Make way for Mistress Yoshino! Make way!" and the crowds were pushed to either side to let her through.

When Seikichi had been in hiding, I had taken Naokichi with me to Taka-mori once or twice to pay our respects to the Yoshino family, and I could remember Mistress Yoshino quite well. But now, here she was sitting before me in my own house.

"In this, your time of sorrow. . . ."

Yes, that's what she said, and then she went on, "My husband has asked that I convey his heartfelt apologies for the many hardships you have suffered these long years."

I collapsed in tears when I heard her words, unable to hold back the flood of emotion any longer. Hardships? I hadn't thought I had suffered. And then, when I heard what she said, it suddenly struck me that these hardships, yes what she had called "hardships," would disappear from my life forever now. And what would become of me! I felt like a cast-off skin.

The funeral procession set out around three o'clock, as I recall. Oaki began helping me dress in the white silk kimono we had prepared the night before. It was cold that day. Round wooden braziers had been lit and placed in every room. Miss Oyuki was beside me; she was also being dressed in a kimono of pure white silk. Yes, you see, I had heard that when a woman wears the white hood and white kimono, she shows the world she has promised never to serve another man. Maybe it wasn't the usual way of things, but I was certain the townsfolk would think it only proper when they caught sight of both Miss Oyuki and me wearing the white. Besides, what good would it do for me to start challenging Miss Oyuki now—especially now?

"My, what a handsome man he's become!" Miss Oyuki cooed as she caught a glimpse of Naokichi. "Would you just look at Young Master Nao —all dressed up in his *haori* and *hakama!*"

My sister-in-law entered the room just then. "You!" she glared at Miss Oyuki. "You ought to be wearing a black kimono, one with the family crest. You've no business wearing white. Take it off!" I'd never heard her speak so harshly.

"Oh now, surely you don't mean this kimono!" Miss Oyuki gave a throaty laugh. "I can't take it off. No, I've my reasons for wearing it." That's what she said. She didn't even bat an eye—just stood where she was, gazing at herself in the mirror.

No one else was in the room at the time, just the maids—and then it was all over. I understood why Mistress Yoshino said what she said. I knew she only meant to protect me. But she was wrong. She was wrong about the kimono and that was all. Yes—I knew that there would be no better way to honor Seikichi than to have Miss Oyuki wear white. And do you know when it was I came to realize this? When I chanced to recall that day of heavy snow, the day Seikichi crawled out to the road. Naokichi ran up behind him and without so much as a word fell upon his father, wresting the knife away. And when he did—that look in his eyes! Oh, it was that look I remembered. Was that the sort of look a son gave his father, the father he had lovingly awaited all those long, long years? Those were frightful eyes!

No, today of all days Miss Oyuki would wear white. I did not care what my sister-in-law said, Miss Oyuki must wear white!

The sound of the sutras filled the valley, echoing all the way to the peak of Mount Odaishi, or so I imagined. Someone told me later that after the funeral procession left our house, it wound all the way to the Norimoto graveyard in one unbroken line. We left the road and headed along the Omizo, following the narrow footpath up into the graveyard—I don't suppose we traveled more than three hundred yards in all. Snow was still falling, soft and powdery. We climbed the frozen paths in sandals made of straw.

This was the path, wasn't it? The very path Seikichi had taken sixteen years ago when he fled on horseback with Miss Oyuki. How heavy his heart must have been then, and he unable to speak a word of it to me! Now he was to take this path again.

My family plot is up there on the crest of the hill where the view of the valley below is best. My ancestors' graves are lined one right after the other, and Okaka's is at the very end. They placed Seikichi's casket in the ground next to her. One by one we took up handfuls of freshly turned earth—earth that had earlier been blanketed with snow—and dropped them down on the casket.

"Osen." I was certain I heard Okaka calling out to me. "I'll take care of Sei now. He belongs to us—to no one but you and me."

Yes. The snow was still falling, but even so the sun was streaming softly through the clouds. I looked down at the others climbing slowly through the grove of withered trees. They were like figures in a shadow play—figures in a dream. And then it happened. There, above the trees, I saw Seikichi, his eyes pulled into lines of laughter. I gasped and, reaching out to the sky, collapsed in the snow.

THIS POWDER BOX

I

This powder box is not ornamented in any way. It is just a plain silver box. Well, it used to be silver. At some point the silver wore away to reveal the nickel underneath. To be more specific then, it is just an old nickel box, and it hardly seems appropriate to use it as a powder case. But that is, after all, what it is.

How did I feel the first time I used this powder box? I don't remember. It was some thirty years ago—the first time I went to his house. When I awoke the next morning, I wanted to fix my makeup, and that is when I found it there beside the mirror.

"I wonder if I could use this?" I must have asked something like that, but I don't remember what he said in reply. I began to use the powder box from that morning on.

It was late when I went to his house. We had been drinking together. I had never even dreamed of spending the night with him, and yet I followed him home without so much as a second thought. I cannot use the liquor as an excuse. I wasn't even that fond of drinking, but there I was, and because I had been drinking I was capable of anything.

His house was surrounded by a thick hedge of cedar. We did not go in through the front door but walked around to the back and stepped up into his room from the veranda. And then I slept with him. I did not notice then because of the darkness, but when I began putting the bedding away the next morning, I found that the quilt we had used was stained with blood. Where the blood flow had been especially heavy it had dried into hard crusty patches. Was this the only quilt he had? Is that why he still used it? I would have thought he would be reluctant to sleep with a woman he had just met in bedding like this. But he didn't seem to mind at all.

Enough of what he thought, though; how was it that *I* was not repulsed by what I had seen? I ought to have fled the house in horror, and yet, even when I realized that I had spent the night entangled in a blood-encrusted quilt, I did not feel particularly alarmed. I really do not understand it myself. Was running off at daybreak too embarrassing? Or, was it that I knew it was too late?

That is how we came to be together, he and I. Neither one of us said a word about wanting to be with the other. I simply followed him home. Acting on the spur of the moment as I did, I hadn't packed a suitcase, and that is why I used the powder box when I discovered it there the next morning. I also used the nightdress and sash that were there as well. Oh, I knew they belonged to someone else, but that didn't bother me—and so begins the mistake that I shall recount in this tale of mine.

2

Two or three days passed, I believe, and then he went out somewhere, leaving me behind alone. I guess he knew I wouldn't go while he was away. Or maybe he didn't care whether I stayed or not.

He had left all sorts of things in his room, things someone there for the first time should not have seen. I had not planned to look at them, of course. No, I hadn't meant to look at them, but there they were scattered about for all to see. And that was only natural, I suppose, since he lived alone. I began to leaf through the newspapers that were stacked in the alcove, not really paying attention to what I was doing. But then I noticed that each paper was from a different press, and each was devoted to the same incident—the love suicide he had attempted a month earlier. He and a woman had tried to kill themselves by inhaling gas from an open outlet. They had cut the artery in their throats, too, just in case the gas failed to do the trick. Even so, someone discovered them in time. That's what the articles were about. He had all sorts of papers there, and the same kind of report appeared in each. I wondered why he had saved them all.

I had heard about it earlier. In fact, I knew all about his suicide attempt, but that still didn't stop me from poring through those articles one by one. I hadn't been particularly interested in the event when I first heard of it, and I suppose I ought to have found it exceedingly impressive now, seeing as how I was practically standing on the very spot where it had happened. But no, I treated it as something of absolutely no concern to me—and that I find strange. I guess my reaction was linked to the feelings I had when I discovered that blood-stained bedding and did not run away.

The newspapers were not the only things in the room. Hanging on the wall was a woman's lavender, arrow-pattern kimono, and beside it was a three-length sash of gauzy yellow muslin. The woman must have been little more than a girl, really, to have worn such a gossamer sash. Leaning against the wall on one side of the room was a woman's portrait—it had not yet been framed. At a glance I could tell it was one of his works. It was abstract and the woman's eyes looked like seashells. I wondered if it were a portrait of her. In a word, the very atmosphere of that room still spoke vividly of the man and the woman. He had left me there—in a room like that—and he didn't even care. *That,* I think, was very strange.

But then, I did not seem terribly concerned either, surrounded as I was by things I did not understand. I wonder if ours was not the kind of depraved mentality you see portrayed these days in the movies and on television. Just when he had been going through a troubled time, so had I. I didn't go so far as a love suicide, but I had done things ordinarily taboo without so much as batting an eye. I wasn't surprised by much.

"I've never met a woman more unshakable than you!" he told me once. He wasn't referring to the fact that I hadn't been scared off by the blood-stained bedding or the newspaper articles. He said this after he had pointed a pistol at me and had pretended to fire it, all as a joke. I acted as though it hadn't even fazed me. Strangely, I took his comment as a compliment. But was being an "unshakable woman" really something to be proud of? Even now I'm not certain.

At any rate, this is how we began our life together. I didn't see the pistol again. The blood-stained bedding disappeared, too, along with the woman's lavender kimono, her yellow muslin sash, and eventually her portrait. They just disappeared one after the other. Perhaps he carried them off while I wasn't looking. And perhaps this was his way of expressing his gratitude to me for staying with him. The powder box was the only thing left behind, probably because I had been using it ever since that first morning, but also because it was such an inconspicuous item. Anyway, I began to think of the box as mine. I guess I never gave it back because it was just an ordinary old silver-plated box; and I guess I never bothered to remind myself that it was hers and not my own.

One thing I found unusual about him during that time was the fact that he never seemed depressed. He never once offered a word of explanation as to why he had turned to love suicide. He had a scar on his neck, but otherwise he looked like any other young artist. Yes, that scar was the only trace he bore. Of course, I should have realized that his heart would not have escaped unscarred, not after what had happened to him. I understand this now all too well, but at the time I fell for his charade. Once all the blood-soaked evidence had been disposed of, I forgot all about the suicide attempt. It wasn't that I didn't want to pry into matters that were none of my concern; rather, I suppose I just didn't care. But later there would come a time when I would be made painfully aware of this attitude of mine.

3

Did I really find him that attractive? Wasn't it just his physical presence that captivated me? He looked dangerous. I like the wild way the young actors look today on television and in the movies. He looked like he could do things normal people could not; that he would think things normal people would not. I don't know. I guess I just like people who arouse my curiosity. He wasn't what you would call a gentleman, not the type of man others find pleasant.

But I won't go on about him. It doesn't really matter anyway. I have to think about myself, about the way I was then. I had just been abandoned by a man I loved, and people said I was going through a period of "despair."

I had loved this man, and yet one day, after living with him for five years, I left. I wanted to see what it was like to leave. I still loved him, but I slept with another man. It was a summer night. I bathed myself in the river that flowed nearby. I didn't think I had done anything wrong, but I did feel as if something meant to last forever had suddenly been snapped in two. Well, if it's been broken once, then what difference does it make if it's broken again, and again? I wonder if this is what people call "despair?"

When I went home, no one was there. He had gone somewhere else—with a young, child-like woman, I was told. I wasn't jealous. No, I couldn't be because I still loved him. I don't know how it is with others, but for me jealousy is tantamount to a profound remorse. And anyway, what right did I have to be jealous when I had done the very same thing to him? I knew where he was but I didn't try to chase him. I cried alone.

Those times were full of things I could not understand. I was like a dog who had broken loose from his chain. I did not care for liquor, but I drank anyway, and I took some kind of German sleeping pills. When I took the pills and liquor together I slipped into a dream world. I slept with other men while I was in this world. One night I slept with a married man. I knew he was married but I didn't care. It didn't bother me that he was deceiving his wife.

And so it went until one night I met him at a bar. "Come home with me," he said. I had no reason to say no. Everybody knew about his love suicide attempt. You could say I found him at just the right moment.

Actually, the timing was perfect for both of us. We were birds-of-a-feather in a way, a dangerous pair—neither knowing what to do. And yet, we didn't do anything. Nothing happened. Once we began living together we put an end to our promiscuity. I find it strange that a man and woman can be wildly licentious one minute and then faithful the next.

For nearly two years we lived together quietly. I suppose everyone has wanted to live a tranquil life at least once.

4

At some point a woman came by to visit. She was his former wife, he told me. When she smiled she had dimples. She came once a month to pick up her living allowance, he said. This was because of the child they had had together. There was nothing in my attitude toward her that would make me wish to deny her this right. And she, too, said nothing, even though she knew there was a new woman in her husband's house. I wonder if this was because I did not threaten her as directly as the other woman, the one with whom he had attempted suicide. Whenever she came I would set our dinner trays side by side in the large sitting room, and we would all eat together, laughing and sharing stories. Then she would leave. It is strange but if he had told me that she and I would have to live together, I believe I could have managed it. It is not love that binds a man to a woman, after all, but rather a sense of vanity.

"You're certainly confident, aren't you!" he told me. I will not forget it.

After that the woman's child would come to visit from time to time—a boy around seven or eight. He was a sweet thing. He often wore a dark blue splash-pattern kimono, and he had dimples like his mother. I was indifferent to him. I just didn't believe that this tiny child would ever play any role in my life with the man.

You couldn't say it was love that bound me to the man. Was it a sense of convenience then? We were like two boats that had accidentally put down anchor in the same port—but were we living together now just so as not to disrupt the tranquillity of the port? When you live in the same house with someone, you find yourself catering to the wishes of that person just to make your own life easier. Do you do it then for selfish reasons? At one point we began talking about building a house. There were still plenty of empty fields on the outskirts of Tokyo. It did not take much to rent land and build a house, and so we began scheming out of our own selfish desires to cater to the wishes of the other.

An acquaintance of ours helped with the building plans. The house I saw in the blueprints, once they were complete, reminded me of a Russian-type building, the kind that would take years to finish. And how were we to finance this house? We had no idea. Our financial plans were as illusory as the house in the blueprints. Since the income I brought in with my work was next to nothing, we hoped that his paintings would sell. No, we decided that they would have to.

We picked out a large field and the construction began. The pillars were placed, the roof raised, and suddenly a majestic house loomed before us. We were caught off guard. Our money-raising scheme and our house-building plan had not been sufficiently coordinated. There we were with a house but no money.

We moved into our new house just the same. Aside from the fact that it was unpaid for, it was flawless. No, it was almost as if to remind us of our debts that the house was conspicuously grand. Even we had difficulty believing we had actually built such a place! It was painted completely white, with a wide lawn spread out before it—a peculiar house for the time. It looked as if it had been built solely as a gesture of bravado, but of what, I wonder, had we meant to boast?

At the time I had no idea what he was thinking, but when I tried to put myself in his place I imagined his thoughts were something like this: "I tried to commit love suicide. But now nothing remains in my heart, and I am living in this house as if nothing ever happened." I didn't know then whether my guess met the mark, but later, much later, something happened that made me realize that his feelings were not at all what I had thought them to be.

And how did I feel to be living in such an outlandish house? My days and nights were filled with surprises. Perhaps this was because he was a painter who painted surprising pictures. I bobbed my hair and wore Western dresses with big, billowy sleeves. I rubbed rouge on my cheeks and drew my eyebrows in thin. We invited guests over to dance. I had never once dreamed that this could be me, and yet I knew that it was.

5

We had a large atelier in our new house and a room where I could do my work. There was also a room for the child and next to it, a guest room. The atelier faced north as did the child's room, the guest room, and my room, and received little sunlight. These rooms surrounded a large, circular parlor, which—facing the wide front lawn—was always bright and sunny. We put a large black-painted table in the parlor. This is where we entertained our guests and hosted our dance parties. Indeed, the life we lived in this sunny parlor was so different from the one we led in our drab little rooms at the back of the house, that it was as if we lived in two separate worlds.

We had planned a room for the child just because it seemed the thing to do, and sure enough he came to live with us before long. From time to time his mother would come, too, and stay the night in the room next to his. I took no notice of the child, or of his mother whenever she chanced to visit. Now that I think of it, I imagine she probably called her son into her room at night and let him sleep with her. She must have hugged him to her as they slept.

Each of our rooms, opening out onto the parlor as they did, was completely independent of the other, and each could be locked from the inside. It was as if the rooms had been planned to accord with the fact that I had no interest in that child or his mother. But what was this indifference of mine? Was it a sign of my virtue? Of my immorality? Or was it arrogance?

All my energy was spent just trying to get used to living in the house. In all of that huge structure we had not made a single Japanese room, and it left me feeling as if I were stopping over at a hotel somewhere. He had said we did not need a room with tatami mats; but as a result the house reminded me of a hotel, an unfamiliar hotel in which I was briefly sojourning before passing on. Can the physical features of a house, the mere features, shape a person's life? I was not aware of it then, but I never felt settled in that house.

I brought the silver-plated powder box with me to our new house, along with my other belongings. I gave the powder box no special thought really; in fact, I had grown so accustomed to using it every day that I thought of it as my own and didn't feel the slightest compunction about keeping it. I went on with my life, never once stopping to consider what kind of person the owner of the box had been. No, it never occurred to me to wonder that maybe, whenever he caught a glimpse of the box, he thought of her.

But then, I never mentioned the powder box to him. After all, I couldn't stand to talk about things that were already over and done with, things that had nothing to do with the present. When we sat across from one another at the dinner table, when he held me as we danced, I could see the scar on his neck—the place where he had thrust the knife into his throat. But even so, all I ever thought as I gazed at it was, "Oh yes, there's his scar." I never allowed myself to think that maybe the wound on his neck went all the way to his heart.

Was this indifference of mine then a sign of my immorality? Was it arrogance? Hadn't I read all about his attempted suicide in those newspapers—the ones I had found in his room when I first began living with him? They ought to have told me something. Indeed, they had described with annoying detail just why it was the two had resorted to love suicide. He was a dissolute artist who could not make a decent living; he had a wife and child to boot. She was the darling of a family that in those days was counted among the privileged—so young, really, she was just a child herself. Who in his right mind would have tolerated a match between a man like that and such a girl? And so they opted for suicide. But what were the true motives concealed within his heart? And was it because those invisible motives were still lodged there that he built this conspicuous house? Did it not occur to me even once that perhaps he had built the house for her?

Much, much later there would come a time when I would be forced to confront the fact that this suggestion, though I had barred it even from my dreams, had become a reality.

And yet our life was quiet and uneventful. The child wore stylish Western garments and frolicked on the front lawn. We kept a long-necked, European-breed dog on a chain outside. The child was already in school, a school where they taught French. I would call him into the room where I did my work and would go over his lessons with him. I didn't do this out of any need to fulfill a motherly role; no, I had been a schoolteacher long before, and I was just reliving my old calling.

Auntie. That is what the child called me. I was not his mother, yet the term implied that I was the person he felt most comfortable with. I liked the sound of his voice when he called for me. I liked that he never tried to disguise the fact that our relationship was one of distance. When I think about it now, I realize that this was because I only allowed the child into a tiny fissure in my heart.

6

We traveled frequently in those days. Well, I don't know that "travel" is the best word for what we did. We would go off to sell his paintings because we found that they sold better outside Tokyo. Oh, I suppose you can call it traveling. He would send a number of paintings off ahead, and we would set out later. We'd stay overnight in a local hotel, or sometimes one of the wealthy families in the region would put us up. We would display his paintings in whatever public hall had been made available, or else we'd carry them around to the houses of whomever had been introduced to us. The point was to sell, and whether we were selling paintings or some other product mattered very little. We had to sell his works, and we had to convince people to buy them even when they were not terribly interested in them.

Strange, strange things took place one right after the other—things that had nothing to do with art. In an effort to sell his paintings he would cozy up to the wives of the local wealth or the wives of company executives—on far more intimate terms than was necessary. He would drink with them and would take them dancing. They would wrap their arms around his back as they danced, flinging their heads back in ecstasy. I could not look at the expressions on those women's faces without feeling something, something akin to jealousy. But was I really jealous? He had to sell his paintings after all. And once he danced with those women his works sold briskly. He and I lapsed into a state of inertia. We were tired. But we did not try to probe for the true meaning behind the things we did. Once he performed these "services" his paintings suddenly became marketable. What he did, of course, did not affect the actual value of his art . . . and yet . . . well, we were very tired after all.

And so we went home, only to find that a police inspector, aggravated by our unpaid bills, had posted a repossession notice on our door. The front lawn had grown into a thicket, and the dog chained there had a glazed look in his eye. The child, too, had become a stranger. We had been away too long. One by one we took care of the events that had occurred in our absence, and as a result we found ourselves short of money again. He began to concentrate on painting, and I began to sell whatever he finished. Yes, I was glad the role of art seller had been passed to me. This way I did not have to watch him dance with those women. And so, before we were even aware of it, our lives became defined by our new roles.

Isn't it strange? I had lived the same kind of wild life one sees on television or in the movies; and I had cultivated the same sort of attitude. Then why was it that, just because I had begun to live with the same man in the same house for a certain period of time, I was jealous of the women with whom he danced? Are love and jealousy natural consequences of living with a given man for a given period of time? I do not know. It's just that I was glad the role of selling paintings was mine and mine alone.

After that I frequently set out on those trips by myself. No, I haven't forgotten. There was a certain pension in a pine grove by the Hanshin train line. I lived in one of the rooms there, along with a large assortment of his paintings. I would tie two or three paintings together with string and would carry them with me as I walked the streets. It was summer and the days were hot. The paintings grew heavy as I trudged up the hill to the station. I didn't care that I was selling art. To my mind's eye I was just as pathetic as any old peddler hawking any old ware. Eating my breakfast alone in the pension left me feeling so miserable I could hardly stand it. And so it was that I began to do behind his back exactly what he had done under my very nose in an effort to sell those paintings of his.

I probably could have sold his paintings without doing what I did. Yes, even if I had just sat at home without lifting a finger—thinking all the while that his paintings would never sell—someone probably would have turned up to buy them eventually. If only our life together had been more modest; indeed, that is just what it should have been—but we were not about to live modestly. He began to paint for money, turning out one canvas after the other. Seeing him like this only increased my misery. And so, whenever I succeeded in selling one of his works, I was especially courteous to the person who had purchased it from me, just as he had been.

Courteous? Would you call what I did "being courteous?" I made no attempt to hide my own relief and pleasure from whomever had rescued me from my predicament. Once, when a customer saw me back to my pension, I invited him up to my room to show him more paintings. But no, this did not happen only once. It all came about very naturally. I even allowed myself the pleasure of being treated to dinner by the man. Yes, that's right. I "allowed" myself. And because I was "allowing myself" I suppose I can avoid calling what I did "prostitution."

The man was a mine operator—or more accurately, I suppose—a mine speculator. He owned some mountain land deep in Hyōgo Prefecture. No, he wasn't a speculator exactly, either. I guess he was just a young businessman. "I'm going out to inspect my land, now," he told me one day. "Wouldn't you like to come along?" Without so much as a second thought I told him that I would. Was going off to the mountains with this man then a courtesy? He had bought three or four of my paintings, after all.

Spring had only just arrived, and there was still snow in the mountains. Night had fallen by the time we reached the inn at the foot of the mountain. Seven or eight other people were with us, I believe. We sat around the hearth eating dinner, and then we began to drink sake. I did not know what this "mountain inspection" entailed, but being the only woman in this party of men made me feel awkward.

"Interesting old place, wouldn't you say?" The man spoke to me very casually. The inn was actually an old mountain house, and the pillars and ceiling glowed with a deep black luster.

"They found this today," he continued, and he held a shiny ore crystal out for me to see. I guess they were celebrating the fact that they had struck a vein. Afterward, when I went off to my room to sleep, he followed me and lay down beside me. I moved closer to him, waiting for what I knew would happen. Did I "allow myself" to do as I did, or did he make me do it? I do not know. But far from filling me with shame, this prostitute's transaction, which took place under the pale glow of the lamp in that dark mountain inn, made me thrill with a sense of freedom. Even now this strikes me as odd.

I gave not a single thought to the one waiting for me in the house in Tokyo. And even farther from my mind were the paintings, the dog, and the child. I could hear the sound of voices calling gleefully to one another deep in the mountains. Perhaps it had started to snow. Had I not been there in the mountains, would I have felt differently about my actions? But no, even when we left the mountains and returned to town, I still had not the faintest regret about being that young man's lover.

7

My life began to take an unusual turn. I left the pension in the pine grove and moved to a little hotel on the other side of town. The hotel was closer to the man's office, the man who had taken me to the mountains. I do not know what I was thinking. All I knew was that if I were nearer his office, he could come to me the minute he finished his work, and we would be together that much sooner. Not a day went by that we did not see one another; and once we were together, we didn't part until morning. That is how intimate we had become. There were times when we could not distinguish morning from night. I wonder if this is the sort of self-oblivion a prostitute feels. Or perhaps we fanned the fires of our passion purposely to make us forget the exchange of money. Whenever we were together, we roused this sort of madness in ourselves.

"MONEY TOO LATE. FORECLOSE TOMORROW A.M. COME HOME NOW." A telegram from Tokyo came for me one day at noon. It was soon followed by another: "ARRIVING 4 P.M. WAIT." He would be here in an hour! I leaped out of bed and began frantically straightening up the room, thinking all the while that under no circumstances could I allow him to find out what had happened.

Nothing in this world is as strange as a human's ability to reason. I set things straight and headed for the station to meet him, determined to keep everything under wraps, at least for the meantime. We had not seen one another for half a month, and when I confronted his dark, scowling face I suddenly found myself turning playful. "I sold four paintings in one shot yesterday!" I exclaimed. "I wired the money to you a while ago but our messages must have crossed. And, I have wonderful news. I've heard that a new building is going up and since they'll need paintings to decorate the walls, I believe they'll want to purchase a number of yours!"

"What does he do?"

I was alarmed. When I had seen his telegram I had made up my mind not to go back to Tokyo. I had pulled together all the money I had made and had sent it off to him. So, half of the story I had just told him was true. It is strange, I suppose, to tell half the truth when you are telling a lie.

"He's a stockbroker. His business suddenly took off so I thought I'd stay here a bit longer."

As soon as I said this I could feel the joy bubbling up within me. I had successfully construed a pretext for why I couldn't go back to Tokyo just yet. I was so happy I wanted to shout for all to hear, "I can stay! I can stay!"

He didn't say anything. After some time had passed he said brusquely, "Let's have dinner in Kobe," and he began to walk off. He had entrusted some of his paintings to an art gallery there. We went by car. He got his money from the gallery and then, as we were walking along the street, he saw a pair of lady's shoes in a store window and went in and bought them for me. I do not remember now if I thanked him or not. We went to a restaurant nearby for dinner, and as we were in the midst of our meal he said, "Introduce me."

"Oh, you needn't bother," I said looking up at him. "It'll be enough if I go and meet him. Really, don't you think that'll be quite enough?"

I could still look him in the eye, no matter how shameless the lies I told.

He walked out of the restaurant without a word and hired a car. We began riding back along the Hanshin National Highway. "Hey?" I said. His silence was ominous, but he refused to utter a word. I think it was around Uozaki or Shukugawa that he suddenly had the car stop. There was nothing in sight but a telegraph pole. "Get out," he said.

"Here?" I asked. But I did as I was told. The car drove off and he began to walk.

"What's wrong! Why are we walking?" I hurried after him. The road stretched far and wide ahead of us and there was hardly a car to be seen. The moon was bright overhead. As he strode off his back loomed massively in front of me—menacingly. Yes, I was afraid of him then. I had never been afraid of him before, and I never would be again. We trudged along the moonlit highway in stony silence. I felt as if we had walked three miles, five miles, maybe farther. I was wearing those new shoes and my feet hurt so badly I could hardly stand it. "Please! I can't go any farther. These shoes are killing me."

We walked quite some distance after that before finally finding a car. It was already past ten, I think, when we reached my hotel. The hotel was small, and there was a reception desk in the entryway, the kind you would find at any Japanese inn. He stopped there briefly to write his name in the registry book. And then he took the heavy book up in his hands and began flipping through the pages. The blood pounded through my veins.

My name was there in bold letters on a page a week back, the page marking the day when I had first come to this hotel with the man from the mountains. The signature was not mine. No, it was clearly written in a man's hand, that man's hand. He had written in thick, careless strokes.

Dear god! The man's name was not in the book. It was clear to all that he had stayed here with me, and yet, his name was not there. I don't know why —perhaps because his family was so well known—but he had written no other name but mine.

He stood there holding the registry book for nearly a minute.

"That stockbroker was kind enough to see me to the hotel," I murmured. I would have said anything to get myself out of the fix I was in. And once I saw that his name was not there, I was capable of almost any lie. We went to my room. He said nothing but turned the latch loudly in the door.

"Please, nothing happened between us. If you'd like I can introduce you to him tomorrow. How would that be?" I threw myself on the floor at his feet and clung to his knees. Yes, I tried my best to beg his forgiveness with my voice and my body; but in my heart all I wanted was to slip away from the oppressiveness he imposed and flee to my man from the mountains.

Just then we heard a knock on the door. "You've a telegram." I'll never forget that telegram. He had only just arrived at 4 P.M., but now he was preparing to leave.

"How many paintings are left?"

"Six."

"See that you sell them tomorrow. And when you do, wire the money."

Yes! Yes! He finally spoke! He was going back to Tokyo. He was leaving me here alone, and he was going back to Tokyo! I was beside myself with joy. At that moment how could I possibly have had the capacity to penetrate this man's heart—a heart so resolute that it would allow me to prostitute myself simply for the sake of selling paintings?

As soon as his car pulled away from the hotel, I raced back to my room and threw myself on the bed with a cry of relief.

8

I don't remember now how much time passed before I returned to Tokyo. The house was smartly decorated. Of course, he had always had an eye for such things, but when I first stepped inside, I found the house so elegantly appointed that I feared I was at the wrong address. Was this really the same house the police inspector had ticketed a month or two earlier, threatening to repossess all our furniture and belongings?

At the entrance to the parlor was a life-size wooden statue of a woman—a sea goddess I was told—from an ancient Dutch sailing vessel. To have a wooden carving as old as that in a parlor as modern as ours created an unbalance that imbued the room with a sensuous charm. Or, was this, too, an illusion evoked by the sudden change in the house? While I was away the house had been completely transfigured, and I could not help but feel that an inexpressible coolness, indeed, a form of rejection, was implicit in this change.

"Auntie! Look how pretty it is!" I will never forget the expression on the child's face as he called happily to me, pointing to the large mirror that was hanging in the parlor. "See what a pretty mirror came while you were gone, Auntie!" he said. "Don't you like it, too?" he added. He was so animated I hardly recognized him. I certainly had never seen the soft velvet tie that was now knotted under his chin. What was I doing here? I felt as if they were all telling me, "Look how well we've managed without you"; or, rather, "Look how much better we've managed with you gone." In fact, while I had been away they had freed themselves from that oppressive financial burden, and perhaps it was the quietness now gripping the house that I found so unnerving.

Had I fallen into a hole I had dug myself? He did not say a word about what had happened at the hotel. He acted as if he couldn't even remember. I suppose his indifference was a type of silent revenge. I was confused. Was it absolutely necessary for me to seek a place for myself in this elegant, unfamiliar house? I did not forget what I had done. Yet, even though my conscience did not bother me in the least, my feelings had changed for the man I had seen nearly every night in that hotel. Strangely, I no longer felt the desire that earlier had been so hot it had seared my heart. Now my memories of him were but a faint wisp when compared to the sharp disquiet I felt in this house.

It wasn't long before I began renting a farm cottage just behind the house. I did my work there. It is peculiar, I suppose; my work is writing but I could never write until something like this had happened. Could you say then that writing was not work for me but rather a form of retreat? I would stay in my cottage from noon and then go back to the house for dinner. After eating, I would return to the cottage to sleep and would not go back to the house until morning. I was not aware of it at the time, but it seems I was much more at ease in the sparse tatami room in that farmer's hut. The loneliness of the room, furnished only with a desk and a few odd dishes, suited my mood at the moment far better than the glittering atmosphere of that house.

"I could live in a place like this." I remembered, however, that this is just what I had told myself when I was staying at that hotel in Osaka, praying all the while that I could leave him, escape from him and my life in that house. But then, if slipping off to this farmer's cottage was a form of escape, it was, I suppose, a very pathetic attempt.

"I'm sorry, but may I bother you for a moment?" A young girl called to me from the veranda one morning. She was a girl from the country, whom we had hired to look after the boy. A year had passed, I believe, since she had come to work for us. While I was away she had taken care of the house as well and thus had become indispensable to us all. We sat on the veranda to talk.

"Well, uh . . . um," she stammered. "Well, there's this man who acted very sweetly to me up to just the other day, but now he won't even look at me. Would it be wrong for me to ask him why he doesn't like me anymore?"

"What are you talking about? Who doesn't like you anymore?"

Even now I cannot forget the way the downy hair on the girl's cheek glistened in the sunlight that poured over the garden that morning.

"Well, it's Sensei," she said, her face downturned.

I knew perfectly well that the reason she did not look at me was because she was embarrassed by what she had to say and not because she wished to avoid the shock that swept across my face. But here she was confessing to me about what had happened with him in my absence. What on earth was I to make of this girl? She, of course, had no idea that her confession would wound me. She had needed to unburden her troubled heart to someone, and she had chosen me. That was all. Yes, I suppose she was just that naive.

Strangely enough I was not disturbed by the confession itself, but I found myself profoundly moved by her innocence. "Darling," I began. "No matter how painful, you mustn't say a word. Now, whether you take the initiative or not depends entirely on whom you are dealing with—and with the *sensei* I'm afraid it's hopeless. Don't say a thing."

She buried her face in her hands. An impulse seized my heart—something that the sight of this powerless girl awakened. What I had to say would be cruel, destructive.

"Act like you don't notice a thing. Even if he doesn't treat you kindly, act like you don't care."

"I couldn't do something like that! I can't!" The girl began to wail.

What stirred my heart at the moment was not the girl's tears. Rather I was spurred to an awareness that he had behaved right here exactly as I had behaved elsewhere. Neither of us had felt any shame or any sense of wrongdoing. Had we imagined that one deed would cancel out the other?

One morning, half a month later, the girl walked out the front door, a tiny suitcase dangling from her hand.

9

From that point on our life together marched rapidly toward destruction. But what, indeed, did we do to alter its course? Had we ever once believed, even from the very beginning, that our relationship would last forever? We had both shared the same vague understanding that we would live with one another as long as it was mutually convenient. It was only natural, therefore, that in a relationship like ours we would not be too conscious of the other, too considerate of the other's feelings. Then how, I wonder, had I had the nerve to behave so outrageously when trying to raise money for the house and for him? I don't know. Probably because I had wanted to. It is strange but whenever I am confronted by adversity, no matter what the circumstances, something hidden deep within me—oh, I suppose you could call it a desire of sorts—compels me to thrust myself into the very midst of the turmoil, where I instinctively try to break my way through. It is as though I were overcome by an animal instinct of sorts. Yes, that's it. I never act on account of my lover. Even when it may seem as though I do, I only do what I do out of some kind of self-directed impulse.

One day I told him that I wanted to move to the city where I could better concentrate on my work. It was a sudden proposal, with no real motive behind it. But then, everything we did, well, everything I did, was always that way. The same thing had happened five years ago when I was living with that other man, the one I had loved. One day I just left the house on my own accord for no particular reason. But was I even aware now of the fact that I was repeating what I had done earlier? Had I ever stopped to consider exactly where it was I was heading, or what it was I was doing? Weren't my feelings like those of a vagabond who leaves the rigid, regimented life behind for one of uncertainty? I do not remember now what he said in reply, or how he reacted to my proposal. I guess that just proves how little I cared about his feelings. I left the farmer's cottage, taking only what I could carry, and moved into a modest, two-storied house near a small railway station in the city.

It was mid-autumn. The tracks of the Government Railway ran right behind the house. Oh, that's right . . . the train line had not yet been renamed the National Railway, so if I count back—yes, it would have been twenty-eight or twenty-nine years ago. Every time a train passed, the house would shake. But aside from that it was comfortable enough and brand new, too. The house looked out over a broad avenue, so even though there wasn't a garden it was pleasant. A maid lived there with me, and for the two of us it was perfect.

I do the same thing whenever I move into a new place; I entertain myself with mental pictures of how the room should look, and then I set about putting things in order, all with a mind to making a pleasant home. I hung curtains in the eight-mat room upstairs and put down a rug. Both were of poor quality—strictly for looks. I guess I was secretly trying to rival the gorgeous splendor of the house I had just spurned.

I put a mirror stand in the upstairs room. This is where I saw to my toilet in the mornings. I had brought the silver powder box with me. I always had it with me. Earlier when I traveled and then when I moved into the farmer's cottage behind our house, that silver-plated box had gone with me. I was so accustomed to using it that I didn't even think about whether to bring it or not—I just packed it along absentmindedly.

It is strange. I had walked out of that house of my own accord. I had left him and had gallantly set off on my own—alone. And yet, in one corner of my heart I never quite believed that I had finished with him or even with the house. No, I imagined that I was only living in a separate dwelling temporarily—just to see what it was like.

"Auntie!" the child would call up to me. He occasionally stopped by on his way home from school. Sometimes I would telephone him. The role the child played at such times elicited a certain sentiment in me—but this should not stand as proof that I loved the boy. Yes, that's right. I had not separated from the man definitely, but had left our relationship open to either option. And because we were free to choose—or to not choose at all—we were content. And we would continue to be content until the time came when we finally had to decide one way or another.

And then one day I called him from the public telephone at the train station. I often called him like that, and I do not remember why I called that day. I probably didn't have a specific reason. I usually didn't. Neither he nor the boy was home.

"He's over at Mr. Kojima's wife's place," the housemaid told me. She was a rather dull-witted woman.

"Mr. Kojima's wife? Which Kojima is that?" I asked automatically, but of course the maid did not know. I was taken by an uncanny feeling. I suppose a month or more had passed since I had left. And now that I was no longer there, what business was it of mine if he had gone to see the wife of someone I had never heard of? She was probably a woman of no consequence whatsoever, and yet, since I had never heard of her before, I had this uncanny feeling. I suppose I was disturbed because I had left him there in that house and now something was happening in his life that did not include me! I called him again the next morning, but he still had not returned.

I have no idea how to describe the way I felt at that moment. I just had to know who this woman was. When I called again that evening he answered. "Who's Mrs. Kojima?" I demanded. I guess I did not really know what I was saying.

"Mind your own business!" he said. "It doesn't concern you." From the tone of his voice I could tell he was laughing.

10

It was not long after that. A young man stopped by to see me—one of his pupils but also his good friend. "Sensei is very happy these days. He's been saying he feels like a kid on summer vacation!"

"Oh? I wonder why?" I said nonchalantly. I did not particularly enjoy being told how he was relishing his freedom now that I was gone. But then, on the other hand, I did not want people saying that he'd been suffering horribly ever since "that woman left." I suppose it would have been only natural for me to have cared nothing for him now. After all, I was the one who had picked up and left. But that wasn't what I felt either. Really! Is there anything more contrary than a woman's feelings at such a time? I was reluctant to analyze my own feelings. Didn't I remember the way he had retreated from that hotel, his heart hardened with resolve? I ought to have spoken coolly to that young man—I should have brushed off what he had just told me. But by the time I snapped back to my senses I found that I had already blurted out "By the way, who is Mrs. Kojima? Do you know?"

A smile flickered briefly across his face, as if I had said something amusing. "You mean you don't know? She's that woman! That woman in the love suicide. She's married and now her name is Kojima."

What was he saying? Suddenly that day long ago floated before my eyes. There was a girl, young enough to be a child—and yes, she was dressed in a lavender arrow-pattern kimono with a yellow sash of soft muslin bound loosely about her waist. I had never once met the woman and of course had no memories of her, and yet, there she was—standing firmly in my path. So, Mrs. Kojima was that woman—that woman who five years ago had attempted a love suicide with him and then had disappeared so suddenly it was as if she had vanished into the mist.

But no, it couldn't possibly be true, I told myself over and over. Not that, anything but that! How had she changed during the five years that I was living with the man? What did she think of my life with him? And what, indeed, were his feelings about all this? Had I ever once taken the time to even consider these questions?

I did not understand it. The fact that I had taken up with a partner in someone else's love suicide had never bothered me before. But, if that were true, then why should I care what she thought about me? Now that the answers to all these questions were popping up before me, I was caught completely off guard. But had all of this really been so unexpected? And still, what devastated me was the fact that it had happened within a month of my leaving—yes, since I had deserted him and had walked out of that house. This is what really had me reeling. And, as was always the case when I ran out on a relationship, I began to imagine that he had tricked me and had forced me to leave.

I would find it much too discomfiting to describe in detail the way I felt at the time. But I did the very thing I wanted most not to do. Perhaps I was led to do what I did by that flicker of a smile on the young man's face when he told me of the woman. As soon as he had left, I raced out to the public telephone by the station. "Hello! Hello? I'm coming home right now," I said. "Did you hear me? I want to come home."

"You can't," he told me. "Why are you saying this now, anyway? It doesn't make sense." His voice was cold and dry.

"Why? Will my coming back inconvenience you?"

The phone clicked loudly in my ear.

I do not remember what I did in the brief period before the sun went down. But I will never forget the wild anger that roared through my breast. All I could think of was how I was not about to hand him over to that woman. Nor was I going to allow him to continue his relationship with her.

Once I was alone I cried to my heart's content. I do not know why I cried exactly. If there is such a thing as selfish tears, then that is what mine were. I had never once considered his feelings while I lived with him. How was it that I now expected him to think of mine? We had lived together on a fifty-fifty basis. We had both wanted it that way. Then why was I so reluctant to allow a turnabout in our lives? No, it was precisely because we had lived on a fifty-fifty basis that I objected to this sudden reversal.

I waited for nightfall and then set out for his house.

II

I did not stop the car on the street in front of the house but had the driver pull in past the gate and all the way up the narrow, pebbled pathway to the porch. I acted like I was coming home after a brief outing. The dog ran out to greet me.

"What the hell are you doing! You're ruining the hedge!" He stepped out through the parlor door, flooding the front yard with so much light it was as bright as noon outside. Because the light was behind him, I could not make out the expression on his face, but from the low tremble of his voice, I could tell he was fighting to control his anger.

"I've come back," I said. "I'll be here from now on."

"Don't be ridiculous! You think you can breeze out of here whenever you want—well, how long do you think you can keep coming and going like this?"

I squeezed past him through the open door and into the house.

"This is my house. You said so yourself, remember? 'If you ever want it, the house is yours,' you said."

"What?"

"Well, you did. And I want the house now. It's my house."

I blurted out whatever popped into my head without even knowing what I was saying. It's just that I hadn't seen the house for such a long time, and my heart was struck by how gorgeous and ample it was, especially compared to my shabby little two-storied flat on that city street. Even so, I certainly did not want the house. I had never once felt any sort of fondness for that house. I had not put any effort into the actual construction, and he was not about to give it up, so I haven't the slightest idea why I said what I did.

"Get out!" he growled.

"Oh my! And just why is it that you want me to leave so badly?"

I have no way of knowing how I looked at that moment. We both said things to each other that we did not really mean, things that we thought would hurt the other most. And, as a result, we did not even begin to tell each other what we really wanted to say, what we knew we needed most to say. When we had come to the end of our savage exchange, he pushed me out the door.

"I've never met a woman I've hated more than you. You're more loathsome than that hysterical woman in Paris!" Those were his last words to me, and he spat them out.

I don't know how much time passed before I came to my senses. The house was in what was then the outskirts of the city, and once night fell it was deathly quiet. I straightened out my kimono coat, brushed the dust off my *tabi* socks, and began walking along the road. Only two, maybe three, cars passed by.

"You're more loathsome than that hysterical woman in Paris!" Was it this —his parting shot—that had slapped me back to reality? More than any of his other insults, this remark cut into my pride. I do not know what kind of woman he was with in Paris. But, to be told that I was more loathsome than a woman he couldn't stand was really the most painful part of this whole pitiable separation.

How long, I wonder, did I walk down that dark, rural road? Others may find this hard to believe, but as I drifted, dazed, along that wind-swept road in the middle of the night, I found my heart filling with an emotion I cannot adequately describe—I guess you could say it was a sort of contentment. Yes,

that's right. I had flung all my unfulfilled passion at him. And now when I
saw that it had had no effect, I found therein an illusory sense of satisfaction.

Suddenly, at the corner up ahead, I saw a black herd of soldiers marching
toward me. There were barracks nearby and I assumed they were on their
way back after a day of maneuvers. They were tired and looked as if they
could hardly take another step. And yet, I do not know how to describe it,
but as they passed, the odor of their young male bodies—smeared with sweat
and dirt—assailed my nostrils, registering in my brain like the smell of something dry and thirsty. I stood rooted to the spot for a long time afterward.

I didn't sleep that night. What was it that was troubling me? I understand
it now as clearly as if I could take it in my hand.

What had hurt me most was not that his heart had turned from me, but
that I had not left him before he had lost interest in me. Why hadn't I left
him that time in the hotel and fled to the man who had taken me to the
mountains? Why hadn't I left him right there on the spot when he made me
walk down the Hanshin Highway? Why hadn't I run to the other man's
house? But it was too late to turn to him now. I had lost all the passion I had
felt for the man in the mountains.

Yes, that's right. I was bitterly disappointed because I had been abandoned
first; because I had not left him before he left me. And, oddly enough, my
disappointment had blurred the image of the woman in the lavender arrow-
pattern kimono, the woman I had assumed was *her*—and she no longer stood
before me as a distinct figure. Her very existence had, without a doubt, been
the catalyst that had driven me to my despair, yet she herself had absolutely
no connection to my sorrow.

Those five years . . . me . . . I had just been an interlude in their relationship—nothing but a filler. Yet, even after I came to understand this, I still felt
no hatred for her. Well, no, it is not that I felt no hatred for her; I suppose it
would be more accurate to say that I was wrapped up in another emotion,
one that was quite unlike hatred. I had carelessly walked into a relationship
with her partner in a love suicide—driven by my own innate indifference—
but this did not mean that I had carelessly trampled on her, or her feelings. I
thought about this afterward on countless occasions. Hidden in my perception of her was something special—something even I could not believe.

12

Not long after we parted—close to half
a year—I began living with another man. I, myself, have difficulty accepting

the way my feelings shift—but then maybe it's not so much that they shift as that I am just not the type to hold too long to any one emotion. And thus it was that the resentment I had felt for him—resentment that I had thought deeply rooted—slipped so effortlessly from my mind that it was hard to believe I was still in possession of the same heart. I was like a different woman in a completely different world.

Three or four years went by, and then, one cold night in early winter, while my new lover and I were out on the town, we happened into a certain nightclub. "He's here," I thought I heard someone whisper in my ear. Or maybe it was just a feeling that swept over me. I knew he had a special business arrangement with this nightclub. He had taken to living flamboyantly with his other artist friends after I had left, and was often commissioned by hotels, department stores, and the like to decorate their walls with his unique frescoes.

Back in those days, drinking spots like this one purposely kept the lights low to create a certain ambience. It was so dark you could hardly find the stairs, much less make out the faces of those inside, but even so I thought I had caught a glimpse of his rugged shoulders.

"So . . . how've you been?"

He was suddenly beside me in the smoky darkness speaking in that low, raspy voice of his. Something akin to relief flooded my heart, soon to be followed by a surge of happiness. I broke into a smile but offered no other answer.

Three or four years had passed since our separation, and after all that had happened, I suppose I ought to have been offended by the casual familiarity of his greeting. But I wasn't. Couldn't you say that with this greeting of his all the raw, pathetic feelings we had harbored during that bitter separation completely evaporated? Wasn't it, in fact, relief that we felt then? Yes, with those casual words, the tumor of anger we had carried was dissolved, and we became, I suppose you could say, just a couple of "former lovers." This made me happy.

As I clutched this happiness to me, I danced with the man who had brought me to the nightclub. "He's here, you know," I said, "and the woman, too. She's wearing white." Having grown accustomed to the darkness, I could see that a woman dressed in white was sitting at his table. She seemed to be holding a glass or something in her hand. A flash ran through my heart like an electric current. "It's *her.*"

You could hardly tell who was standing in front of you, it was so dark— how was I so sure, then, that it was her? She was so slender she looked as if she might disappear at any moment, and the white lace dress she was wearing complemented her figure. "So, that's her." I was overwhelmed. Yes, for the longest time she had been hidden in the mists and had not allowed me a single glimpse—and now here she was. I ought to have borne her a grudge, I suppose, since I knew she had moved in with him the minute I left. But what was it then that I was feeling?

It was something that had been hidden deep within my heart, deeper than I could fathom. He had never once told me a thing about her or that incident while we lived together. And, I had never once asked him to. Of course, it was my nature to have no interest in the past, but more than that, I think, was the fact that I felt I couldn't ask about what had happened—afraid that it was something I should not touch.

For whatever reason, they had resolved to die together, and they had tried to carry out their resolve. Theirs was a promise that belonged to a special world—a world cut off from this one—a different, hidden world where others could not go. No, he was not like others—but what of her? She was no more than a child, an innocent child with a heart so sweet and simple she turned all of her attention and obedience to him. It was this sweetness of hers, I suppose, which struck my heart most forcibly. Yes, the fact that she had tried to kill herself with the man I had lived with was not nearly as disturbing as her innocence. To put it another way, her innocence was like that of a growing plant. Was it for this that I felt a certain longing? Yes. I suppose the word "longing" would best define my mental state then. But it was only later, much, much later when I tried to put my thoughts in order, that I came to understand this. At the moment, of course, I was moved by only a vague emotion.

The memory of my chance meeting in the nightclub that winter lingered with me for a long, long time to come.

13

After we parted I came to understand perfectly just what she had meant to him. I realized that he had left me because of her, and yet I came to feel that this was, after all, inevitable. Perhaps he had never forgotten her but had continued to think of her even while he and I were living together. Perhaps, as he was building that oddly shaped white house, he was imagining all along how it would be to live there with her. It was only natural. After all, there was no reason to expect that the two would sever their relationship completely—not after such a shocking event.

But by the time I came to understand this it was already too late. It didn't matter anymore that I had become the cast-off lover.

The war came and went and eight or nine years passed. I rarely thought back on what had happened—after all, it had been more than twenty years since he and I had separated. It was just our way—or perhaps it is the way of the world in general—to forget the recklessness of the past, and to settle down to a comfortable, quiet life.

A number of my writings had been collected and published in a book, and one evening there was a party to celebrate. The country was at peace then, and the party was not so much to laud my accomplishments as it was just an excuse to celebrate. On the spur of the moment my publishers decided that I should give a show of the kimonos I had been designing in my spare time. They also arranged to have someone sing. It was his daughter, Akemi, whom they asked—the daughter he had had with that woman. She was not yet known as a singer but was just making her debut. Others had told me of her, and so I knew a bit about her. Even so, I could hardly believe that the daughter he had had with that woman was now so grown up. Had so much time passed? I do not know whose plan it had been, but I was pleased that there was still something between him and me—something that would render it only natural for his daughter to sing in my honor.

This was the first time I had ever seen Akemi. She was somewhat plump but nicely firm, and she wore a white dress of shimmery silk. She sang a song in a foreign language while she accompanied herself on the piano, playing with calm assurance. He stood next to her at the piano, as if he were guiding her through the piece. I could hardly believe my eyes.

"Thank you, Akemi," I said, as I pushed my way through the throng of people to greet her. Perhaps I was just excited by all the celebrating, but I was given the impression that what they were demonstrating to me, there before everyone else, was their friendship.

Afterward I selfishly believed that there was something between him and me that was more intimate than a mere acquaintanceship. Considering all that had gone on between us, it was rather alarming for me to feel this way. But I did not think there was anything so unusual about it. Soon I was going off regularly to attend the autumn art exhibits he was affiliated with. Or else I was showing him the paintings of one of the young men who worked for me, asking him to include them in his exhibits.

And then one day I received a phone call:

"Hi! This is Kazuma. Mind if I drop by?"

"Kazuma! Is that really little Kazuma?" I asked.

Yes, the voice was familiar. Long ago when I had lived with the man I would sometimes get telephone calls from the boy. He would come by to visit us. I had not given him a second thought from the day the man and I broke up, and yet, the minute I heard his voice, I forgot this fact.

"I'll make a pot of oyster stew. Do you know how to get here?" And then a certain scene flashed before my eyes. Indeed, the scene had appeared to me the second I heard his voice—the voice of a boy I had not even remembered. It was in the child's room in that white house. The boy was crying. He had thrown himself down on his bed and was clutching a teddy bear, or some little stuffed animal, tightly to him as he cried. "What's wrong, Kazuma?" I asked. He did not answer, but the trembling of his tiny shoulders conveyed something to me. But what could I do? The child was far removed from the tense passion I shared with his father. I hardly thought of him as my step-child. No, he was just another woman's child, living in the same house with me. It had never bothered me that I treated the boy as a stranger's child and nothing more. And now this boy was coming to see me.

I prepared dinner and waited.

"Hello there!" he called as he stepped inside. He had a present of some sort tucked casually under his arm. He acted just as though he were a regular visitor.

"Well, if it isn't little Kazuma!" I cried, completely drawn in by his casual air. It was entirely inappropriate for me to call him "Little Kazuma," of course. He was ten or eleven when I left his father, and since I had not seen him for over thirty years, it was a wonder that I was even able to recognize him at all. We stared at each other long and hard. Here a sturdy man of forty stood before me—yet when he smiled I saw that he still had the same dimples that had dotted his babyish cheeks so many years ago.

"Well, at last I'll be able to get a good-night's sleep!" Kazuma said happily. "Really, I don't know how many times I called you over the last fifteen years or so, but somehow I just couldn't get you to see me."

He was exaggerating, of course, yet I did not find his complaint displeasing. His words had the ring of an entreaty—the kind of thing countless men had whispered in my ear long ago—and so it was odd, I thought, that I was not offended. Furthermore, I had never expected to hear Kazuma speak so warmly and wistfully of the past—for still burned in my memory was the image of the boy curled up in the corner of his drab, dimly lit room, his tiny shoulders hunched as he cried. My heart swelled with relief when I saw that this pitiful child had grown into a jovial, world-wise man. Yes, it was this relief and this relief alone that surged through my heart. But perhaps even this feeling too was just the sort of selfishness a stranger feels.

"Not surprisingly you take after your father!" I said with a laugh. With his rugged shoulders and firm bearing he was the exact image of the man!

After Kazuma left I felt as if I had been set free. I felt an idleness almost everyone has lapsed into at one time or another. Perhaps it was because I had grown older, but I was happy to learn that even my life, as turbulent as it had been, had finally settled into a quiet calm.

14

It was in the autumn last year. I received a notice from the art association he belonged to informing me of a gathering they were hosting to celebrate their founding. The gathering was to take place in an elegant, newly constructed hotel. They had arranged for a band and everything and no doubt had intended for the party to be a very gala affair. Unfortunately though, on the day of the celebration it poured rain from evening on. The hotel entrance was soon jammed with people trying to get in and out of taxis. All the party preparations had been completed and the meeting hall stood ready, but there was only a smattering of guests present for his party. The heaping trays of food, the flowers, and the glittering candles were painfully conspicuous in the emptiness.

"What a shame," people murmured. It was so quiet in the hall one could hardly imagine the tumult created by the downpour outside. The room was almost eerie, it was so deserted.

Time passed. The other members of the association were there with him, along with his daughter Akemi. That woman was there, too. How long had it been—some twenty years since I had seen her at the nightclub? I had not seen her since. With so few people in the room her presence now was unavoidable. She was dressed in white lace, as she had been that time twenty years ago. And yet I was shocked to discover how her slenderness had turned to frailty over the years. Her face was so peaked it was hard to believe she was actually the same woman.

I do not know who took the initiative, but we approached one another and exchanged greetings.

"Do drop by sometime," she said.

"I hear you have a game of mah-jongg now and then. I'd love to join in."

"Is that so? Then come tonight."

She spoke to me as if she were handing down an order. That's right, as if she were "ordering" me about. Here was this woman for whom I had felt on that day long ago a sweet "longing." And now, now that she had finally spoken to me, her words reverberated in my ears like some kind of command.

The party did not liven up. A few more guests trickled in, and finally he stood up to the microphone. "Thanks for coming in all this rain," he began, and he launched into his opening speech, describing the background of the association from its formation to its present state. Something of his own past, too, found its way into this long and complicated history, and yet, as I listened, I felt as if I were hearing a completely unfamiliar account.

The band began to play. A young man invited her onto the floor, and she began to dance. Gradually other couples made their way out onto the floor. I followed her with my eyes. As I watched her I felt suddenly that I was beholding my own self. And then, in her withered, wraithlike form I thought that I could see how her sorrows had piled up over those thirty some years. Why? Why was it sorrow I found? I do not know. But I suppose I was led to feel this way because I could sense in this woman for whose innocent purity I had once felt a "longing," yes—I could sense as vividly as if I were witnessing the process with my own eyes, how her innocent dreams had been torn asunder, how her pure, childlike spirit had been sullied. And the same would have happened to her even if she had never met him but had spent her life with another man.

The party finally drew to a close and people began to leave. He stayed behind for awhile, but she had already walked through the front entryway with two or three guests. It was still raining. Doormen were running this way and that with their umbrellas, and amidst the confusion I saw her car glide slowly around the curb.

"Coming?" she called to me.

It was pouring, and the car's headlights cut through the darkness like lightning. She was sitting at the wheel of a large, white car of foreign make —a type I had never seen before—and when she glanced back at me from over her shoulder I felt myself shudder.

If it had not been raining so hard; if it had not been so late . . . would I have gone with her?

"No, some other time." But the white car glided away before I had a chance to answer.

What took place that night remained in my heart for a long, long time. The way it rained—yes, I felt that it had to have rained like that. And in that woman, in her wasted state, I thought I could see reflected perfectly the brutality of time—a brutality whose vengeance is apparent in my face as well. Yes, even in me. And yet . . . and yet, precisely because I understood this, I felt that I could finally see the cruel truth that passion too withers and fades, and there is nothing anyone can do to prevent it from doing so.

I still use her powder box every morning. But today when I lifted the lid from the box—the silver plating so badly worn that the nickel shows through—it was as if I were seeing it for the first time. "Tomoko," I said, as though I were speaking directly to her, "I've been using this powder box of yours ever since that first time I went to his house. And look . . . just look at it now."

Notes

CHAPTER I

1. Uno Chiyo, *Ikite yuku Watashi* I (Tokyo: Mainichi Shimbunsha, 1983), 12.
2. Uno Chiyo, *Aru hitori no onna no hanashi*, in *Uno Chiyo zenshū* 7 (Tokyo: Chūō Kōronsha, 1977), 12. *(Uno Chiyo zenshū* hereafter cited as *UCZ).*
3. Uno Chiyo, "A Genius of Imitation," in *To Live and to Write*, ed. Yukiko Tanaka (Seattle: Seal Press, 1987), 190.
4. Uno Chiyo, "Kokyō no ie," in *UCZ* 7:205–206.
5. Interview with author at Uno Chiyo's residence in Tokyo, June 21, 1984.
6. Uno Chiyo, "Michiyo no yomeiri," in *Shinsen Uno Chiyoshū* (Kaizōsha, 1929), 325–326.
7. Uno, *Aru hitori no onna no hanashi*, 17–18.
8. From author's June 21, 1984, interview with Uno.
9. Ibid.
10. Uno, "A Genius of Imitation," 189–190. The two stories she mentions, "One's Own Sin" (Ono ga tsumi) by Kikuchi Yūho (1870–1947) and "A Bride's Abyss" (Yome ga fuchi) by Ogasawara Hakuya are examples of *katei shōsetsu* (domestic fiction), a kind of fiction thought to be suitable for "domestic readers," that is, women and children. Stories in this category were ponderously melodramatic, sentimental, and overplotted, but they were believed to instill "a proper moral attitude," in that virtue was always rewarded and vice duly punished.
    The offerings of *A Flower of the Capital (Miyako no hana)* were of a different sort. These stories espoused the traditional attitude that fiction was little more than frivolous and titillating entertainment. They celebrated, among other ills, notoriously evil women and greed-driven men.
11. *Onna daigaku* (Greater Learning for Women), believed to have been written by Kaibara Ekken, was a guide to proper feminine behavior and education. Based on Confucian precepts, it taught primarily that women were inferior to men, their "thinking shallow," and that they should be subservient to men in all things. Furthermore, women were instructed to guard against the five infirmities that afflict the female nature: indocility, discontent, slander, jealousy, and silliness.
12. See, for example, Joy Paulson's explanation of Meiji marriage laws in Joyce Lebra, Joy Paulson, and Elizabeth Powers, eds., *Women in Changing Japan* (Stanford, Ca.: Stanford University Press, 1976), 14:

Under Meiji law, marriage was still a transaction between two families rather than two individuals. . . . A marriage was not legally binding until it was registered. The groom's family usually did not register a marriage until the wife had proven she could adjust to the family or until she had borne an heir.

13. Uno, *Ikite yuku Watashi* 1:30–31.
14. Uno, "A Genius of Imitation," 190.
15. *Seitō* (Bluestocking) was a magazine founded in 1911 by the feminist Hiratsuka Raichō. Originally established to encourage women to develop their creative talents, it soon took on a decidedly political nature, advocating economic and political freedom for women, as well as the abolition of prostitution and the feudal marriage institution. The group also spoke out for abortion and "free love," and because many practiced what they preached Seitō women were thought to be self-indulgent, irresponsible, and oversexed "new women."
16. Uno, "A Genius of Imitation," 191.
17. Uno, *Ikite yuku Watashi* 1:52–53.
18. Uno Chiyo, *Watashi no okeshō jinseishi* (Tokyo: Chūō Kōronsha, 1984), 118.
19. Ibid., 80.
20. Uno, "A Genius of Imitation," 192. Uno refers to Hiratsuka Raichō's essay "Genshi josei wa taiyō de atta" (Original Woman was the Sun, 1911), in which she boldly suggests that originally women had been powerful, but that they had been eclipsed by men and now resemble only the pale light of the moon. Raichō's rhetoric was revolutionary, and her assertion became the battle cry for many newly emerging feminists.
21. Uno, *Watashi no okeshō jinseishi*, 10–13. Osome and Oshichi were well-known historical-literary characters, their tragic lives the subject of many stories and plays. Both were doomed by their uncontrollable passion. Osome committed suicide with her lover Hisamatsu. Oshichi, in love with a temple acolyte, set fire to her house in a naively plotted attempt to force a meeting with him. As arson was a crime in 1682, punishable by death, Oshichi was burned at the stake.
22. Ibid., 166.
23. Uno Chiyo, "Watashi ni totte haha to wa," in *Shiawasena hanashi* (Chūō Kōronsha, 1987), 26.

CHAPTER 2

1. Matsui Sumako was the most famous actress in the Taishō era. She achieved recognition in 1911 for her performance of Nora in Ibsen's *A Doll's House*. In 1914 she starred in an adaptation of Tolstoy's *Resurrection*. On January 15, 1919, shortly after her lover, Shimamura Hōgetsu, had died in an influenza epidemic, Sumako hanged herself in one of the back rooms of the Ushigome theater.
2. Uno, *Watashi no okeshō jinseishi*, 36–37.
3. Ibid., 21.
4. Ogawa Mimei was a minor writer, though he won the Noma Prize for litera-

ture in 1946. He is known mostly as a forerunner to the New Romantics and as a writer of children's stories. But when Uno met him he was closely involved in the anarchist movement, and his works showed strong Socialist tendencies.

5. Kon Tōkō, "Kafue Enrakuken no hanagata," *Fujin Kōron* (November 1958), 86–87.

6. Anthony Chambers, trans., *Naomi* (Tokyo: Charles E. Tuttle Co., 1986), vii.

7. Uno, *Ikite yuku Watashi* I, 95.

8. Uno, *Watashi no bungakuteki kaisōki,* in *UCZ* 12:124.

9. Miyake Kikuko, "Uno Chiyo, Chotto Jiden, Furisodezakura," *Croissant* (November 25, 1989), 50.

10. Uno, *Ikite yuku Watashi* 1:96.

11. Kon Hidemi, "Shotaimen, bijo to yajū," in *UCZ* 9, *Geppō* 10:1–2.

12. Akutagawa Ryūnosuke, "Negi," in *Akutagawa Ryūnosuke zenshū* 6 (Tokyo: Shinchōsha, 1950), 5. Takehisa Yumeji (1884–1934) was a famous Taishō artist and illustrator, whose pictures of women with sad, elongated faces are said to symbolize the Taishō era.

13. Uno, *Watashi no bungakuteki kaisōki,* in *UCZ* 12:124.

14. Akutagawa, "Negi," 14.

15. Uno Chiyo, "Jidenteki ren'ai ron," in *UCZ* 12:79.

16. Uno, *Ame no oto,* in *UCZ* 8:228–229.

17. Uno, "Mohō no tensai," in *UCZ* 12:12. August Bebel (1840–1878) was the co-founder of the German Social Democratic party. His work *Die Frau und der Sozialismus,* 1883 (English translation: Woman and Socialism, 1904), was his most successful work. It was translated in 1923 into Japanese by Yamakawa Kikue (1890–1980), renowned feminist and Socialist. See also Uno, "A Genius of Imitation," in *To Live and to Write,* Yukiko Tanaka, ed., 193.

18. Uno used her married name, Fujimura, until 1924, when she reverted to her own name. In the newspaper announcement, her given name is listed as Chiyoko, a name occasionally used to refer to her in early articles. She may have adopted the name for literary effect, since at the time female names ending in "ko" had become fashionable.

19. Uno Chiyo, "Shifun no kao," in *UCZ* 1:13.

20. Uno, *Watashi no bungakuteki kaisōki,* 128.

21. Uno, "Mohō no tensai," 12–13. See also Uno, "A Genius of Imitation," in *To Live and to Write,* Yukiko Tanaka, ed., 193.

22. Fujimura Chiyo, "Haka wo abaku," *Chūō Kōron* (May 1922), 112.

23. Ibid., 107.

24. Ibid., 76.

25. Uno, "A Genius of Imitation," 194.

CHAPTER 3

1. Uno, *Watashi no bungakuteki kaisōki,* in *UCZ* 12:132.

2. Iwaya Daishi, "Magome-mura shinseikatsu, Uno Chiyo: hito to bungaku 6," in *UCZ* 1, *Geppō* 7:8.

3. Uno, "Jidenteki ren'ai ron," 92.

4. Haruyama Sakura, "Wakakitsubame den," *Fujin Kōron* (January 1928), 158.

5. "Uno Chiyo," *Shinchō* (February 1931), 116.

6. From author's June 21, 1984, interview with Uno.

7. Katō Kan'ichi, "Sanjūnengata sentanteki kekkon" 2, *Fujin Gahō* (July 1930), 156.

8. Kondō Tomie, *Magome bungaku chizu* (Chūō Kōronsha, 1984), 20–21.

9. Ibid., 25.

10. Uno, "Mohō no tensai," 15.

11. Kitagawa Chiyoko, "Uno Chiyo shi ni tsuite kanjita koto," *Wakagusa* (June 1926), 43.

12. Kondō, 27.

13. Ibid., 105.

14. Uno Chiyo, "Atarashiki seikatsu e no shuppatsu," *Fujin Kōron* (December 1928), 149.

15. Ozaki Shirō, "River Deer," in *A Late Chrysanthemum,* Lane Dunlop, trans. (Tokyo: Charles E. Tuttle Co., 1988), 43.

16. Uno, "Atarashiki seikatsu e no shuppatsu," 140.

17. Uno, *Watashi no bungakuteki kaisōki,* 141.

18. Hirotsu Kazuo, "Shōwa shonen no interi sakka," in *Shōwa bungaku zenshū 48: Hirotsu Kazuoshū, Uno Kojishū* (Kadokawa shoten, 1954), 15.

19. Sharon Sievers, *Flowers in the Salt* (Stanford: Stanford University Press, 1983), 14–15. According to Sievers, calls for shorter, more practical hairstyles for women began to be heard in 1871. But in 1872 short hair on women was made illegal, and any woman who needed to have her hair cut, even for health purposes, had to have a license from the government before she could do so.

20. Takada Giichirō, "Modan gāru no honke-hommoto," *Josei* (October 1927), 285. These creatures are described as falling because apparently, unused to their high heels, they did just that!

21. Ibid.

22. Kondō, 79.

23. From author's June 21, 1984, interview with Uno.

24. Edward Fowler, *The Rhetoric of Confession: Shishōsetsu in Early Twentieth-Century Japanese Fiction* (Berkeley: University of California Press, 1988), xvi. See this work for a detailed study of the early *watakushi-shōsetsu.*

25. Uno Chiyo, "Shitsuraku no uta," in *Shinjin kessaku shōsetsu zenshū* (Tokyo: Heibonsha, 1930), 448.

26. Uno Chiyo, "Tanjōbi," in *Shinjin kessaku shōsetsu zenshū,* 367.

CHAPTER 4

1. Uno, *Ikite yuku Watashi* I:148.

2. Uno Chiyo, "Aisubeki tsurukusa—Tōgō Seiji to Watashi," *Fujin Kōron* (September 1930), 166.

3. Ibid.

4. Uno Chiyo, "Atogaki," in *UCZ* 2:379.

5. Uno, "Aisubeki tsurukusa," 167.

6. Ibid., 168.

7. Ibid.

8. Uno, *Watashi no bungakuteki kaisōki,* 159.

9. Uno Chiyo, "Kono oshiroi ire," *UCZ* 5:234.

10. Uno, "Jidenteki ren'ai ron," 119.

11. Uno Chiyo, *Aru otoko no dammen* (Kōdansha, 1984), 27.

12. Uno, "A Genius of Imitation," 196.

13. Uno Chiyo, "Tōgō Seiji no eikyōryoku, in *UCZ* 9:292-293.

14. Uno Chiyo, "Danro," in *UCZ* 3:27.

15. Uno, *Watashi no bungakuteki kaisōki,* 169.

16. Ibid., 172.

17. Ibid.

18. Uno, "Jidenteki ren'ai ron," 70.

19. Ono Kiyoshi, "Tōgō Seiji to wakareta Uno Chiyo," *Hanashi* (May 1935), 233.

20. Uno, *Watashi no bungakuteki kaisōki,* 173.

21. Uno Chiyo, "Wakare mo tanoshi," in *UCZ* 4:39.

22. Uno Chiyo, "Miren," in *UCZ* 4:70.

23. Fowler, *The Rhetoric of Confession,* 143-144.

24. Basil Hall Chamberlain, *Things Japanese* (Kobe: J. L. Thompson & Co., 1927), 503.

25. Sandra Gilbert and Susan Gubar, *The Madwoman in the Attic* (New Haven: Yale University Press, 1979), 36.

26. Uno, *Aru otoko no dammen,* 47.

27. Uno, *Watashi no bungakuteki kaisōki,* 173.

28. Kamei Katsuichirō, "Sakuhin kaisetsu," in *Nihon gendai bungaku zenshū* 71 (Tokyo: Kōdansha, 1966), 386.

29. Saeki Shōichi, "Uno Chiyo ni okeru seijuku no himitsu, in *UCZ* 7, Geppō 8:5.

30. Uno Chiyo, *Confessions of Love,* Phyllis Birnbaum, trans. (Honolulu: University of Hawaii Press, 1989), 3.

31. Saeki, "Uno Chiyo ni okeru seijuku no himitsu," 5.

32. Uno, *Confessions of Love,* 152.

CHAPTER 5

1. Uno, *Watashi no bungakuteki kaisōki,* 175.

2. Jay Rubin, *Injurious to Public Morals: Writers and the Meiji State* (Seattle: University of Washington Press, 1984), 264.

3. From author's June 21, 1984 interview with Uno.

4. Uno Chiyo, "Tsuma no tegami," in *UCZ* 4:285.

5. Uno Chiyo, "Bunraku to Watashi," in *UCZ* 10:175.

6. In Tanizaki's work the two Chinese characters in the puppet maker's name are read "Hisakichi." Uno Chiyo, however, in the 1984 interview, indicated that the name was to be read "Kyūkichi."

7. Uno Chiyo, "Ningyōshi Tenguya Kyūkichi," *UCZ* 5:8.

8. Donald Keene, *Dawn to the West* (New York: Holt, Rinehart and Winston, 1984), 1134.

9. Miyao Tomiko, "Kaisetsu," in *Ningyōshi Tenguya Kyūkichi, Sasu* (Tokyo: Shūeisha bunko, 1978), 173.

10. Kawamori Yoshizō, *Gendai Nihon bungaku zenshū* 45:422.

11. Tanizaki Jun'ichirō, *Zoku Tanizaki Jun'ichirō—Shōwa bungaku zenshū* 31 (Tokyo: Kadokawa shoten, 1954), 410. Indeed, when Kyūkichi died on December 20, 1943, his grandson Osamu took over the business briefly; but when he, too, died there was no one to succeed him. The Tenguya Shop closed forever. On December 20, 1957, fourteen years after Tenguya Kyūkichi's death, Uno erected a stone monument to him in Wada, Tokushima.

12. Uno, "Bunraku to Watashi," 175.

13. Uno Chiyo, "Ningyōshi Tenguya Kyūkichi," in *UCZ* 5:56.

14. Kamei, "Sakuhin Kaisetsu," 385.

15. Uno Chiyo, *Watashi wa itsudemo isogashii* (Tokyo: Chūō bunko, 1988), 31.

16. Uno, *Watashi no bungakuteki kaisōki,* 184.

17. Uno, *Ikite yuku Watashi* 1:192.

18. Uno, *Watashi no bungakuteki kaisōki,* 203.

19. Uno, *Ikite yuku Watashi* 1:235.

20. Uno, "Ohan ni tsuite," in *UCZ* 12:241.

21. Uno Chiyo, *Ohan,* in *The Old Woman, the Wife and the Archer,* Donald Keene, trans. (New York: Viking Press, 1961), 51.

22. Ibid., 116.

23. Ibid., 118.

24. Kamei, "Sakuhin Kaisetsu," 384.

25. Okuno Takeo, "Uno Chiyo," in *Joryū sakkaron* (Tokyo: Daisan bummeisha, 1974), 39.

26. Takahashi Hideo, "Kanjō no katachi," *Umi* (August 1976), 161.

27. In this love-suicide play, Jihei, a paper merchant, falls in love with the courtesan Koharu, forsaking his family and business. Osan, his wife, begs Koharu to release Jihei. Out of respect for Osan, Koharu tricks Jihei into believing that she no longer loves him. But when Osan realizes that Koharu intends to kill herself, she confesses to Jihei and urges him to redeem Koharu, even though it means she will lose her role as Jihei's wife. Osan is taken back to her parents; Jihei and Koharu turn to love suicide.

28. Uno, *Ohan,* 114.

29. From author's June 21, 1984, interview with Uno.

30. Uno, "Bunraku to Watashi," 177.

31. Uno, "Ohan ni tsuite," 243.

CHAPTER 6

1. Keene, *Dawn to the West*, 114.
2. Uno Chiyo, "Onna no inochi," in *UCZ* 10:47–48.
3. Uno, *Watashi no bungakuteki kaisōki*, 210.
4. Uno, "Kono oshiroi ire," 252.
5. Uno Chiyo, *Sasu*, in *UCZ* 6:61–62.
6. Ibid., 35.
7. I am grateful to Professor Tetsuichi Hashimoto of International Christian University for this information.
8. Uno, *Watashi no bungakuteki kaisōki*, 211.
9. Uno, *Ikite yuku Watashi* 2:39.
10. Uno, *Sasu*, 101.
11. Ibid., 99.
12. Hagiwara Yōko, "Kaisetsu," in *Ohan, Kaze no oto* (Tokyo: Chūō bunko, 1975), 221.
13. Uno Chiyo, "Ichiban ii kimono wo kite," in *UCZ* 10:100.
14. Setouchi Harumi, "Sainō no yama ni tsuite," *Bungakkai* (February 1966), 128.
15. Gilbert and Gubar, *The Madwoman in the Attic*, 23.
16. Chamberlain, *Things Japanese*, 505.
17. Uno, "A Genius of Imitation," 196.
18. Uno Chiyo, "Yoyo to nakanai," in *UCZ* 10:27.
19. Uno, *Watashi no bungakuteki kaisōki*, 217.
20. Annis Pratt, *Archetypal Patterns in Women's Fiction* (Sussex: Harvester Press, 1981), 21.
21. Uno Chiyo, "Mizu no oto," in *UCZ* 6:227.
22. Uno Chiyo, "Nasu no ie," in *UCZ* 10:149–150.
23. Setouchi Harumi, "Bōkansha no me no iro," *Umi* (May 1972), 177.
24. Ibid., 176.
25. Uno Chiyo, *Ame no oto*, 146.
26. Fukuda Hirotoshi, "Uno Chiyo ron," *Gunzō* (March 1975), 190.
27. Translation from Earl Miner, *An Introduction to Japanese Court Poetry* (Stanford: Stanford University Press, 1968) 84.
28. Uno Chiyo, "Happiness," in *Rabbits, Crabs, Etc.*, Phyllis Birnbaum, trans. (Honolulu: University of Hawaii Press, 1982), 134.
29. Uno Chiyo, "Atogaki," in *UCZ* 8:263.

CHAPTER 7

1. Uno Chiyo, "Nani ga shōsetsu no zairyōka," in *UCZ* 10:235.
2. From author's conversations with Uno Chiyo in April 1985.
3. Uno Chiyo, "Usuzumi no sakura," in *UCZ* 8:7.
4. Ibid., 67–68.

5. Ibid., 37.

6. Ibid., 120.

7. Uno Chiyo, "Watashi no isshō ni kaita sakuhin no naka de," in *UCZ* 10:229.

8. Ibid.

9. A movie actress and TV star, Yamamoto Yōko is best known for her highly publicized affair with a man twenty years her junior.

10. Uno Chiyo, "Ningyōshi Tenguya Kyūkichi," 25.

11. "Mullion," *Asahi Shimbun* (August 27, 1987).

12. Uno, "Kaze no oto, sono hoka," in *UCZ* 10:140–142.

13. Uno Chiyo, "Futatsu no shigoto," in *Zoku kōfuku wo shiru sainō* (Tokyo: Kairyūsha, 1983), 79.

14. From author's conversations with Uno Chiyo in November 1987.

THE PUPPET MAKER

1. *Keisei Awa no Naruto* (The Tragedy of Awa), a *jōruri* play written in 1768 by Chikamatsu Hanji and others.

2. Tenguya Kyūkichi was born in 1858.

3. *The Household-Precept Letter Writer,* a collection of model letters, is believed to have been written by the Buddhist priest Gen'e (1279–1350).

4. En'ya Hangan, the lord whose involuntary seppuku is avenged by the loyal *rōnin* in the *Chūshingura*.

5. Oboshi Yuranosuke, leader of these *rōnin*.

6. A famous carpenter and sculptor of the late sixteenth and early seventeenth centuries, he is credited with making the "sleeping cat" of the Tōshōgū Shrine in Nikkō and the "nightingale" floors of the Nijō Castle in Kyoto.

7. Another *Chūshingura* character, Bannai is a loyal henchman of the villain Ko no Moronao.

8. Legendary artisan Hida no Takumi is said to have directed the construction of the Imperial Palace when the capital was moved to Kyoto in 784. In one of the *Konjaku Monogatari* tales he engages the famous artist Kudara Kawanari (782–853) in a duel of skills. Hidari Jingorō is described above in note 6.

9. A Tengu is a mythical creature thought to live deep in the forest. Masks depicting this creature are generally red and have a long, grotesque nose. "Tengu" is also used to refer to someone who brags, exaggerates, and tells lies.

10. Kumagai Naozane (1141–1208), the Genji warrior who beheaded Taira no Atsumori (1169–1184) at the battle of Ichinotani and, overcome by remorse, became a monk.

11. A character in *Yoshitsune Sembon-zakura* (Yoshitsune and the Thousand Cherry Trees).

12. Masatsura (d. 1348) was the son of Kusunoki Masashige (d. 1336), the famed warrior in Emperor Go-Daigo's forces whose heroics are portrayed in the *Taiheiki* and in various plays.

13. The famous *gidayū-bushi* chanter Toyotake Yamashiro no Shōjō (1878–1967).

Originally named Kanasugi Yatarō, he succeeded to the professional name of Toy-otake Kōtsubodayu in 1909. Prince Chichibu granted him the court title of Yamashiro no Shōjō in 1947.

14. Kyūkichi is here referring to the *"eejanaika"* outbreak of 1867. Rumors began to circulate that sacred amulets from Ise Shrine were falling from the skies over Nagoya, prompting a rash of near-hysterical celebrations that swept through the Kansai. The common people, long suppressed by the government and baffled by the many changes taking place, interpreted the amulet rumors as a sign that good times were ahead. They dressed in gaudy costumes and took to the streets, bursting into the houses of the wealthy and feasting on whatever they could find, all the while exclaiming *"Eejanaika!"* (Why not! Anything goes!)

15. Daikoku is the god of wealth.

16. The Toba-Fushimi Battle, first of several conflicts accompanying the Meiji Restoration. Shogunate troops stationed at Osaka Castle marched to Kyoto to rout the Satsuma and Chōshū forces but were intercepted on January 27, 1868, at Toba-Fushimi and defeated.

THE SOUND OF THE WIND

1. Iwakuni dialect for *Okaasan,* or "Mother," which in nuance is roughly equivalent to "Mama" or "Mummy."

Select

Bibliography

WRITINGS BY UNO CHIYO

Fujimura Chiyo. "Haka wo abaku." *Chūō Kōron* (May 1922): 71–119.

"Minato no zatsuon." *Chūō Kōron* (August 1922): 63–123.

Uno Chiyo. "Aisubeki tsurukusa—Tōgō Seiji to Watashi." *Fujin Kōron* (September 1930): 163–169.

Akutoku mo mata. Tokyo: Shinchōsha, 1981.

Aru nikki, Nokotte iru hanashi. Tokyo: Shūeisha bunko, 1983.

Aru otoko no dammen. Tokyo: Kōdansha, 1984.

"Atarashiki seikatsu e no shuppatsu." *Fujin Kōron* (December 1928): 134–149.

Ikite yuku Watashi 1 & 2. Tokyo: Mainichi Shimbunsha, 1983.

Ippen ni harukaze ga fuite kita. Tokyo: Chūō Kōronsha, 1989.

Shiawasena hanashi. Tokyo: Chūō Kōronsha, 1987.

Shinjin kessaku shōsetsu zenshū. Tokyo: Heibonsha, 1930.

Shinsen Uno Chiyoshū. Tokyo: Kaizōsha, 1929.

Uno Chiyo zenshū 1–12. Tokyo: Chūō Kōronsha, 1977.

Watashi no okeshō jinseishi. Tokyo: Chūō Kōronsha, 1984.

Watashi wa itsudemo isogashii. Tokyo: Chūō bunko, 1988.

(Zoku) kōfuku wo shiru sainō. Tokyo: Kairyūsha, 1983.

TRANSLATIONS

Birnbaum, Phyllis, trans. *Confessions of Love.* Honolulu: University of Hawaii Press, 1989.

———. *Rabbits, Crabs, Etc.: Stories by Japanese Women.* Honolulu: University of Hawaii Press, 1982.

Chambers, Anthony, trans. *Naomi.* Tokyo: Charles E. Tuttle Co., 1986.

Dunlop, Lane. *A Late Chrysanthemum.* Tokyo: Charles E. Tuttle Co., 1988.

Keene, Donald. *The Old Woman, the Wife and the Archer.* New York: Viking Press, 1961.

Tanaka, Yukiko, ed. *To Live and to Write.* Seattle: Seal Press, 1987.

SECONDARY SOURCES IN ENGLISH

Chamberlain, Basil Hall. *Things Japanese*. Kobe: J. L. Thompson & Co., 1927.

Fowler, Edward. *The Rhetoric of Confession: Shishōsetsu in Early Twentieth-Century Japanese Fiction*. Berkeley: University of California Press, 1988.

Gilbert, Sandra, and Susan Gubar. *The Madwoman in the Attic*. New Haven: Yale University Press, 1979.

Keene, Donald. *Dawn to the West*. New York: Holt, Rinehart and Winston, 1984.

Lebra, Joyce, Joy Paulson, and Elizabeth Powers, eds. *Women in Changing Japan*. California: Stanford University Press, 1976.

Pratt, Annis. *Archetypal Patterns in Women's Fiction*. Sussex: Harvester Press, 1981.

Rubin, Jay. *Injurious to Public Morals: Writers and the Meiji State*. Seattle: University of Washington Press, 1984.

Sievers, Sharon. *Flowers in the Salt*. Stanford: Stanford University Press, 1983.

SECONDARY SOURCES IN JAPANESE

Akutagawa Ryūnosuke. *Akutagawa Ryūnosuke zenshū* 6. Tokyo: Shinchōsha, 1950.

Fukuda Hirotoshi. "Uno Chiyo ron." *Gunzō* (March 1975): 188–190.

Hagiwara Yōko. "Kaisetsu." In *Ohan, Kaze no oto*. Tokyo: Chūō bunko, 1975.

Haruyama Sakura. "Wakakitsubame den." *Fujin Kōron* (January 1928): 152–154.

Hazue Tsuyuko. "Yūme josei inshōki." *Fujin Salon* (April 1930): 41–42.

Hirotsu Kazuo. *Shōwa Bungaku zenshū* 48. Tokyo: Kadokawa shoten, 1954.

Itagaki Naoko. *Meiji Taishō Shōwa no joryū bungaku*. Tokyo: Ōfūsha, 1967.

Itō Sei. "Kaisetsu." In *Gendai Nihon shōsetsu taikei* 44. Tokyo: Kawade shobō, 1950.

Kamei Katsuichirō. "Sakuhin kaisetsu." In *Nihon gendai bungaku zenshū* 71. Tokyo: Kōdansha, 1966.

———. "Uno Chiyo no *Ohan*—mono no aware wo kaku." *Shūkan Asahi* (June 1954): 66–67.

Kawamori Yoshizō. "Uno Chiyoshū." In *Gendai Nihon bungaku zenshū* 45. Tokyo: Chikuma shobō, 1954.

Kitagawa Chiyoko. "Uno Chiyo shi ni tsuite kanjita koto." *Wakagusa* (June 1926): 43–45.

Kondō Tomie. *Hongō Kikufuji Hoteru*. Tokyo: Chūō Kōronsha, 1983.

———. *Magome bungaku chizu*. Tokyo: Chūō Kōronsha, 1984.

Maruya Saiichi. "Kaisetsu." In *Nihon bungaku* 46. Tokyo: Chūō Kōronsha, 1969.

Miyao Tomiko. "Kaisetsu." In *Ningyōshi Tenguya Kyūkichi, Sasu*. Tokyo: Shūeisha bunko, 1978.

Nagano Haruyo. "Migatte sugiru." *Fujin Gahō* (May 1931): 138–140.

Nishizaki Mitsuko. "Gufū ni norite." *Fujin Kōron* (July 1935): 170–180.

Okuno Takeo. *Joryū sakkaron*. Tokyo: Daisan bummeisha, 1974.

Ono Kiyoshi. "Tōgō Seiji to wakareta Uno Chiyo." *Hanashi* (May 1935): 232–233.

Ozaki Shirō. *Ozaki Shirō zenshū* 6. Tokyo: Kōdansha, 1966.

———. *Watashi no bundan seikatsu wo kataru*. Tokyo: Shinchōsha, 1936.

Saeki Shōichi. "Kaisetsu—*Ohan, Ame no oto.*" In *Shinchō gendai bungaku* 7. Tokyo: Shinchōsha, 1978.

Setouchi Harumi. "Bōkansha no me no iro." *Umi* (May 1972): 176–177.

——. "Sainō no yama ni tsuite." *Bungakkai* (February 1966): 122–129.

Sugiyama Heisuke. "Uno Chiyo to Hayashi Fumiko." In *Bungei gojūnenshi.* Tokyo: Masu shobo, 1942.

Takada Giichirō. "Modan gāru no honke-hommoto." *Josei* (October 1927): 285–295.

Takahashi Hideo. "Kanjō no katachi." *Umi* (August 1976): 160–164.

Tanizaki Jun'ichirō. *Shōwa bungaku zenshū* 21. Tokyo: Kadokawa shoten, 1954.

——. *Tanizaki Jun'ichirō zenshū* 21. Tokyo: Chūō Kōronsha, 1968.

Index

About the Author

Rebecca L. Copeland was born in Fukuoka, Japan, and raised in North Carolina. She received her Ph.D. in Japanese literature at Columbia University. Uno Chiyo was the subject of her dissertation, and she has had the good fortune of meeting with Uno on several occasions. Dr. Copeland is currently assistant professor at Washington University in St. Louis. In addition to translating Uno Chiyo's works, Dr. Copeland is working on a historical survey of modern women writers.